THE EMPTY BEACH CHAIR

A NOVEL BY
RENEE PROPES

THE KIMMER GROUP

Copyright © 2024 by **RENEE PROPES**

All rights reserved. No part of this publication may be reproduced, distributed or transmitted in any form or by any means, without prior written permission.

THE KIMMER GROUP, LLC

Publisher's Note: This is a work of fiction. Names, characters, places, and incidents are a product of the author's imagination. Locales and public names are sometimes used for atmospheric purposes. Any resemblance to actual people, living or dead, or to businesses, companies, events, institutions, or locales is completely coincidental.

Book Design – 99Design-Aaniyah.ahmen

The Empty Beach Chair/ Renee Propes. – First Edition
ISBN 978-1-7348219-8-7 PB

To my precious granddaughter, Emmy.
You are loved beyond measure.
Pippa

Chapter One

The car horn blared, and Natalie Howard-Nieman rushed out the door of their Macdonough Street Brownstone—a posh neighborhood in Brooklyn, New York; at times, she still couldn't believe the townhouse was theirs.

She looked toward the curb, and there it was—the fire engine red convertible...it was love at first sight.

Her husband, Paul, was already out of the car, standing on the sidewalk, arms folded, looking at her with that mischievous expression that drove her crazy. She ran down the steps, straight to the driver's side of the 911 Porsche Carrera. Just as she reached for the door handle, he brushed her hand away—quickly flashing that charming smile to soften the sting of his action.

Her lifelong dream to own a convertible... finally fulfilled, and it was *his* baby. For months afterward, he wouldn't let her touch the vehicle, much less drive it. It had stung, but she'd learned to choose her battles. She loved how he smiled when he was behind the wheel and the way the wind whipped through her hair as they drove around the city with the top down.

Now, it was hers. She loved it and she hated it, this shiny red monkey's paw. The new car scent still lingered—for the almost two years since his death, she'd stored the car in a private garage and had taken the bus to work each day.

Back then, they were playfully known as Mr. and Mrs. Hollywood by their friends, dubbing Paul "Tom Cruise," and Natalie the "Duchess of Cambridge."

But that was then, and this is now.

***

Natalie shook away the memory as she lifted the hem of her skirt. She was hot and sweaty, and the scorching southern sun had already blistered the tops of her legs. A black Tahoe swiftly cut in behind her. Was that the same vehicle she'd passed a few exits back?

They're probably trying to get a closer look at the car. It often happened when she took it out for a drive. It *was* a cool car—it had taken her almost a year to start thinking of it as her own. Now, two years after the tragic taxi-cab accident that had derailed their picture-perfect life, she still imagined she could smell his sandalwood aftershave in his most valued possession, the Porsche.

She was tired and cranky from being in her cramped vehicle for thirteen hours. Natalie looked from one side of the highway to another as she passed the exit to Hilton Head Island in South Carolina. She'd recently resigned from a coveted job in one of the top trauma centers in the country, a position she'd prepared for her entire educational career. It was the most difficult decision of her life, but with Paul gone, the excitement of living in the "Big Apple" had lost its appeal.

Yet now, she found herself in an unfamiliar place. A southern state, with humidity so high, her sun-kissed hair started frizzing the moment she crossed the Mason-Dixon line. She had spent the better part of the previous Saturday afternoon in a salon chair, hoping to achieve a glow like the pictures of the cute southern girls in the fashion magazines she'd flipped through at the local bookstore. But more importantly, she wanted to blend in with the casual southern lifestyle. Otherwise, had she left her hair untreated, she would have stood out like a... well, like a true New Yorker.

Thirty minutes later, as she crossed the Georgia state line, the black Tahoe was two cars back. As the temperature rose, she smelled the peculiar, rotten-egg stench of sulfur. Natalie cranked up the AC, wrinkling her nose at the offensive, industrial smell that, in her experience, probably signaled the presence of a nearby paper mill.

A single drop of hot sweat rolled from Natalie's forehead to the tip of her nose and dripped onto her cleavage. Sadly, her own perspiration just magnified the offensive scents of the region.

She'd talked to herself throughout the entire day... out loud, not in her head... in an honest-to-goodness conversation. The self-talk had started the days following her husband's death. Perhaps she'd get a dog when she got settled. Or find a therapist. Then she'd have someone to talk to instead of herself.

She pressed her back against the seat in a makeshift stretch. She rarely sat for any length of time. Between the constant motion of her twelve-hour shifts and the three five-mile runs she clocked each week, her legs were as toned as a marathon runner. But now, her extremities felt rubbery from being confined to one seat for so long.

Only one more hour of driving in the scorching Georgia sun, and she'd reach her destination.

Her heart fluttered when a sign announced Exit 29 for US-17. It was the road that would take her to St. Simons Island, off the coast of Georgia.

She reached for a bottle of water from the cooler. As she twisted the top and took a long swallow of the icy drink, she remembered the joy in Thomas Baldwin's voice the last time they had spoken. He was her mentor, and she had finally agreed to check out his practice for six months. It was just enough time for her to know if the change in scenery would help her get through the grief of losing her husband. The last time they spoke before she'd made her decision, she'd heard something in his voice. He didn't exactly beg, but there was a hint of desperation. He needed her, and perhaps she needed him, too. At least, she owed the elderly man that much, but quitting her job and leaving the three-story brownstone where she and Paul lived throughout their marriage was much more difficult than she had anticipated.

Natalie opened the console and reached for a wipe. She rubbed her neck and chest with the cool cloth.

What was I thinking? Well, at least she'd worn the cool coastal white clothing on the trip down. Leaving the salon on Saturday, feeling like a million dollars with her new hair color, Natalie made a mad dash to her favorite store in Manhattan in search of casual clothing to take on her trip. It had taken three hours to process her hair to achieve the desired look and less than twenty minutes to choose the casual beach wardrobe. Still, she had left the boutique with the same satisfaction she felt as she completed her Christmas shopping on the afternoon before the holiday.

Natalie smiled at the memory as she smoothed the top of her skirt. She couldn't believe she'd left New York City for this weather. It was hot in the city, and yes, there was also humidity up north, especially during September. However, there was so much to do indoors up there. Not in the South… as she had learned while reading southern beach books, every activity revolved around an outdoor venue. Even the most sophisticated soirees occurred on a covered veranda overlooking a large body of water, in the backyard pool area of someone's home, or in the neighborhood cul-de-sac. Yellow jackets, ants, and gnats *be damned*. Southerners hated the bugs. They may even swear at them during an event. Still, it would never impede their enjoyment of a picnic during the sweltering summer months.

Natalie glanced in the rearview mirror, realizing she needed an attitude adjustment, and pondered what Paul would say to her if he were still alive. Paul looked at the world through rose-colored glasses, always seeing the glass as half full. Natalie, not so much. She tended to worry a lot, but their extremes kept each other balanced.

Finally, she saw a billboard in the distance but couldn't make out the words. Her eyes stayed fixed on the sign until the words Paradise Point were clear, advertising a new waterfront residential community on the southeastern coast of Georgia.

She flipped on the radio to a local station. Eddie Money was singing *Two Tickets to Paradise*. She smiled despite herself, knowing that was Paul's answer. The message was as plain as if Paul were sitting in the passenger's seat, looking at her with his ridiculously gorgeous smile and telling her that she was on her way to *paradise*.

Fresh tears formed in her eyes as she remembered his smile. And she could imagine him pointing that crooked index finger, telling her that coming to the coast was an opportunity to start over.

A few minutes later, she turned onto a two-lane highway. The road was lined with large oak trees dripping with layers of Spanish moss hanging so low they almost scraped the windshield of her car. It was a beautiful sight, and if she had ever experienced a soulful moment from the beauty of nature, this was it. Suddenly, the weight of anxiety released from her body as she looked at the moss cascading from one tree to the next for as far as the eye could see. It was a visual commensalism, whereby one species benefitted from a relationship while the other was not affected in the least. She'd heard this explained by her mentor. The vision before her was even more beautiful than Dr. Baldwin had described. The urge to raise her hand and grab a handful of moss was almost too much to resist.

The mercury quickly dropped ten degrees, and the shade on Natalie's face as she approached the beach town felt good. But it wouldn't last long. The sun was making its descent when Natalie caught a whiff of the nearby ocean. The salt air smelled delicious, and what was that other fragrance?

Is it honeysuckle or magnolia?

She'd never been able to distinguish one scent from the other. But the sweet aroma lingered, just the same. Natalie shoved her Ray-Bans onto her head and looked through the trees, hoping to get a peep at the water.

Without warning, a break in the wooded area provided the long-awaited view of the Atlantic Ocean. Natalie whipped the sports car into the next blacktop drive, which supported a fresh produce stand. She cut off the engine, grabbed her purse, and quickly jumped out of the car. Then, nodding to the attendant, she said, "Do you mind if I park here for a second while I dip my toe in the water?"

She caught a glimpse of the black Tahoe speeding by as the attendant looked at the license plate on her car and his eyes danced with excitement "… just getting here?"

Natalie nodded and wiped the tears from her face. "My first trip to the 'Golden Isles.'"

"I remember that feeling." He motioned to the ocean with his hand. "Be my guest… enjoy!"

Natalie walked to the water's edge; she could almost feel her husband's warm breath on her neck. She turned and looked around… but nothing, no one. She was alone. Then she slipped off her flats, lifted the hem of her cotton skirt, and walked into the ocean. She reached over, scooped up a handful of water, and brought it to her chest. A few dribbles streamed down her blouse. It felt invigorating… she closed her eyes, allowing her mind and body a quick refreshment. Then she licked the remaining water from her fingertips.

Oh, my god, she thought as she tasted the salt water.

Although New York City was situated on a large natural harbor along the Atlantic coast, the Golden Isles differed. There was a tropical feel in the south… the water was much warmer, too. Driving across the F J Torras Causeway, a lump had formed in her throat. It was a sense of relief, wonder, and awe when she saw the large yachts and waterfront cottages on her right and the beautiful marsh and mystery beyond on the other side. It was an emotional but welcoming force.

As Natalie stood looking out over the ocean, with her hands planted in the small of her back, a posture she often favored because of the long hours standing in the ER, she could barely distinguish where the water ended, and the sky began. It was the same as her connection to Paul. Even in his absence, he was always with her. A peaceful feeling soothed her raw nerves as she dampened her lily-white arms with water. Then, closing her eyes, she crossed her hands over her chest and absorbed the sounds and smells of the ocean.

Coming down here could very well be the perfect place for her heart to heal.

Okay, Paul. As usual, you win.

Chapter Two

Paul - Seven Years Before

Paul Nieman had just finished reading an article in the Wall Street Journal when he looked up and saw her walking into the restaurant. Her long brown hair—flecked with snowflakes, her eyes as bright as fluorescent lights, and that smile, the image of her beautiful smile, forever engraved in his mind. Paul envied her confidence. Her full-length, winter-white coat stood out like a breath of fresh air in a city where black was the predominant color worn during the winter months. He had never been so glad that his colleagues had gone home to their families after a few happy hour drinks at Rue 57—or that he had hung around for a light dinner before heading out into the cold.

He watched, entranced, as her slender fingers reached to loosen the taupe-colored scarf from around her neck. Then she stopped, looked around the restaurant as if expecting to meet someone, and descended the steps to the lower level.

When she returned to the dining room, shoulders slumped, a profound look of disappointment had replaced her beautiful smile. Like a seasoned model, she sauntered through the restaurant and paused to speak to the *maitre'd*. Her disappointment grew even more pronounced as the *maitre* looked at the lectern and shook his head. Finally, she glanced back at the front door, then moved to the window and looked up the street.

Before he could talk himself out of it, Paul did something entirely out of character. He walked over to the window, touched her elbow, and with as much confidence as he could muster, said, "Hi, I'm Paul Nieman. Would you like to sit with me while you wait?" She turned toward him, a question in her eyes, and he hurried to answer it. "I've learned that when people see a single man eating alone in a restaurant, they feel the urge to stop and make conversation. You look like you'd be a lot more interesting to talk to."

She hesitated as she took one last glance through the dining room. "Thank you, but I'm…." She paused. Her gaze flitted to the snow-covered streets and then back to the front of the restaurant. She seemed about to escape through the front door. Then she turned toward him, straightening her shoulders as her mouth tightened into a smile. "Of course. Why not?"

He led her to his table and held the chair for her. "Would you like a drink…?"

She extended her hand. "I'm Natalie Howard."

"It's nice to meet you, Natalie Howard. May I order you a drink?"

Her eyes lit up again, and she took her seat. "Yes, a glass of Prosecco would be lovely."

Paul ordered her drink and signaled the waiter to delay dinner until Natalie had time to review the menu. She sat upright, her back as straight as a steel rod, barely touching the back of the chair. He still wasn't sure she would stay. Perhaps, she'd make a quick getaway before their drinks arrived, leaving him with both. That would be just his luck. Paul hated Prosecco.

At last, they agreed on a charcuterie board to share. While they waited for it to arrive, Natalie peppered him with questions about himself. Paul told her he worked as an investment banker for JC Mellon Bancorp. Without thinking, he mentioned they had received a global ranking for being the best private wealth manager for mega-net-worth clients. Their clientele included some of the wealthiest mercantile owners in the city. He paused, afraid of sounding arrogant, but she was nodding, her face alight with interest.

When the drinks arrived, her shoulders relaxed, and her smile seemed more natural. Paul carried the conversation about his life growing up in a middle-class family in Detroit, Michigan. "My dad worked for General Motors. I have two older, very doting sisters, a history teacher and a financial advisor." Paul chuckled. "And I blame them for every flaw in my personality."

At her urging, he shared a few anecdotes about his sisters—how they'd pick out his school clothes for him each night before bedtime, which had led to his expensive taste in suits. Afterward, they'd read him books about finance, theory, and the masters of rhetoric. Finally, the entire family recognized his strengths and charted a trajectory toward a successful career path.

Natalie smiled as she rubbed the rim of her champagne glass. "How about your mother? Did she have a career?"

"Oh, no. My mom's career was her family." He took a small sip from his water glass before continuing. "Met us at the school bus each afternoon, and had dinner on the table every night at five-thirty. But she did do alterations for women in the community to make extra money for the family. She was an excellent seamstress."

When the cheese board arrived, Natalie reached for a hunk of bread. "She sounds lovely... tell me about your childhood."

Paul took a deliberate moment to dip into the gooey, baked brie. *Dang, this girl is actually eating.* Then he continued, "Every night at dinner, we discussed current events. My father received a college scholarship, but his dad died the summer after his senior year of high school. He was the oldest of five children, and his mother was unwell, so he stayed home and went to work to support the family."

Natalie made a sad face. "That's unfortunate. He must have been a brilliant man." She chose a slice of salami and wrapped it around a piece of cheese. Then, looking up, she smiled as she took a large bite.

Paul nodded, eyes misting at the memory. "He was brilliant. He decided his children would be well-read. We enjoyed a lively discussion each night—answering questions about the classics. The three of us received a literary education from our parents." He missed those conversations. His father had laughed and said Paul's mind was like a sponge. "I was thirsty for knowledge, and Dad recognized that. After junior high, he visited the city's only private high school. He somehow convinced the headmaster to enroll me in the school."

"Well done, your dad."

"Yeah, it was a bold move." Paul smiled. "The private school I attended handled my scholarship to Harvard, but when I learned the price of tuition and the cost of living in Cambridge, the least I could do was pay for my own MBA."

Paul couldn't believe he had told this mere stranger about his family. He was good at business talk and felt comfortable with it. Small talk, especially with women, had never been his strong suit. It surprised him how good it felt to talk about his childhood. How good it felt to talk to *her*.

He explained that after finishing graduate school, he'd received multiple proposals from central investment banks.

Turning down several with higher starting pay and more opportunity for advancement, he'd accepted an entry-level position with JC Mellon Bancorp.

Natalie tilted her head. "What made you choose them?"

"JCMB had the most prestige. They have an impressive reputation and are known for quality work. That was important to me. So, I started out working the regular twelve-hour days and spent my free time studying the investment habits of our client base."

"So, you're smart and ambitious." When he continued pulling at his ear, a nervous habit he said he'd had since childhood, Natalie raised her flute and finished the last of the Prosecco.

She had finally relaxed. Elbows on the table, her fingers picking at the remnants from the cheese board, occasionally reaching for a piece of fruit from Paul's plate.

Looking down at the plate, Paul realized he had eaten very little. Not wanting to dominate the conversation, he asked, "What is it *you* do for a living, Natalie Howard?"

He finished the cheese board and listened to her describe a typical day as the medical director at New York Memorial. A trauma specialist. Had he been a betting man, he'd have wagered she was a model... not a medical doctor.

"Do you wear scrubs to work?"

She laughed. "I change when I get there. If I wore scrubs on the subway, I'd get inundated with questions about everything, from how to treat the common cold to how to lower cholesterol."

Paul couldn't believe someone with her level of intelligence and beauty was still talking to *him*. On the other hand, he tried to act as casually as possible, not wanting to seem overly impressed by her career.

A medical doctor. He would've never guessed.

Natalie had finished eating and took her turn talking about her job. Now spellbound... Paul held her gaze as she spoke. It wasn't so much what she said, but her mannerisms, the way she used her hands to emphasize a remark. Her speech's simplicity and rhythm, and the flutter of her soft brown eyes, were captivating.

A younger guy in an expensive suit turned around as he walked past their table. A few minutes later, he walked by again, but Natalie was oblivious to the attention her beauty attracted.

She underscored her attachment to the patients she worked with by saying, 'my patients.' They weren't just random people who showed up at the hospital to be treated. For example, they'd brought an elderly man in one evening by ambulance, and his wife sat by his bed in a wheelchair. Natalie had held his hand and spoken to him in a soft voice, then found his wife a heated blanket and placed it over her arthritic shoulders. As Natalie told this story,— Paul heard the passion in her voice. Yes, she was beautiful, but she was also a natural healer, and the people about whom she spoke were *her patients*—each one... meaningful, memorable, and with a unique story.

Natalie was different from any girl Paul had ever met. Compassionate, thoughtful, and very real. As she sat across the candlelit table, against a backdrop of large snowflakes peppering down outside the window, the golden flecks in her dark brown eyes flashed in concert with the light. She seemed angelic— somehow living a dream, enveloped by a considerable sheath, both natural and ethereal.

When the evening was over, they walked out into the freezing temperatures. The snowflakes had stopped falling, and the stars shone in the black sky. Shivering, Paul looked at the landscape as he hailed a cab for her. The dream-like state extended to the streets of NYC—a scene worthy of a Hallmark

Christmas card. Between the stars and the streetlights, the blanket of snow sparkled like glitter.

As a yellow cab stopped, they quickly exchanged contact information. At once, Paul committed Natalie's cell number to memory, knowing he would call her as soon as he got home.

Paul held the door while Natalie slid into the back seat of the taxi. "I forgot to ask," he said. "Were you meeting someone tonight?"

Natalie closed the door and hesitated while rolling down her window. Was she going to ignore the question? Then, as the cab pulled away, she smiled, shrugged, and yelled, "I don't remember."

Chapter Three

The Island – Now

Fourteen hours after leaving New York City, Natalie pulled into the pebbled parking lot of a place called Rosie's Diner. The air was heavy, and at 7:30 in the evening, the temperature was still a balmy 89 degrees. Natalie glanced into the rearview mirror. With her face shrouded by damp ringlets, she barely recognized herself.

She locked the door and stood beside the car as her legs adjusted to the pebbles beneath her feet. Finally, she walked toward the front of the diner. It had a vintage aluminum exterior, similar to the old Airstream trailers she used to see parked at camping areas along the northeastern coast. The doorknob dripped with condensation, and cool air escaped from the aluminum door frame. The windows were fogged over, and when she finally opened the door, she was met with a wave of arctic air that almost took her breath away.

Natalie looked over the room; the diner was filled with tanned individuals wearing shorts, T-shirts, and flip-flops. She walked past the only available booth, leaving it for a larger party. Darting to an empty seat at the end of the bar, she suddenly felt over-dressed. As she climbed onto the stool, her legs tingled from sitting in the car all day.

A loud discussion ensued between the server and the customer sitting at the other end of the lunch counter. "You're just a thirty-eight-year-old building contractor with no wife, no family... not even a girlfriend that I know of. You're pathetic."

The customer retorted, "You don't know that. Besides, you've been dying to date me since I first stepped foot into this diner."

Although put off by their teasing, Natalie continued to follow the conversation while pretending to scroll her phone. She would never admit it, but his deep voice and strong personality attracted her.

His name was Jake Ellis, she learned, as he and the owner of the diner bantered back and forth like old friends. He was a tall man dressed in washed-out jeans and a rust-colored T-shirt underneath a thin blue chambray shirt. Silver rimmed aviator sunglasses hung from the center neckline of his T-shirt, and carefully rolled up sleeves revealed a platinum watch on his left wrist. She couldn't help but notice the ring finger on the same hand was empty and evenly tanned. Not even a pale line where he might've worn a ring during his off time. Not that she cared about that.

The messy blond hairstyle conflicted with his understated intelligence and perfect diction. There was something intense about his blue eyes... a knowing. But the restricted pupils told Natalie all she needed to know about the man at the end of the lunch counter. Opioids. He seemed too functional to be addicted, which meant it was probably from a prescription following an injury. She wondered what had happened.

Well, well. Natalie had been there less than ten minutes and had already witnessed a budding romance. The owner looked to be in her early forties. She wore a white uniform—it looked more like the top of the pants suit—similar to a style worn in the early eighties. Although it covered her thighs, it was much too short for a woman of her age. Worse, it hugged her hips, showing the outline of her skimpy underwear. The top was also a tad low in the front and showed her ample bosom. But her hair color…that got Natalie's attention.

Once brown, her hair had not seen the tip of a Clairol bottle in several months. Her root growth had left a three-inch area of silver, while the lower part remained a brassy brown. Natalie stared at it. Ombre? Wasn't that the name the stylist had used? At least, the fashion world called it Ombre, but this was in reverse. Natalie wasn't sure it would qualify.

Either way, it wasn't a good look. A short bob or a pixie style would better accentuate the woman's beautiful skin and would be an adorable cut for her. Natalie gave herself a wry smile. Was she a hair stylist now? She'd spent one afternoon flipping through beauty magazines, looking at current hairstyles, and she thought she was an authority. Anyway, who was she to pass judgment on a stranger?

Besides, the waitress moved about the diner with such confidence that Natalie doubted she would care what anyone thought about her silver roots. When she reached for the coffee pot, Natalie saw her uniform had her name embroidered above the pocket on the left side.

Rosie. The hairstyle didn't fit, but the name sure did.

Rosie walked around the lunch counter carrying a coffee pot in one hand, a pitcher of iced tea in the other, and a dingy white dish towel tossed over her shoulder. She chatted with every male who walked through the door.

She stopped when she got to Natalie, "Hi, hon, what can I get for you?"

"What's your special?"

"Hon, everything at Rosie's is special," she looked toward the end of the counter and winked, "especially our customers."

"I know you're talking about me, Rosie. You know that's rude." Then stretching his neck toward the plate of desserts temptingly displayed under the glass dome near Natalie, Jake said, "How about grabbing me a slice of that key lime pie on your way back over here, please?"

Natalie chuckled at his constant teasing. She'd done her research. St. Simons Island was a golden island, home to a luxury, beachfront resort with a casual elegance unlikely found in other coastal towns. This little piece of paradise, which originated from over ten antebellum plantations, was only twelve miles long and three miles wide. The island was roughly the same size as Manhattan Island in New York, but with one and a half million fewer people.

Unfortunately, Jake seemed to try a bit too hard to act as if he had rough edges in a place where it wasn't required.

One thing was for sure: he was trying to fit the role of a rugged contractor. But he was also good-looking, with an air of professionalism. His table manners were impeccable, too—he chewed his food slowly, almost methodically, and then he wiped his mouth and placed the napkin to the left of his plate, a sure sign he'd been raised in a decent home. Then, when he slid his toned body from the barstool, she saw the well-fitted jeans and work boots. His windswept hair, lightened from long hours working in the sun—was a good style for someone living on the coast. Natalie had spent five hundred dollars and several hours in a salon chair to achieve the same look. Although the arrogance he'd displayed in his conversation with Rosie distracted her, Natalie couldn't help but glance as he walked toward the men's room—rubbing his shoulder along the way.

Jake's presence filled the room as he glided through the diner with a confidence few men could pull off. He was tall and lanky... well built, with chest and arm muscles that showed either years of manual labor or a lot of time spent in a gym.

There was a stirring inside... a feeling she hadn't felt since Paul. She dropped her head behind the plastic menu, ashamed of her reaction to this stranger. Her husband had been dead for less than two years. How could she even look at another man?

By the time he returned to his seat, Rosie had stopped to take Natalie's order. "What'll you have, sweetheart?"

Natalie tapped her menu. "I've decided on the grilled shrimp dinner."

"Hon, we deep-fry everything... and usually smother it with gravy." Rosie winked at Jake.

Jake coughed. "Little lady," he said in a playful tone. "If you want something grilled, a new restaurant just opened on Market Street. The owner's from Atlanta. I understand it's pretty good." He grinned as if he'd just imparted a vital news release.

Natalie looked at him with pursed lips. She knew Rosie was flirting with him, but she couldn't decide if he was flirting back or just enjoying the banter. He'd asked for more sweet milk when she walked into the diner, and now he wanted her to bring him a piece of the pie. Were they a couple, or was it possible that the man at the end of the lunch counter was a needy narcissist?

"Hon, pay no attention to him," Rosie said. "He's just an old Georgia redneck."

Natalie glanced at the end of the lunch counter and considered the comment. No, he wasn't a redneck. Finally, glancing at the menu, Natalie said, "Okay, I think I'll take the fried shrimp dinner, please."

"Do you want coleslaw or a tossed salad with that?"

"I'll take a salad with oil and vinegar dressing on the side. Water to drink."

Rosie smiled. "I've got Thousand Island and Ranch dressing. That's it." She paused and looked around the cafe. Her hand flashed to her hips in a stance that meant *times up* or *hurry*.

"Ranch... on the side," Natalie said.

"Good choice." Rosie turned toward the bar separating the kitchen area from the restaurant. She said, "One shrimp dinner with salad and a side of Ranch." Then she placed the ticket on the top of the bar for the cook to put in the queue with the other orders.

After she finished her meal, Natalie walked to the register to pay her bill. "Rosie," she asked, "do you know Dr. Thomas Baldwin?"

Rosie leaned on the counter and tilted her head. "Hon, I know everybody on this island."

Natalie smiled. "Somehow, I thought you did. How far is his office from here?"

"Mmm... a fourth of a mile down the road on the right. It's a white house with black shutters and a bright yellow door. There's a tall white sign in the front yard. You can't miss it."

Jake got up from his barstool and towered over Natalie. "I'm going in that direction. You can follow me down there."

Intimidated by his height, Natalie turned to Rosie with a questioning look. "It's a straight shot, right? No turns... just go down the road?"

"That's right, sweetheart. Just go down the road to the white house with the yellow door." Rosie chuckled. "It'll take you less than five minutes."

Natalie looked from Rosie to Jake, "The directions seem simple enough. I believe I can find my way." She flashed Jake a tight smile. "But thank you, just the same."

"Suit yourself," His tanned face turned red as he placed a couple of bills on the counter.

Natalie walked out the door and down the steps to the parking lot. She was proud of herself for not taking him up on his suggestion… from the look on his face, he wasn't used to being turned down by a member of the opposite sex.

She threw her purse over the seat when she got into her car, slowly pulled to the exit sign, and waited for a vehicle to pass. As she pulled out of the parking lot, she misjudged the loose gravel on the four-inch incline. Pressing the accelerator, she winced as the tires spun and rocks flew beside the car. She glanced back at the diner. Jake stood on the steps outside, watching her leave. He laughed, his head tilting backward.

"Dammit!" she said, as she flew out of sight.

Chapter Four

The Mentor

Natalie slowed as she spotted the clinic ahead. Rosie's description of the white, cottage-style building, black shutters, and yellow door were spot on. Carefully, she pulled into the small parking lot, the sound of the crunching pebbles grating on her nerves.

As she got out of the car, a horn blew behind her. Natalie jumped. Her head twisted toward Jake's silver truck. Still laughing, Jake turned back to wave. Natalie smiled to herself. For years, she'd walked the streets of New York City without being recognized. It felt good that someone in this town already knew her. Of course, it was just a hunch, but perhaps she had met her first friend on the island.

She pushed through the clinic's front door as a young family was leaving. A young boy around the age of ten held his arm wrapped in a sling. Several people had already signed the freshly cast neon yellow arm. Natalie looked beyond the family. Dr. Baldwin was standing just inside the arched doorway. She barely recognized her old mentor and friend. She'd met him in medical school, when the medical college had invited him as a guest lecturer. He spoke about the importance of primary care medicine in maintaining the total health and welfare of patient care. She approached him after the lecture, and he'd taken her under his wing.

The past fifteen years had not been good to her friend. Dr. Baldwin looked feeble, and his skin was an ashen color. She saw his trembling hand and wondered if he still maintained a full schedule of patients.

A look of relief spread across the doctor's face when he saw her. "I've got one more patient waiting to see me. Have a seat… I shouldn't be long." His blue eyes sparkled with joy. Just like Jake's. The memory of the handsome contractor laughing at her from his truck came unbidden to her mind.

He turned toward the examining room, and she walked into the receptionist area. The large clock struck nine o'clock, and any receptionist or nurse who might have worked that day was long gone. The reception desk was clean and tidy. There was a short stack of manila files on the top of a filing cabinet. Someone had placed a few opened bills on the desk next to the phone. In bold print, a yellow Post-It note on top of the stack read *Needs approval*.

It was a homey office. Unfortunately, scents of coffee, antiseptic, and human sweat permeated the walls and fabrics of the old medical facility. After looking around the cramped lobby, Natalie wondered why the doctor hadn't moved to a larger building.

Around 9:30 p.m. as Dr. Baldwin followed the last patient to the door, he turned the sign on the window to *closed*. "Would you like a cup of tea?"

Natalie smiled, closed the magazine, and followed him into the kitchen area, where he filled a kettle with water. The doctor slowly opened the refrigerator door and assessed the contents. He must have been hungry, but he only removed the container of cream and closed the door. The doctor combed his fingers through his thick white waves and made small talk while watching the kettle. He was shorter than Natalie remembered. She'd thought he was around six feet tall. Clearly, he was more stooped than the last time she'd seen him. But he was gentle and kind, and there was something in his demeanor that made her want to hug him.

When the water was ready, he removed the kettle from the stove and placed a cup of tea in front of Natalie. Then he pulled a key from his silver key ring and slid it across the table as if she'd automatically know whether it fit the front door of the clinic or the door to his house.

She did not.

"Do you have a place to stay tonight?" he asked, turning to fill a second cup with water.

She nodded and reached for the shiny new key. "King and Prince."

"Good. They'll treat you well over there." He poured a small amount of creamer into his cup and stirred. "Have you had dinner?"

Natalie explained that she'd stopped at the diner down the road.

"Hmm, so you've met Rosie."

"Yes, indeed," she said, with more attitude than she had intended.

He looked over his glasses. "She's a lovely lady and a successful entrepreneur." He hesitated, then continued, "Rosie is a lot like you, but don't be distracted by her façade."

Thirty minutes later, as they walked to the front door, Dr. Baldwin said, "Get some rest tomorrow and meet me back here on Monday at about ten o'clock. You can shadow me for a couple of days."

Chapter Five

Shadowing

The following two days were a whirlwind of activity as Natalie learned to navigate her way around the clinic. Dr. Baldwin kept a full schedule Monday through Saturday. His was the only medical facility on the island; most days, it was more like an urgent care facility. Between his regular patient appointments and walk-ins, he also drove over the causeway to the Brunswick Campus of the Southeast Georgia Health System to check on hospitalized patients. It was a grueling schedule, serving an island of just under sixteen thousand people. A man half his age would struggle to meet the demands of this clinic. Yet, Natalie was in awe of his ability to keep the fast pace.

The time passed quickly, and Natalie seldom had a spare moment to think about the life she'd left behind in New York City. Instead, she enjoyed working in the clinic with her mentor. He was old school, the kind of doctor who prescribed the age-old remedies of licorice candy for curing a cough or warming vegetable oil to stop a child's earache. Still, he'd come to trust the latest discoveries in medicine, depending upon the newest technology afforded by the hospital in Brunswick. He quickly learned to access the electronic medical records used nationwide to manage and store medical information.

Natalie marveled at the information each patient shared with the doctor. Only yesterday morning, Dr. Baldwin had run into Mrs. Tribble at Rosie's Diner. The sweet-natured woman had shared that Mrs. Butterfield, her eighty-four-year-old neighbor and the doctor's oldest patient, struggled to walk through her house without getting winded. Moreover, the elderly woman's feet had swollen to twice their normal size. Dr. Baldwin had called Mrs. Butterfield the moment he arrived at the office and persuaded her to come in that very afternoon.

Was it the small-town way of life that caused the patients to speak openly, or was it the soft-spoken and unassuming manner in which the doctor dealt with each person? It was obvious from the first day that Dr. Baldwin's practice was more about knowing the patient. He was kind and jovial, regardless of the patient's gender or age, and always unhurried, allowing him to reach a personal level of communication quickly. Whether it was talking about their grandchildren or a beloved animal, Dr. Baldwin made it a point to form a relationship with each person who entered his clinic. A patient might enter the clinic as a perfect stranger, but Dr. Baldwin made certain they'd leave a trusted friend.

Now, as Natalie restocked the supplies behind the examining table, she watched him treat his oldest patient as if she were his grandmother. He pulled over a chair, so they were face to face, and rubbed the stethoscope over the fabric of his slacks. When the small metal device had warmed, he placed the stethoscope on Mrs. Butterfield's chest. He took her hand and said, "I'm hearing some things that concern me. I'm afraid we'll have to transport you to the hospital."

She jutted her chin and said firmly, "No way I'm going over that bridge in an ambulance. So, you can just forget about that!"

Natalie paused in her work, wondering how Dr. Baldwin would handle the elderly woman.

"I understand," he said gently. "Unfortunately, you have what we call congestive heart failure, and you'll suffocate unless we remove some of that fluid from around your heart."

With teary eyes, Mrs. Butterfield pursed her lips and silently considered her options. Finally, she said, "My heart feels fine. And I don't like ambulances. Or hospitals."

Dr. Baldwin stroked her hand. "I'm just trying to keep you alive for another holiday season." He winked as a broad smile fell across his lips. "You know how much I love your homemade candy."

Mrs. Butterfield's face softened. "Is it really that serious?"

"I'm afraid so."

She drew in a long breath and lowered her head in assent.

Afterward, as the ambulance pulled away with Mrs. Butterfield inside, Natalie smiled at Dr. Baldwin. "You should teach a class on bedside manner. That was masterful."

"It would be a very short class," he said, laughing. "Good morning, class. People know when you genuinely care about them—and when you don't. Class dismissed."

Chapter Six

The Fall

The fourth day since Natalie's arrival on the island was Tuesday—meatloaf day at Rosie's Diner. Dr. Baldwin picked up two meals as he returned from the hospital to check on Mrs. Butterfield.

When the last patient left, they settled into the kitchen to eat dinner and discuss their day. Dr. Baldwin took a cup from the cabinet and poured the steaming water over the tea bag while Natalie got a bottle of water from the fridge. Twisting the top of the water bottle, Natalie slid into her chair and watched the old man with affection. His feet shuffled as he crept around the small kitchen. Finally, after adding a splash of milk, Dr. Baldwin placed the paper towel holder on the table. Then he hesitated, placing both hands on the back of the chair, and stared at the table.

"How is the little Jones girl?" he asked. "I saw her come in this afternoon."

"Hairline fracture," she said. "Right foot, navicular bone." She took a swallow of water, then described how the patient had suffered an injury earlier in the afternoon from a bicycle accident.

The scuff of the chair on the wooden floor made her look up. He was teetering, his hand on the back of the chair for balance.

He slid the chair out and bent as if to sit. Then he toppled sideways and tumbled to the floor.

It happened so quickly that Natalie scarcely had time to think. She rushed around the table and knelt beside him... eyes rolled back in his head, saliva drooling from the corner of his mouth. She felt for a pulse—faint. Then she leaned her head over his face... his breath was shallow.

No, oh no.

She'd been away from the emergency room for almost a week, dealing with bug bites, fractured bones, allergies, and stomach viruses. Still, she returned to trauma mode as soon as she recognized the signs of cardiac arrest. Never taking her eyes off the patient, not even for one second, Natalie reached across the table, grabbed her phone, and pressed 9-1-1.

"Hello, what is your emergency?"

In a matter of seconds, his face had turned from an ashen gray to a sickly blue. Frantic to keep him alive until the emergency medical team arrived, she began chest compressions and CPR, answering the operator's questions between breaths.

Pump, two, three, four... she heard a rib crack. Five, six, seven... Thirty compressions, two breaths, begin again. And again. Until her hands cramped, and her arms ached. Pump, two, three, four... She pumped for what felt like hours, her old friend's life in her hands.

Hurry, hurry, please.

A siren screamed in the distance, and she stole a glance at the clock, surprised to see how little time had passed. The emergency medical team had arrived in record time.

The door burst open, and she made way for the paramedics, who administered a lifesaving shot of Epinephrine and loaded him onto the gurney and straight to the ambulance. But, before the last medic entered the ambulance, he yelled, "Follow us to the Southeast Georgia Health System Brunswick Campus."

The door slammed shut, and the ambulance squealed out of the parking lot.

Natalie jumped into the Porsche and let out a deep breath. She fumbled for the emergency lights… it was the first time she'd needed them, and she wasn't sure how to activate the flashing lights. Then, with a stroke of luck, she figured it out, spun out onto the highway, and sped up to catch the ambulance as they crossed the causeway.

Don't you die on me, old friend. Don't you dare.

She lurched to a stop at the traffic light in front of the medical center and glanced around to get her bearings. The hospital was much smaller than New York Memorial. Still, she'd heard it was an excellent facility. It was a salmon and beige modern stucco structure with lots of glass and a bit of brown brick at the base. The view from the main road was impressive, with easy access to the entrance and ample parking throughout the campus.

She went straight to the visitor's lot, parked, and ran toward the emergency area, her rising dread a stark reminder of the night of her husband's accident. One fellow from the EMT group was standing at the front desk, providing patient information to the nurse. He turned just as Natalie walked through the double doors of the emergency room.

"There she is," he announced. "She was with Dr. Baldwin when he collapsed at his office."

With that quick introduction, Natalie became her friend's point person. Outside his fall and apparent cardiac arrest, she knew little about his health. When the emergency room staff learned Natalie was the trauma doctor from New York City that Dr. Baldwin had been telling them about, they elevated her to "rock-star" status without warning.

It was almost midnight before they finished the diagnostics and determined a course of treatment. Natalie slept as best she could in the emergency room, in a chair next to Dr. Baldwin's gurney. Each time she woke, she looked at the vital signs on the monitor. It was interesting how different being an observer felt from being part of the medical staff. The sterile environment... watching the clock above the nurse's station... the sounds of ambulances coming into the hospital emergency entrance... the hushed conversations between the medical staff and another patient's family member... the sniffs and moans of a heartbroken spouse or parent, and the smells of antiseptic. More reminders of the night Paul had died.

Once, when Natalie looked at the gurney, her husband's face looked back at her with that charming smile. She blinked twice, then realized it was only a dream. She stood up and stretched, then she stepped outside the curtain that divided the units in the emergency room.

The numbering on the wall stopped her short. Dr. Baldwin's unit was the same as Paul's the night he'd died. A wave of unease washed over her. Looking across the way, she noticed another number, 3-B, the unit number where the woman, the one the nursing staff had mistaken for Paul's wife, had received treatment.

Natalie's eyes filled with tears, but she blinked them away. This was no time to become emotional. She was finished with that. Instead, she took a deep breath and headed toward the nurses station for fresh coffee. As soon as the head nurse saw her, she reached for a pad and got up from her seat. Natalie could tell she had a million questions already formulated in her mind.

But Natalie knew nothing.

The only thing she could tell the nurse with any certainty was that she had arrived on the island four days earlier, fulfilling a promise to check out Dr. Baldwin's medical practice. But that wasn't enough; the head nurse wanted more information about the doctor's health.

"I was told you will replace Dr. Baldwin at the clinic. Is that correct?"

Natalie hadn't even had time to find a permanent place to stay, much less decide about taking over the clinic. Still, she nodded. "Yes, I suppose I will run the clinic for the unforeseeable future."

When she returned to check on Dr. Baldwin, they were preparing to transfer him to the ICU. She carried his belongings and followed the gurney to the third-floor intensive care unit. Once she helped the nurses settle him in, Natalie squeezed his hand and left the hospital.

On the way back to the clinic, it hit her. She was in charge. The clinic, his clinic, was now her responsibility. The night air was heavy, and it seemed darker than when she'd followed the ambulance over the causeway earlier in the evening. She felt sad and alone, her sadness magnified by the limited number of vehicles on the road in the early hours.

A light from the passenger seat blooming in her peripheral vision caught her attention. A reflection of some kind, a trick of the moonlight on an exhausted mind. At the next stoplight, when she turned to look, it was Paul, not entirely in his human form, but enough so that she recognized him.

He looked almost angelic, sitting in the passenger's seat, an aura around him, looking at her with that beautiful smile. That look… her heart skipped a beat. That look drove her crazy… the look he used to get her to do anything he wanted. Engulfed by loneliness, at that moment, she would have stopped the car and followed him to any point on the globe. But she looked away when the light turned green, and when she glanced back at the passenger's seat, foot poised over the accelerator, he was gone.

***

Natalie pulled into the clinic's parking lot in a daze. She couldn't even remember driving over the causeway. Cutting off the ignition, she leaned her head back onto the seat and closed her eyes. Just for a moment. Just long enough to gather her thoughts.

Then she walked to the front door and removed the key from her pocket. It was tarnished, the metal of the jagged edges grainy looking. It looked like the kind of key you'd have to jiggle to make work—if it worked at all—but it slipped easily into the lock.

She sighed with relief as she turned the doorknob.

Natalie turned on the lamps in the waiting area and walked through each room, gaining a new perspective with each moment. The standard diplomas on the doctor's office walls were surrounded by plaques commending him for various acts of community service on the island. There was also an impressive collage of pictures—double-matted in an expensive frame. Dr. Baldwin grinned out at her, in one photo grasping a nine-iron and in another, mugging from a golf cart.

How was it that she'd missed these earlier? He'd never mentioned his love for golf.

The top center photo was of the Augusta National clubhouse, where the Master's Tournament was played each year. In the middle was a picture of Dr. Baldwin and three other gentlemen standing behind their golf clubs. At the bottom of the frame was the winning scorecard. Natalie stared at her friend's face and marveled at the likeness of the man she'd last seen in the hospital. Despite the photo being over forty years old, Dr. Baldwin's face had changed very little except for a few smile lines and silver hair.

Exhaustion set in. She'd been shadowing Dr. Baldwin for only two days, but they'd been long ones. Natalie had been naïve to think healthcare in a coastal area would move at a slower pace.

Gingerly, she pulled the large leather chair from behind his oversized oak desk, collapsed into it, and closed her eyes. For a few minutes, she drifted. Then her eyes snapped open. She looked at her watch. It was 5 a.m. The piercing intrusions of sirens had startled her from a sound sleep. In contrast to the perpetual noise of New York City, the island was deathly silent from ten o'clock at night until the early morning. More so at the clinic. Her mind reflected on her current situation.

She was in charge. The implications of that struck with the force of a tidal wave. She needed to make a list of items to order, reschedule an annual physical for one of Dr. Baldwin's patients, and go through the outstanding invoices. A dozen more tasks leaped into her mind, and she scrambled to make a list of things she needed to attend to before the clinic opened.

Who needed sleep, anyway?

By the time she heard the key fit into the back door, she'd caught a few hours of sleep, gotten through most of her list, and made a quick call to the ICU. No change in Dr. Baldwin's condition. She glanced at her watch. A little after 9 a.m.

A young woman walked into the office and stopped short when she saw Natalie. "Who are you?"

This must be Donna, Dr. Baldwin's receptionist. She had taken a few days off and was due back at the clinic today. Natalie had been expecting her.

When Natalie told her what had happened, the woman's eyes grew wide, "Is Dr. Baldwin going to be okay?"

"It's too soon to know."

Donna looked her up and down. "But what are *you* doing here?"

Natalie gave a self-conscious laugh. Of course, the woman had been taken by surprise. She'd been expecting her boss and found a stranger in his place. "Dr. Baldwin has been after me to come down and work with him in the clinic."

The woman's face flushed. "He never mentioned that to me." Her shoulders straightened. "If he didn't respect me enough to tell me he was bringing in another doctor, he clearly doesn't need me as much as I thought he did." Hands shaking, she removed her key from her keyring. "Please give him my regards."

She stalked out of the room, slamming the door behind her.

For the next few days, Natalie took care of the patients at the clinic. At the end of each day, she'd rush to the hospital to check on Dr. Baldwin, pick up a bite to eat, and return to the clinic to sort through the day's files and the stack of mail. At last, when she was too exhausted to read another word, she'd amble over to the sofa in the waiting room or the one in Dr. Baldwin's office and slept. It wasn't the leisurely beach adventure she thought she'd signed on for, but her friend needed her, so it had to be done. And, if she were completely honest with herself, a part of her loved it.

Each morning before opening the clinic, she'd go to Rosie's for breakfast and then to the hospital to check on her friend. Then, on the seventh morning, one week after her arrival on the island, she woke earlier than usual. With a subdued sense of urgency, she pulled on a pair of jeans and an old sweatshirt, brushed her teeth, and grabbed her keys on the way out.

When she walked into the ICU unit, Dr. Baldwin was asleep. Natalie sat and waited, careful not to make a disturbance. Then, finally, the new day dawned as she stared at the large picture window. The Sidney Lanier Bridge, the largest bridge in Georgia, was in plain sight. She sat up in her chair and soaked in the view. Natalie was grateful for the beautiful moment she would have missed had she not awakened so early.

Dr. Baldwin opened his eyes. They were wet and glassy, and his skin was ashen. His hands were cold as he pressed a scrap of paper into her palm and closed her fingers over it. Then, he grabbed the bed rail with one hand and gasped. "There is a safe… in the closet of my office." They were the first words he'd spoken to her since his heart attack.

He took another shallow breath, a tiny sip of air. "The papers are inside. Everything needed to settle my estate." His eyes closed, and his hand released the railing.

Natalie looked at the tiny piece of paper she clenched in her hand. It revealed the combination to the safe, and when, at last, it dawned on her she was in charge of his estate, he reached and squeezed her hand. A veil of peace fell over the room, and a scant smile appeared on his lips. A holy moment—unlike anything she'd ever experienced. She had slept very little since the night of his hospitalization and was so emotional she couldn't speak. As she held back tears, his grip loosened. His hand dropped to the mattress as he exhaled his last breath.

Gone.

Natalie leaned over and kissed her friend's cheek. He had left this world with a smile on his face. And although tears now streamed from her eyes, she couldn't help but smile, too.

Chapter Seven

Natalie

Still numb with grief, Natalie tried to focus on the hospital administrator's comments about Dr. Baldwin's legacy in the Brunswick-St. Simons area. "I don't know what we're going to do without him," the woman finished. "I've never known anyone so good with difficult patients." She gave Natalie an apologetic smile. "But you must have come here for a reason. What can I do for you?"

"Yes, I need someone to answer the phones at the clinic and fill in for me for a couple of days," Natalie said. "I wondered if we could use the hospital's answering service and one of your P.A.s until after the funeral?" They probably didn't have a physician's assistant to spare, but you'd never know if you never asked.

The administrator tapped her long red nails on the top of her desk and said, "Well, what about his assistant?"

Natalie explained the assistant's unexpected departure and then added, "I know it's a lot to ask, but I can tell you care about this clinic, so I wondered if you'd be able to spare someone for a few days." Following a lengthy discussion, the administrator said, "You're welcome to use our answering service, and I think I can provide a P.A., but I'll need him back in three days."

Relieved, Natalie rushed back to the clinic, cataloging all the things she had to do before the clinic opened. She printed a message about Dr. Baldwin's passing, taped it to the front door, and recorded a voice message explaining the telephone calls would be forwarded to the hospital in Brunswick.

When she could put it off no longer, she went into the dreaded closet. It smelled of sweet vanilla, musk, and mothballs. It was a unique combination. She had only gone into the closet on one other occasion to hang up Dr. Baldwin's cardigan sweater that he'd laid on the back of the kitchen chair the night she'd arrived. Gently, she touched the shoulder seam of the light blue sweater and lifted the sleeve to her nose. Closing her eyes, she inhaled the scent. The sweet scent of the vanilla pipe tobacco the doctor enjoyed at the end of the workday. Just as she remembered. A smile formed on her lips as she ran her index finger over the scribbled numbers on the torn paper. Then she wiped her eyes and looked down at the safe.

The safe, a cast-iron cube the same color as the dull side of a piece of aluminum foil, came almost to her knees. It had been in the same spot for a very long time, judging from the amount of dust that had accumulated around the floor.

She squatted on the floor and turned the safe dial to the left until she reached the number ten, then dialed back to the right to nineteen, and then back to forty-three. It was a convenient number to memorize since it was the doctor's birthdate. On the first attempt, the lock popped, and the door released. She opened the door to look inside. On the safe floor lay one legal-sized manila envelope. It was thick. She removed the envelope and felt around in the back to ensure she hadn't missed anything.

She hadn't.

Natalie rubbed her hand over the envelope's smooth surface and glanced at the closet full of clothing and shoes. She felt so alone. Coming to the island was supposed to provide an escape from the life she had left behind in New York City...a time to slow down and find herself after Paul's untimely death. And now, she was faced with planning a funeral for a person she had known and cared about for over fifteen years. True, he was her mentor, not a family member, but his absence left a hole in her heart. Even with the nine hundred miles between them, she'd always known she could depend on him. And now he was gone.

As if on cue, she heard Paul's voice say, "You can do this, Nattygirl. You'll get through it. You always do." It was his retort to every concern she'd mentioned throughout their marriage.

Natalie closed the safe door, lifted herself off the floor, and opened the envelope as she returned to the study. It took over an hour to read through the documents. Dr. Baldwin had been thorough... birth certificate, marriage license, his deceased wife's death certificate, medical license, deeds to properties, statements of financial accounts, and his Last Will and Testament. It was all there. By the time she turned over the last page, a detailed description of the funeral he'd planned, her vision was bleary, and her eyelids felt leaden. She leaned back in the oversized leather chair, rested her head, and closed her eyes.

Knock, knock.

Startled by the loud thump, she sat straight in her chair. Then, wide awake, she sat frozen, barely breathing...another moment passed.

Knock, knock, knock.

She rushed to the front door and glanced through the small, rectangular window cut into the wood. Jake stood on the porch watching the traffic pass. Natalie glanced at herself in the mirror. Ugh. She looked like she felt rumpled and exhausted. Oh well, there was nothing she could do about it. She raked her fingers through her messy hair and unlocked the door.

"Hi, Jake."

He turned to face her. "I just heard the news about Dr. Baldwin and thought you might need a cup of Rosie's coffee and a breakfast sandwich."

Natalie had been so involved in reading Dr. Baldwin's documents and thinking about his funeral that she hadn't even thought about coffee, much less breakfast. Jake handed her the brown paper bag but held onto the two cups of coffee.

"That was thoughtful of you. Would you like to come in?"

"Sure." He followed her into the small kitchen area and stood against the counter while Natalie removed a paper plate from the cabinet and reached for a knife.

They talked for a few moments about Dr. Baldwin. Then Natalie mentioned the detailed instructions he'd left about the cremation of his body and the memorial service.

"Let me know if I can help." Jake shuffled his feet and took a sip of coffee. "Planning a funeral can be a daunting experience. I'd hate for you to have to deal with it alone."

Natalie's back was to Jake, but she could hear the compassion in his voice. She smiled to herself, every nerve ending aware of his presence behind her.

As he continued to talk, she sensed this was the softer side of the man she'd met at Rosie's diner the day she pulled into town. The arrogance from the previous week was gone. His hair was still wet from his morning shower, and the potent scent of maleness added a touch of vulnerability to the long-legged man leaning against the counter. He was so close she could feel his body heat.

The powerful urge to touch him surprised her, but she managed to keep her voice steady when she said, "Please, sit down." She removed the paper wrapping from the thick sandwich. "I can't eat all of this. Why don't you eat half?"

She clamped her mouth shut, recognizing her own nervous chatter.

Jake didn't seem to notice. He chuckled, then pulled out a chair and said, "I just finished breakfast, but I'd never turn down one of Rosie's breakfast sandwiches."

As soon as he drained the last of his coffee, she made a fresh pot and then sat back down to finish her breakfast. "According to the notes," she said between bites, "Dr. Baldwin wanted the memorial service to take place the day after his passing." She got up, refilled Jake's coffee, and continued, "We can schedule it for later in the afternoon, but tomorrow is still awfully soon. Wonder when the cremains will be ready?"

"Thank you." He nodded at his cup. "Tomorrow, if they use the place in Brunswick. Let me know, and I'll ride over and get them."

Relieved, Natalie reached over to touch his arm, then caught herself and grabbed her coffee cup instead. "Thank you," she said without looking up, fearing he might see something in her eyes she wasn't ready to give.

Chapter Eight

The Funeral

The entire town of St. Simons turned out for the funeral at The Wesley United Methodist Church at Frederica on Sunday afternoon.

At the appropriate time, the service began. After the minister's opening remarks and a reading from the Old Testament, he invited friends to take a few minutes to share stories about Dr. Baldwin.

A middle-aged woman stood and cleared her throat. "When John Junior was a little over a year old, he got his leg stuck in the slats of a wooden highchair. As many of you will remember, John Junior was a chubby baby. We tried to free his leg but couldn't do it without him screaming like a banshee. So finally, we called Dr. Baldwin and asked him to meet us at the clinic. He laughed and asked if we had any olive oil.

"I said, 'Yeah, we have a bottle of olive oil.'

"Doc told us to rub the oil over John Junior's leg, and it should slide right out. It worked, and he didn't even send us a bill for his services." Everyone broke out in laughter.

The second person who spoke was a short African-American man with prickly silver hair. Erickson Brown was obese and almost as wide as he was tall. He'd suffered a myocardial infarction five years previous. Brown told of how Dr. Baldwin had kept him alive until an ambulance arrived to take him over the causeway to the hospital in Brunswick. Erickson cited the food he'd consumed at the Fourth of July celebration when he'd gotten sick. Hot dogs, hamburgers, homemade ice cream, and apple pie. He let out a hearty cackle, "Truth be known, it was that rack of Ethel's baby-back ribs that started my heart racing." He looked around the church until his eyes fell on Ethel Johnson, an attractive black woman with a huge bosom. "That's the truth, Ethel." The church exploded in laughter as Ethel shook her head in denial.

The last speaker, the one Natalie would never forget, was Jennifer Stephens. She was a twenty-eight-year-old mother with three little girls, all under the age of five. They clung to her legs as they peeked around and sheepishly smiled while their mother told of Dr. Baldwin's kindness and generosity at the most crucial time of her life. Jennifer's husband had left her the week before she gave birth to their third child. On the day she went into labor, Jennifer was penniless, with very little food in the cupboards and no one to watch her children. When she went to the clinic, Dr. Baldwin gave her money to pay rent for the next six months, with enough left over to buy all the groceries she would need for a month. Jennifer sobbed as she concluded her story about Dr. Baldwin's kindness.

Natalie had only been on the island for eight days, but after hearing the townspeople speak, she already felt like a part of the community.

At the end of the service, as Natalie made her way to the back of the church, she noticed Jake sitting next to a blonde woman. She was whispering to the person to her left, preventing Natalie from seeing her face.

Not that she cared who Jake sat with.

After the service, Natalie stood at the large wooden door and greeted each person who came to pay their respects. Unfortunately, Jake and the blonde slipped out the side entrance without speaking to her, which raised her curiosity even further. Who was the blonde woman? And why did Jake seem so eager to avoid introductions?

**

As per Dr. Baldwin's written instructions, a reception was held at the King and Prince. As it turned out, no one could have planned a better celebration of life. Posh food and alcohol had a way of encouraging people to speak confidently in front of a large group, who ordinarily would never speak in public. So the town folk took turns unself-consciously telling stories about the years Dr. Baldwin had worked in the small clinic on the island.

After everyone was served, Natalie invited the guests to walk out to the beach to spread the ashes. When she pushed the door open, she gasped in surprise as a gust of wind whipped her skirt and hair. While they had been inside enjoying the delicious food and reminiscing, the wind had increased.

Clinging tightly to the shiny urn that held her friend's cremains, she pushed into the wind and led the assembly to the beach. When everyone had gathered. Natalie turned and said, "When I came here eight days ago, I never thought I'd be standing here today saying goodbye to my friend."

There was so much more she wanted to say, but with the men's ties whipping around their faces and the women holding their hats with one hand and holding down skirts with the other, she cut her speech short and signaled to the minister.

As he finished the last of his prayer, a huge spray of ocean water reached the beach. Drenched and shivering, everyone scurried back inside the King and Prince.

Everyone but Natalie.

Finally, the winds ceased, and she was alone. The salt sprays on her lips tasted like tears. She watched as the ashes swirled on the surface of the water. Although her fist was clenched, she slowly opened her right hand and realized that, without thinking, she still had one small handful of her friend's ashes.

As she gave the last grains to the sea a movement from her left startled her. She turned and looked over her shoulder. Jake stood a few short feet away. His eyes were clear, but he rubbed his shoulder. Maybe she'd been too hasty to judge him.

Natalie could almost feel his sorrow. Unfortunately, the sadness in her own heart was replicated in his eyes.

With a knowing smile, he reached for her hand.

Later that night, while lying on the sofa at the clinic, she tried to remember the name of each person who had attended the memorial service. Natalie never forgot a face and was generally good with names, but it would be a challenge to remember the name of each person she'd met throughout the day. Jake was the first person who came to mind. She wondered again who the woman was with him. Had she misinterpreted Rosie's comment about Jake not having a girlfriend?

That guy is taking up too much space in my head!

Frowning, she turned her thoughts to the mourners. Mr. Sworshenzi was from Poland and came to the States in search of better health care. He'd been one of Dr. Baldwin's patients for over twenty years. Then, there was Mrs. Templeton. She'd moved to St. Simons Island forty years ago after her husband returned from the Vietnam war. Dr. Baldwin had nursed him through the final months of his life, but sadly, he had died of Parkinson's Disease, a complication from Agent Orange exposure during the war.

In New York, she'd never had the time to get to know her patients so well. She hoped she could serve them as well as Dr. Baldwin.

She quickly made a mental note to contact Jennifer Stephens about working at the clinic. Jennifer could even bring the children to work
with her. They could set up a small table in the doctor's office for the children to play during the day. An area of the backyard was already fenced, and she could get someone to build a sandbox and swing set to keep the children entertained. Having them at the clinic would save Jennifer the cost of childcare.

Natalie was sure Dr. Baldwin would be pleased by the decision. She clearly needed help in the clinic, and Natalie could trust Jennifer. If she agreed to take the job, Natalie would enroll her in a C.N.A. program at the hospital in Brunswick and hire a sitter to watch the children while Jennifer went to class.

They would make a good team.

The last thought Natalie had before she'd fallen asleep was about Rosie. She hadn't seen Rosie at the funeral. Dr. Baldwin ate breakfast at the diner every morning and picked up dinner almost nightly. The diner was closed on Sunday, so where was Rosie?

Chapter Nine

The Friendship

Natalie sat on a bar stool at Rosie's diner, sipping black coffee and marveling at the bustle. The place was humming for a Monday morning, with many of the townsfolk gathered over breakfast, talking about the turnout for Dr. Baldwin's memorial service the previous afternoon. She'd lived through two stressful situations within two years. Now, because Dr. Baldwin's loss had come so soon after her arrival, she vaguely considered if staying in the beach town was in her best interest.

She still wasn't sure, but regardless, she had promised him when she arrived that she'd wait six months before making a firm decision.

While sipping her coffee, she watched Rosie dash around the restaurant, waiting tables and greeting each customer as they walked through the door. Rosie had missed her calling by owning a restaurant; she met people so easily, maybe she should run for public office.

Her phone pinged, and Natalie pulled it from her purse and punched in her passcode to read the message. It was an offer from the hospital administrator to extend their services until Tuesday morning.

Natalie smiled and typed her response. **Thanks, I owe you one**.

As Rosie made her way back through the restaurant, she paused to refill Natalie's coffee with a practiced smile.

Natalie said, "Rosie, I didn't see you at the funeral yesterday. Were you ill?"

Rosie cut her eyes at Natalie and lowered her voice. "I was there," she said. There was a refinement in her speech that Natalie had not heard earlier.

"Oh, I must have missed you."

"The service was beautiful," Rosie said, "but this morning's buzz was about the reception over at the King and Prince. How did you put that together so quickly?"

"Doc had everything planned," Natalie said. "I just followed his instructions."

She finished the last of her breakfast and said, "That might have been the best omelet I've ever eaten."

Rosie pulled a stack of tickets from her apron and sifted through them. Then, without looking up, she asked, "Are you staying at the clinic?"

"Yes. I've been so busy, I've not had time to find a place. The first couple of nights, I stayed at the King and Prince, which was wonderful. But before I knew it, I was working later and later and would end up crashing on the sofa at the clinic. So I moved my things there this weekend."

Rosie leaned over the counter and lowered her voice. "Here's my address," she said as she slid a piece of paper toward Natalie's plate. "Come by Sunday afternoon around five o'clock. It's my day off, so please don't get all dolled up. We'll have a cocktail and a light dinner on the porch. Then we'll discuss finding you a place to stay."

***

By Saturday evening, Natalie had met almost thirty patients and familiarized herself with the files of several hundred more. She'd learned how to run the new X-ray machine and the coffeemaker and had interviewed five potential receptionists, none of whom seemed like a good match. She felt like she'd wrestled an anaconda ball. Thank God the clinic was closed on Sundays.

The next morning, she slept until noon, and since Rosie's Diner was closed on Sunday, she made herself a light lunch. She found a jar of peanut butter in the cabinet and noticed a few mellowed apples in the basket on the table. Natalie sorted the apples, turned around to the sink, and washed them. She cut off the dark spots, opened the peanut butter jar, and removed a large spoonful. With the slices well slathered and arranged, Natalie sat on the back steps and enjoyed her lunch while reading the paper. In New York, everyone she knew got their news online, but Dr. Baldwin still subscribed to The Brunswick News. Basking in the smell of warm newsprint in the sunlight, she thought she might continue his subscription.

She spent the day hand-washing a few personal clothing items, then she showered in a small bathroom adjoining Dr. Baldwin's office. Remembering Rosie's remarks, she pulled on a white skirt and a black camisole. In Brooklyn, they would consider the combination casual. But would a skirt be too "dolled up" for a beach town?

She stepped back, appraising the outfit in the bathroom mirror. It seemed casual enough, but it still needed something.

After a moment, she grabbed a matching floral cardigan from her suitcase and rechecked her reflection. Better.

She pinched some color into her cheeks. Then, smiling, she slid on a pair of black flip-flops, applied a pale pink lip gloss color, and piled her damp hair into a bun on the crown of her head.

Not bad.

She grabbed the hostess gift she'd picked up at the market the previous day and checked her watch. It was already 4:55, and she would be late if she didn't get moving.

A nervous shiver shot through her stomach as she taped Rosie's address and directions to the dashboard. Her first real social call in her new town, and she felt like a child on her first day of school.

Rosie's house was a beautiful little cottage on the beach. As she pulled into the pebbled driveway, Natalie got a better view of the pale-yellow exterior with the white shutters and trim. But when she cut off the ignition, she just sat and marveled at the scenery. Imagine, coming in from work each day to the sights and sounds of ocean waves.

After staying in the car to admire the view a tad longer than intended, the back door swung open, and a woman she barely recognized yelled at her, "Hello, Natalie. Get out and come in!"

Who was that woman? Southern and refined. The touch of vocal gentility she'd noticed earlier was on full display, and the voice change took her by surprise. Her redneck dialect was all but gone. But it was her hair that caused Natalie to look twice. Rosie wore a wavy bob with caramel lowlights that added a depth of color to the otherwise blonde curls, all one length that struck her at mid-neck—short but sassy.

As Natalie walked closer to the cottage, Rosie pointed to her hair. "This is mine. I wear a wig to work." She wore a floral sundress with bright pink sandals. A touch of tinted lip-gloss and mascara—just enough makeup to cause her dark brown eyes to sparkle. "I'm Rosie at work, but when I leave the diner, I'm Rosemary. Rosemary Delaney."

"That's quite a transformation," Natalie said as she stopped in front of the door.

"Isn't it, though?"

"What's up with the dual identity?"

"I'm a writer," Rosie–Rosemary said. "I work hard at the diner to pay the bills, but out here, I want complete anonymity."

"You were with Jake at the funeral, right?"

"Yes. Please don't blow my cover. No one has caught on that Rosie from the diner and Rosemary from the beach are the same."

Natalie gave her an appraising look. Rosemary did look like a different person. Amazing what the creative application of makeup and a ridiculous wig could do.

Natalie crossed her heart with a finger. "Your secret's safe with me."

As Natalie got to know Rosemary over a meal of garlic-butter-seared scallops and salad, listening to the entrepreneur explain methods and investments, she realized the woman deserved an Academy Award for her redneck act. Underneath that façade was an intelligent and formally educated woman whom Natalie quickly learned to trust.

After dinner, they sat on the screened porch and watched the twinkling lights from the pavilion at the King and Prince, where a local band was warming up. Rosemary lit a few more votive candles throughout the porch. Just before the sun set, a bronze-colored Lab ran up from the beach and stopped at the screen door, the leash and his owner dragging behind.

Rosemary waved a beckoning hand. "Jake, why don't you and Copper join us for a drink?"

Jake walked over to the porch. The soft light provided just enough light for Natalie to recognize his boyish features.

Jake grinned as he released Copper from his leash. "Hello there," he said to Natalie. Then he turned toward Rosemary and said, "I think I will."

While Rosemary went inside for another glass, Jake watched Copper for a few moments, ensuring the lab would stay close by. Then he removed a napkin from his pocket and methodically dusted the sand from his feet. Just as he opened the back door, Rosemary returned with the remaining wine from dinner, a bottle of bourbon, and one liquor glass.

Jake pointed to the surfboard next to the door and asked, "How long has this been here?"

"Two or three days." Rosemary grinned and handed him a glass.

He looked at it and tilted his head. "You know me well."

Rosemary raised her eyebrows, swung her head to one side, and ran her fingers through her hair. Natalie looked at Jake, but he had missed the performance. Instead, he was busy pouring himself a drink.

Natalie watched as Rosemary eyed the handsome neighbor. *Oh, yes, she knows you very well.*

Jake gave Rosemary a quick hug. "Thanks for letting me crash your girls' night." There was an awkwardness to the embrace, followed by a deafening silence.

Jake looked around for a seat. "So you're from the 'Big Apple,'" he said to Natalie. At her look of surprise, he added, "I saw your car tag."

"Very observant." Natalie smiled and took a deliberate sip of her wine. "Do you know the origin of that appellation?"

Rosemary looked from Natalie to Jake with knitted brows.

Jake cocked his head to the side. "Well, of course!" He reared back until the chair rested on the back legs. "A sportswriter back in the 1920s coined the phrase."

Natalie added a teasing tone to her voice. "And his name was?"

He held her gaze as he deliberately stirred the drink with his finger and licked the excess liquid. Then, clearly enjoying the game, he cleared his throat as if he were about to orate a big announcement. "John J. Fitz Gerald."

"Very good."

Rosemary chimed in, too. "Everyone knows that New York State is known for the size of their apples."

"That's true, my friend," Jake said. "But the Big Apple moniker was first mentioned in connection with horse racing. Isn't that right, Natalie?"

Natalie raised her eyebrows and nodded as she lifted her glass in approval.

Jake continued, "John Fitz Gerald was a New York City newspaper reporter. One day, he heard a couple of stable hands in New Orleans say they were going to 'the Big Apple.' It was a reference to New York City, whose racetracks were big-time venues. So, Fitz Gerald began mentioning the Big Apple in his newspaper columns."

Rosemary cut her eyes at Jake, her face flushed with emotion and clearly annoyed with his ability to impress her guest. "How do you know so much about the history of New York City?"

"I follow horse racing. The Belmont Stakes is in Elmont, just east of New York City."

A stilled silence followed.

When the pause grew uncomfortable, Natalie changed the subject. "It's a little late to be on the beach... Do you live around here, too?"

"Yep." Jake pointed to a house a short distance from Rosemary's.

Natalie followed the direction of his hand. "Next to the house with the 'for rent' sign I passed on the way here?"

"The very same."

"Do you know the owner?"

"Yeah. I know the owner." Jake tugged at his right ear and said, "Would you like me to talk to him for you?"

"Oh, thank you! That would be great. I've been so busy at the clinic that I've not looked for a place yet." She chuckled. "When I arrived on the island, I wasn't even sure I would stay. But now that I've been here a few weeks and have gotten to know the townspeople…." Natalie looked out onto the glistening water and smiled. "This place suits me."

Jake and Rosemary exchanged a knowing look.

"Well," Jake said, "I'll see what I can find out."

Chapter Ten

The Door Panel

The following Thursday, Jake stopped by the diner for breakfast. As he pulled into the parking lot, he smiled at the sight of Natalie's Porsche parked catty-cornered at the side of the building. The back end of the car stuck out about a hand's breadth from the allotted space, and a transfer truck was inching forward and back, trying to get past it.

He knew Natalie had pulled an all-nighter because the lights were still on at the clinic when he passed it on his way to an early morning property inspection. That had been happening a lot since Dr. Baldwin's death. He held up a palm to the truck driver and signaled his intent to find the Porsche's owner. The man gave a curt nod and put his vehicle into Park.

When Jake walked into the diner, Natalie sat on her regular stool at the end of the counter. She looked so tired she could hardly keep her eyes open. When Rosie placed her breakfast on the counter, Natalie immediately dove in, obviously ravenous. She was so engrossed in eating her meal that she seemed oblivious to anything beyond the edge of her plate.

Jake walked toward her. "Hey, Natalie. You're blocking a delivery truck. Do you want me to move your car for you?"

With her mouth full of hashbrowns, Natalie tossed him the keys.

Jake ambled outdoors to the side of the restaurant and nodded to the delivery driver. He fiddled with the electronic key lock until he heard a beep, and the door opened. The interior resembled the cockpit of a 747 plane with colorful instrument panels on the dashboard. A sweet ride, no doubt about that. He slid into the creamed-colored leather seat and positioned it to accommodate his long legs, breathing in the new-car smell. When he'd folded his body behind the vintage steering wheel and moved the sports car out of harm's way, he let himself explore the inside of the vehicle before cutting the engine.

He ran his hand across the leather seats. They were as soft as a baby's bottom. But it was the steering wheel that would cause any guy to abandon all logic and disregard the exorbitant price tag.

Jake's heart skipped a beat as he ran his index finger around the edges of the wooden steering wheel. He marveled at the sleek finish, a result of high-tech polishing. It had a futuristic component: a round metal disc outlined with elegant screw heads with the Porsche gold, red, and black insignia positioned in the center. Three metal arms connected the large disc to the steering wheel. Porsche, a maker of the most elitist of automobiles, used wood steering wheels and hub adapters manufactured to the highest standards using top-quality materials. The alloy parts, machined from prime stock solid billet aluminum, were triple-polished to a mirror finish.

He was still marveling at the engineering when he realized the car was still running. The engine was so quiet he'd forgotten to turn it off. And with the interior temperature set at a comfortable 68 degrees, he'd lingered longer than he should.

He gave himself a few more moments to feast his eyes on the interior. Then reluctantly, he removed the seatbelt and reached for the door handle. When he jerked the handle, the inside panel popped open. Inside were bundles of what appeared to be large-denomination bills.

He stared at the neatly stacked bills. Carefully, he slid his hand inside the panel and removed a package. Holding the bundle between his knees to keep it out of view, he fanned the hundred-dollar bills and added the sum in his head. It was a large sum.

He slid his hand back down the panel and counted ten rows of packages. He'd always been good with numbers, so he quickly did the math. Half a million dollars, give or take a little, hidden behind the panel. So, what was Natalie doing with this much money in her car?

Jake looked at the panel on the opposite side of the vehicle and wondered if he'd find the same amount on the passenger side.

He wiped the beads of sweat from his upper lip and glanced into the rearview mirror—knowing he'd discovered something he wasn't supposed to see. He slid the package of bills back into place. Careful to position them perfectly, he pounded the panel back into position. Then Jake looked around the inside of the car. Natalie had left a scarf lying on the console. He grabbed it and wiped off the steering wheel, gearshift, and door handle. Jake quickly climbed out of the car and locked the door. The shiny sports car had quickly lost its appeal, and he wanted to get as far away from it as possible.

When he returned to the diner, he placed the keys next to Natalie's plate.

"Thanks." Natalie patted the stool beside her. "Sit and join me."

Jake slid onto the stool and considered whether he should ask her about the loose door panel. But the bigger question was why she would hide that much cash in a car. It was a weird place to hide money. Creative, yes, but odd.

Was Natalie a fugitive? He glanced at her from the corner of his eye. She certainly didn't look like one. She was a high-profile specialist from New York City. He had googled her name and read that she'd recently been promoted to medical director. She was legit.

Jake's father had always said that people from the state of New York were slightly more accomplished and refined than folks down here. That was perhaps the ideology of someone from New York or a total myth. Regardless, she was a beautiful and intelligent woman who didn't fit the profile of a thief or a fugitive. On second thought, she may not even be aware there was money hidden in her car. What a surprise that would be!

Rosie strolled over and pointed to her order pad. "What will you have, Jake?"

"I, uh…" Jake stammered and then shook his head as if to clear his mind. "I'll have an all-star breakfast sandwich and black coffee, please." He waited as Natalie finished her meal and was sipping her coffee. Then he said, "I've been meaning to stop by the clinic. I talked to the owner of the cottage next to my place. I've got you a contract." He removed a piece of paper and placed it on the bar. "The lease is $3,000 a month."

Natalie smiled. "Thank you, Jake." She briefly scanned the front page of the document. "Is that a fair price for that area?"

"I should think so." Jake hesitated as he looked over the restaurant, conscious of those sitting nearby. "But, of course, the owner knocked off a grand since you're taking over the clinic." Then he chuckled and said, "You're getting a great neighbor and a view of the best sunrise on the island."

Natalie brushed her hand on his arm. "Thank you so much. I'm looking forward to sleeping in a proper bed again."

Jake looked down at his arm and glanced at her sideways. A lopsided grin spread across his face. "Why don't you stop by my place tonight when you finish at the clinic?"

Natalie quickly removed her hand from his arm. "Why?"

His eyes danced with mischief. "Well, for starters, it's fish taco night."

Chapter Eleven

The Dream

Natalie eased into the clinic's parking lot, relieved that no one was there. She had scheduled her first appointment at 2:30, but sometimes there were walk-ins. If she was lucky, she had six hours to catch some sleep. As she cut the engine, she noticed two black Chevrolet Suburban SUVs parked on the wooded access road just beyond the facility. The vehicles reminded her of a secret service detail, but no one had said anything about a dignitary or celebrity visiting the island.

She got out of the car and trudged through the clinic's back door and sank onto the sofa, pulling out her phone to set the alarm. The date flashed up at her. June 6th. Her wedding anniversary. With a stab of guilt, she realized she'd been so busy with the clinic that she'd lost track of the days.

Natalie closed her eyes, and Paul's gorgeous face formed in her mind. His piercing green eyes, firm jaw, and perfectly straight teeth.

Oh, Paul.

She pulled the afghan up and curled herself around the sofa pillow. As she drifted into sleep, she could almost smell the sandalwood scent of his aftershave.

***

The New York condo smelled of fresh-baked bagels and hazelnut coffee. Natalie looked at the date on her Apple watch. Their fifth wedding anniversary was exactly five weeks away, and Paul had yet to say anything about making plans.

As she handed him a plate of bagels topped with cream cheese, she asked, "Have you thought about our anniversary? It's coming up fast." She reached for the coffeepot.

He looked up from his phone. "No, I've been so busy at work that I've not given it much thought. What would you like to do?"

Smiling, she refilled their coffee. "Since you're so busy right now, I'll make the anniversary plans." She brushed his face with her hand. "It'll be fun."

Fortunately, the big day fell on a Wednesday. Paul's colleagues met for drinks immediately after work each Wednesday afternoon, providing him an excellent excuse to leave early himself.

As the weeks passed, Natalie was very mysterious about her plans. Paul had orchestrated their anniversary dinners in the past, and they were always elaborate and meticulously arranged evenings that Natalie loved. This year, she wanted to do the same for him.

She watched the website for days, waiting for tickets to become available for *Tina: The Tina Turner Musical*. They both loved Motown Music, and Natalie wanted the best seats in the house. But, as excited as she was about the evening, she took every precaution to keep her plans a secret from Paul. She was pleased to note that the suspense drove him crazy.

The tickets stated a seven o'clock start time, and she booked a 10 o'clock reservation at their favorite restaurant Rue 57, a French-American brasserie in Midtown Manhattan. It was a convenient four-minute walk from Central Park, and she hoped they'd have time before dinner for a drink at The Plaza.

"Please tell me what you've planned for our anniversary?" Paul's pleadings had become somewhat of a daily game. He was a control freak who hated being in the dark about anything.

Finally, as they lay in bed on the morning of their anniversary, Natalie said, "I've planned a spectacular evening for us tonight."

Paul turned over, opened one eye, wrapped his arms around her, and kissed her neck. Then he brushed her bottom lip with his thumb and said, "Please, tell me where we're going tonight!"

The banter continued over breakfast. Paul was spreading jam on a bagel when he looked up and said, "I'll tell you what I've got you for our anniversary if you'll tell me your plans for tonight."

"Well..." Natalie pretended to play along. "It involves food and an expensive bottle of champagne."

"We better have champagne—a nice bottle, none of that cheap stuff, either!"

Natalie jumped up from the table and grinned. "That's all I'm saying about it. You'll just have to wait and see."

After breakfast, as Paul got ready to leave for work, Natalie walked with him to the foyer. He checked himself in the mirror, and Natalie reached over to straighten the knot in his tie. With a wicked grin, she said, "If you leave the office at five-thirty and come straight home, we can ride together. It'll be just like a real date night."

"I'll try." He leaned over to kiss her goodbye. "You know I'd love to stay home with you today." His index finger followed the indentation of her décolleté.

"Why don't you call in sick and stay home?" she said with a husky voice. "I promise it will be an anniversary to remember."

To her surprise, his briefcase dropped onto the floor beside them as he looked at her with those dreamy eyes.

"Don't tempt me." He nibbled at her neck as he pressed her body against the front door. At first, it was a few playful kisses. Then he untied her bathrobe.

"Oh, Paul."

His passion increased as his warm hands expertly caressed her bare skin—then he delivered a slow, passionate kiss. Her excitement intensified with every touch.

His lovemaking was strategic... similar to a chess game. Never hurried nor miscalculated. His every move was designed for her pleasure.

As she savored the sensations of their bodies mingling, the alarm on his Apple watch sounded. It was time for him to leave, or he'd miss the bus.

"Must you go now?"

"If I wait to catch the next one, I'll be late for work." He reluctantly released her, still gazing into her eyes. "I love you, sweet Natty."

Finally, he straightened his tie, finger-combed his hair into place, and picked up his briefcase before walking out the front door.

It was over.

The last thing he said before leaving for work was, "I'll leave the office at five-thirty. I promise." He paused and flashed that gorgeous smile. "And tonight, I'll finish what I started."

She had taken the day off, hoping he would do the same.

The ache in her upper torso was unlike anything she'd ever felt. If she hadn't known better, she would have thought it was a heart attack. Unresolved passion could play havoc with the female anatomy.

But he was gone. Natalie watched from the window as he walked down the sidewalk to the bus stop.

She spun around, went into their bedroom suite, turned on the shower, dropped her bathrobe onto the floor, and stepped inside. The water was icy. She stood under the pulsating water until the desire in her body had passed.

Then, to pass the time before the celebration, Natalie gathered up Paul's dress shirts and took them around the corner to the cleaners. Watching pedestrians walk around the city seemed like a glimpse into another world.

So, this is what people do all day while I'm at the hospital. Since she was close to the market, she stopped and picked up a salad for lunch.

When she got home, a dozen long-stem yellow roses sat on the porch. Her favorite. She bent to breathe in their sweet scent and read the note written in Paul's perfect script.

Looking forward to tonight, babe. You just wait until you see the gift I've got for you!

A thrill ran through her—he was thinking of her too!—and as she placed the arrangement on the table in the foyer, she was humming.

Seated in front of the television, she ate her salad while trying to concentrate on the local news, but her mind kept conjuring images of the passion in Paul's eyes from that morning. She looked at her watch for the hundredth time and then prepared a charcuterie board for them to enjoy when he got home. She washed the fruits and left them on the kitchen counter to dry while she arranged the cheese board.

Then, she texted Paul, as she had done throughout the day. Each time, he flirted with her. And each time, the ache in her chest returned and grew stronger.

She removed the champagne chiller from the sideboard and placed it in the refrigerator. Then she returned to the dining room and laid out the clear white plates and cocktail napkins.

She took her time getting ready. At 6 o'clock, she paced around their Macdonough Street Brownstone like a young girl waiting for her prom date. When she could stand it no longer, she went into the bedroom and slathered her long silky legs with Chanel No. 5 lotion.

She hung up a few items of clothing, removed the new piece of lingerie from the shopping bag, and laid it on the chair in the corner. It was a red chemise—no lace, just a soft silk, classy little slip with matching panties. Now she wondered if she should have bought the black one instead. The black one was elegant, and it had more lace. But she'd read somewhere that men liked red lingerie. Red with a capital R. Not pink or salmon, but red. A poll of male readers determined that red was the color of love and passion.

By the time Natalie had slipped into a shimmery sheath dress and a pair of stiletto heels, it was 6:15. She texted Paul again:

Where are you, Paul?

He replied:

I'm about to leave. Let's meet at the restaurant to save time.

She replied:

Dinner will be later. Meet me at The Lunt-Fontanne Theatre on 46th Street-seven o'clock start time.

Her phone rang, and Paul was chuckling. "Oh, Natty, this evening is going to be epic! I was hoping you'd get tickets to see

Tina!" He couldn't contain the excitement in his voice. "If we each leave within the next five minutes, we'll arrive at the theater with at least fifteen minutes to spare."

"Okay," she said, trying to hide her disappointment. "I'll see you at the theater."

On the way out, she paused at the table in the foyer and gently touched one delicate petal of a long-stem yellow rose.

A stubborn smile spread across her lips. She inhaled the sweet fragrance and tried to contain her aggravation with her husband. Despite her initial disappointment, the day had been nearly perfect, with all the texting and flirting they'd done. She'd hoped the evening would be a complete surprise, but because of his delay, she had to tell him where to meet her, upstaging her plans.

The sun had already begun to set, and the New York skyline was dotted with lights. Remembering the elaborate spread on the dining room table, she rushed into the adjoining room to remove the food. The impressive cheese board sat in the middle of the dining room table, with colorful edible flowers interspersed between the various delicacies and the rich golden Krug Grande Cuvee brut champagne sweated in the silver chiller. The chandelier lights reflected off the crystal flutes and the silver chiller. It was a beautiful sight.

Now, a total waste.

She popped an edible flower into her mouth. Goodness, the silky confection simply melted on her tongue. A rush of sugar infiltrated her veins. Paul would've had a hey-day with those flowers. Well, maybe for a late-night post-dessert dessert.

She smiled, remembering the night they met. When he had approached her at the restaurant he seemed short, barely five-foot-seven. In heels, she stood an inch or two taller, and she'd wondered if he'd felt uncomfortable. But Paul was secure—the most secure man she'd ever known. His height hadn't mattered at all.

She was smitten when she looked at his gorgeous face, the silky mahogany-colored hair, and that charming smile with those pearly white teeth. When he looked at her with those deep green eyes—it was like he could see her soul. Nothing else had mattered.

Natalie released a sigh. All she wanted was to enjoy a relaxed evening with her husband. Looking over the flowers in the mirror, she noticed the V-shaped furrow on her brows. That wouldn't do. She smoothed the frown from her face and stopped to check her makeup. She liked the dramatic eyes, but her lipstick had faded. Deftly, she reapplied it. Then she bent her head over and shook out her hair. When she flung her head back, her long curls fell into a perfect position. She could already imagine Paul's appreciative stare.

Satisfied with her appearance, she shook off her frustration and walked out of the condo. In less than an hour, she would meet her husband.

The evening was going to be perfect.

Chapter Twelve

The Clinic - Now

The two o'clock alarm sounded too soon. Natalie squinted from the scorching afternoon sun streaming through the window. She turned over, remembering the layout of the beautiful brownstone where she and Paul had lived.

She was exhausted. After a couple of hours of sleep, she'd awakened from a dreamy state. Her mind flooded with crystal-clear memories of Paul. At some point, she had floated in and out of consciousness, then finally, she drifted off to sleep again. But she wasn't sure how much she'd actually slept in the past six hours.

Natalie rubbed her eyes and hit the snooze button as she thought about the dream. It had been bittersweet. She wasn't certain how much was dream and how much was memory, but it couldn't have been any clearer had it happened yesterday, especially the warmth of her husband's arms wrapped around her naked body. Even now, she could almost feel his gentle touch.

The edible flowers… Whatever made her think about that? Pretty and delicate, white with purple edges, and some were a poppy pink.

Natalie sat up straight and stretched her arms. When Paul hadn't left work at the agreed-upon time, she had been furious. And now, after two years, she still felt the anger of that evening. He'd be alive today had he kept his promise. She knew it was part of the grieving process to want to place blame.

But there it was! Then she remembered the eagerness of his breath on her body and the passion of his last kiss. Her anger faded as her body tingled with desire.

The alarm sounded again, and she hit the snooze button for the second time. Finally, she got up and went into the bathroom. It wasn't long until she heard the clinic's front doorbell signaling the patient's arrival.

When she'd finished with the two-thirty appointment, four additional patients were waiting to see her. It was a busy afternoon, between the Thompsons' youngest son's fractured arm and Mr. Ziegler's gallbladder attack. Mr. Ziegler was her last patient of the day, and she followed him to the door. "Be sure to get this prescription filled on your way home and keep a record of items you eat that cause you discomfort." Natalie quickly locked the door. It was after 6:00, and she rushed into the back office to get ready for her meeting with Jake.

She took a quick shower, dried off, and stepped into the first sundress she saw. Maybe it was because of the scrubs she wore to work, but getting dressed to go out had always been fun. Paul's death had leeched the joy out of it, but she couldn't help feeling a lift in her spirits as she smoothed the dress over her curves.

As she walked out of the office, she grabbed a straw hat. Then she looked around for the colorful scarf. Where was it?

When Natalie unlocked her car, she saw it. The scarf was a perfect match for her pink sundress. Straight away, she tied it around the hat, reached into her purse, and pulled out the lip gloss before cranking the car.

Pulling an all-nighter usually left her looking washed out and haggard, but the shower had somehow rehydrated her skin. Her brown eyes looked perfectly rested, and the golden flecks gleamed in the light.

The evening was just dinner with an acquaintance to review a contract for a rental. Otherwise, she would have taken much more time to dress, but as she pulled onto the road, she admitted she wanted to impress Jake. She wasn't interested in a romantic relationship just yet, but if she were, he'd be the guy.

She drove five minutes to the beachfront road where Jake lived. As soon as she turned, she saw the black Chevrolet Suburban SUV, with its tinted windows and a University of Miami silver inlaid mirrored tag. She hadn't given it a second thought earlier, but now she wondered if this could be more than a coincidence. It looked like the same black SUV that had followed her on the interstate on her way down from New York. Natalie slowed as she went past the vehicle.

Just as she pulled into Jake's drive, the black SUV turned around and went out the way she had entered.

Chapter Thirteen

Taco Night

Jake looked out the kitchen window toward Rosemary's house. He wondered how Rosemary would feel when she found out Natalie was coming to dinner, and he hadn't invited her. They'd been sort of a couple—a platonic couple—since Rosemary had moved to the island two years prior. They attended events together, kept a watch out for each other's homes, and shared an occasional drink on the beach. It was a friendship between a guy and a girl. Nothing serious.

He hoped she wouldn't feel left out. Yet, the moment Natalie walked through the door of the diner, Jake knew she was someone he'd like to get to know.

He'd finished peeling the second avocado and discarded the seed when he heard Natalie's sports car pull onto the gravel driveway.

She's here. He quickly rinsed his hands, dried them on the kitchen towel, and walked to the porch to let Copper inside. His stomach gave a nervous little flip. He'd wanted to invite Natalie to dinner for several days, and the contract gave him the perfect excuse. Now that she was here, though, he wished he'd sprung for the lobster. You only had one chance to make a good first impression.

When Jake glanced at the driveway, Natalie was sitting in her car with a cell phone to her ear. She looked at Jake and waved. He waved back and motioned for her to come in when she'd finished her call, wincing at the ache in his shoulder.

While Copper waited by the door, Jake made a quick dash to the bathroom to get a pain pill. Hopefully, the meds would ease the pain in his shoulder and maybe even calm his nerves. He looked inside the prescription bottle, only two more pills remaining from his last refill. Then he'd begin six months of physical therapy.

Then he returned to the kitchen and finished slicing the lime on the cutting board. It was a full ten minutes before Jake heard Natalie's door shut. He had just finished unloading the dishwasher when the back door screeched open.

"You're here!" Jake said. "Let taco night begin!"

Natalie giggled as she patted Copper, closing the door behind her. "It smells good in here."

Her demeanor and the meds had calmed his nerves, and he smiled as he watched Natalie kneel down and whisper to Copper.

"Thanks." He stepped back, appraising her. "I like that hat!"

Natalie smiled, touching the brim.

Jake handed Natalie a glass of ice water from the counter and pointed toward the table. "Let's start with the guac and chips."

She took a long swallow, moved to the table, and dipped her chip into the guacamole. "Is this homemade?"

He nodded and smiled, then grabbed two small plates from the cabinet, pulled a couple of beers from the fridge, and ripped a few paper towels from the roll.

While Natalie nibbled at the chips, Jake finished setting up the taco bar on the kitchen counter. He'd made a salsa from avocado, kernel corn, tomatoes, red onion, cilantro, lime juice, and garlic. Now he added a small bowl of chopped lettuce, sour cream, and grated cheese on a serving tray to balance the meal. Waving a hand toward the bounty, he said, "Make yourself at home. Grab a fresh plate and build your taco." The conversation between them was light as they filled their plates.

He'd intended for them to enjoy dinner on the screened porch, He'd set the table and found a candle in the closet, hoping to create a romantic mood overlooking the beach. But when Natalie plopped down at the kitchen table and looked so comfortable, he decided to roll with it.

She took a small bite of the fish and looked at Jake with surprise. "Oh, my gosh! This is delicious. Where did you learn to cook fish like that?"

Jake's gut unclenched at her approval. Grinning, he shared his secret—he'd marinated the fish with olive oil, lemon juice, and assorted herbs. Then, ten minutes before Natalie arrived, he'd cooked the meat on the grill for three minutes on each side.

"I may be a tad jealous of your culinary skills." Natalie reached for one last bite of the guacamole.

Jake laughed. It had been a long time since he'd been interested in a woman with whom he could be himself. Natalie seemed at ease with him, too. He caught a whiff of the fresh scent of her shampoo and was surprised by the stirring within him. She was even more beautiful without the scrubs he was used to seeing her wear.

Yet, it was much more than that. Natalie seemed interested in him as a person, interested in his profession, political opinion, and also his literary preferences—a first for Jake. He'd never reached this level of comfort with a woman so quickly.

Confident the evening had gone well and judging from how smoothly their conversation flowed, Jake thought they might move to the porch now.

"Would you like another beer?" he asked. He'd have to pace himself because of the oxycodone.

"Sure." As Natalie pushed back from the table, her smile faded as she quietly remarked, "I looked at the calendar today and remembered this is my wedding anniversary."

And with that one remark, her demeanor had changed. As soon as the words came out of her mouth, Jake grabbed a second beer from the fridge. The comment had come out of left field.

Jake knew she'd been married. He'd read on the internet that her husband had died in a car accident. So how was he supposed to respond to this? He could ruin everything if he handled it wrong.

There were really only two choices. He could show compassion, listen to Natalie talk about her deceased husband, or change the subject by directing her to the porch.

He opted for the former. He twisted the beer top, leaned against the counter, and listened while Natalie told him about her fifth wedding anniversary.

Before he knew it, the sun had set, and he had moved to a chair at the table. There were moments when her eyes lit up with excitement… and her smile stabbed at his heart. Jake had never experienced a love affair like the one Natalie had with her husband.

Lucky bastard.

Natalie had been there three hours, and they'd not even discussed the contract. Instead, she'd talked about the elaborate anniversary plans she'd made for the guy whose heart still beat inside her. Jake listened without interruption. No questions… no judgment. He just listened.

Once, when her eyes could no longer contain her tears, he reached for her hand. Five slender, well-manicured fingers intertwined with his own. He brushed the top of her hand with his thumb. He knew if ever given the opportunity, he would deem it an undeserved blessing to scale the mountaintops and valleys of life with someone like this remarkable woman—grateful to hold her hand every night for the rest of his life. Until this point, Jake had no idea what kind of person he wanted for a wife. Now he knew.

But tonight, Natalie needed a friend. No romance, no patronizing... just a friend. So instead, he memorized every detail of her elegant hand, squeezed it, and then let go. Otherwise, Jake clung to his empty beer bottle and nodded when he thought it was appropriate.

Finally, at 10 o'clock, at Copper's insistence, Jake strolled onto the porch to let him out. While waiting for his dog to finish his business, he blew out the candle, removed the fresh flowers from the mason jar, and placed them in the trash can to the side of his house.

Natalie had already cleared the table when he and Copper returned to the kitchen. "I apologize for unloading on you. I'm not sure what happened to me tonight." She wiped off the kitchen table and continued, "It's not like me to share personal information with a stranger."

Jake's eyebrows went up. "Well, I'm not exactly a stranger."

She touched his arm, "Of course not. But you know what I mean."

Not wanting the tension to ruin the mood of the evening, "Think nothing of it, Natalie. You obviously needed a friend tonight, and I'm glad I could be here for you."

"I hope you don't think I'm some weepy widow who unloads on every person I meet."

He reached for a dry dishcloth, hoping to change the subject. "Not at all. I'd meant for us to walk through the rental after dinner, but time just got away from us."

"It did, didn't it?" She looked at the clock on the microwave. "Goodness, I didn't realize it was so late. We've not even discussed the contract."

He couldn't believe they'd talked nonstop. Natalie didn't seem concerned about the late hour or that they hadn't walked next door to the cottage.

Jake watched her hands as she rinsed the dishes and handed them to him to place in the dishwasher. Then she mentioned she had read the contract, and the wording was acceptable. She gave him a mischievous grin. "Please thank the 'owner' for such generous terms."

When they'd finished cleaning up the kitchen, Jake walked her outside.

"I enjoyed dinner. Thank you."

"You're welcome."

There was a comfortable silence between them now, and it felt good. It was like an epiphany had occurred, and neither felt the need for chatter.

Finally, Jake leaned down and looked at Natalie as she was about to drive off. "Call me tomorrow when you get off work, and I'll meet you next door so you can check out the house."

Natalie smiled, and without a sound, she squeezed his hand, pulled onto the blacktop road, and turned left toward the clinic.

As he watched the taillights of her car fade in the distance, Jake realized that the evening had become much more than a romantic candlelight dinner overlooking the ocean. He had no idea if there was a place for him in Natalie's life, but he now knew he wanted more than a superficial relationship with a beautiful, intelligent woman. He also wanted her heart.

Jake reached down, and rubbed the back of Copper's head, then headed toward the back door. "We've got our work cut out for us, boy."

Chapter Fourteen

The Beach Chairs

Natalie moved into the cottage two weeks after signing the lease agreement. She'd spent a couple of evenings removing the garbage left behind by the previous renters and cleaning the place. What made people leave behind moldy blankets, drawers full of old pens, and a sink full of coffee grounds? She'd die of embarrassment to leave a mess like that for a stranger to clean up. The following weekend, Jake and Rosemary helped her paint the interior walls a soft white. In the meantime, Natalie purchased linens and kitchen items. She hadn't brought any from New York. Everything she owned reminded her of Paul.

She closed the clinic early one afternoon and stopped by B&B Design and Consign, an upscale consignment shop. They had just received a truckload of furniture from a couple on Sea Island, and she found a bedroom suite and a Victorian-style sofa in Prussian blue that would look beautiful in her cottage.

Her regular clothes and scrubs, which she'd kept in a suitcase and strewn across the backs of chairs in the doctor's office at the clinic, now hung in the small closet in the master bedroom. The closet was full, even though she'd pared down her winter wardrobe and only brought a few items to the coast. After cramming her stuff inside the closet and slamming the door, she realized she'd need to customize the area for it to work for her long term.

The following Friday afternoon, when Jake walked over with a pound of grilled shrimp and a salad, he knocked on the back door and then walked inside, Copper trailing his heels.

Natalie reached over and rubbed the top of Copper's head. "How are you, boy?"

"You should keep your doors locked, Natalie. You never know when a stranger might walk up from the beach and try to get in."

Natalie stopped, her eyebrows scrunched. "You're kidding, right?"

"No, I'm not kidding."

Jake explained there had been three unsolved murders in this part of the state in the past two years. So, it was best to keep her doors locked or get a dog for protection.

It seemed like an overreaction. The southern part of the state was a large area. Three murders in two years? That was nothing, compared to Manhattan. With a polite smile, Natalie said, "I appreciate the warning, but now that you've delivered it, do you think you could take a look at the bedroom closet and draw up a proposal for me?"

Jake walked toward the master bedroom and stopped at the door. "May I?"

"Yes. Of course. Go on in." She followed him and Copper into the bedroom and opened the closet door. "See what I mean? It's very cramped in here."

Jake looked around the room and nodded toward the mattress and box spring on the floor. "Are you sleeping on the floor?"

"For now. I'm about to put the final coat of paint on the bed and nightstand." She pointed to the other wall. "I'm pleased with the dresser."

"Yeah. It looks good."

He assessed the space, then he pulled out a pen and pad. "I can add built-in shelving to store your accessories if you like."

Natalie nodded as she looked at the mess in the tiny closet. "I like that idea." Then she looked toward the kitchen. "Take your time. We can eat when you're finished."

Jake made notes as he measured the closet's dimensions, returned to the kitchen, and straddled a chair at the table.

She looked over his shoulder and asked if she could see his plan. Jake put down the pencil and rubbed his hands together. "Let's eat. This is going to take a little thought in order to utilize every inch of space."

After dinner, Jake continued to sketch on the pad, and when he completed the design, he pushed the drawing across the table for Natalie to approve.

Natalie studied the paper for a second. "I like it. It's sort of like what I had envisioned." She nodded her approval. "When can you start?"

"As soon as I get a lull in my schedule. Hopefully, seven to ten days."

While Jake helped clear the dishes from the table, Natalie asked if there was a store on the island where she could get two Adirondack chairs. She'd hoped the Design & Consign store owner could find a small table for her to refinish; he had promised to call her when he found something. However, the previous renter had left a firepit between the house and the beach, and Natalie thought that would be the perfect place to sit and enjoy the view of the ocean.

Jake leaned against the counter, pulled out his phone, and punched the keyboard. "What color do you want?"

"Hmmm. Either seafoam green, yellow, or white. Do you see anything with a distressed finish?"

Jake flipped his phone around and showed her the picture.

***

The morning the chairs arrived by UPS, Jake removed their packaging and placed them near the fire pit in the backyard, throwing the boxes in the back of his truck to take to the dumpster.

It was after six o'clock when Natalie finished with her last patient. It had been a busy day at the clinic. Besides her regular appointments, Mr. Ziegler had another gallbladder attack, and Mrs. Cronmiller turned her ankle while playing golf. As a result, the only time Natalie sat down was for a few minutes to eat her lunch.

She saw the yellow chairs beside the fire pit before she pulled into the drive. Although dead tired, she changed into a swimsuit and cover-up, poured a glass of sparkling water, grabbed the container of leftover pasta from the fridge, and went outside.

The thermometer on her screened porch registered 90 degrees, but after living in a cold northeastern climate for many years, she welcomed the warmth. She leaned back in the chair on the right, enjoying the sun on her face as she soaked up the fresh breeze from the ocean, and for the first time in twelve hours, she could totally relax.

As her eyes closed, she heard a voice. "These chairs are more comfortable than they look."

Natalie sat up in her chair and looked at the empty beach chair. She knew that voice. "Who said that?"

"Nattygirl, it's me, Paul."

She shook her head. She must be more exhausted than she thought. Uneasily, she settled back into her chair and sipped her water.

"Your friend Jake seems like a nice guy. What does he do besides hit on pretty women?"

Without thinking, Natalie answered. "He's a contractor. And he's agreed to customize the tiny closet in the master bedroom."

"Good. I want this place to feel like home for you."

It felt so natural to sit here chatting with Paul. If she closed her eyes, she could almost see him sitting beside her, and when the breeze shifted, she caught a hint of his cologne. Real or not, it felt good.

And so it continued. The firepit area soon became Natalie's favorite spot. At the end of a long day at the clinic, she'd rush home, make dinner, and go outside to sit in her new chair—often taking a plate of food or a glass of wine to enjoy while watching the surf. It was relaxing. The breeze from the ocean often carried the sweet scent of the delicate and fragrant Confederate Jasmine vine, which trailed outside the screened porch. The graceful formation of seagulls flying overhead, dozens of pelicans parading on the beach, the salty air, and a small amount of vitamin D provided a relaxing end to an otherwise stressful day.

After all these many years, Natalie had finally found her happy place on the southeastern coast of Georgia. Each afternoon, as she cleared her mind of clutter from the exhausting day at the clinic, Paul would start a conversation about their previous life—as if he were sitting in the empty beach chair beside her.

During those visits, they relived memories they'd shared, and occasionally, he would tell her about his work—things he'd shared with her previously, but she had forgotten. Natalie couldn't tell if the conversation occurred only in her mind or if her deceased husband was actually visiting her. It no longer mattered.

***

"Do you remember the night I told you about the head of global sales summoning me to the ivory tower to meet our largest client?"

"Uh-huh." Natalie had drifted into a peaceful state, somewhere between beta and alpha waves, but she remembered the evening. "You were such a meticulous eater; I should have known something was up when you took that huge bite from your roll."

"Remember, I told you that you'd never guess what happened that day?" He'd recently been assigned to a team of financiers responsible for the highest net-worth clients in New York City, including a prominent family whose patriarch was the 'boss' for the east coast operation.

"I remember." Natalie took a sip of water. She was awake now and knew better than to try to catch a nap. "I'd just received the third text from the trauma center that night, and you were mad at me for responding to text messages during dinner."

"I wasn't mad, but I did point my finger at you."

Natalie nodded. "If I remember correctly, it was the first time you'd ever pointed that crooked finger at me."

"My finger's not crooked!"

Natalie rolled her eyes. "Whatever…."

"When I told you that Mr. Steelton, the executive vice president of global sales and marketing, had invited me to meet with the head of our largest account, you just brushed me off."

She ignored the comment. Sometimes Paul would make a controversial statement, hoping to start a stimulating conversation. Today, Natalie wasn't in the mood. She'd received plenty of stimulation at the clinic and preferred to sit quietly and enjoy her peaceful little section of the beach.

"You asked me if it was a big deal. Remember?" He paused.

Natalie sat up in her chair to position the pillow. "Yeah, you said, 'you're damn right, it's a big deal.'"

"The day they assigned me to our largest client was when Mr. Steelton asked if he could use my car to take 'the boss' to lunch."

She settled back into her chair. "You should never have told me about that meeting."

"I know... I could've lost my job for that. But I knew you'd forget all about the 'boss' by the time we went to bed."

The area between Natalie's eyebrows scrunched. "Your meeting 'the boss' didn't make an impression on me, but loaning your car to Steelton really made me livid."

"Well, he was the executive vice president and *my superior*."

Natalie strummed her fingers on the chair arm. "You'd never let *me* drive the Porsche, but when your boss asked, you threw the keys on the table!"

"I told you the executives often asked to borrow a car to take a client to lunch. So, it wasn't a big deal. Besides, you're driving it now."

Natalie removed her shades as she looked toward his voice. "It sounded fishy... the suits on the eighteenth floor had a company car and a driver at their disposal."

"Yeah, you're still pissed, aren't you?"

The vein in her neck throbbed, and she continued, "Why would he ask someone at your level to attend a meeting with the top client, anyway?"

"At my level?" Natalie sensed him drawing away, his voice husky with hurt. "I told you, I was next in line for VP."

Chapter Fifteen

Natalie

Natalie stood at the island in the center of her tiny kitchen and sorted through the mail. The last item caught her eye—an official Georgia Department of Public Health envelope. After a steadying breath, she tore open the envelope. It contained Dr. Baldwin's death certificate. Holding it in her hand made it feel more real. She wished they'd had more time to work together the way he'd planned. At least now, she could begin the process of settling his estate.

No time like the present. She called his attorney to schedule an appointment. When she ended the call, she opened her calendar to record the date and realized today was the twenty-fourth—Paul's birthday.

The thought made her miss him even more. Maybe if she showed up in their special place, he would be there, too. She grabbed the pimento cheese sandwich and a handful of carrot sticks and headed for the Adirondack chairs in the backyard. There was no sign of Paul. She nibbled at her light dinner, trying to suppress her disappointment.

***

"Aren't you going to wish me a happy birthday?"

Natalie jumped at the sudden, disembodied voice. "Paul! You scared the crap out of me."

"Sorry, Nattygirl. But it's not like I can give you advance notice."

"Why not?" She still wasn't sure exactly how it worked. These visits were, from a rational perspective, impossible. Still, much as she enjoyed her chats with Paul, it would be nice to know when he planned to show up.

She shook her head. Twenty-four months ago, she would have given anything for a single conversation with him. Her annoyance at his unannounced visits seemed ungrateful.

She smiled. "Happy birthday, honey. I should have bought a couple of cupcakes to celebrate?"

Paul laughed. He'd never liked cupcakes. For his birthday, he'd always requested a chocolate cake with silky chocolate buttercream icing from the bakery around the corner from Rockefeller Center. He wasn't much of a sweets eater, but he enjoyed a small bowl of that silky icing after dinner. It contained the perfect amount of sugar to make it good without causing a spike in his blood sugar.

As a surprise for Paul, she'd order a cake for every holiday or memorable occasion. The icing was their favorite, and she could almost taste the light, silky confection on her tongue.

As if reading her mind, he said, "I'd be happy with a small serving of buttercream icing. Rubbing the icing on your face with my finger would be fun." He paused. "Remember the night I did that with the whipped cream? You almost slapped me, and then you got so tickled, tears rolled down your cheeks."

Natalie smiled at the memory. "That *was* a good time." Then, with a pause and somewhat of a segue, "I need your advice. The check engine light came on in the car today, and I don't know where to take it for service."

"You better take it to a reputable dealership. One of those shade tree guys won't understand the complex mechanics of a Porsche."

She pulled out her phone and punched in *car service*, and a list of dealerships and garages in the Brunswick area popped up. Then, as an afterthought, she mentioned receiving Dr. Baldwin's death certificate in the mail that day. "I made an appointment with his attorney for next week."

"That was quick! How long did it take for the State of New York to process my death certificate?"

Natalie tilted her head and scrunched her eyebrows. She couldn't remember. The period following Paul's accident was still a vast blur in her mind. Had it not been for her close friend and colleague Alex Martin, she'd never have gotten through those first six months.

A screen door slammed, and Paul said, "It doesn't matter." She felt him shift in his chair. "Here comes your contractor, Nattygirl. Catch you later."

She turned and saw Jake walking toward the firepit. He was carrying a bottle of water.

Jake waved and yelled, "Hey, Natalie, is that seat next to you taken?"

Natalie jumped up. "Here, you can sit in mine. I need to run inside and put a load of clothes in the dryer. I'll be back in a few moments." On her way inside, she glanced back at the empty chair.

When Natalie reached the house, she opened the screen door and yelled back to ask Jake if he'd like a glass of iced tea on the porch—anything to get him away from Paul.

She couldn't help but wonder if Paul could interact with his environment. It didn't matter if his appearances were part of a dream or if he was real. Either way, she just wanted to keep him to herself.

Chapter Sixteen

Fourth of July

Each day, the clinic got busier, and the roster of patients increased as word spread of the young female doctor who, like her predecessor, took time to listen to their needs. Still, she kept a tight schedule. A patient could usually get in and out of the clinic within an hour, much less time than a trip to the hospital in Brunswick. Of course, the hospital had the latest equipment, and the clinic needed updating to twenty-first-century standards.

Natalie was trying to upgrade the old-fashioned ways Dr. Baldwin treated patients, but it would take time and funding to do so.

When Natalie met with the attorney about settling Dr. Baldwin's estate, it surprised her that the doctor had left the clinic and the property to her. However, the will stipulated that she sell his cottage and use the proceeds to pay for indigent care for the homeless community surrounding Brunswick. She wasn't sure when she'd have time to get it all done. Besides working at the clinic, she spent her free time settling his estate and was too busy to think about much else.

The following week was the Fourth of July, and Natalie looked forward to a day of fun and celebration. As much as she'd thrived in her fast-paced life in New York, she looked forward to settling into the beach town's more relaxed lifestyle. She had already announced in the local paper that the clinic would be closed on the Fourth. However, she hoped to catch a break, close early on the third, and perhaps even take July 5th off as well. Natalie had alerted the hospital in the Brunswick area of her intent to close. They assured her that the few days leading up to the holiday would be slow for the hospital and agreed to send a physician's assistant to fill in for a few days. She made a mental note to talk to Jennifer about the position soon.

Natalie smiled. She couldn't wait to experience the excitement of the holiday parade. A fun day with her new friends was exactly what she needed.

Natalie woke around seven o'clock on the morning of the Fourth. The smell of brewing coffee was enough motivation to get her out of bed. While the coffee dripped through the coffeemaker, she grabbed the newspaper from the front steps. Then she poured the hot liquid into her Yeti cup and went down to the beach for a few moments of quiet time. Already, people were running on the beach. Young families enjoyed the cool breeze coming off the ocean while couples tossed pieces of driftwood for their dogs to retrieve.

The early morning sky was breathtaking, with soft pink and blue hues. When Natalie looked out across the ocean, the beauty mesmerized her. The first day she'd driven across the causeway and onto the island, her eyes couldn't soak in the sights fast enough, and each day since had provided a repeat experience. Nowhere she'd ever lived had mesmerized her like this island;

the beauty of the marshes, the Spanish moss hanging from the large oak trees, and the seaweed that washed up from the ocean were all gorgeous visions. However, nothing could compare to the sunrise on the beach. The view from her Adirondack chair was breathtaking.

She could grow old here. And, against all hope, she might even do that with her dead husband.

Picking up the newspaper, she finished reading an article about the parade route that was scheduled to start in a few hours. Then, a large object in the ocean held her attention... a surfer popped out of the water. He'd caught the wave perfectly—legs slightly bent, arms outstretched, and a massive smile.

Was this a dream?

She couldn't ignore that gorgeous smile. When Paul came to shore, he grabbed his board, placed it under his arm like a professional surfer, and walked in her direction. He flopped down in the empty chair, splattering water everywhere. "How'd you like that, Nattygirl? Didn't know I could surf, did you?"

Natalie looked around, making sure no one was watching.

Am I crazy?

She'd just watched her deceased husband surfing in the Atlantic Ocean, and now he was sitting in the chair beside her.

Not sure if he was corporeal or not, Natalie reached for his hand but felt nothing. Paul grinned as she pulled her hand back and reached for her coffee cup.

"You looked good out there," she said.

Embarrassed that she had tried to touch him, she closed her eyes, remembering the passion of his last kiss. Oh, what she would give for one more afternoon of lovemaking.

He said, "Are you going to the parade?"

"Yes. Jake should be here in about thirty minutes to pick me up."

Paul stood and walked toward the ocean. "You should go shower now, or you won't be ready."

Natalie leaned forward in her chair. "But I'd rather spend the day with you."

Paul turned around and grinned. "Yeah, me, too. But you should go... and enjoy yourself!"

Jake blew the horn outside Natalie's cottage. Determined to enjoy herself, she ran out the door wearing white shorts, a light blue linen shirt barely tucked in the front, over a white camisole. A large canvas bag hung over her left shoulder as she pushed the key in the door to secure the lock. Her long hair was covered with a pink cap, and her ponytail extended through the open area in the back. As Natalie hopped into the front seat, Copper reached up and licked her face.

"Oh, Copper! It's good to see you, too."

Jake ran his hand down Copper's back. "You may be the only woman on the planet who appreciates Copper's affection." He gave Natalie a sideways look and ran a hand through his damp hair. "I'd hoped to get up in time to run in the one-mile fun run, but I took my board out for a few minutes of surfing instead."

Her mind flashed back to her vision of Paul on the surfboard. "I went out early, too. There were several surfers out this morning."

"Yeah, I saw you out at the firepit."

"How were the waves?"

"Strong. Just the way I like them." He laughed and drove a couple of hundred yards to Rosemary's place. The music from the Jeep's radio was blaring "California Girls" from *The Beach Boys' Greatest Hits*. The open-air Jeep was the perfect vehicle for a beach town.

Jake honked the horn. Finally, Rosemary stuck her head out the back door, "Aren't you coming in?"

Jake motioned for her. "Let's go, Rosemary. I want to get a decent spot."

Copper welcomed Rosemary with the same affection he'd given to Natalie. Rosemary pushed him away and said, "Jake, must your dog slobber on me every time he sees me?"

Natalie turned around in the seat and motioned to the dog. "Come up here with me, Copper."

Jake glanced at Natalie and winked.

At 8:35, Jake pulled into the parking lot of Parker's Convenience Store in time to get the last parking space facing Ocean Boulevard. The July Fourth celebration began with a 9 am parade starting at the traffic circle just past Malcolm McKinnon Airport.

People of all ages, dressed in shorts, flip-flops, and sunshades, lined the streets. Natalie said, "This reminds me of watching the fireworks in New York City. Every year, millions of people would line the Hudson River to celebrate with family and friends."

"I'd like to see that myself," Jake said.

Natalie felt as giddy as a five-year-old. "Look at the people! They're standing three and four rows deep."

Jake said, "Yeah, July Fourth is a big deal around here."

The July Fourth parade had always attracted families vacationing in the area. Now it seemed everyone on the island had shown up to celebrate their country's birthday.

Natalie stretched her neck for a better view of the town. There were police officers everywhere—at every major intersection and several in between. "Wow! The city planners thought of everything."

In the rearview mirror, Rosemary rolled her eyes. "I'm sure to a big city girl like you, it comes as a surprise that we small-town folk can put on an impressive event."

Jake grinned back over his shoulder. "Aw, Rosemary, your claws are showing."

The Grand Marshall of the parade was the Mayor of St. Simons Island, and he rode in the front seat of the fire truck. The police department was there only to maintain order. The long flatbeds carrying colorful floats, little league baseball players, soccer teams, cheerleaders, local and state politicians, and a barbershop quartet glided through the streets. Shiny antique cars driven by their owners and loaded down with young children positioned on the backs of the seats threw individually wrapped candy to the people along the route. The crowd loved it!

Jake caught a piece of candy and popped it into his mouth. "There's an arts and crafts show from 10 a.m. - 5 p.m. at Postell Park, in front of The Casino, if you ladies are interested."

Jake, Natalie, and Rosemary were at the corner of Mallery Street and Ocean Boulevard and had a clear view of the 9 a.m. parade as it went down Frederica Road from the Redfern Village and the post office. It passed under the red light at Fern Island Causeway and continued on Frederica until it reached Lawrence Road. The parade took a slight right on Lawrence Rd. and ended at the King and Prince Resort.

The night before the Fourth, the island paper quoted the mayor as having announced that the official band of the state's national guard would be on hand to perform for the celebration. When the band was within earshot, Copper moved to the front seat and hid in the floorboard in front of Natalie's seat. Natalie placed her hands over the dog's ears so the sounds of the instruments wouldn't alarm him.

"Look at the golf carts," Natalie said. "It's crazy! Does everyone on the island own one?"

Jake said, "Most do, according to the owners of St. Simons Bait and Tackle in the village. They organized the golf cart parade."

The golf cart parade was scheduled for 2 p.m. at Mallery Park. The paper stated it would go down Mallery Street into the village, make the loop at the pier, turn down Beachview to the swimming pool, turn around in the parking lot, and sweep back through the pier area one more time. Participants decorated their carts in red, white, and blue patriotic themes. Toward the end, Jennifer and her three children rode past in the back of a cart. As soon as Jennifer spotted Natalie, she waved and motioned to her children.

When the last cart trundled by, Jake suggested they return to the Jeep and drive down to the restaurant to eat their lunch.

"Give me a minute, Jake." Natalie said, "I need to speak to Jennifer about coming to work at the clinic."

Rosemary rushed to Jake's side and placed her hand on his arm. Jake wiggled his arm free and veered off to the side of a building for Copper to relieve himself.

Natalie ran back to the truck with a huge smile on her face.

Jake asked, "Well, do you have a new employee?"

"I do!"

Fortunately, they quickly found a parking space at The King and Prince. Then they followed a group of young people heading toward the grassy area at the back of the property overlooking the beach.

Natalie stopped, appreciating the elaborate setup. It was the added touches, like the strings of tiny white lights on the huge white tent, that made the event more festive. A makeshift bar was housed inside the tent, and it also kept the food and drinks shielded from the sun. The wait staff replenished the food supply throughout the day. And, at four o'clock, a band set up poolside overlooking the ocean and played oldies and beach music.

Rosemary, Natalie, and Jake settled in at a table around the pool to enjoy their dinner. Natalie nibbled on a perfectly smoked rib and closed her eyes in ecstasy. "Oh, my goodness! This may be the best barbeque I've ever tasted."

Jake laughed as he wiped his mouth with his napkin. "Rosemary, our new friend loves food as much as you."

"True. I enjoy preparing the food, and Natalie enjoys eating it." She smiled, but it seemed a little strained.

After they finished their meal, they hung around to listen to the music. Finally, Jake extended a hand toward Natalie. "Would you like to dance?"

"I'd love to!"

Rosemary looked around the pool at the young families and couples. Then she crossed her arms and said, "I'm going to the ladies' room."

Jake took Natalie by the hand and went to the concrete area roped off for a dance floor. Natalie was nervous. It had been a very long time since she had been dancing. She wondered what Paul would think about her dancing with another man.

But he'd told her to enjoy herself.

Jake placed his right arm around her waist and pulled her closer. His scent was familiar, and it felt good to be in his arms. She looked up at his face. He was at least five inches taller than Natalie. Jake closed his eyes, and she suddenly felt a sense of security.

When Natalie and Jake returned to the table, Rosemary was already there. She raked her fingers through her hair and said, "We need to get down to The Village… the fireworks will begin soon."

Jake glanced at Natalie. "Are you ready to leave, or would you rather watch the fireworks from here?"

Seeing the disappointment on Rosemary's face, she said, "Let's go to The Village. We can spread out our towels and sit on the grass."

The look on Rosemary's face told Natalie that where they watched the fireworks wasn't the problem. Instead, it was clear Rosemary though of Jake as her man.

Chapter Seventeen

The Fireworks

Watching the crowd through Jake's front windshield, Natalie could hardly believe the number of people swarming from every direction in hopes of getting a good view of the fireworks. The roads were lined with vehicles as far as the eye could see, and the congestion surrounding The Village created intense conditions for even an experienced driver like Jake. He cut through a couple of backstreets and patiently waited while a guy strolled across the street from Palmer's Convenience Store with a brown paper bag under his arm. The man quickly jumped into his truck and sped away, leaving a parking spot at the corner of Ocean Boulevard and Mallery Street. It was as close to The Village as they could hope to get, and they only had to walk across the street, past the restaurants and shops, to secure a spot on the grass.

The atmosphere was electrifying. People weaved in and out of the local boutiques, buying ice cream cones and sprinklers or just killing time until the fireworks began. All the while, a band played beach music next to a food truck set up to sell beer near the pier. The music energized Natalie, and she thought about how Paul would have loved the lead singer's smooth vocals.

Jake had Copper leashed, but the big bronze Labrador walked a few steps away from Natalie, pausing when she paused, attuned to her every movement. Natalie enjoyed having Copper around. As much as she loved dogs, her unpredictable work schedule would've made it challenging to keep an animal in her New York condo. But now that she was living on the coast, it seemed like people had their dogs leashed to their wrists everywhere they went. Maybe it was time to get a puppy.

The large cargo freighter that would be launching the fireworks floated half a mile out into the water. In the past, Jake explained, the freighter had unleashed the light show from farther down the beach, but the city planners believed that staging it from the village area, which had a pier and devoted green space for families, would allow more people to see the display. Of course, some people still insisted on watching the festivities from the sandy beach—traditions on the island were hard to break, but most residents seemed to have found their way to the south part of the island to enjoy the annual fireworks display.

Pointing beyond the cargo freighter, Natalie asked, "What's the name of the island across the way?"

Jake's gaze followed her pointed finger. "That's Jekyll Island. We'll have to ride over there one day soon."

Natalie nodded and spread two beach towels on the grass. Copper scooted on his bottom ahead of her. Jake sat next to her, with Rosemary on his other side.

Jake nodded toward Copper. "I think he likes you, Natalie."

Rosemary snorted. "Of course, Copper loves everybody. He follows the mailman halfway down the beach every morning."

It was still daylight, and they enjoyed watching the smaller boats arriving to observe the fireworks display. Jake offered Natalie and Rosemary each a bottle of water from his backpack. It wasn't long before a dark wave of clouds floated across the sky. Then the sun disappeared behind the trees, and dusk fell over the water. The boats' red, green, and white lights twinkled in the distance as the three sat on the cool grass, listening to the music and relishing the evening breeze off the ocean.

When it was almost dark, the whistle of a bottle rocket cut through the chatter of the crowd, followed by a boom and a large display of bright blue stars. An instant later, bold red and white stripes lit up the sky. In the pause that followed, Natalie leaned forward to cover Copper's ears. Jake grinned at her as the Labrador dug his head under her folded legs. Then the band started one more set of songs before officially starting the Fourth of July fireworks extravaganza.

Jake leaned back on the towel, his arm resting on Natalie's back. "Loud noises don't affect Labs as much as other dogs." He smiled as he looked at his dog's head nestled under her leg. "He's just flirting with you."

Natalie laughed and nodded to a couple sitting close to them. Their little Yorkie was shaking uncontrollably. "The owner should take it home," she said. "Those dogs are terrified by loud noises. Sometimes, they even run off and get lost."

Jake whispered, "You sure know a lot about animals."

"What did you say, Jake?" Rosemary asked, frowning. She must have noticed Jake leaning in toward Natalie.

"I just said that Natalie knows a lot about animals. Don't you think so?"

Rosemary rolled her eyes. "She's a regular encyclopedia." With an exaggerated yawn, she said, "The fireworks seem a little lacking this year. I don't know about you, but I'm ready to go home."

Chapter Eighteen

Rosemary

Rosemary dropped her beach bag on the tiled floor and let the screen door slam behind her.

She had to scrub that canine stench from her body; she only tolerated the dog because she was fond of Jake, but it certainly hadn't been worth it tonight. Still fuming at the way Jake had ignored her, she stalked to the bathroom and slid out of her clothes. After a quick shower, she dressed for bed and walked back through the house to cut off the lights. The cottage had been closed all day, and the warm air was stifling. It had been a long day, filled with two parades, lots of food and drink, and extreme temperatures, and she was both exhausted and on edge. Her muscles felt as tight as if she'd spent the past four hours slinging hash and bussing tables.

Rosemary rummaged through the refrigerator and found the aloe vera gel. Rubbing a handful of liquid over her bare shoulders, she stood in front of the open door and smiled, enjoying the cool air circulating her body.

A memory flashed through her mind: Jake rubbing the fine hairs on Natalie's wrist as they sat on the lawn waiting for the light show to begin. The intimacy struck her like a bombshell. She slammed the fridge door and walked through the house.

A loud noise from outside startled her. Rosemary stepped onto the screened porch. The music had stopped just before the official start of the fireworks display, and she could see them from her porch. She watched briefly as the dark sky burst into white sparks. It looked like a vast kaleidoscope had rained down on the ocean. The next few were brilliant colors of red, blue, and purple. The sounds of children's laughter filtered through the screens.

Rosemary looked toward Jake's house. His driveway was empty, but two doors down, his Jeep was parked in Natalie's driveway.

She sighed. It looked like Jake was going to watch the fireworks on the beach with Natalie.

A breeze from the ocean brought with it the scent of cigar smoke. Again, she looked toward Natalie's cottage. The silhouettes of two people moved around behind Natalie's place, the outlines of their bodies illuminated by the lights from the porch. Finally, they lit the fire pit, and a red light appeared as Jake inhaled from the cigar. It was his nightly habit, a good cigar and a bourbon. It was how he relaxed at the end of a stressful day.

She hated that it was Natalie he was enjoying them with tonight.

Rosemary locked the wooden door before going to bed. She pattered back through the house and saw the bottle of bourbon on the kitchen counter. She pitched the bottle of liquid into the trash can, realizing it was time she finally admitted that Jake was falling for Natalie. Rosemary was sure that Natalie wasn't aware of Jake's feelings. Perhaps she was still grieving the loss of her husband. All the same, it was clear that, for some reason, Jake was crazy about her.

She climbed into bed, but sleep would not come. Tired as she was, the jumbled thoughts running through her mind kept her awake. The loud pops of the fireworks and the shrills and laughter from the people on the beach enjoying the light show didn't help. She rolled over and clamped her pillow over her head to block the sounds.

Later, as a light rain pattered on the roof, Rosemary snuggled under the cool sheets. Her mind wandered back through the day, remembering every word spoken between Natalie and Jake. Not that she didn't like Natalie; she did. She liked her a great deal. In fact, she had considered Natalie a friend, but the way Jake melted in her presence felt like hot stones in Rosemary's throat.

Jake had been her closest friend since she'd moved to the island two years ago. There was no room for Natalie in that relationship. Natalie had to go.

Chapter Nineteen

The Corporate Dining Room-Seven Years Before

The corporate dining room on the eighteenth floor was quiet for a change. John Steelton wanted a sandwich, and he always got what he wanted. Not just an ordinary sandwich but a croque Monsieur. A classic French delicacy with a generous portion of ham and cheese between two slices of crispy buttered bread. The soft fried egg elevated the jambon beurre to a gourmet equivalent.

These gourmet meals, prepared by a chef trained at a five-star restaurant in Paris, France, were an added perk of his job, a benefit he seldom discussed with his peers. The chef, a medium-height guy with graying blond hair, was masterful at creating spectacular lunches for the executive staff. Steelton was fairly certain they had added the chef for his benefit. One of the many perks to keep him from considering one of the countless other companies that would have liked to lure him onto their own payrolls.

John relished having a corporate dining room fifty yards from his office. He could entertain clients at lunch without leaving the building. There was no lunch-hour traffic to deal with, no valet parking tickets to document for his expense report, and it also protected him from the heat and cold of the various seasons.

He had plenty of time to savor his lunch while appreciating the view of the financial district and the Hudson River. On occasion, he'd bring a file to review while waiting for his lunch to be prepared, but not today. His next appointment wasn't until 2:30. He'd have plenty of time to prepare for the next meeting when he returned to his office.

When he finished his lunch, he nodded to the chef and gave him a thumbs up. The chef smiled, and just as Steelton was about to exit the dining room, he yelled, "Always keep your knives sharp and your belly full." It was a throwback to the chef's culinary school days.

Steelton chuckled as he raised two fingers to his temple in a mock salute. Then he closed the door behind him and strolled toward his corner suite.

At his approach, his receptionist raised an eyebrow and warned, "You have a visitor waiting…."

That could mean only one thing. The boss was back in town.

"Thank you," Steelton said, his skin suddenly clammy. He wiped his mouth with a monogrammed handkerchief and opened his office door.

He flashed a practiced smile and said smoothly, "Hello, my friend. How was your trip?"

***

Mario Bernardi looked out the window at a Schooner America 2.0 sailboat moving down the Hudson River. His face was stoic, and he never blinked when Steelton entered the room.

After a moment, Bernie spoke with a strong Sicilian accent. "Where's my money, Steelton?"

Steelton walked around his desk and glanced at the three messages taped to his phone. "What money?"

Turning from the window, Bernie folded his arms high on his chest and followed Steelton's every move with resolute eyes. "The five million dollars you hid for us a couple of years ago. We've secured a new place, and I'm here to get the money."

Retrieving an item from his pocket, the boss approached Steelton and added, "I was told you hid another $2M for my brother at the same time. Did you forget to tell me about that drop?"

Steelton's gaze fell to his desk as he anxiously inquired, "We wired ten million to the offshore account. Are you sure you didn't get it?"

The boss walked toward Steelton and reached into his pocket. Then, in one sweeping gesture, he shoved Steelton into his chair, grabbed his head yanking it backward, and placed the knife under his throat.

Bernie towered over him as he pushed the leather chair back and stepped into the gap.

He had Steelton in a precarious position. He'd gone chalk-white, and he looked about to throw up. Bernie let up for a minute, just long enough for Steelton to cough.

He struggled to speak… his face still red from coughing. "I don't… have… your… money."

Lying little weasel.

Bernie jerked his head back for the second time and whispered, "You've got about three seconds to remember where you put my money."

It had been over two years since the boss had dropped a sizable brown satchel with Steelton at a lunch meeting. He'd left it in the car during lunch. When he exited the vehicle at the end of the meeting, Bernie pointed to the bag and asked if he knew what to do with it. It was a much more significant sum than the previous drop.

Talk on the street said the boss was losing his edge and that maybe dementia was setting in. Steelton thought he must have forgotten about the money after that length of time.

Steelton could hear his heart beating through his chest as his brain raced to think of a scapegoat. Tiny beads of perspiration covered his forehead, and the drenched armpits of his dress shirt stuck to his skin. He could usually think fast under pressure. But, today, he was drawing a blank.

Finally, a name popped into his mind: *Paul Nieman.*

He was at a vulnerable point, and he knew if he spoke, his voice would likely quiver. At last, he opened his mouth. "I... gave it... to Paul... to hide."

Bernardi pressed harder on the blade, glaring into Steelton's eyes. "Good try... Nieman's dead, remember?" He paused before continuing. "I've always liked you, Steelton, but you should've picked a simpleton for the job. Nieman was an institutionalist... a rule follower and my intellectual equal. He was an ethical guy and too damn smart to collaborate against me." He shifted his weight. "I'm certain he would have contacted the FBI if you'd tried to involve him. So, think about your answer before saying anything stupid."

It was true... everything Bernie said about Paul was unequivocally correct. Steelton's mouth went dry, and his stomach continued to churn. Then he remembered the three-story brownstone Paul's widow had recently sold. He envied her. She'd moved to the beach, or so he'd heard from a colleague.

Without warning, he could almost smell the briny scent of the white-capped waves rolling in from the Atlantic Ocean.

Of course, by now, he was shaken, but he tried to articulate his thoughts. His story must sound plausible because one more jerk to the head and his neck would snap. "You're right about Paul. He was sharp." Steelton gasped for air, and his voice steadied. "But he wasn't the choir boy you thought he was. He told me he'd hidden the money... behind the mahogany-paneled wall in his study... on the top floor of his townhome." It was a complete fabrication. Paul was innocent, but he was dead. And with the wife gone...no harm, no foul.

A scene from his earlier life flashed before him—a snow-covered boxwood next to a freshly plowed walkway in front of his childhood home. The large multi-colored bulbs on the Christmas tree in their living room. His beautiful mother was wearing a long-sleeved red wool dress and a starched white apron with holly leaves on the pocket. His eyes welled at the memory.

Then his mind sped back to the present day.

Steelton had only been to Paul's townhome on one occasion. The young asset manager and his wife had hosted a New Year's party six months before Paul's death. Steelton's wife was visiting her sister in Vermont, and Steelton had no plans for the evening, so he accepted the invitation.

He'd arrived early, and although it was obvious Paul's wife wasn't ready to receive a guest, she seemed to think nothing of it. Paul suggested they tour the house to pass the time. The view of the Hudson River from the mahogany-panel study was spectacular—a tinge of jealousy swept over Steelton as he realized it was better than the view from his corner executive suite. They had a drink and waited for the other guests to arrive. To avoid small talk, Steelton had used his time to read the spines of the many books in Paul's personal library. It surprised him to find many 1st editions signed by authors, some leather-bound, some hardback books that had been banned and removed from circulation.

Bernie's voice jerked Steelton back to the present. "Don't lie to me, Steelton. I told you the day I left the satchel that your office was just one of several locations we used, and I'd return for it as soon as we secured a larger vault in the States." Bernie released the tension on his neck, grabbed the back of his head, and slammed his face onto the desktop. Pain exploded in his skull, a black wave washing through his mind. Blood gushed from his nose, and when his vision finally cleared, he saw splatters of red across several documents his assistant had placed on his desk before lunch.

He gagged on his blood and grasped at an answer he hoped might save him. It was a long shot, but it was the best he could come up with under such extreme pressure. Of course, the boss would kill him when he found out he was lying, but there was a good chance he'd kill him, anyway.

In a voice rich with feigned confidence, Steelton spun his tale.

Chapter Twenty

Natalie

The screen door slammed as Natalie headed out to the fire pit area to enjoy her coffee and read the morning paper. She'd no more than sat down when she heard her husband's familiar voice.

"Looks like you had a merry ole time watching the fireworks last night."

Natalie looked at the empty chair and said, "You're back."

"My dear, I've never left."

Natalie rolled her eyes as she opened the newspaper. "You could've fooled me."

"Why are you so angry with me, Natty?"

"I never said I was angry with you."

"Not saying it is not the same as not being it."

Natalie sighed. Maybe on some level she was upset with him, but she wasn't ready to deal with that yet. "I love you, but this is my quiet time. I allocate a few moments each morning before I start my busy day. It's become spiritual for me."

Paul was silent for a few moments as Natalie began reading the first-page article. The caption read: **Funding approved for a roundabout near the east beach.**

"Maybe next time I come, we could discuss our life together. Talking about our memories could be healing for both of us."

Natalie folded the newspaper, wrapped both hands around the mug, and sipped her coffee.

"By the way," Paul said. "I'm only here because some part of you wants me to be here."

She looked out over the water and said, "Why can I see you on some days, and today, I can only hear your voice?"

Paul laughed. "I don't know. I don't make the rules."

When Natalie got to the diner later that morning, she sat at her usual place at the end of the counter. She glanced over the first page of the morning paper and waited for Rosie to take her order. Jake was at the other end of the bar at his normal place. Natalie glanced in his direction. He lifted his coffee cup and winked. She tried to suppress a grin and then pretended to read her paper.

Finally, Rosie stopped in front of her, "What will you have this morning, Natalie?"

Natalie looked up from the paper. "Are you okay?"

Rosemary looked like she'd been awake all night. The dark circles under her eyes were accentuated by the fact she was not wearing a smidgen of makeup. The wig she wore to the diner had not been combed, and her hands shook as if she'd spent the night drinking numerous pots of caffeinated coffee.

"I'm fine," Rosemary said. "What will you have?"

Setting aside the paper she still hadn't had time to read, Natalie said, "Coffee, a veggie omelet, toast with butter on the side, please."

When her order was delivered, she got a Texas omelet, a slice of heavily buttered toast, and a small glass of orange juice. Natalie looked at her plate, then looked up at Rosemary who didn't seem to notice the error. Rosemary was also ignoring Jake, which was a rarity for her.

Rosemary must be in a funk this morning.

While Natalie ate her breakfast, she watched as Rosemary pointedly ignored Jake. When he asked for a coffee refill, she walked into the kitchen. When he tried to catch her eye, she turned her back and engaged another customer.

Something had obviously happened between the two before Natalie got there.

When she'd swallowed the last of her breakfast, Natalie glanced at Jake. He wasn't in a hurry to leave. When she got up, Rosemary followed her to the cash register, a scowl still planted on her face.

"Rosemary..." She glanced at Jake to make sure he was listening. "Why don't you and Jake come over for dinner on Friday night?"

With one hand on her hip, Rosemary immediately turned toward Jake as if to judge his reaction.

Jake nodded in response.

A couple of seconds passed, but then Rosemary seemed to have an epiphany. "Sounds good. What can we bring?" She flashed a radiant smile at Jake, like they were suddenly a couple again.

Natalie placed a single bill on the counter. "Not a thing. It's my turn to entertain you." She started for the door, then turned and said, "Come over around 6:30, and come hungry, I'm planning a seafood boil."

Chapter Twenty-One

Rosemary

After Natalie left the diner, Rosemary reached for a fresh pot of coffee and said to Jake, "I never got you that refill."

"Yeah, you've pretty much ignored me all morning. What's up?"

"Oh, I was just thinking about my next book. It was nice of Natalie to invite us for dinner."

"Uh, huh."

This invitation to dinner on Friday could be a game changer for Rosemary; she would approach the evening with a different mindset than the day they spent together on July Fourth. The long day watching Jake coddle Natalie had taught her a valuable lesson. This time, she'd bring her A-Game and win.

Rosemary and Jake had hit it off almost immediately when she came to the island, but she'd taken their friendship for granted. This could be her chance to make Jake see her in a different light and possibly get Natalie out of the picture for good. Of course, it would take a killer outfit. J. McLaughlin had recently advertised a pair of white pedal shorts with a matching top. It was the perfect outfit for a summer shrimp boil. She reached for her phone and called her stylist to schedule an appointment. A trim and a few highlights would add some much-needed sparkle to her look. Game on!

With a smile, she handed Jake a small plate with a hot apple Danish. "Thought this might go well with your coffee."

She no longer wanted to share him with Natalie. A three-pronged relationship wouldn't work for her. She'd secretly vowed to give herself five years before jumping into another romantic relationship; yet, here she was, jumping. Ironically, she and Natalie were at the same point in their grief journey, two years in. Rosemary's fiancé, whom she thought she'd spend the rest of her life with, had died. His death certificate said it was a heart attack.

Rosemary smiled.

As she scrubbed the lunch counter, she pondered her scheme. First, she needed to clean her aura and improve her image—she could become anyone she wanted. Then, still smiling, she looked toward Jake, who was looking at his phone. This could be as much fun as creating a character in a novel. Jake had always said that she was cold and indifferent. Reserved was another adjective he'd often used. Of course, he was kind and always a gentleman, but he had gotten his point across.

When they met, a platonic friendship with Jake was ideal for her delicate heart. However, Jake had never pushed her for anything more than friendship. She paused and checked the coffee level remaining in the caffeinated pot. Come to think of it, Jake had never even tried to kiss her. It saddened her to think that he might not have found her attractive. He'd never pushed for sex, that was certain, but... to never even try to kiss her?

She brushed the thought from her mind. Of course, he would have found her sexy. They had a healthy friendship. Rosemary had once read that men prefer to marry women with whom they had initially forged a friendship. They found those relationships to be a strong foundation on which to build a lasting marriage.

And then came Ms. Sparkle! Rosemary should have known the first day Natalie arrived on the island that she was going to cause trouble. She was right. Natalie had ruined everything! But only for a short time.

Jake got up from the lunch counter and headed toward the door. "Bye, sweetie!" she yelled. The diner grew silent as all eyes turned to Rosemary and Jake. His face reddened as he darted out the door.

Rosemary smiled again. Her first declaration that Jake was hers!

***

Jake looked forward to the seafood boil at Natalie's house, although he'd rather it just be the two of them. He knew Natalie was just trying to ease the tension with Rosemary. He hoped it didn't backfire.

The thing about a federal holiday, like the Fourth of July, was that when it fell on a weekday, the shorter work week was easier to get through. Hump day arrived one day earlier, and after that, Thursday and Friday were a sweet downhill slide. Many of Jake's workers had taken the week off, and although he checked the construction sites each day, he also knocked off earlier than usual.

On Friday afternoon, he stopped by the bookkeeper's office to drop off his month-end paperwork, and when he left, he stopped by Palmer's to pick up a twelve-pack of beer and a bottle of rosé wine. Then he rushed home, quickly changed into swim trunks, and took Copper for a short walk on the beach. As they waded in the surf, Rosemary's words the previous morning came back to him. What had she meant by yelling "goodbye, sweetie" inside the diner full of customers? Could she not tell her remark embarrassed him?

When he returned to the house, he jumped into the shower, listened to the news, and watched the time as he shaved and dressed in a pair of khaki shorts, a seafoam green golf shirt, and flip-flops. It was almost 6:15. He removed the beer and the bottle of wine from the refrigerator and placed them in the cooler at the screen door. Then he leashed Copper, grabbed the cold beverages, and headed down the trail to Natalie's cottage.

As he should have expected, Rosemary was already there. He could hear her laughter when he opened the porch door. A half-bottle of wine sat on the kitchen counter. Two sparkling glasses sat untouched next to the bottle. Three striped kitchen towels and a small bowl of lemon wedges lay next to the wine bottle. The cottage smelled of seafood, sausages, and lemon juice.

Without announcing his arrival, Jake stopped and leaned against the wooden framework of the kitchen door and admired Natalie's handiwork.

When Natalie looked up, Jake was smiling at her. There was a softness in his eyes that she didn't want to think too hard about. All she knew was that she liked it. As the two exchanged a nonverbal hello, Rosemary's glass dropped onto the tile floor and shattered.

"Come in, Jake," Natalie said as she finished arranging the seafood items onto a large wooden platter and turned to wash her hands. "Watch the glass."

Jake touched Natalie's back and then stooped to pick up the shards of glass. When Natalie finished drying her hands, she reached into the cupboard and retrieved a clean wine glass for Rosemary.

"Thanks, Jake," she said and pointed to the cabinet under the sink. "You can put the broken glass in there."

Jake wiped off the floor with a damp rag to ensure no broken pieces remained. Natalie filled three glasses of ice water and went out to the porch.

While Jake washed his hands, and as Natalie returned to the kitchen, Rosemary pointed to a hostess gift on the sideboard. "I brought Natalie a copy of my book."

"She'll enjoy reading it. I could hardly put it down once I got started." Jake tore a paper towel from the roll and dried his hands.

Rosemary brushed his arm with her hand, "Thanks for cleaning up that mess."

"No problem. You seem jumpy tonight. Are you okay?"

Rosemary winked at him. "I'm fine."

Natalie grabbed the three striped dish towels and the large wooden board piled high with seafood, corn on the cob, bite-size pieces of sausages, and small red potatoes and headed back to the porch. Jake picked up the bottle of wine, cut off the overhead light, and followed her to the table.

The table on the porch was round, and Natalie had positioned the chairs equally distanced from each other. Rosemary seemed a little tipsy. "I'm not sure which one is most adorable, Jake. You or Copper." She continued flirting with Jake as he checked on Copper before settling in at the table.

He glanced again at his beloved dog. When Jake finally came to the table, his face was flushed. "Wow! That's a ton of food on that board."

Rosemary said, "It's almost too pretty to eat."

Natalie reached for the wine bottle and poured a small amount for Rosemary. "Well, thank you, but let's dig in. There are no rules of etiquette for eating a seafood board, thank goodness."

Jake grabbed a beer from the cooler and removed the top. "There's a nice breeze coming off the ocean tonight. The lower humidity has been a nice change this week."

Rosemary filled her plate first, then waited for Natalie and Jake to do the same. "Jake and I usually go down to Sal's for dinner on Friday night, don't we, sweetie?" Her hand rested on Jake's arm as she looked at him with dreamy eyes.

Natalie wondered what Rosemary was trying to do. Of course, they were all friends, enjoying the end of another week. But for Natalie, it was also a celebration of spending her first holiday in her beach cottage. For Rosemary, it was clearly about establishing Jake and her as a couple.

Based on Jake's uncomfortable expression, she was trying a little too hard.

Natalie glanced at Rosemary with amusement. "Perhaps a good pizza is in order, following a week of barbeque, hamburgers, and hotdogs." She snapped a crab leg with a louder crack than was intended. Smiling, she glanced from Rosemary to Jake. Her eyes flitted to Rosemary's hand, possessively holding onto Jake's arm. "I hear Sal makes a fabulous pizza pie."

"You're right," Jake said. "I eat at Sal's at least once a week. You'll have to go with me one night." He managed to withdraw from Rosemary's grasp as he reached for the seafood board and scooted it closer to his plate, sliding his chair a few inches from its original position.

Thanks to Rosemary, Natalie's first dinner party on the island had started as a tension-filled evening. Jake tried to ease the strain by asking Natalie about the food. "The fresh shrimp and crab legs are delicious," he said as he peeled another shrimp.

"Thanks. I now wonder how I've eaten seafood from the freezer section at the market," Natalie said. "The difference in the taste of the fresh seafood from the dock is like night and day." The crab legs were firm and opaque. They'd allegedly been flown in from the upper coastal area.

When Natalie brought the dessert to the table, a mint chocolate sorbet in small bowls topped with whipped cream and a mint leaf, she found Rosemary slumped in her chair with her head resting on the table. She'd had too much to drink again. Natalie hoped her friend wasn't struggling with an alcohol problem. Rosemary remained in the same posture while Natalie and Jake chatted and completed their meal.

Jake helped clear the table, and later, he took the garbage out to the dumpster while Natalie cleaned up the dishes.

When Jake got ready to leave, he nodded to Rosemary, who was still passed out on the table, and said, "I should probably take her home."

"You could move her over to the sofa."

"I'll just take her home." He leaned over and tenderly kissed Natalie on the lips. "I had a good time tonight. Thanks for inviting me." Then he gently picked up Rosemary and carried her toward the door.

Natalie stepped ahead of him and held the screened door, "Stop back by on your way home if you like."

Jake winked and said, "Thanks, I'm ready for a strong bourbon and cigar."

"I may join you." After the tension of the evening, she relished the thought of relaxing by the fire with a friend.

Chapter Twenty-Two

Rosemary

Rosemary was neither asleep nor altogether conscious when she jerked the comforter back, exposing the pale blue sheet. The night air was humid, and her white shorts and spaghetti strap top clung to her damp body. She opened one eye and glanced at the digital clock on the nightstand. 1:30 a.m.

As her eyes adjusted, she inhaled the surrounding air, remembering the security of Jake's muscular arms as he carried her home from Natalie's house. His scent still clung to her clothes.

She lay in the darkness, remembering with disgust the way Jake looked at Natalie when he entered her kitchen. He'd never looked at her that way. The jolt was so severe she'd shattered one of Natalie's new pastel-colored wine glasses. The faux pas looped through her mind like an old movie reel. Clearly, there was no point trying to get back to sleep.

Rosemary swung her legs over the edge of the bed, biting her bottom lip as she tried to figure out a way to eliminate the threat Natalie's presence had created. Smiling, she knew. A few minutes later, she turned on the light, grabbed her laptop, and started the outline for a new story. Writing suspense allowed her to hide behind the characters, but now she would write a book that would show Jake she had the same qualities he admired in Natalie. By the time Jake finished reading this book, he would *see* her, really see her, and know she was the only woman for him.

Perhaps, she'd never have Natalie's natural openness and vulnerability—but she was smart, energetic, and driven. Jake was right about her being prickly—she was a private person and kept her feelings to herself, but that didn't mean she didn't have them. She would pour them all into this story to create the perfect character… the perfect Rosemary.

Of course, she couldn't call the book's main character by her own name. She'd have to choose a different one. Since rosemary is a spice, maybe this new character should be named for one, too.

Sage…yes!

After a couple of hours, she saved her work and went to the bathroom. When she climbed back onto the bed, she realized this book would be the scariest thing she'd ever done—because it would force her to face her demons.

Sage, like Rosemary, had completed her latest novel the year before moving to the island. After her fiancé's death, she'd felt restless and empty, certain her creative juices were diminished. She'd doubted she'd ever write another book. So when her uncle's estate settled, and the deed to the diner was in her possession, she set off to St. Simons Island.

Rosemary tapped her fingers on the laptop, thinking about her father's only brother. Uncle Buck was the youngest of seven children, and his siblings had called him the rebel. Nevertheless, she had always loved him—he was the cool uncle. He was fun.

She jotted a few sentences about Sage's cool uncle—maybe call him Bob—then let herself drift into the past.

Owning a diner wasn't something she'd ever considered. The only time she'd waited tables was a short stint of time before she landed her job with The Chicago Tribune.

Driving across the causeway and onto the highway leading to the beach town, it was like the heavens had opened and released a load of pixie dust. Not literally, of course, but the sensation of entering an enchanted island devoured her. The enormous oak trees and the Spanish moss flowing from the branches captivated her soul.

By the time she pulled into the diner's driveway, she felt like she'd found her way home, and in that moment, she felt the spark of her muse—the knowledge that she would, and could, write a second book.

On that first day on the island, sitting inside the diner, still intoxicated by the warmth of the drive through the Spanish moss and oak trees, Rosemary decided to keep the business for a few months. The stress of her previous life had already disappeared. Moving to the island was a welcomed respite, and with the easygoing lifestyle the coast would offer, a bestseller would undoubtedly emerge. She would write about island life. It wasn't something she knew much about, but she would learn.

Rosemary had displayed a picture of her uncle on the bookshelf in her bedroom. Her eyes flitted to the picture. She smiled, remembering the large tattoo on his forearm and the smell of pipe tobacco and peppermint.

He'd carried peppermint candy in his pockets for her. At least, she thought he'd brought the candy for her, but now that she was older and more mature, she realized it was to avoid smoker's breath.

She would definitely use that in the book.

It took her the rest of the night to get her initial thoughts on the page. Re-reading her hours of work, she realized the eight thousand five hundred words were just random beliefs about her uncle, her journey to the island, and the role the diner would play in the story. Lots of emotion, little structure. Still, it was a good beginning.

Rosemary walked through the cottage, waiting for the coffee to brew. The lights from a distant shrimp boat out in the ocean twinkled in the predawn hours, and at last, the memory of Jake and Natalie blurred. Although she hadn't slept, she felt refreshed. Sure, she looked like hell, but the adrenalin rush would get her through the morning.

When the coffee was ready, she took a cup out onto the screened porch. As the sun peeped beyond the ocean, she watched the King and Prince Resort staff moving around the beach area, setting up beach chairs and umbrellas for the hotel guests.

When Rosemary glanced in the other direction, Natalie was sitting at her firepit, reading the morning paper. Bile rumbled in Rosemary's stomach. She couldn't wait for the book to be finished. She had to do something... plan something...*now*... and an idea came to mind.

Rosemary went back inside and stopped in front of a closed door. She reached above the door frame, removed a slender silver key, and unlocked the spare bedroom door. As she walked inside the room and looked at the various props she'd used throughout the years, a brilliant idea about casting Natalie as the antagonist burst into her mind, and her creativity heightened. Rosemary aka Sage, the protagonist, and Natalie, the antagonist—a perfect pair. She would pull out all the stops and give it everything she had! She'd sell the diner if necessary or hire a temporary manager to run the day-to-day operations while she wrote.

Rosemary rushed back to her laptop to outline the ending scene. Ideas kept popping into her mind as her creative juices flowed. She would spend the summer or however long it took, to complete the manuscript. As she looked over each chapter's description, she realized that, just like her previous book, the plot would read like a true-to-life story, but this one was sure to be a bestseller.

There was one more thing to do before getting ready for work. Rosemary pressed the insert button and added a blank page at the start of the outline: *A Southern Suspense Novel by Mary Rose.*

Chapter Twenty-Three

Natalie

Early Saturday morning, Natalie returned to the beach for a few moments of reading and coffee before getting ready for work. Then, just as she finished reading the paper's front page, she heard his voice. "Well, looks like your carpenter friend stayed pretty late last night. Nice of him to take the neighbor home before coming back for a nightcap."

Natalie ignored him. Was talking to the deceased one of the stages of grief? Besides, if anyone on the beach heard her talking to a chair, they'd probably have her medical license revoked.

There was a period of dead silence, and then Paul said, "Do you remember those tickets you bought for our fifth anniversary? I sure wish I could have seen that musical, but I was more disappointed that I didn't get to see you in that beautiful black dress you bought for that evening."

"Yeah. Me, too." Natalie thought back to the night of her husband's accident: "I'd spent weeks planning it, and on the ride to the theater, I remember thinking I'd never spent a day in a state of such anticipation."

"I got detained," Paul said. "We were expecting a delivery by special courier, and I couldn't leave until the guy made the drop."

"I suspected as much." She wrapped both hands around her cup to capture the warmth. "When I arrived, there were so many people in the lobby that I was afraid we'd miss each other, so I stood inside the door and watched for you. Later, as I turned toward the door, I saw the ambulance flying down 46th Street, followed by a second and a third. I checked my phone, but no messages."

Natalie took a swallow of coffee and continued. "I kept checking my phone, hoping you'd either send a text or call. The lights flickered, and you still weren't there. And when Tina began singing 'What's Love Got to Do with It' in her raspy voice, I wanted to scream for her to stop the show until you could get there. You missed the best opening on Broadway."

"Believe me, I'd rather have been there," Paul said. "What did you do when you realized I wasn't coming?"

"Well, at the intermission, I stayed in my seat and rechecked my phone messages. Nothing. So I looked around the theater, and I thought I saw you. Same dark hair, same sexy walk. I was halfway out of my seat when I saw it wasn't you. Then I got a horrible feeling and went out front to call you."

"I bet you were pissed!"

"More like panicked. When I came down the stairs into the lobby, a police officer was just coming in. I could tell something bad had happened, and somehow I knew he had come for me."

"You must have been terrified."

"It was the scariest moment of my life. I remember thinking he looked like a TV cop. Square jaw, wide shoulders, and lots of muscles. Which meant that, whatever he said, none of it was real."

"I'd hardly made it to the hospital," Paul chuckled, "and you were already checking out the policeman."

Natalie grinned. "He was nice looking—thick black hair and olive complexion. But not as hot as you." As her story unfolded, it all came back as if it were happening all over again.

The officer had stopped and looked around the room. His eyes settled on Natalie and lingered a little longer than was necessary. A shiver went down her spine. She reached for the handrail and then slowly continued down the steps. When she looked over at the mirror-covered wall, a reflection of the officer walked in her direction.

"Excuse me, ma'am," he said. "Are you Natalie Howard-Nieman?"

She couldn't speak. Her heart pounded in her throat.

As he walked her out of the building, he brushed her arm with his hand as if trying to brace her for a fall. "Ma'am," he said. "I'm Officer Rhodes from NYPD. I'm sorry to have to tell you, but your husband was involved in an accident. I'm here to escort you to New York Memorial."

She glanced over to where she thought Paul should be.

"Did you think I was dead?" he asked.

"I don't remember thinking you were dead, but I knew you'd never miss seeing Tina Turner on Broadway!"

For a moment, she felt a warm breeze on her hand, as if he had brushed it with his fingers.

"You got that right," he said.

Chapter Twenty-Four

Jake

Early Sunday morning, before dawn, Copper jumped off the end of the bed and howled like a crazy hyena.

Jake turned over onto his side. "Come on, Copper. Quit the yapping. You'll wake the neighbors."

Copper laid his snout on the edge of the bed and nuzzled Jake with his nose. Jake groaned and pulled the pillow over his face. When the insistent nudging continued, he finally opened his eyes. A beam of bright light shone through the house.

What the...?

While Copper continued to bark, Jake hopped up and followed the light. He looked out the kitchen window. Just past Natalie's cottage, there was something in the sky. It wasn't an airplane; it was way too small to transport humans.

Jake turned off the fluorescent light above the sink so he could get a clearer view and watched the object move over Natalie's house. Copper paced back and forth, his barking reduced to a pitiful whine.

He patted Copper's head and said, "No worries, boy. It's just a drone...nothing to get excited about." He had read about unmanned aerial vehicles or vessels that navigated autonomously for military missions, but this was the first he'd seen so close.

At last, Jake flipped on the coffeemaker and went back to his bedroom to dress. When he'd slipped on sweatpants and running shoes and poured coffee into an insulated cup, he took Copper outside to do his morning business. Afterward, they lingered on the beach for a while. Copper finally stopped whining and was enjoying his morning stroll when Jake noticed an object with two bright purple lights hovering overhead.

Another drone? He hesitated, then walked on when Copper tugged the leash. As they wandered farther down the coast, Jake glanced over his shoulder toward home. The object had risen higher into the clouds.

He waited until full daylight before removing Copper's leash. The dog waited, patient as a coiled spring, until the snap came free. Then, tail wagging with delight, he darted away to prance in the surf and sniff the holes in the sand while Jake sipped his coffee.

Over the ocean, the clouds made way for the blue sky, and the air smelled clean from the overnight rain. It was like the heavens opened and someone had poured buckets of water from the sky. The lasting effect was pristine, clean air, but the ocean waves were massive and much too strong for surfing. Jake counted back to the last time he'd been on his board. It had been almost two weeks. He shrugged. Since meeting Natalie, his heart was not as interested in his beloved hobby as it had once been.

Jake finished his coffee and followed Copper down the coast when he noticed the Labrador was winded. As they walked back, Jake saw the object again, still hovering over Natalie's cottage. By then, the sun had peeked through the clouds, and he could see it was shiny, silvery-colored, and shaped like a small space rocket positioned on a four-pronged metal foundation.

Two of the prongs twinkled with lights from the front. The purple flashes from earlier were now clear, bright lights. Something about the darkness had caused him to visualize the color purple.

The drone's spotlight stopped directly over Natalie's car, completely encircling the vehicle in a clear bubble created by the light. One. Two. Three. Flashes sparked from above. The drone rose slowly into the atmosphere as the bubble moved from the car to the cottage. Another set of flares sparked at the house.

Soon, the kitchen light appeared, and Natalie walked onto the screened porch. Even though the sun was coming up over the water from the other direction, sleeping with those intense lights shining in the windows would be difficult. Natalie walked out to the fire pit wearing pajama shorts and an oversized T-shirt and looked up at the sky. By then, the light had faded, and the drone had disappeared.

As Jake approached his house, he noticed Natalie's Porsche parked in the driveway. He stopped, and Copper halted at his side. The money. Was this a government surveillance? He wondered if there was any connection between the drone shining over Natalie's cottage and the money he'd found stashed inside her car's door panel.

Chapter Twenty-Five

Afternoon at the Beach

On Sunday, Rosemary and Natalie had planned to spend the afternoon at the beach. When Natalie arrived at Rosemary's cottage, she placed the cooler on the porch steps and hollered inside.

Rosemary called back, "I'll be out in a second."

Once they got their beach towels spread over their chairs and placed the cooler between them for easy access, they were ready for a quiet afternoon.

Natalie pulled a paperback book from her beach bag. "I've been reading your novel. It's fascinating. Have you always known you wanted to write?"

"Pretty much," Rosemary told her about her Uncle Buck. Beginning when she started middle school, they'd go to the local bookstore on her birthday each year. The first classic he gave her was *Anne of Green Gables*. It was her most prized possession. After that, he gave her another classic each year to add to the collection.

"And you've loved reading ever since?"

"Yeah," Rosemary said. "When I got home from the bookstore, I'd lock myself in my room and read my new book in one sitting, and the next day I'd read it all over again. I was twelve years old when I knew I wanted to be a writer."

"So how did you end up in a coastal town with a diner?"

Rosemary looked out over the ocean and grinned. "I inherited the diner from my father's youngest brother." Then her eyes brightened. "This is a great story about the day I came to the island. I was sitting at the end seat at the lunch counter—where you typically sit each day. I was reviewing the profit-and-loss statement while sipping a cup of coffee, still unsure if I'd keep or sell the business. My uncle always said you could judge the success of a restaurant by the quality of the coffee.

The restaurant's profit margin was higher than I expected. I could tell the restaurant had a huge customer following by the foot traffic during that two-hour visit, and the waitress was constantly brewing more coffee. Then they brought me the best hamburger of my life."

Natalie said, "You're joking, right?"

Rosemary raised her hand. "I promise. True story. The burger had two fresh ground beef patties, caramelized onions, pickles, crisp lettuce, yellow cheese, and a generous dollop of Thousand Island dressing crammed inside a steamed bun. I bit into that double-decker burger, and my taste buds exploded."

"And to think," Natalie said, laughing, "I've never even tried your burgers. They must be fabulous!"

Rosemary nodded. "I've never told a single soul, but the burger sealed the deal. I quickly changed my mind and decided to keep the diner." She smiled. "It was nothing more than a gut instinct. My journalism professor used to tell us to compile as many facts as possible, but in the end, trust your gut."

"So, you were a journalism major," Natalie said. "Where did you go to school?"

Rosemary took a long swallow from her water bottle. "I grew

up in the Midwest. After graduating from the University of Illinois, Chicago, I got a job at the Chicago Tribune and rented an apartment in the Lincoln Park area."

"Good for you. That's a good place to start a journalism career… It's cold in Chicago, though."

Rosemary gave a mock shiver. "Extremely cold." She twisted the cap onto the plastic bottle. "When I arrived at the Tribune, one of my first assignments was to interview a young Chicago native who was running for the United States Senate against an incumbent."

"I remember that race," Natalie said. "He was remarkably articulate and brought fresh ideas to the campaign."

Thirty-year-old Chadwick Rockwell came from a prominent family in Illinois. They had groomed him for politics from a young age. If elected, Rockwell would be the seventh youngest United States Senator in U.S. history.

The article Natalie had read said he was an avid runner.

Rosemary said, "At first, I thought the guy was a pompous ass, and I just wanted to finish the interview and get the story turned in to the editor by the end of the day. The interview lasted longer than I intended. As I listened to him answer questions about how he intended to support the younger population moving into Illinois, I was mesmerized." She lowered her shades and gave Natalie a sideways glance. "I mean, who wouldn't vote for him? He was gorgeous, intelligent, well-connected, and articulate."

Natalie reached for a sandwich from the cooler. "The best politicians usually are!"

Rosemary sipped her water and said, "At the end of the interview, he suggested we take a break and get a cup of coffee."

That was a smooth move, thought Natalie as she bit into her sandwich. Olympic athletes used caffeine to improve their performance.

By the end of the interview, they were on a first-name basis. That was the start of a four-year love affair. Rosemary tucked a strand of hair behind her ear. "Chad wasn't married. I couldn't even find any romantic links. That's when we started seeing each other regularly."

At first, they would meet for dinner once a week, on a Thursday night. Chad explained he needed to use the weekend to travel around the state. He would board a bus on Friday and return late Sunday night or early Monday morning. His schedule was busy, so their Thursday night dinner date just stuck. Occasionally, he would ask Rosemary to go with him on a weekend excursion. During those weekend getaways, they went to his family cabin at Camp Beach at Cedar Lake, about a five-hour drive from Chicago. It was a four-bedroom, three-bath cabin with a wood-burning fireplace in the large family room and a screened-in porch across the back of the house overlooking an Olympic size swimming pool.

"Sounds like a gorgeous place," Natalie said.

Rosemary shifted in her chair, her eyes animated. "It was... Cedar Lake has beautiful nature trails. It didn't take long for Chad to figure out I have extraordinary organizational skills and ask me to get involved in his campaign for the Senate. I should have realized something was wrong when the first photograph appeared in the local newspaper of Chad and me running on the campaign trail, and he had the audacity to introduce me as a speechwriter."

Natalie nodded. Yeah, that should have been a red flag, but women always seemed ready to give the benefit of the doubt to the men they love.

Rosemary went on. "I guess I didn't see it because he seemed to appreciate me so much. If anyone on his staff asked about my role in the campaign, he would say I was the engine that kept the machine moving. And I was, too." She ticked off the evidence on her fingers. "Before Chad met with a group of potential supporters, he'd give me a list of names. I'd dig around for every bit of information I could find that might prove helpful. Chad went into every meeting with an extensive list of the strengths and weaknesses of each person he met. He was a walking encyclopedia of knowledge, from where they vacationed each year, their political views, and their net worth. All because of my efforts." She gave a bitter little laugh. "I almost single-handedly got him elected to the U.S. Senate."

Natalie said, "Your journalism background paid off."

Rosemary nodded as she grabbed a sandwich from the cooler. "For all the good it did me."

Natalie said, "Tell me more about the Senator."

While the women ate their sandwiches, Rosemary shared her story. The night of the November election, around 11:30, a picture of Chad and Rosemary appeared on the front page of every Illinois newspaper, their hands joined in the air and broad smiles on their faces. She was sure his election to the U.S. Senate would mean an engagement announcement by year-end.

"Once Chad began his term in January," Rosemary said, "he bought a townhome in the Old Town neighborhood of Alexandria, Virginia. It's known for its historic, colonial-era charm, with stunning views of the Potomac River, and there were running trails close by. I oversaw the remodel of the condo and dealt with the designers to create a comfortable space for Chad. Of course, I was disappointed that he'd not proposed over the holidays, but I never lost sight that the townhome would someday be my second home. I started leaving a few outfits there."

Chad joined the ranks of Congress, but it wasn't enough. He aspired to do more. "We dated through three summers, but going into the spring of the fourth year, something changed."

When he first moved to Alexandria, he'd call Rosemary every night when he got in from work. But then the calls decreased to once or twice a week. Chad seldom returned to Chicago, and Rosemary's visits to the townhome were less frequent, too. They'd dwindled from regular weekly visits where she arrived on Friday afternoon and flew out around ten o'clock on Sunday evening to one visit every four to six weeks.

"I hadn't seen Chad for, I don't know, probably six weeks or more… when I was assigned an interview with the Majority Leader on the hill. On the way to the interview on a Monday afternoon, I flew into Dulles Airport, then rented a car and drove to Alexandria to pick up my favorite jacket in the townhome foyer closet."

Rosemary wadded the sandwich wrap tightly in her hand. "I remember looking down as I slipped the key into the lock. Chad's running shoes were next to the door. He always removed his shoes to let them air after a run." She shook her head. "As I entered the townhome, I thought I heard something, but it was only a noise from outside. Then I checked out the new rug in the foyer."

Natalie looked at her with suspicion. *He could've been there all along.*

As Rosemary walked to the living room, her eyes flitted to the bookshelf. A picture of a redhead holding a baby in a christening gown had replaced the photo of her and Chad in the sterling silver frame they had bought at Tiffany's on their first trip to New York City. Her stomach churned when she saw the size of the engagement ring on the woman's left hand.

Natalie leaned forward in her chair. "How did you keep from throwing that picture against the wall?"

Rosemary exhaled. "I didn't want to damage the place. At that point, I still thought of the townhome as mine." A look of malice distorted her beautiful face. "But I would've killed that man if I could've gotten my hands on him."

Numb with disbelief, Rosemary went into their bedroom. A picture of the redhead had replaced Rosemary's in the frame that sat on the bedside table, and the enormous walk-in closet Rosemary had designed had been converted into a nursery. The built-in dresser drawers now housed beautiful baby blankets and tiny pink outfits neatly folded on the shelves previously designed for the senator's shoes. Someone had removed her designer clothes from the closet, and her favorite robe was no longer hanging on the back of the bathroom door.

Rosemary's voice rose an octave as she lifted her outstretched hands. "The guy I'd dated for four years, from whom I had expected a marriage proposal the past two, had developed a relationship with this woman and fathered her child."

Natalie said, "That must've been painful for you."

"It was terrible." Rosemary stared past her water bottle. "When they were throwing out my belongings, they somehow missed the jacket I stored in the foyer closet. I grabbed it and searched the pockets. There was a credit card receipt in the pocket from our dinner the last time I was in Washington. Chad had drawn a heart over his signature."

Unbelievable. Paul hadn't been perfect, but Natalie couldn't imagine him doing something like that. Then she thought of the unidentified woman in the emergency room and wondered if she'd known him any better than Rosemary had known Chad.

Rosemary reached for the sunscreen and applied the lotion to her shoulders. "I'm not proud of this, but I couldn't help myself at the time. I stormed through the bedroom door, placed the restaurant receipt on his pillow, wadded the coat up, and threw it on the floor at the foot of the bed, and that's where I left it."

Natalie gave a little laugh of surprise. "This has all the makings of a bestselling novel."

Rosemary laughed, too. "I agree. By the time I'd discovered the truth about the senator, his name had already been tossed around as the keynote speaker for the Democratic National Convention. And he was being groomed to run for President of the United States in 2024."

Rosemary had been instrumental in helping her cheating boyfriend establish a platform the millennial population of Illinois would support. His staff organized rallies to get the young people of the state registered to vote. As soon as he caught wind of speaking at the convention, he texted Rosemary a list of talking points for her to research. Rosemary was clever and tenacious, he said, and the perfect speechwriter. Without so much as a face-to-face conversation, he expected her to outline the speech.

She reached for the cooler and removed a beer. "Three weeks before his appearance at the 2020 Democratic National Convention, I shredded the speech and deleted the outline from my iPhone and laptop computer. I was done. Finished."

She took a long swallow from the bottle. "Later the same day, I met with the Majority Leader, then headed straight to the airport. After finishing a second glass of Chardonnay on the flight back to Chicago, I made a life-changing decision."

"What was that?"

"I sublet my apartment, then packed my belongings and headed south to check out the restaurant my uncle had left for me in his will. At that moment, I was done with politics, and I was done with men and their eloquent lies."

"What happened to the senator?"

Rosemary lowered her sunshades and said with a smirk, "He died of a heart attack later that night."

Chapter Twenty-Six

The Boss – Seven Years Before

The next meeting in Mr. Steelton's office lasted most of the morning. After they'd finished the analysis of an acquisition their largest client was negotiating with a rival company, Paul prepared a quick PowerPoint of the data. He projected it onto the screen for Steelton to review.

Steelton nodded. "This is excellent!"

The praise came as a surprise. Steelton rarely appreciated contributions other than his own. He was a dynamic figure within the financial district. He exuded a sense of superiority unmatched by anyone in the company. Perhaps his feeling of importance was related to his height. He was a tall man, well over six feet tall, with bronzed skin from the hours he enjoyed on the golf course and a head full of white hair that had begun greying in his early thirties.

Then again, Paul's success would naturally reflect on him. So maybe the accolades weren't so surprising after all.

"When The Boss gets here, I'll provide the quarterly overview and you can discuss the PowerPoint of the acquisition. He keeps a tight schedule; he won't be here long. Thirty minutes tops."

Paul was nervous and excited at the same time. This was his first encounter with the firm's largest customer. From the looks of Steelton, he was equally anxious. As he walked around the office, he clicked the silver pen he held. An unusual habit that told Paul the man was under considerable pressure.

During the previous week, Paul had analyzed the stock purchases to ensure a robust stock-to-bond ratio, but today his primary objective was to convince their largest client that the business acquisition was worth the investment and that the services his bank offered were worthy of the enormous fees they charged.

The office was deathly quiet after the nonstop chatter of preparing for the meeting. Paul's mouth was dry, so he reached for a glass and carefully poured water from the Waterford carafe on the shiny mahogany table. The offices on the eighteenth floor where the top brass resided were appointed with elaborate furnishings, unlike the small offices and cubicles on the third floor.

Steelton returned to his desk and was checking emails when his assistant buzzed to tell them that Mario Bernardi had just arrived.

"Thank you," Steelton said. "Send him in."

Paul stood, waiting to meet the legend himself. He'd heard of Bernardi, but he'd never met him, and neither had any of the other financial advisors working on the third floor. The very first day on the job, he'd googled Bernardi's name, using every alias he could think of but was unsuccessful in finding any viable information. It was almost as if the man did not exist.

Mario Bernardi stormed into the room with the speed and sound of a mountain lion. The Boss, as they often referred to him in private, was a fast-talking man of Sicilian descent with shiny black hair, combed straight back, olive complexion, and a face covered in pockmarks. He wasn't conventionally handsome, but the monochromatic and particular color palette of khaki, off-white, and cream created an ageless and classic look. Keeping with the chic style of most Italian men, he wore Santoni loafers without socks.

Bernardi was slightly shorter than Paul, barely five-foot-six. Paul waited for Steelton to finish his greetings and make the introductions. Then, when the openings were over, they settled around the conference table. Steelton quickly finished his overview and nodded to Paul.

Paul handed the men a copy of the reports. "Mr. Bernardi, we've prepared a PowerPoint of your portfolio. If you direct your attention to page one of the document, we'll run through the information. We'll address your questions as we go along."

He'd just flashed the data onto the screen when Mr. Bernardi's Apple Watch pinged. He looked down, read the message, jumped up, and said, "Thank you, gentlemen, for putting this together. I'll read through it during my commute home tonight and let you know if I have any questions." He removed a piece of paper from his pocket and slid it across the table to Steelton.

Steelton read the note, looked up, and nodded. And without further discussion, the meeting was over. Paul watched as Mr. Bernardi left the room.

When Paul looked over at Steelton, he appeared relieved. As Paul closed his laptop, preparing to go back downstairs, Steelton walked to his desk, picked up the phone, and placed his hand over the receiver. "Paul, would you like to join me for lunch in the corporate dining room down the hall?"

It was the first Paul had heard about a dining room on the eighteenth floor. "Sure."

"Two for lunch," Steelton said. "We're on our way down."

Steelton hung up the phone and said, "We've hired a French chef. Pierre's steak sandwich is the best New York City has to offer. You've got to try one."

Paul couldn't believe his good fortune. Side by side, like peers, they walked down the corridor and stopped at a polished nickel door with a keypad entry positioned next to the door frame.

The guys on the third floor would never believe this story. He'd just met with the legend himself, and now he was about to have lunch in the corporate dining room. Of course, he could never discuss what had happened on the eighteenth floor with anyone. Those were the most sensitive accounts, which required the utmost discretion.

Steelton punched in a few digits, and the door swung open. The entire situation caught Paul completely off guard. Besides not knowing about the dining room, neither had he heard about the world-renowned chef. But there he was…standing in the kitchen with his white coat and hat, looking all French.

Steelton introduced Paul to the chef.

"Bonjour."

"Can we get two steak sandwiches, please, Pierre?"

The chef nodded, pulled a couple of thick steaks from the sub-zero refrigerator, and pounded them with a food mallet. Within seconds, he tossed them onto the hot grill next to a handful of onions, green peppers, and mushrooms. The meat sizzled, and the smell of the steaks frying on the grill made Paul's mouth water.

In fewer than ten minutes, Pierre arrived at their table with their food. As they enjoyed their lunch, Steelton talked about his new custom-made golf clubs, and Paul listened while savoring his lunch. He should try to play more often—he'd been a pretty good golfer in college—but his weekends were spent hanging out with his wife. He wasn't willing to sacrifice their time to improve his game.

Steelton finished his sandwich first. "Did you drive to the office today?"

Paul nodded and folded his napkin. "Yes, sir. I did."

"Great! I need you to go over to the Staten Island Ferry terminal. A courier will meet you there with a parcel—I'll give him your car description and tag number. Wait and let him approach you. He'll most likely be riding his bike."

"What kind of parcel is it?"

Mr. Steelton finished the last of his iced tea and got up from the table. "He'll be expecting you at 3:30. Bring the parcel to my office when you return."

Chapter Twenty-Seven

Chris Rhodes - Now

The following Monday morning, Rosie had just cleared out the regular natives and the travelers, who typically awoke early to get ready for a workday and somehow couldn't readjust their internal clocks for a short week of vacation. When the late crowd started drifting in, Rosie saw a tall handsome guy with dark thick hair come in ahead of a group of suits. He had on a pair of blue swim trunks and a yellow T-shirt with the slogan *Life's a Beach* printed on the front. The attractive man looked like anything but an islander. Even in his dressed down vacation attire, he carried himself as a professional... perfect posture accentuating his six-foot frame. Exuding a heightened sense of awareness, his well-trained, intelligent eyes scanned the interior of the diner.

Funny how quickly Rosie could spot vacationers. There was an intensity about them at the start of the first week that they had yet to release. By the second week in June, they had relaxed and blended in with the other islanders. However, Monday morning after arrival, was way too early to shed the layers of stress brought on by the habits of the previous nine months.

As soon as Rosie served the orders the cook placed on the bar, she grabbed a clean cup and a fresh pot of coffee and headed over to Mr. Not From Around Here's booth. Even with his olive complexion, it was obvious his muscular legs had not seen the light of day in quite some time.

"Morning, Hon. Here's a cup of coffee to get you started." Rosie handed him a menu and winked. "Take your time. We're beginning to get a bit backed up."

"Thanks."

Rosie served another customer and then returned. "Hi, Hon. I'm Rosie. Are you here on vacation?"

"I'm Chris Rhodes." He extended his hand. "It's nice to meet you Rosie. I'm here for work, but I hope to enjoy the beach while I'm here."

Rosie asked how long he planned to stay.

"Through Labor Day." Chris studied the menu, Rosie continued to talk to him about the island. Finally, he looked up from the menu, "I understand a young doctor took over the clinic earlier this year."

Rosie nodded, intrigued by his remark. Had he come to town just to ask about Natalie?

She asked where he was from. It was a safe question that she asked all the vacationers who came into the diner. Most people were more than happy to disclose where they lived.

"New York City."

That explained the accent. "How was the drive?"

Long and boring, he said. It had taken fourteen hours, and he was unprepared for the humidity, which had zapped him of his energy. "Have you ever been to New York?"

Rosie placed one hand on her hip and said, "Yeah, once or twice." She pulled her order pad from her pocket. "The French

Toast is to die for, but of course, the All Star Breakfast is a big hit, too."

She laid the ticket on the bar for the cook to fill and went to check on the other customers.

When Rosie set the plate of French Toast and bacon on the table, he said, "Thanks. By the way, do you happen to know Natalie Nieman?"

Wow. He didn't waste any time.

The chatter in the diner suddenly stopped. The noise from the kitchen staff stopped. Every eye in the building looked at Rosie, hanging onto her next word. Even the chatty young professionals who came in between 8:30 and 8:45, and preferred to grab a coffee and breakfast sandwich to-go, stopped talking and directed their attention to Rosie.

If Rhodes had shown up thirty minutes earlier, Natalie and Jake would've been sitting at the lunch counter drinking coffee. He'd barely missed them. Now that would've been interesting…watching Jake as this gorgeous man asked about Natalie. Rosie wondered what Jake would have done.

She finished wiping the counter and then threw the dish cloth over her shoulder. "Yes. I know Natalie. She's a friend of mine." Well… *friend* wasn't exactly the right word, but she could be if Jake hadn't got all goo-goo eyed for her. They'd all been having such a good time before he had to go and ruin it. Then Rosie had an idea. She dropped the redneck act and lowered her voice to barely a whisper. "She took over the medical clinic vacated by our long-standing doctor. Dr. Baldwin passed away the week Natalie arrived on the island."

At the mention of Dr. Baldwin's death, Rhodes leaned in and made an inaudible comment.

By the time the breakfast crowd began to clear out, with only three other customers remaining in the diner, she and Chris Rhodes were on a first-name basis. Rosie poured herself a cup of coffee and took a break while pumping Chris with questions about Natalie's life in New York City.

After a few minutes, he said, "Do you think Natalie would mind if I dropped by the clinic to say hello?"

"Oh, no! I'm sure she would love to see you."

Interesting. Chris had come all the way from New York City. Normally Rosie would never be so open with information about one of her customers, but this might be the perfect solution to keep Natalie away from Jake.

"Will you write down her address for me?" Chris asked.

Mr. I'm Not from Around Here, you may be the answer to my prayer.

Rosie quickly jotted the clinic's address on a napkin. She slid the paper across the counter and smiled.

"And just to be clear," he asked. "Were you in New York once or twice?"

Chapter Twenty-Eight

Rhodes

Officer Rhodes had fallen in love—or at least, was infatuated with the memory of Natalie gliding down the staircase at the theater. As he looked at her now, standing inside the medical clinic with her hair pulled back in a ponytail and dressed in her blue medical scrubs, she was just as beautiful as the first night he saw her. Her slender hands held the back of a young boy's head as she evaluated a cut on his forehead, she was every bit as beautiful as he remembered on the night of her husband's accident.

***

"Are you okay?" Officer Rhodes fastened his seat belt as Natalie settled into the backseat of his patrol car. She seemed to be about the same age as his younger sister.

"Hmmm. I guess so…" Her damp eyes glanced at the rearview mirror, "I should've known something was wrong the minute I heard those sirens going down 46th."

THE EMPTY BEACH CHAIR

She fought back a sob that barely escaped her mouth, then bit her fist before continuing. "Today is our fifth wedding anniversary. I'm a doctor at New York Memorial and my husband is an investment banker. We both work brutal hours and barely get to see each other. This was supposed to be a big night out for us."

A milestone anniversary. She was dressed for a rare evening with her husband. Like his sister, the lady in the backseat was a classy woman. She reminded him of someone famous. Who was it? A movie star... no, an aristocrat. The one who wore expensive jewels and looked demure while waving at the people in the crowds.

She'd just draped a shawl over her black cocktail dress and touched the window as if waiting for the next bomb to drop in her lap.

Her shoulder-length hair was chestnut brown with golden highlights that accented her soft brown eyes. The red lipstick was the perfect touch. Not every woman could pull it off, but the shade was the ideal complement to her dark hair and alabaster skin. His image of her at the theater... he would never forget the sight of her gliding down the curved staircase. It was a shame her husband had missed seeing her there. Rhodes glanced once more in the rearview mirror, somehow knowing the stark lights of the hospital emergency room would not lend the same effect as the soft lighting inside the theater lobby.

He ran every red light on the way to the hospital, then skidded to a stop at the ambulance bay and shepherded Natalie inside. Dr. Martin was emphatic that the officer should not leave her side until he came face to face with him at the hospital. It was one order he was happy to obey.

Rhodes now worked for the FBI. He'd been recently assigned to a special task force. He had been waiting for this opportunity his whole career. He flipped through the pages of a magazine as he waited for Natalie to finish with her patients. He wasn't in a hurry. In fact, quite the opposite. Perhaps one of her former neighbors had contacted her already. Rhodes considered how he would broach the subject. Should he ease into it, or should he just come out and tell her without softening the news? He didn't know how she would react to her former townhome in Brooklyn being vandalized, or that the FBI had linked her deceased husband to 'The Mob.'

Chapter Twenty-Nine

Rhodes & Natalie

The door to the examination room opened, and Natalie emerged with a young boy and a woman who must have been his mother. The boy said something that made Natalie laugh. Rhodes looked at his watch. It was 5:30. He'd spent the day familiarizing himself with the island, just like an actual vacationer. Vacation. Now, that was a foreign concept. He hadn't taken one in ten years. Like most of the officers he worked with, Rhodes was passionate about the job. Some might have said too passionate—especially his ex-wife, who'd left him after two years to run off with a guy she'd met at the gym.

On her way out the door, she'd given him a bitter smile and said, "Being married to a cop is like being the other woman, but without the fun parts."

Rhodes looked down at his shirt and wondered why he'd grabbed the pink one. He knew that eating ice cream in the stifling 90-degree heat was a mistake, but he couldn't help himself when he spotted the Moo Cow Ice Cream shop on Ocean Boulevard, so he stopped and went inside. It was a cool shop. The Georgia Peach flavor was the best ice cream he'd ever eaten. He was in heaven. When he dropped his napkin into the garbage can, he realized a few drops of cream had landed on his shirt. So, at the last minute, he'd returned to the hotel, showered, and changed into a pair of khaki pants and a fresh golf shirt. It wouldn't look good for him to show up at her office wearing a soiled shirt.

Natalie was still smiling when she walked into the waiting area with the patient and his mother. As soon as they were out the door, Natalie turned toward Rhodes. "Have we met?"

Rhodes stood and smiled as he tossed the magazine on the table. He extended his hand. "I'm Chris Rhodes from the NYPD." Natalie's eyebrows knitted. He paused momentarily, allowing her to process the information. "Dr. Martin sent me to the theater to get you the night of your husband's accident."

He wished she were more transparent; he couldn't read her thoughts. But in his years of experience, he'd learned it was best to give small bits of facts at a time rather than trying to blurt out a series of events.

Finally, Natalie nodded. "Yes, I remember. I thought you looked familiar when you came in, but I couldn't quite place you."

"I'm investigating a vandalized townhome."

Natalie ran her hand through her hair and sat in a straight chair facing Rhodes. "You've come to the coast to investigate a crime?"

Rhodes followed her lead and sat down on the sofa. "Sort of...The townhome belonged to you and your husband."

Natalie bit her bottom lip and glanced at the picture window. "How long will this take?"

He shrugged, following her gaze, "It may take a while."

Natalie nodded. "Excuse me. I'll be right back." She went into the office and cut off the lights.

He stood when she returned to the waiting area, her purse and car keys in her hand.

"I'm hungry," she said. "If you don't have dinner plans, would you like to get a bite to eat while you conduct your investigation?"

"Sure. We can do that."

Rhodes wasn't happy about it, but Natalie insisted on driving her car. It would've been nice had she let him drive. But what the heck, he'd never ridden in a fancy Porsche. He detected a slight new car scent when he closed the car door. The inside was immaculate.

Natalie opened the convertible top before pulling out onto the road. Rhodes wondered if she'd driven the car down from New York. Owning a car in New York City was a luxury few young professionals could afford. Most people used the Metropolitan Transportation Authority. Of course, she'd need transportation to get around down here, but he would never have expected her to own a new vehicle, much less an expensive one like this.

Finally, he asked, "Where are we going?"

"The Rooftop at Ocean Lodge serves a grilled shrimp scampi to die for. They also have a fabulous burger if you're a burger guy." She slowed at the traffic circle. "The views from the rooftop are spectacular."

Rhodes smiled to himself. He might not have driven, but he couldn't complain about her choice of eating places. He'd never been to a rooftop restaurant.

After they'd eaten, they went across the street to the beach. Rhodes asked a few questions as they walked along the coast to let their food settle. "Tell me about Paul's job. What does an investment banker do?"

Natalie explained that Paul had helped other businesses manage and grow their money. That may mean issuing stock, floating a bond, negotiating the acquisition of a rival company, or arranging the sale of a company.

Her description was surprisingly eloquent, and Rhodes was more engaged than he'd thought he would be. It caught him off guard. Of course, she told him more than he needed to know, but that was okay, too. The longer she talked, the more relaxed she became around him.

When she was done, he explained that the home of John Steelton, Vice President of Global Sales and Research, had been vandalized the previous month. Also, the perpetrator had left several messages about turning over the remaining money.

Her eyebrow shot up. "What money?"

Rhodes lifted a shoulder. "That's what we're trying to find out."

Natalie assured him she knew nothing about it. "How does that involve my townhome?"

He watched her face carefully as he laid out what they knew. The Mob had allegedly targeted various people throughout the New York and New Jersey areas for money laundering. However, the authorities had only stumbled upon the scheme when Steelton offered the information in return for twenty-four-hour surveillance after his house was vandalized.

"Does that mean he knew who did it?"

Rhodes chuckled. "I would say so…"

Later, as they walked back to the restaurant's parking lot, Rhodes mentioned the scene at the hospital. "I need to ask you about the night your husband died. Do you remember his saying anything about his firm's involvement with the Mob?"

Natalie's head snapped around to face him. "Are you kidding? Paul never regained consciousness after the accident." Tears sprang to her eyes. "I can't believe this! After two years, you're trying to link my deceased husband with Steelton and the Mob?"

Damn. He'd moved too fast. He had a sentimental attachment to Natalie, and it had made him let his guard down. It happened sometimes when two people were thrown together in a crisis. He didn't sense the same connection from Natalie, but he felt a strong emotional bond with her.

His hand brushed her arm. "I was hoping Paul had mentioned Steelton's involvement, perhaps during drinks and dinner or at night before you went to sleep. You know how couples share things about their jobs at the end of a long day."

Natalie reached into her pocket for the car key. She seemed to accept his explanation and to understand that he was gathering information for a case. After a few minutes of silence, she said, "You mentioned someone had vandalized our townhome. Was it a random act?"

"No. It wasn't random." The brownstone had been ransacked, but the destruction appeared to be systematic.

"How do you know?" she asked.

"The perpetrators took a chainsaw and cut through the mahogany paneling in the upstairs study. It's likely they were looking for something hidden behind the walls."

"Was a chainsaw used at Steelton's house?"

"Yes."

They were standing next to the car in the restaurant's parking lot. Natalie looked out over the ocean. "It sounds like they thought Paul or Steelton had something that belonged to them."

Chris nodded and opened the driver's side door for her.

"What could it possibly be?" she asked.

Without flinching, Chris declared, "Five million dollars."

Chapter Thirty

Jake and Natalie

Jake had rolled down his windows and removed the top of his Jeep to enjoy the fresh air and sunshine. The Friday before the start of the Labor Day weekend was always a bittersweet day on the island. It was the start of the last official holiday of summer. The bright yellow school bus stopped in front of him at the traffic light, a reminder that the Glynn County School System had been in session for eighteen days. From the looks of the kids piled into the last rows on the bus, roughhousing with each other, the students were ready for a few days off.

When the light changed, the bus went straight, and Jake turned right toward the clinic. He'd wanted to take Natalie out on the sailboat—perhaps have dinner on the water, complete with wine. Jake had cleaned the boat earlier in the week and strung tiny white lights around the rails. He thought it would be romantic to throw a tablecloth over the deck and enjoy a simple meal together at the end of a long week.

Jake smiled. Only one other car, besides Natalie's, was at the clinic. He pulled into the parking lot and cut off the engine. In a few moments, the front door opened and an elderly lady and a younger woman, possibly her daughter, came out and walked down the steps toward their car. Jake waited for them to leave the parking lot before going in. He was nervous—he wiped his damp hands onto the front of his jeans.

At last, Jake got out of the vehicle and hesitated again. He walked up the steps, turned the door handle, and let himself inside. Natalie was standing in the office area, reading a chart. When she looked toward the door and saw him, a huge smile spread across her face. "Did you take off early today?"

He could tell by the playful tone of her voice that she was in a cheerful mood—an excellent sign.

"Yeah. I did. If our jobs are running on schedule, I let my crews leave early the day before a holiday, as long as they've worked hard the other four and a half days."

It was a win-win for everyone concerned, he explained. Then, he mentioned taking the sailboat out later in the afternoon.

"You've got a sailboat, huh?"

"Yep, I do." Jake grinned and asked if she'd like to have dinner on his boat when she got off work. He knew she'd had a rough week, starting with the investigation by the FBI.

Natalie closed the file. "You know, the hospital is sending over a temp in about an hour to fill in for me this weekend." She returned the file to the cabinet and turned around to face him. "I've worked late all but one day this week and had cereal those nights for dinner. I'm ready for a good meal."

He'd been pondering taking Natalie out on the boat since she came to the island, yet he hadn't given the meal much thought. As he lingered in the waiting room, it finally dawned on him. "Let's see, I'll grill a couple of lobster tails and make a salad." He reached for the doorknob. "Message me when you get home and change.

***

The weather was perfect. The day's high had been 83, but the thermostat registered 74 at six o'clock. Natalie had never seen the sky so intensely blue since she got to the island, and the ocean was as tranquil as ever.

Jake wore white shorts, a navy-blue T-shirt, and deck shoes with no socks. His long, toned legs were bronzed from the time he spent outside. He removed his shirt and stuck it in his backpack.

Natalie nodded at the scar on Jake's shoulder and said, "An old sports injury or rotator cuff surgery?"

He touched the scar and said, "Old sports injury."

Jake was a skilled boater and was deft at navigating the sails. When he was satisfied with their direction, he reached into his backpack and removed a tube of sunscreen. He lathered his face and arms and then pitched it to Natalie. "You better use some of this."

Natalie took the sunscreen and rubbed it over her arms. "I know a little about sports pain…ran Cross Country back in the day." She looked up at him and continued, "Are you still taking opioids for pain?"

Jack looked at her without blinking as he held tightly to the sails. "No. Just physical therapy. The pain is much better now."

When they got a couple of miles out, Jake mentioned that the wind reached ten knots at certain times of the day.

Natalie knew little about boating, but Jake's talk about the change in wind velocity fascinated her. "What are they registering now?" she asked.

Jake smiled before answering. "They're registering four today. Perfect conditions for a smooth sail."

The wind decreased even more, and the boat slowed to almost a stop. The boat drifted for a few minutes until they were only a couple hundred yards from shore. Jake jumped up, pulled a tablecloth from the picnic basket, and laid out a spread of food, ranging from shrimp cocktails, lobster tails, Caesar salad, olives, cheese, and fresh melons. He popped open a bottle of Prosecco.

Natalie watched him pour the liquid into two tall champagne flutes, realizing she had made an inaccurate judgment about his drug use the first time they met at the diner…an occupational hazard. Now she was relieved she had not jumped to conclusions and had given him the benefit of the doubt.

They discussed the events of their week as they enjoyed their meal. Jake wanted to spend the night out on the boat. He had a bed on the lower level, but he wasn't sure if Natalie was ready for that kind of commitment. Natalie was quieter than usual. Her mood had changed from earlier in the day, and he felt like she wanted to discuss something, but he wasn't sure.

Finally, she said, "The FBI agent said something the other day that's been bothering me. He said someone had vandalized my Macdonough Street Brownstone." She looked up from her plate to register his reaction. "They used a chainsaw on the wall in the library upstairs. A chainsaw! Can you imagine?"

Jake wasn't sure how to respond. All he could think of was a story he'd read about The Texas Chainsaw Massacre from the 1970s. Judging from Natalie's face, it didn't freak her out. She just needed to talk about it. "Were they looking for something specific?" he asked.

She nodded as she picked at her lobster tail. "Apparently so."

That wasn't much to go on, but something was wrong. The only news coming out of New York these days involved drugs, murder, and burglaries. It reminded Jake of the money he'd found stuffed in the car door, which caused him to wonder if there was money hidden in the upstairs library in Brooklyn. He tapped off her glass with more champagne, thinking he would mention it, but he didn't yet know all the facts. The money in the car could be completely unrelated to the break-in.

He glanced at Natalie, who was only picking at her food and didn't seem overly concerned. Jake was cautious not to frighten her. Maybe she—or someone else—had already retrieved the money from the car doors. Maybe later he should check to be sure.

He rubbed the rough edge of the lobster tail while pondering what he would say to Natalie. Then he noticed the expression on her face as she gazed across the water.

It could wait. He'd mention it to her later.

The sun began its descent and hung low in the sky. He'd been thinking of this evening for weeks, and it had finally arrived. Beautiful shades of yellow, orange, and red scattered across the horizon. The brilliant sun looked like it might explode as it communicated with the water.

It would be unconscionable to spoil the ambiance of this lovely evening by bringing up something so unpleasant.

Chapter Thirty-One

Natalie

Natalie woke on Saturday morning looking forward to a carefree holiday weekend. Between the clinic's regular patients and the summer influx of tourists stricken with various illnesses and injuries, it had been a busy few months at the clinic. Natalie was ready for a break.

She yawned and stretched, already sweltering in the extreme heat. Barely seven o'clock, and already her camisole clung to her torso. Just her luck. It was the first day she could sleep late, and here she was, staring at a ceiling fan that didn't work. She made a mental note to ask Jake to replace it when he got a chance.

The thick air was humid, and her first instinct was to jump into a cold shower. Then she thought about the breeze at the water's edge. If she planned to jog, she should do it now, because the heat would only intensify. Afterward, she planned to make a much-needed grocery run to the local market.

As she ran toward the beach, Natalie purposely paused at the Adirondack chairs near the firepit. Secretly yearning for Paul to make an appearance, she thought of all she had to tell him. Why had it been so long since his last visit? How would he react to the news about their brownstone?

These thoughts crowded her mind as she ran at a steady, moderate pace. Feeling invigorated, she stopped once again at the chairs on her way back to the house. Still, no Paul.

Disappointed, she went inside, showered, dressed, and drove to the market.

Miles of traffic jammed onto Fredericka Road on the way to Harris Teeter Market. Sitting in traffic, Natalie worried that Paul's visits were over. There was still so much she wanted to tell him. She was tempted to make a U-turn and return home, but needing the groceries more, she chose to patiently wait it out.

Later that afternoon, she moved the grill onto the concrete pad and lit the briquettes. While the charcoal heated, Natalie made a quick salad, then removed the white butcher's paper from the fresh piece of fish she'd purchased at the market earlier and placed the filet on a plate.

While applying herbs and seasoning, she looked and caught a glimpse of Rosemary as she dashed across the backyard. Her hair tumbling into a loose bun, she was dressed in all black except for the bright neon yellow flip-flops. She shoved the large tote into the back seat, jumped into her cobalt blue Mini Cooper, and spun out of the driveway. Where was she going in such a hurry?

Later in the evening, as Natalie cleaned up the kitchen and got ready for bed, she noticed Rosemary's porch light was still on. There was no sign of her car, though. Maybe she'd left the porch light on to make it look like someone was home. Or maybe she was planning to come home sometime after dark. But Sunday evening came and went with no sign of Rosemary.

On Labor Day morning, Jake stopped at Natalie's cottage and honked his horn. As she hopped in and closed the door to the

Jeep, he asked, "Do you know where Rosemary went this weekend? She's been gone for a couple of days."

"She left late Saturday afternoon, and I haven't seen her since."

Jake pulled onto the paved road and slowed down in front of her house. "She left the porch light on, but I noticed last night there were lights on inside." As they drove toward town, he said, "Can't believe she's gonna miss the last holiday celebration of the summer!"

Once again, the town put on a spectacular Labor Day parade. Natalie and Jake spent the day together on the beach, then walked to the King and Prince later in the afternoon for the community cookout. They filled their plates and found a table in the pool area near where the popular East Coast Rhythm and Blues band had set up to perform. Copper curled up at Jake's feet and watched the crowd.

As soon as they settled in, they were joined by one of Jake's crew members, Chase, and his wife, Rhonda. Jake introduced Natalie and invited them to share their table. While Jake and Chase chatted about baseball, Natalie and Rhonda talked about fashion and hairstyles for beach life. After the band got warmed up, Natalie put her hand over her mouth and said to Rhonda, "How are we going to get these two to move?"

Rhonda grinned. She got up and extended her hand to Chase, "How about a dance?"

Chase cut his eyes at Jake and said, "Excuse me, once the music starts, you can't keep this girl in her seat."

As they walked away from the table, Jake leaned over and said, "Why don't we join them?"

Just as they got to the dance floor, the band switched to "Sittin' on the Dock of the Bay," by Otis Redding. Jake reached for Natalie's hand and grinned. Their bodies molded into each other. The same as her body used to mold into Paul's. It felt right and completely natural. Secure in Jake's arms, Natalie rested her head lightly against his cheek. It was a perfect first dance!

They laughed, danced, ate, and chatted with Chase and Rhonda and the crowd sitting around the pool. Natalie was pleasantly surprised by how many people she knew from the clinic and around town. It really was beginning to feel like home.

When the band was on their last set, Jake leaned in closer and said, "Let's go home and build a fire in the pit. I've got a bottle of Cava chilling in the fridge."

On the way home, Natalie said, "This has been an idyllic ending to the summer season. I enjoyed meeting Chase and Rhonda. It's nice to see a married couple who still have so much fun together… let's invite them to dinner."

"Sure. We can do that." Jake reached for her hand and squeezed it. "By the way, I told Chase that you enjoy running on the beach several times a week. He asked if we'd like to hike Cannon's Point Preserve with them since you enjoy the outdoors. It is the highest of all the trails on the island."

"I'd love it!"

They spent the next mile reminiscing about the songs the band had played. Suddenly, Jake started singing "Be Young, Be Foolish, Be Happy" by The Tams.

For the first time in over two years, Natalie felt young and happy. Then, she joined in, and they were belting out the chorus when Jake rounded the curve.

The words caught in Natalie's throat as she stared at her house. There were lights on in every room.

She couldn't breathe. It felt like her heart was about to explode.

Someone might still be inside. What should she do?

As soon as Jake pulled into his driveway, Natalie reached behind the seat for her beach bag. Jake hurried around to open her door. With a troubled glance at her house, he said. "Do you want me to go inside with you?"

She hesitated, staring at the cottage. "Maybe you should. I don't remember leaving all those lights on."

They approached the house cautiously, from the rear. On the back stoop, Natalie noticed a cigarette butt with a larger, dark object beside it. "What is that?" she asked.

Jake reached for the object. "Looks like a black garden glove."

The screen door was slightly ajar, and the wooden door was wide open. Natalie said, "I know I locked the door before I left this morning."

"You did," Jake whispered. "I watched you."

Jake went inside first, with Natalie close behind. The smell of stale cigarette smoke still lingered in the air.

The room was a mess. The drawers on either side of the farmhouse sink hung from the hinges. Whoever had been there had pilfered through the shelving of each cabinet, leaving the doors open. Some of the contents had spilled onto the granite counter, and someone had dropped cigarette ashes onto the countertop.

Natalie couldn't seem to move past the kitchen. "I can't believe someone would break into my cottage." Unlike New York City, which was rife with dangers, this was a safe place to live. Burglaries were a rarity on the island. Natalie seldom even locked her doors unless she knew she'd be gone for a long time. Detective Rhodes's words came back to her. There was no sign anyone had used a chainsaw on her cottage, but this break-in came too soon after his visit to be a coincidence.

Numbly, she followed Jake through the house, assessing the damage. Her neat cottage had been ransacked. In the bedroom, clothes hung from every drawer in the dresser, and her neatly arranged closet was in total disarray. Someone had broken in through the bedroom window, leaving shards of glass on the bedroom floor.

When they returned to the kitchen, Natalie stopped short and stared at a note on the table. When she'd read it, she looked up at Jake with tears in her eyes.

"What does it say?" he asked.

Natalie handed him the note, and watched his face tighten as he read the words that had left her shaken: *We're watching you.*

Chapter Thirty-Two

The morning after Labor Day

It was a few minutes after seven a.m. Rosie yawned as she stood at the coffee station, dumped the used coffee grounds into the trash, and added fresh water to the pots. The morning after a holiday was always busy at the diner, especially the morning after Labor Day. She had promised herself every year to take an extended vacation at the end of the summer, yet here she was again, exhausted from the long holiday weekend and stuck in the diner with ravenously hungry people.

The door opened, and two men in suits walked in. They weren't regulars—but looked vaguely familiar. At first, Rosie paid little attention to them. When she filled the dispenser with fresh coffee, she eyed the gentlemen and decided she may have seen one of them during her days as a reporter.

Four other couples were ahead of them for coffee, and a family of six had just come in. The summer people had already loaded their cars with more stuff than they'd brought and needed a quick bite before getting on the road for the long trip home. The regulars—well, they just wanted the summer people to leave so they could enjoy a peaceful breakfast and reclaim their island.

She opened the diner six days, beginning the week of Labor Day until the week before Spring break, and she closed at 2 p.m. She looked at the clock on the wall; only seven more hours until she could go home and sleep.

Rosie struggled to keep up. Three coffee machines, and it still wasn't enough. As she hurried around the diner, refilling coffee cups, she noticed the two men were wearing suits made from lightweight wool. Clearly, neither man had spent much time out of doors in a while. It was obvious they weren't from around here and were unlike anyone she'd ever seen on the island.

When she heard them speak, paranoia set in. Something interesting happened when people from Chicago spoke. Short vowels underwent a change that linguists called a vowel shift. It was hard to explain, but she recognized it when one guy mentioned the hat belonging to the kid sitting in the booth next to them. The sound of the short "a" in the word "hat" was shortened and emphasized so that it sounded more like "hay-it."

Yep! They were definitely from Chicago.

Fortunately, she had dropped her Chicago accent while working on the senatorial campaign. It had taken some time, but it was all but gone by the time she started reporting from The Hill.

No one from Chicago knew where she'd fled. She'd left no forwarding address through the postal service. Not even her closest friend at the Tribune knew where she was going. She never intended on returning, either. The morning she left, she'd texted her boss and told him she'd decided reporting the news from The Hill wasn't for her.

She had rallied for almost a year to get the position. In her opinion, being a member of the White House Press Corps and getting to report the daily news briefings from The Hill was the most exciting assignment in the business. She still missed it, but continuing as a reporter/journalist in the news industry now would be too big a chance for her to take.

Whenever she remembered the day preceding her departure from Chicago, she would break out in a cold sweat. Rosemary was sure Mrs. Kravitz, the older lady living in the adjoining condo in Alexandria, Virginia, had seen her arrive at the townhome. The delivery man stopped at the curb in front of her place and rushed up the steps. Mrs. Kravitz came to the door to accept the box of groceries, and when her gaze fell on Rosemary's car in the drive, she stepped onto the stoop. Rosemary quickly slipped inside the condo and closed the door behind her, escaping an opportunity to be questioned by the nosey neighbor.

Pinching the area between her eyebrows, she erased the scene from her mind. Then she grabbed two clean cups and returned to the booth. Conscious of her need to keep her speech consistent, she said, "Hi, I'm Rosie. I'll be serving you today. What can I get for you?"

The older man looked at Rosie and said, "We'll take a cup of coffee for starters, but give us a minute to read over the menu."

"Take your time. Let me know when you're ready to order."

She overheard a couple of remarks they made while she poured the coffee. One of them mentioned finding the house. He just needed to get inside and lift some prints, and then he mentioned a frame. A picture frame? Or were they trying to frame someone? It sounded more like the latter. But frame whom, and for what?

It wasn't so much what they said that bothered Rosie; it was the silence that followed each spoken word. She realized that there was meaning in the combination of their words and silences—like a code. She had read somewhere that such codes were common in the underground world of drugs. The article explained that, since silence referred to the lack of verbal communication, it left room for other messages in actions, eye contact, and gestures. A second of silence, in the absence of verbal signs, could also convey a message. Rosie had not fully understood the article, but now, seeing it in action, it was beginning to make sense.

As she hung around their booth, she noticed a pattern of speech. One word or one short sentence, followed by a pronounced silence. A head turn, a flick of an eyelid, a subtle movement only someone paying close attention would notice. At last, she overheard them discussing the height of the blonde. She could have heard wrong. But she was pretty sure they were talking about her.

She had just removed a tray of food from the counter and started toward the family of six when the younger guy asked, "Well, how tall was Alison McKay? The report doesn't give her height."

Did he just say Alison McKay? Rosie almost dropped the tray when she heard her birth name. The diner was packed with people and buzzing with noise. Surely she had misunderstood. The older man looked around the diner. His eyes rested on her. "She was a tad taller than Rosie there." He continued to appraise her. "Yep, she was taller than Rosie."

She felt queasy and lightheaded, and her stomach churned with anxiety. When her hands stopped shaking, she placed the tray on the table and served the family. Perspiration covered her upper lip.

Rosie hovered around the men's booth as they continued to question the accuracy of the police investigation—the information given to them by the family and the people living in the condo next door. At one point, the first man pointed to the untouched jar of strawberry jam and said, "The concrete garage floor was as red as that jam, but it's the smell I'll never forget." He shook his head in disgust.

By the time the two men left the diner, Rosie couldn't be sure but thought the men might have tracked *her* to the island. If that was the case, then that could be a serious problem.

Chapter Thirty-Three

Rosie-Parker-Rhodes

The following morning, Officer Ben Parker from the Glynn County Police Department flopped down at the counter, pulled several paper napkins from the dispenser, and wiped his damp face. After a long night, the intense humidity only added to his frustration.

Across the counter, Rosie reached for a clean mug and a fresh pot of coffee. "You okay?"

He crumpled the paper napkins into a tight ball. "Yeah. Worked the eleven to seven shift last night but got detained following a routine check of the island. I'll be fine as soon as I get a cup of your strong coffee."

Rosie poured the steaming liquid and said, "Isn't the graveyard shift typically uneventful around here?"

He barked a laugh. "Yeah. It was pretty quiet until about five this morning…that's when I found myself staring at a rental car with two people slumped over in the front seats."

"Dead?" Her eyebrows lifted.

Parker nodded. He'd radioed back to dispatch and requested a member of the Criminal Investigations Division. After making the call, he stayed at the scene and assisted the CI Division after his shift ended.

Rosie refilled the coffee mug of another customer, sitting two seats down. When she looked back at Parker, he motioned that he was ready to order.

"Can I get an All-Star Breakfast?"

She wrote the order on her pad, tore the sheet off, and laid it on the counter for the cook to see.

When the customer sitting next to Parker got up to leave, Rosie grabbed a clean cloth, removed the dirty dishes, and wiped off the counter. She and Parker looked up just as the door opened. A tall dark-haired man with a buzz-cut walked in and sat in the only empty seat at the counter—next to Parker. Parker shifted in his seat and assessed the newcomer, who scanned the room and settled onto the stool, his shoulders half-turned to give him a clear view of the door. A cop. Had to be.

As Rosie waited on the stranger, someone from the end of the counter said, "Hey, Parker, who were those folks you found dead outside the hotel this morning?"

"We don't have any names. The CI Division is still working on the scene. It'll likely take a few hours to track down their identities."

The loudmouth at the end of the counter said, "Someone said it was two women from Atlanta...died of carbon monoxide poisoning... said they found a green garden hose in the car. Still had the tags on it. Is that true?"

How the hell did he know about the hose? The reporters hadn't even started sniffing around the case yet.

Parker sipped his coffee and ignored the questions. The guy had gotten a few things wrong. The deceased were two men rather than women. They weren't from Atlanta either, but that wasn't relevant in the grand scheme. He had gotten the details right. Someone had placed a garden hose on the exhaust pipe and run it through the back car window. It was a well-organized and executed plan.

Parker glanced at the windbag and thought back to the early morning hours. He remembered a lone person dressed in a bright yellow reflective safety vest running along Downing. At the end of the road, the man had turned left onto Arnold. Perhaps he had circled back around, standing in the shadows, watching the initial investigation. Definitely a connection worth looking into. He'd wait until the loudmouth left and ask him some questions in the parking lot.

Chris Rhodes ordered coffee as he peered from the corner of his eye at the officer beside him. The local guy at the end of the counter explained what he'd heard to his table mate.

When Rosie brought his coffee, Rhodes asked, "Did he say they found two women dead in a rental car this morning?"

"That's what he told us," Rosie said. "Parker here worked the scene, but the CI department's got the case now."

Rhodes gave Parker a friendly nod, then ordered breakfast and scrolled his phone until he found an article that stated in the past year, over four hundred and twenty accidental deaths were attributed to carbon monoxide poisoning. During the same period, CO poisoning caused over two thousand one hundred unintentional deaths.

He stopped scrolling. When someone breathed in carbon monoxide, the poison replaced the oxygen in their bloodstream, starving major organs of oxygen. Not a bad way to die. Most people just drifted off. Still, it was weird. Women tended to take pills, and double suicides were rare. But if they hadn't done it themselves, there was a killer on the island. Maybe in this very establishment.

THE EMPTY BEACH CHAIR

He glanced around the diner.

Parker pushed away his empty plate. The meal seemed to have given him a new burst of energy. "Where're you from?"

Rhodes phone pinged. He glanced at his phone. Then turned his attention back to his seatmate. "New York City."

"You're a long way from home. Vacation or work?"

Chris picked up his phone. Trying not to appear too eager for conversation.

The text message read:

Times up. Two Chicago agents dead on the island. Looks like suicide—drugs involved. We need you here to help with damage control.

Chris lifted his knife and methodically spread butter on a slice of wheat toast. He explained he had just completed an investigative fact-finding search for work and had planned to stay a few days to enjoy the beach.

Parker tilted his head, a flash of curiosity in his eyes. "So, you're from NYPD?"

"FBI," Chris said, before taking a bite of his toast. "And it looks like the beach is going to have to wait."

Chapter Thirty-Four

Natalie

The break-in frightened Natalie more than she cared to admit. Those who lived on the beach side of the island loved being there. Some had inherited their real estate from a family member or moved from another area, some after retirement. Others just decided early in their marriages to move to the coast. Now, it seemed her neighbors were all on edge.

While living in New York, she'd expected crime and was always cautious as she wandered through the city. One of the main reasons she'd moved to the coast, other than an offer by her mentor to work in his clinic, was the lower crime rate of living in a smaller town. Yet, as she faced the demons of the previous weeks, it seemed like the big city crime had followed her to the island.

She wouldn't stay overnight at the cottage. Most nights, she slept on the sofa at the clinic with the burglar alarm turned on. Once, she'd stayed at Jake's house, but it didn't seem right for her to take over his bedroom while he slept on the daybed in the guest room.

More than anything, she missed Paul. He had been a great problem solver and would know what to do, but he hadn't visited the beach chair in several days. She wondered what he would make of the message on the note. Each time she read the script, she felt someone was haunting her.

We're watching you.

It was bizarre. Who was watching and why were they watching her?

On Wednesday morning, while eating breakfast at the diner, Chris Rhodes read in the local paper that Natalie's house had been ransacked. He finished the last of his coffee and left a tip on the counter. Pulling out of the diner's driveway, he turned left toward the clinic.

Natalie was standing in the office when he walked into the waiting room. She immediately came out to meet him.

"Have you got a few minutes?" he asked.

She nodded and led him to the back door. They went outside and talked on the porch.

"I read about the break-in at your house," he said. "Have you encountered any unusual people since moving to the island?"

When she pulled the note from her pocket and handed it to him, tears formed in her eyes. His first instinct was to hug her, but he was a professional and had to refrain from showing his true feelings.

He said, "I don't mean to invade your space here, but I might be able to find something."

Natalie wiped the tears from her face. "Thanks. I appreciate it, but the local law enforcement guys have already finished their search. They found nothing. Not even a fingerprint."

He shuffled his feet, folded his arms, and leaned against the porch railing. "I don't mean to pry, but I'm a forensic investigator. I'm sure the local force gave it a thorough sweep, but I might find clues an ordinary patrol officer might overlook."

"I didn't know that about you. Where did you go to school?"

Rhodes smiled. "Cornell University in Ithaca. I have an undergrad in chemistry and a master's in forensic science." He continued telling her about his success with other cases in New York, Chicago, and on the West Coast.

It took a few minutes, but Natalie relented. "You think you can uncover something?"

"I'd like to try."

"Hold on," Natalie went inside and returned with a key. "This goes to the back door. I haven't been back since the local officers were there. The place is a mess."

Rhodes removed the key from his pocket and let himself into her cottage. She was right. The kitchen was a mess. The drawers and cabinet doors were still open, and the contents were strewn all over the counter, but that was a good sign. It looked like the local guys had done a great job preserving the crime scene's integrity.

He removed his research tools from the case and dusted the kitchen surfaces. He started with the top cabinets because the perpetrator had opened each door—perhaps looking for cash hidden in a canister or envelope. Next, he dusted the countertops, the top, and the inside of the fridge. It was interesting how burglars went through people's food. He'd yet to investigate a break-in where the robber had not violated the refrigerator and pantry.

A few breadcrumbs were on the countertop. Although he doubted it, those could have been there before the break-in. After his unsuccessful attempts to lift fingerprints, he moved over to the kitchen table. He didn't see that anything there had been tampered with. Salt and pepper shakers and a small napkin holder were neatly aligned on the table. A package of unopened cocktail napkins had been placed in the holder.

Rhodes moved into the living room and looked around. Again, nothing seemed to be disturbed, but he dusted the surfaces anyway. Before he finished, he removed the cushions from the small loveseat and chair. Nothing. Clean and clutter-free.

It was a different story in the bedroom. The mattress had been turned over to reveal the box springs. They'd bundled up the comforter and thrown it on the floor. The sheets were hanging on the bed. The dresser drawers were open.

They had scattered Natalie's clothes all over the bedroom. Workout clothes…swimsuits…underwear, and every other item of clothing she owned was violated. A black cocktail dress was tossed across the back of a chair. Gingerly, he lifted the delicate dress. It was the same silk blend dress she'd worn to the theater the night her husband died. It angered him that some thug had touched the beautiful garment.

When Rhodes looked inside the small closet, he marveled at the detail of the space. Whoever had built it was a true craftsman. Now, all the contents had been gone through, each shoe box opened, and every storage container searched.

When he finished brushing every inch of the bedroom and every container that might have been handled by the perpetrator, Rhodes returned to the kitchen and looked around.

The first search of any scene was like a quick look. The obvious items would jump out at you. It was the second look that often revealed a minute, inconsequential item or bits of trace evidence. It could be something normal, like an ordinary, everyday object, requiring added diligence on the part of the investigator. Rhodes typically used contracting spiral patterns in his search. In this case, the spiral began at the periphery of the crime scene and circled inward toward the spot where the actual criminal act took place.

Rhodes retraced his steps. He had less than six hours to meet the chartered plane and fly home. The boss wanted him back in the office the very next morning, but first, he wanted to finish the search of Natalie's house.

He walked outside, and after a few moments, reentered the kitchen. He made another assessment of the countertop and cabinets. Turning toward the kitchen table, he saw a few tiny crumbs. Maybe the locals had missed something since the table appeared to be untouched. He moved it to the middle of the room and dropped to his knees, eye level with the surface. Then, starting at the farthest corner, he brushed a small section at a time until he reached the other end, where he was sure Natalie would typically sit. There were only two chairs. When he got to the last section, he wiped the crumbs from the table and brushed the area thoroughly for prints.

He'd lifted several latent prints too large to be Natalie's. It was like the perpetrator had gotten careless and removed the glove from his right hand before sitting at the table. Rhodes jumped up from the table and opened the breadbox on the counter. Sure enough, there was a fresh loaf of wheat bread opened. The tie was lying on the floor of the breadbox. This was the lucky break he'd been hoping for. The perpetrator had made a sandwich and eaten it.

Rhodes glanced into the deep farmhouse sink. At the bottom lay a silver butter knife with remnants of mayo on the blade. He immediately put on his gloves and dusted the handle.

The silver knife had captured a perfect print.

***

Jake sat in his regular seat at the end of the counter, his phone in one hand while scrolling the morning news and a fork in the other as he ate his breakfast. Rosie came out from the back of the diner with a folder, placed it on the counter in front of him and said, "Read this chapter of my new book and tell me what you think?"

Jake opened the folder, removed the stack of papers, and jokingly remarked, "So, I'm your book editor now?"

Rosie said, "Very funny. Just read it and tell me what you think." She reached for the coffeepot and refilled his cup while he began reading.

When Jake finished, he placed the pages back into the folder.

Rosie grabbed a cup of coffee and sat next to him at the counter. "What do you think?"

"It's good. It's clear, concise, and has good sentence structure. The story grabbed my attention from the very first line." He sipped his coffee and then gave Rosie a broad grin. "It was brilliant to model your villain on a sweet girl like Natalie. But don't you think your heroine is a little bit of a Mary Sue?"

Rosie grabbed the folder and swatted his arm. "No, she's not!"

He was oblivious to her subtle message about a woman who had been friends with a small-town journalist, only to realize that she was really in love with him when a new girl came to town. Rosie had spent the past two months working on the chapter, making certain the story flowed the way she intended, but when Jake read it, he failed to see the irony of the plot. Rosie did not know how to make him understand they were more than friends. She loved him.

Jake laid his money on the counter to leave. "Good luck with your story. Natalie will be moving back home this afternoon. I'm going to finish cleaning up her cottage.."

Rosie's face burned with rage as she watched him leave the diner. When she went back to the kitchen, she murmured, "Of course you are!"

Chapter Thirty-Five

Natalie

On Friday afternoon, after the last patient left the clinic, Natalie decided it was time to move back to her cottage. The longer she stayed away, the more she missed home…staying away appeared foolish and irresponsible. Living alone made the decision more difficult, but she was an intelligent woman and had to confront her demons.

Jennifer, her assistant, walked through as Natalie made a final notation on the file folder. "Do you want me to take your scrubs home and wash them?"

"No, thanks. I appreciate the offer." Natalie had kept a few extra pairs of scrubs behind the bathroom door for convenience. A quick trip to Red Fern Village to purchase toiletries had made her stay at the clinic bearable, but it wasn't like being at home.

Bathing at the clinic in the tiny shower stall was creepy. It was obvious they'd remodeled the bathroom during the sixties because of the tiny yellow tile. The entire shower stall had the same tile: walls, floor, and ceiling—the ugly yellow one-inch squares reminded Natalie of nicotine stains.

Her inner voice had been pushing her to return home all week, but Jake's offer to clean up the cottage after Investigator

Rhodes finished his sweep had settled the issue. He'd only left at lunchtime to distribute payroll checks to the job sites for his crew. Otherwise, he'd worked the entire day at the cottage. They had talked at different intervals, discussing several minor repairs required to restore her home to its original state.

After returning the patient folders to their rightful file, Natalie went straight to the bathroom and gathered her dirty scrubs and makeup bag. Jennifer said, "Are you going back home?"

"Yes. Jake will think I'm ungrateful for all his hard work if I don't go home tonight."

Jennifer shook her head. "That guy sure does like you."

Natalie laughed and slung her head around. "Are you ready to go?"

"Right behind you."

Natalie locked the door, got into her car, and waved at Jennifer as she pulled onto the road. She considered going to the market for groceries, but she had the leftovers from lunch and was eager to get home. As she rounded the curve, the view of the Atlantic Ocean took her breath. She pulled over to the side of the road and soaked up the view. How could she have forgotten how beautiful it was out there?

She stayed until the day's tensions had burned away. Then she drove the rest of the way home and parked in her driveway. When she walked in the back door, the cottage smelled clean. She stopped and inhaled. It smelled the same way her townhome in Brooklyn smelled after the cleaning lady had been there.

Her gaze fell to the table. In the center stood a large arrangement of fresh flowers and a note: *A bottle of wine chilling in the fridge.* She opened the refrigerator door, and a bottle of Cava was on the top shelf.

Smiling, she walked through the cottage. Jake had put the bedroom back together. Fresh sheets were on the bed. He had turned back the top of the comforter like a picture in a magazine. She opened the top drawer of the dresser. He had folded and organized various T-shirts and shorts.

Natalie searched through every drawer and closet and found the same result, but her hand went to her chest when she opened the nightstand drawer. Jake had neatly placed each of her bras with matching panties. The second drawer contained her gowns, and her pajamas were in the third. It felt a little strange to know that Jake had seen and touched her most private pieces of clothing.

In the kitchen, she stopped in front of the flower arrangement, hugged herself, and smiled.

For dinner, she had the leftovers from her Chinese lunch plus a fistful of fresh blueberries Jake had left in the fridge. Standing over the kitchen sink and eating from the cardboard carton, she was thankful she didn't have to mess up her spotless kitchen.

Later, when she got into bed, sleep wouldn't come. At last, she turned on the light and opened Rosemary's novel. She was about halfway through the book, but by the time she got to the end of the next chapter, thoroughly engrossed in the whodunit story, she hardly registered Copper barking in the distance.

It was almost five a.m. when, eyelids drooping, she reluctantly closed the book. She had only a few more chapters left before the sleuth was sure to gather the suspects in the parlor, but when she'd snapped awake the third time, she knew the solution would have to wait. Still pondering the clues, she turned out the light and snuggled under the covers.

She'd barely closed her eyes when the alarm clock went off. Blearily, she fumbled for the clock. Almost seven. Two hours wasn't enough, but the coffee pot had already brewed her morning coffee, and the aroma of dark roast Colombian filled the cottage. She tossed back the covers, stepped into her comfy bedroom slippers, and went to the kitchen.

When she filled her thermos cup and headed out to her beach chair, the sun was already showing its beautiful face.

She yawned, still exhausted from another sleepless night. Paul said, "Natalie, you need to watch that Rosemary. She's trouble."

Natalie pressed her lips together and continued to look out over the ocean. She was in no mood to fight with him.

"Natty, did you hear me? You need to watch out for your neighbor."

Natalie gripped her Yeti cup, remembering the late nights he'd worked when they were living in their Macdonough Street Brownstone. "What makes you such an authority on women?" she said in a tone much harsher than intended.

How many times had she envisioned another woman in his arms? If that were the case, why did he keep showing up like this? The old Paul…her husband who loved her completely… it was like he was back and the six months before he died had never existed.

"I didn't say I was an authority on women, but I know her type. She'd stab you in the back in a minute."

Natalie paused. Although she loved Paul, it was time to admit that their relationship had been strained for several months before he died. They had both worked long hours, but his had stretched beyond reason, sometimes without explanation. She'd finish her twelve-hour shift at the hospital, rush home to prepare a heart-healthy dinner, only to sit at the dining room table staring at the empty chair at the other end. She would finish her meal, leaving Paul's dinner on the stove for him to eat when he got home. Sometimes, he wouldn't even bother coming into the bedroom. Instead, he'd sleep in the guest room or crash on the sofa. The next morning, he'd give her a distracted smile and say he hadn't wanted to disturb her.

The pattern repeated itself three or four times each week. The only bright spot was the weekend. To Paul, Sunday morning was synonymous with family—the day he fulfilled his marital obligation. Sometimes it felt halfhearted, much like a conjugal visit. But sometimes it was still magic.

If she were being honest with herself, the main reason she'd insisted on planning their fifth-year anniversary was because she wanted them to enjoy something so over the top, she hoped they could recapture the passion and romance they'd shared when they first got together. Maybe they could even start their family before her biological clock stopped ticking.

And it had almost worked. Paul had made a concerted effort to get home for dinner more often. Not every night, but more often than not.

She'd created enough suspense throughout the weeks leading up to their anniversary that Paul had almost returned to his old self. As proof, the few moments at the door before Paul left for work the last morning were as passionate as anything they'd experienced in a long time.

Realizing he had to hurry to get to the bus, he'd kissed his index finger and rubbed it across her bottom lip, the way he'd done during their first years of marriage. On his way out the door, when he flashed that gorgeous smile and promised to finish what he'd started when he got home from work, she'd smiled back, certain he'd planned his schedule around leaving the office early.

He'd promised, without fail, to leave the office in time to get home, shower, and change clothes so they could ride together—just like a proper date.

But none of that had happened. Once again, Paul failed to honor his promise.

Whatever the reason, Natalie felt like someone else was getting the better part of her husband. As Paul's wife, she deserved more than a few leftover crumbs. As much as she wanted a child, it wouldn't be fair to have one until she was sure it would have two fully committed parents.

Natalie shuffled in her seat. "Well, Rosemary has been a good friend to me. If I hadn't met her when I first came to the island, I would never have found this great cottage."

"Well, I hate to be the one to break it to you, but it wouldn't surprise me if she didn't have something to do with the break-in on Labor Day."

He was being ridiculous. Rosemary lived next door—well, almost. There was one cottage separating them. Why would she vandalize Natalie's home? Anyone who lived in that area of the beach would recognize her as the lady who lived in the pale-yellow house below the King and Prince.

"Natty, honey, I love you and want you to be safe. Please let Jake and the FBI officer take care of you."

She continued to look out over the ocean. Paul's voice rose an octave in frustration. "I know you, Natty! You'll just shut down and never sort this out. You're one of the smartest and most accomplished women I've ever met, but sometimes you can be very naïve."

That was enough. She jumped up from her seat and stormed toward the house. "I think it's time I get a dog."

Paul chuckled. "That might be the smartest thing you've said in a while."

Natalie yelled over her shoulder. "Be nice!!!"

Chapter Thirty-Six

Natalie and Jake - Now

Each afternoon, Natalie was comforted that Jake watched for her to come home from the clinic. He was such a thoughtful guy. If she hesitated before going inside, he'd walk over and go inside with her.

Exactly six weeks after Labor Day, when Natalie pulled into her driveway, she noticed a bright yellow paper protruding from the mailbox next to the back door. She got out of the car and walked onto the porch, staring at the yellow paper for a moment before reaching inside to retrieve the mail. There was an envelope from the utility company, a brochure from the local hardware store, and a half-torn sheet of paper. The same type of paper as the legal pad she used at the clinic to scribble notes.

She immediately recognized the perfect script as used on the note when her cottage was vandalized. Stunned, she turned over the note, but there was nothing written on the back. Natalie's hand shook, and she heard her heart thumping inside her chest.

Through teary eyes, she read the note for a second time.

Turn over the car—if you know what's good for you.

What car? Paul's Porsche?

She looked next door and Jake's Jeep was parked in the driveway. Leaving the back door locked, she walked over and knocked on the screened door.

"Come in!" he said. "You don't have to knock."

Her hand shook as she gave him the stack of mail, the yellow paper still on top.

As Jake read it, his jaw tightened. He turned away and dropped his head, grabbing the kitchen counter with both hands.

Natalie sank into a chair at the breakfast table, her chest tight and her eyes burning. Someone was watching her home. Why? And for how long? The thought was unnerving, and the threatening note only made matters worse. Propping both elbows on the table, she covered her face with her hands and choked out a sob.

Whoever had vandalized her cottage had obviously returned. They had walked up to her back door and delivered their threatening message. She closed her eyes and shuddered. What if she hadn't stopped to admire the view on her way home? Would she have rounded the curve and seen a stranger standing outside her cottage, tucking a note into her mailbox?

She wondered if she would ever feel safe there again.

Jake grabbed a couple of bottles of water from the fridge and pulled out the chair across from Natalie. "I want you to listen to me for a moment."

Natalie sat back and looked at him through tearful eyes. "Okay. What is it?"

"You can't let this guy get inside your head. You've got to remain calm and alert. Otherwise, he wins."

Natalie wiped her face with her hands. "How do you know it's a man?"

Jake raised his eyebrows. "You got a point there, but I wouldn't think a woman would try to torment another woman like this. Do you?"

She sat straight in the chair and pulled her hair up off her neck, remembering the comment Paul had made about Rosemary. "I don't know. Perhaps not."

They sat in silence for a few more minutes. Jake looked at the kitchen counter, "I was planning to do a light shrimp boil for dinner. Why don't you join me?"

She smiled, suppressing a sniffle. Since moving to the island, Natalie felt like she was always imposing on Jake. He had become her go-to person, the one she depended on for everything.

"Great!" he said. "I'll open some wine and we can move out to the porch while I grill dinner." He reached for a bottle of Pinot Grigio from the fridge and removed the cork, chatting away about a new recipe he'd found online to grill the shrimp, sausage, corn, and potatoes in aluminum foil.

As they sat on the porch after dinner, he said, "Let's take a few days off. I'll let the foreman check on my jobs and you can get a temp to cover the clinic for a couple of days. We could use a little time away from here. Maybe go to the mountains, rent a cabin on the river, and do some trout fishing…read a few books…watch some movies."

Natalie smiled again. "That sounds nice, but running away won't solve our problems."

He twisted the top from his water bottle. "Maybe not, but a change of venue couldn't hurt, either."

"Perhaps," she said. "But promise me you won't tell anyone we're leaving."

Jake leaned forward and placed his hands over hers. "Not even Rosemary?"

She hesitated. Rosemary had seemed like a good friend, but the certainty in Paul's warning made Natalie give her head a firm shake. "Especially Rosemary!"

Chapter Thirty-Seven

Rhodes

Rhodes had skipped breakfast, something he seldom did. At 6 a.m., when the alarm went off, he hit the snooze button twice. A luxury he rarely allowed himself, but it meant sacrificing the bagel and peanut butter he usually had for breakfast.

Ten minutes before eleven, he forwarded his office calls to his cell and walked around the corner to the local delicatessen to grab a bite of lunch. He was the first customer when the owner unlocked the door. He had timed his visit perfectly. After ordering his sandwich, he grabbed the table in the corner next to the window so he could watch the people on the street. When his phone rang, he'd just taken the first bite of his Reuben sandwich.

"Meet me in my office in five minutes." FBI Director, Colin Armstrong spoke in a raspy voice—from years of smoking three packs of cigarettes each day and drinking cheap bourbon.

"Boss, it may take me a little longer than that," Rhodes said. "I'm at lunch."

"Well, cut it short. We need to talk about the Rockwell case."

Ten minutes later, Rhodes glanced at his watch as he walked into the building. Why would Armstrong want to discuss an almost three-year-old, open-and-shut suicide?

It had been nearly a month since his trip to St. Simons Island. During that time, he'd done his best to handle damage control about the two agents found dead in their rental car on the island. It was never good when agents died, but the combination of drugs and suicide was a PR nightmare.

Rhodes shook his head. He'd worked with the two dead men on the Rockwell case, and they'd been good agents then. Whatever had happened to change that, it was a damn shame.

He'd barely stepped into Armstrong's office when the director, jacked up on black coffee said, "We're reopening the Rockwell case." He lit another cigarette, took a deep drag, and tilted his head, creating a spiraling circle of smoke toward the ceiling. "This is what we know. About an hour ago, Tonya Rockwell sent us a photo taken by her neighbor on the morning of the senator's death. It shows someone entering the townhome on the morning he died."

"Any idea who?"

"She's convinced it's Rockwell's campaign manager, Alison McKay."

The elusive Ms. McKay. Interesting. During the initial investigation, the police contacted everyone who'd worked on the senatorial campaign, except for Ms. McKay. She'd disappeared from the Chicago area, and in light of the senator's apparent suicide, no one had bothered to look for her. People picked up and left every day, especially when their high-profile employers upped and died on them.

Rhodes nodded toward the folder on the director's desk. "Why are we just now hearing about this?"

Tonya Rockwell had always held the belief that there was a cover-up in the case. Her husband had worked too hard to win the senate seat to throw it away—especially on the cusp of his greatest victory. The keynote address he'd delivered at the 2020 Democratic National Convention had elevated him to a distinctive status within the political arena. He found himself bombarded with threatening calls, but since his name was being thrown around for the 2024 presidential election, they had assumed it was a normal occurrence when playing on the national stage. It hadn't seemed to bother him. If anything, it had fueled his ambition,

The director went on. "Apparently, she just found out about it this morning. Two things Mrs. Rockwell asked me: First, she wants to find Alison McKay and question her about the senator's use of recreational drugs or opioids. Second, she wants to know if Ms. McKay and her husband were lovers."

Rhodes removed the toothpick from his mouth. "She said that? She wants to know if they were lovers?"

The director took a sip of coffee from the heavy mug and shot him a sly grin. "Well, she's pretty torn up about the picture taken of Ms. McKay outside their Alexandria home. The neighbor said she was a regular visitor. Without the picture, we might not pay as much attention to the eccentric neighbor next door, but that picture proves Ms. McKay was at their home on the morning of the senator's death. Admit it, if they were lovers, that would introduce an interesting twist in the case."

Rhodes shrugged. "I would suspect so."

Armstrong wrote something on the legal pad before him, grabbed some papers from another stack, and said, "Turns out our two agents were moonlighting on the case."

Rhodes frowned. Outside work was strictly forbidden by the agency. Mrs. Rockwell must have made them a hell of an offer.

Armstrong's voice was flat as he pushed the folder toward Rhodes. "Here are their autopsy reports."

Rhodes placed the toothpick back in his mouth, reviewed the first report, glanced at his boss, and then read the second report. "Wait a minute, Boss. Fentanyl is the same drug that killed Rockwell."

"Are you sure about that, Rhodes?"

He continued to look at the autopsy reports and nodded. "Yes, sir. I'm certain."

The director sat up straighter. "Take those home with you and spend some time getting yourself up to speed. Then we need you to get back to St. Simons Island and find out what happened to our men."

Chapter Thirty-Eight

Natalie and Jake

In between patients, Natalie arranged for a temp to cover for her at the clinic. While completing paperwork, ordering supplies, and approving last minute bills to be paid, Natalie had eaten only a few bites of the Chinese takeout that Jennifer had ordered for her at lunch.

It was almost five o'clock when Natalie finally checked the time. Where had the day gone? Throughout the day, she'd felt an underlying nagging—a sense of guilt and disloyalty toward Paul. But the note she'd found in her mailbox had frightened her more than she cared to admit, and she looked forward to getting away with Jake and Copper for a few days.

She dreaded going home. If she could just get through the night, tomorrow would be a better day.

When they closed the clinic, Jennifer hugged her and said, "Try to enjoy your day off! The temp and I will handle any issues that come up."

Natalie shrugged and sighed.

Jennifer arched an eyebrow. "There's not a woman on this island who wouldn't give their right arm to spend the night on the water with Jake."

Natalie laughed. "It's just one night on a boat...not a romantic weekend at The Ritz."

"Okay," Jennifer said. "Just saying. There are a lot of women around here who would make sure Jake Ellis kept coming back for more nights on the water."

"Point taken." Natalie waved, jumped into her car, and sped off toward her beach cottage. A wave of relief swept over her when she got home from work. Jake was sitting on the back porch, scrolling through his phone.

Her convertible top was down. "What are you doing?" Natalie called.

He looked up from his phone. "Hey, you! Did you find a temp?"

"I did."

"Have you talked to the mechanic about your car yet? We could drop it off on our way to the dock in the morning."

She smiled and grabbed her bag from behind the seat. "Talked to him this morning."

When she reached the porch, Jake reached for her keys to unlock the back door. "Good job."

He held the door open for her, and they continued to discuss their plans as they walked inside. Jake said he wanted to get started by 9 a.m., and she promised him she would be ready.

When Jake left, Natalie got busy, grateful for the distraction of preparing for their excursion. She cleaned out the fridge, saving a few items to throw in the cooler the following morning. She hurriedly placed the house plants into the bathtub with a few inches of water. She checked her watch. There was still enough time to climb into bed and finish reading Rosemary's novel.

The next morning, Natalie gathered a few items for their adventure. While they planned only a short trip, she was determined to take advantage of as much restful. sun-soaked time as she could before the days grew shorter. Natalie grabbed her overnight bag and flung in two of her favorite swimsuits and cover-ups, the bright Lilly floral suit and the hot pink one featuring ruffled shoulders and a matching sarong. She was confident either outfit would work well should they venture to one of the local restaurants by the bay.

The third swimsuit she chose was her absolute favorite—a red and white polka dot bikini. After throwing in a sweatshirt and a pair of jean shorts, she was ready for the trip.

As Natalie headed out the door with a duffle bag in hand, she ripped a piece of paper from the notepad on the countertop. On it, she had written the name and address of the car repair shop in Brunswick and the mechanic's name with whom she'd spoken earlier in the week.

Jake followed Natalie to the shop and went in to meet the guy. The mechanic assured Jake he'd have the car serviced and the transmission fixed within a week.

Before they left the shop, Jake opened the driver's side door and said, "Have you got everything out of here that you might need?"

Natalie shrugged. She hadn't thought about that. She always kept the Porsche immaculate.

Jake sat in the driver's seat and reached across the console. "Do you need this scarf?"

"Thanks. I shouldn't leave it in the car." She grabbed the scarf, a flowered silk piece Paul had given for their second Valentine's Day, and crammed it into her pocketbook. "Let's get out of here!"

She jumped into the Jeep and hugged Copper's neck. "Hey, boy! We get to spend a couple of days together."

THE EMPTY BEACH CHAIR

They drove to the docks, loaded their gear onto the boat, and set sail. The sky was clear, and the wind was perfect for a day on the water. At midmorning, the temperature was a comfortable 78 degrees. Natalie removed her swimsuit cover-up and positioned herself on the back of the boat. Once the sunshine hit her body, she forgot about the note she'd found in the mailbox.

She scanned the area for her wide-brimmed hat that went perfectly with her red and white polka dot swimsuit. When she turned to reach for it, she noticed Jake had taken off his shirt. He was tanned, and his torso had the lean muscles of a boxer. His fingers nimbly handled the ropes and controlled the boat's sails. When he stepped over her to get to the other side, she could have reached up and touched his strong hands. Natalie looked away.

After a couple of hours of sailing, Jake brought out his cooler. "I got up early to prepare a picnic for you, Natalie."

"What did you bring?" she asked.

He cut his eyes and grinned. Natalie had never seen that look before. It reminded her of Paul's grin when he'd done something he was sure she would love, but with Paul, it was more of a tease. Not so with Jake. He'd meant for the sexy glance to have a specific effect on her. And it did.

He lifted a container of pimento cheese and fruit from the cooler. Then he reached into a recyclable bag for a loaf of white bread and a bucket of fried chicken. They chatted while Jake filled their plates. He was thoughtful, organized, and comfortable waiting on her. Somehow he knew just what she wanted. He even cut the sandwiches into triangles. Apparently, he liked them that way, too. Then he settled in the back on the other side of the boat from where Natalie was sitting to enjoy his lunch.

Natalie bit into the chicken leg. "This isn't very healthy, Jake." She tore off the bread crust and fed it to Copper.

Jake cut his eyes again. "I know that, but it sure is good! It's the perfect picnic meal for a day sailing on the ocean. My mom used to serve pimento cheese sandwiches and fried chicken during the summer. It was her go-to for picnics."

Natalie set down the chicken leg and nibbled at her sandwich. It really was delicious. "Did she make her own or buy it?"

"Are you kidding?" He jumped up and reached for the cooler and removed two water bottles. "It was homemade!"

He tossed a bottle of water to Natalie, refreshed Copper's water bowl, and then settled back in his seat. While the boat drifted in tranquil waters near a cove, they enjoyed their lunch. With the vacationers leaving the island each day and the schools already in session, the traffic on the water was minimal. It was like they had the entire Atlantic Ocean to themselves. She couldn't believe Jake had prepared this lovely picnic of his favorite childhood foods for her. He must've gotten up early to get it all done. She thought back to Jennifer's remark from Friday afternoon—no wonder so many women had him in their sights. And here he was, with her.

After lunch, they sailed in a different direction. When the white, domed-shaped lighthouse came into sight, Jake pointed and gave her a quick history lesson about the island. It was built by the first lighthouse keeper, James Gould of Massachusetts, and was destroyed by Confederate forces in 1861. Being a history buff herself, Natalie listened to every word as she admired the beauty of the lighthouse. It stretched skyward, a commanding presence against the horizon.

Later on, after several hours of sightseeing, they stopped at a remote camping area and set up camp. Natalie wasted no time unzipping her overnight bag and removed a pair of white palazzo pants to put on over her swimsuit.

"Have you ever slept outside on the ground?" Jake asked.

Natalie grinned. "No! My idea of camping is a Sunday afternoon nap on the sun porch."

"Well, this will be an adventure, for sure!" At any rate, sitting out under the stars might be an adventure to get her mind off the note.

They fished for their dinner, and Jake laughed at Natalie as he watched her clean the whitefish while he built a fire to cook dinner. Then he returned to the boat to get his supply box and found the aluminum foil. He pitched it to her along with a bag of herbs and seasonings. She prepared the fish for baking over the open flame and made a quick salad of cherry tomatoes and cucumbers while Jake gathered more firewood. They made a good team. He hoped she thought so, too.

Jake dropped his last armful of wood as Natalie removed the fish from the fire. While she was finding the silverware in the supply box, Jake pulled a bottle of wine from the cooler. He watched as she pulled back the aluminum foil to create a makeshift plate. Clever. She made cooking dinner look effortless.

Listening to the ocean waves, they sat around the fire and chatted while enjoying their meal.

Jake said, "Tell me more about your life in New York? What was your favorite place?"

Natalie took a sip of wine and her eyes flashed to the heavens. "Well, my favorite place in New York would have to be our Brooklyn condo. It was my sanctuary."

He tried not to wince. Of course, her best memories would be from her marriage. *Just listen, Jake. Be the friend she needs.* His head tilted to the side. "How do you mean?"

Natalie smiled, a faraway look in her eyes. "Well, my husband and I both worked stressful jobs. I worked three twelve-hour shifts. The night shift rotation can put a strain on a marriage. The last year Paul was alive, he worked twelve, sometimes fourteen-hour days." She leaned forward in her chair, put her wineglass on the ground, then extended her arms and rubbed her hands together. "When I got home each day after a long shift at the hospital, it was like a wave of happiness swept over me."

"What was your condo like?"

"We called it a condo, but it was actually a townhome. It was a happy place. Good karma—if you will."

Jake nodded in all the right places as she told her story, but all he could think of was that good karma and how it had left this remarkable woman a widow.

If that was good karma, he hated to think what the alternative would be.

When they finished eating, Jake tossed his aluminum foil on the fire and did the same with hers. Then he collapsed in his chair and topped off his glass with more wine.

Deep in thought, Natalie continued to watch the sparks in the fire. When Jake finally shuffled in his chair, she realized her thoughts were many miles from the campsite.

"What are you thinking about, Natalie?"

She gave a nervous laugh. "I can't figure out if the writer of the note was referring to my car or not."

Jake shifted in his chair. "There's something I've been meaning to tell you, and this seems like the perfect time. But first, please know I'm not trying to pry into your business." He told her about finding the straps of bills in her car panels the day he moved her car outside the diner.

Natalie's eyes grew large, and her face glowed from the fire.

"So you found money in the door panels of my car, and yet you said nothing about it."

"Yes. At the time, I didn't want to be intrusive and ask a bunch of questions. We'd only just met a month earlier. The day before yesterday, when you showed me the note about the car, I thought the person who wrote it could've also planted the money in your door panel."

In a tone much sharper than intended, she said, "Did you ever consider the money could be mine?" She couldn't believe he'd withheld such an important detail from her.

Jake laughed, "Not even for a moment! You don't look like the kind of person who would rob a bank."

His good nature soothed her pique, and they talked late into the night while Copper slept. Even though they had packed sleeping bags and pitched a tent, they both fell asleep sitting beside the campfire.

The next morning, Natalie woke up first. She looked over at Jake. They were the same age, but slumped in the low chair, he looked so young with his disheveled blond hair. His high cheekbones and strong jawline just added to his charm. Something stirred deep inside her. Why had she never noticed that before? Of course, she knew he was a good-looking man. It was the first thing she'd noticed the day she saw him at the diner, but something about him had changed. The cockiness had vanished—he was more compassionate than when they first met.

Or had she changed? Had his kindness over the past month altered how she viewed him? Natalie put her hands over her face and shook her head back and forth. What about Paul? She still loved him. Was it possible to be in love with two men at once?

The water splashed against the boat, making soft hypnotic sounds. Natalie could almost drift back to sleep. Instead, she leaned back in her chair and watched Jake sleep. He was so still—she could hardly make out his breathing pattern.

Watching him, she questioned why he'd kept the discovery of money inside the door panel a secret from her. She sat up straight. Copper's head popped up and gave her a questioning look.

Could the money still be there? If it was, what would happen if the mechanic inadvertently found it?

She needed to go to the bathroom and tried to avoid fidgeting in her seat. Any movement on her part might awaken Jake. She maintained complete stillness while observing him sleep.

Not once could she recall watching Paul nap during their time together. He needed far less sleep than she did—Paul was the last to bed and first to rise.

Jake woke up about thirty minutes later and started another fire right away. Natalie had an overwhelming urge to do something for him. She found the tin pot and made coffee. While it was perking, she pulled a couple of protein bars from her bag and found the container of fruit left over from the previous day's picnic.

Jake prodded the fire with a branch. "How long have you been awake?"

Natalie shrugged. "Don't know. I was just enjoying my quiet time."

She explained that each morning when she got up, she brewed a cup of coffee and went out to the beach chairs for her quiet time. She handed him a steaming cup, an apple, and a protein bar. "Here's breakfast."

They reclaimed their seats, and Jake said, "What do you do during your quiet time?"

Natalie chuckled. "Not sure you'd believe me if I told you."

"Try me."

Should she? It sounded crazy, even to herself. But his eyes were kind, and his head was again tilted in what she'd come to think of as his listening posture.

Haltingly at first, then with growing confidence, she told him about Paul's visits, and how, more often than not, it was during her quiet time that he came to visit her. She paused and watched Jake's facial expression for any sign of alarm. There was none.

She went on about how comforting it was to know Paul was still close enough to communicate with her. About how they conversed about events throughout their marriage, and how she was still haunted by the thought of the woman in the vehicle the night of the accident. How she'd avoided mentioning the woman to Paul. Even though she suspected he would tell her, she wasn't sure she wanted to know.

Natalie gave Jake a quizzical look. "I'm having a conversation with my deceased husband! Does this sound like bizarre behavior to you?"

"Not at all." Jake shrugged. "Who am I to judge you? I've never lost a spouse to death." He sipped his coffee as he looked out over the water. "But I read a lot. Living alone, there's not much to do other than watch television or stay on social media sites, so I read."

"You read about grief?"

Jake wiped his hands on his shorts. "Not necessarily. But one thing I've learned through reading books over varied genres is that grief manifests itself in many unusual forms."

He paused for a few moments and then cleared his throat. "Natalie, if you're comforted by Paul's visits, then you shouldn't be ashamed to talk about it with anyone, especially with me. It was obvious from the start that you guys were close, and I'm not threatened by him. I realized when you came here that it would take time for you to get comfortable with me."

He was well read...*and* intuitive. After a few minutes, Natalie reached for the coffee pot and poured the remaining coffee into Jake's cup.

"Thanks," he said, and changed the subject. "When we leave we'll head north. I want to show you Sea Island. It's a beautiful island separated by the Black Banks River. If we time it right, we'll get to Jekyll in time for lunch."

"It sounds perfect," Natalie said. "But I'd love a shower, especially if we go on land for lunch."

"You look fine. You don't need a shower."

She made a goofy face and finished the last of her coffee.

A little later, Jake approached Natalie, leaned down, and gently kissed her. His lips felt soft and gentle. At first, he teased her a little, slightly brushing her lips—his breath warmed her cheeks, and a tingle spread through her body. She wanted more. As if he'd read her thoughts, his lips parted, and she tasted the sweet coffee on his tongue. It sparked a need inside her.

They had spent the night sitting across from each other, overlooking the fire. He'd never even hinted at wanting a romantic evening. He had listened to her go on about Paul—interested in her every word. Now, it was time to head out for a day of sightseeing, and his kisses engulfed her. Her desire increased. Jake never rushed. It was as if time was no measurement for this one kiss.

Natalie wondered if a future with Jake would mirror this moment. Slow. Deliberate. Unrushed. Then, he withdrew and winked. "I'll take a walk and gather more firewood for the next people who land here. While I'm gone, you can take a quick bath in the ocean. I have a bar of soap and a towel in the boat's hub. It's nothing fancy. Just plain soap. Watch out for passing vessels. The boat will shield you if any come by."

"Thank you! I'll be much better when I get a bath." Natalie knew Copper wouldn't let anyone get too close without making a noise.

Jake looked deep into her eyes, his fingertips barely touching her neck, "Someday, you'll get to a place where joy and contentment will replace your anger and blame. And when you do, I'll be here for you."

Natalie smiled and squeezed his hand. She sensed their friendship was quickly becoming something more. Was she ready for this?

Chapter Thirty-Nine

Wednesday on the Water

They had just finished their lunch of cobb salad and oysters on the half shell at The Wharf at Jekyll Island and were now back on the boat. September was coming to an end, and soon the evening temperatures would begin to cool. This afternoon, however, the heat was blistering.

They puttered to the main body of water, ready to head back to the St. Simons docks. By Natalie's estimation, they had ventured a few miles out at sea when she noticed a boat in apparent distress. A young woman wearing cutoff jean shorts over a swimsuit was waving her arm to get their attention. Jake made a sudden move and swerved in the boat's direction.

Natalie cupped her hands around her mouth and yelled to him, "Where are you going?"

Jake pointed to the stalled boat ahead.

Natalie got up and grabbed the side rails as she moved toward Jake. "How are you going to help her? Are you a marine mechanic?"

Copper stretched his neck and barked.

"No," Jake said. "But I wouldn't want you to be stranded on the water like that for any length of time. Maybe we can call for help when we get back to land. She might only need a couple of gallons of gas." He put his arm around Natalie and continued to watch the boat in the near distance.

"Please Jake," Natalie said. "Let's not get involved. We don't even know her. She could be hauling drugs in that boat for all we know."

"Seriously? Look at her! She looks more like a sorority girl than a drug dealer."

Natalie rolled her eyes, her shoulders tensed as she looked back toward Jekyll Island.

He reached for his shirt and pulled it over his head. "You're not in New York City anymore. We tend to trust each other down here. Besides, that girl could be someone's sister or daughter."

Copper rubbed his snout on Jake's leg.

Realizing there was nothing she could say to sway Jake from helping the young woman, Natalie went to the back of the boat and grabbed her flip-flops and the cornflower blue Lilly sarong.

Once they got close to the boat, Jake cut the engine. "Hi, I'm Jake, and this is Natalie." He hugged Natalie's shoulder. "What seems to be the problem?"

"I'm Charli." She had high cheekbones and raven hair, braided like a Desi Indian. She was tall, maybe five-nine or taller. "Thanks for stopping," she said. "We're not sure what's going on. We filled up with gas before leaving the docks at Sea Island." She looked at the soft waves hitting the side of the boat and shook her head. "We'd only been out here for an hour when the boat stopped."

Natalie looked at the boat's deck. "We? Charli, who's with you?"

She blinked, then waved a hand absentmindedly. "My little sister's in the cabin, sicker than a dog. I told her to take Dramamine! Anyway. I panicked when the boat stopped running...afraid we might be left out here alone all night."

Jake asked a few questions about when she'd last serviced the boat. Finally, he asked if she wanted them to come on board to check the engine.

Charli flashed an appreciative look and quickly checked him out.

Copper barked angrily, and Natalie stepped back. Why did she need to get on the boat? She knew nothing about repairing a water vessel. They didn't even know this woman. Charli said she'd come from Sea Island, but that didn't mean she lived there. She could have made that story up to put them at ease. Natalie looked over at Jake. Like a kid, he was already checking out the boat. She preferred to speak with Jake privately before she hopped on their craft, but that seemed impossible now.

As Jake stepped behind Natalie, Copper snapped at his ankle.

"Come on, Copper," Jake said. "Stop that. Can't you see we're busy here?"

He kissed Natalie's nose, "Natalie. You stay here with Copper while I go on board and check out the engine. Hold his collar to keep him from jumping out of the boat."

Copper's barking was almost deafening. Jake patted Copper's head and looked into his dog's eyes. "Don't be afraid, buddy. Everything is good here."

Jake tied his boat to the larger one, reached for Charli's hand, and jumped on board.

Natalie's eyes narrowed when Charli held on to Jake's hand a bit longer than necessary, causing him to stumble. He regained his balance, looking around for the steps down to the engine.

Natalie gave Copper the stay signal. Something was off with Charli. Jake needed someone to watch his back. She placed her hand on the rail and asked, "Is this a cabin cruiser?"

Charli extended a hand. "Yes. Come on board, and I'll show you the lower level."

As Natalie stepped across, Charli yanked her on board, and two men holding guns stepped from behind the cabin. Natalie fell onto the deck. Before she could scramble to her feet, a man stood over her—the gun barrel pointing at her chest.

***

Jake rushed toward Natalie.

In two swift steps, the second guy shoved Jake to the boat's edge and struck him in the temple with the butt of his gun. Jake lurched backward, ears ringing and a pounding in his head. He heard Natalie scream his name as he toppled over the side into his boat.

Chapter Forty

Jake

Beads of sweat formed on Jake's face as the boat rocked back and forth in rhythm with the ocean's waves. Barks echoed in the distance. His head pounded, and he couldn't seem to open his eyes. Copper's wet tongue covered his cheek, and he could smell dog breath on his face. He swallowed hard, choking back the hot acid in his throat. Then, bit by bit, his eyelids lifted.

The sun was almost directly overhead. He felt like he'd been sleeping for hours. Yet, something told him it hadn't been nearly that long.

"Hey, buddy," Jake croaked and gave Copper's ears a stroke. The dog whined as Jake pulled himself into a seated position and checked his watch. At first, all he could see was a blazing glare, but after a minute of blinking and squinting, the large white letters of the Apple watch came into focus. Thursday, 2:25 p.m.

Jake had spent much of his spare time on the water and could navigate the area surrounding the three islands better than anyone. Now, though, his internal compass seemed to have failed him. He couldn't even remember why he'd taken the boat out in the first place.

After a while, he got his bearings and bore north, toward St. Simons. Gradually, his stomach settled, and the pounding in his head dulled to a throb. An hour and a half, after he'd started for the docks… a single pier appeared in the distance. That didn't seem right.

He shaded his eyes with one hand and steered the boat closer. Was that…? It was. Somehow, he'd ended up at The Wharf at Jekyll Island.

He patted Copper's head. "This is the wrong direction, boy. I feel like we're going in circles." He turned the boat around and headed north toward St. Simons.

It was 4:30 by the time Jake made it back to the docks. A trip that typically took fewer than thirty minutes. What the hell was wrong with him?

As he unloaded the boat at the dock, a lady's overnight bag caught his eye. He reached for it, then frowned. The sleeves of Natalie's sweatshirt were tied to the handles. Unzipping the bag, he saw a red and white polka dot bikini. Jake held up the top. He'd seen it before. It belonged to Natalie. As he dug deeper into the bag, he found a pair of white palazzo pants and a hot pink swimsuit.

What was her stuff doing on his boat?

Shaking his head, Jake threw her bag along with his gear into the back of his truck and signaled for Copper to hop into the front seat. He'd sort it out when they got home.

By the time he unlocked the back door to his cottage, Jake's head had cleared a little, but the pain was still a pulsing ache, and there was a constant sting above his temple. He went to the pantry and poured a generous serving into Copper's dish. It was the first thing he did each day when he got home. Today, the ritual made him feel more grounded.

While Copper ate, Jake went into the bathroom and showered, gingerly washing the tender spot above his temple. Afterward, when he rubbed the steam from the bathroom mirror, he saw the gash on his head. He dabbed away the blood and rubbed some antiseptic over the cut.

How had that happened? A vision of a young woman waving from a boat in the middle of the ocean came to mind. Had he imagined her? If not, who was she?

Jake found a bandage in the medicine cabinet and dressed the wound. When he finished, Copper seemed anxious and followed him throughout the house, going back and forth between the front and back doors.

"Who are you looking for, Copper?"

The hound's persistent barking caused Jake's head to hurt even worse. Why couldn't the dog just be quiet for a few minutes? How could anybody think with all that racket going on?

Finally, Jake went out to the truck to unload his gear. There was Natalie's bag again. Where was she? The memory niggled at his mind, just out of reach.

It was much quieter outside. A nice breeze blew off the ocean. He leaned against the truck and tried to clear his head. He remembered the delicious whitefish she'd cooked over the fire. Was that yesterday or last week?

Jake listened to the calming sounds of the ocean waves. His head still hurt, but not like before. Feeling himself drifting away, he lay back onto the truck bed and placed Natalie's overnight bag under his head for support. His eyelids grew heavy as he breathed in the scent of her sweatshirt. Drifting away...

Just as he was about to fall asleep, a man's voice jolted him awake.

"You've got to take care of my Nattygirl, Jake."

A blast of cold air flashed over his face. Jake sat straight up. The quickness of the movement only enhanced the pain.

"What? Who are you?" he asked.

But there was no one there.

He looked toward Natalie's cottage. It was late afternoon. Not a single light. The screened porch light that typically stayed on was not burning. The red Porsche wasn't there, either.

The voice came again. A dream, maybe? Or a hallucination? But it sounded real enough. "She's in trouble, Jake, and you're the only one who can help her."

Where had she gone? Why couldn't he remember?

There were no more messages from his invisible visitor. But whether he'd dreamed it or not, Jake couldn't stay in the back of the truck, and he surely couldn't go back inside and listen to Copper's barking. He got inside his truck and slowly pulled out onto the road.

At first, Rosie ignored Jake when he got to the diner, but she eventually saw him frowning at the menu. It was upside down. She walked over and dabbed his arm. "Are you okay? You don't look so good, Jake."

He put down the menu and shifted his gaze to the air-conditioning vent overhead. "It's hot in here, Rosie. Do you mind adjusting the thermostat?"

"You're blistered!" she said in a tone much more challenging than intended. "Did you forget to use sunscreen?"

He lifted his left arm and observed the sunburn.

Rosie glanced at his eyes. He looked disoriented. His hair was wet, and a bandage haphazardly covered a nasty gash on his forehead where spots of dried blood seeped through. She went into the kitchen to get him some water, and when she returned, Jake was looking around the diner as if expecting someone.

Rosie waited a few moments while Jake drank the water and then asked, "Did you spend the night on the boat? He held the cold glass to his face and shook his head. She looked around the diner. The late lunch crowd had cleared out—two people at the counter and three couples sitting in the booths.

Rosie sat down on the stool and rubbed his arm. "What's wrong, Jake?"

He responded with a vacant look. Rosie had never seen him like this. Jake was always so confident and quick with a retort.

After some prodding, Jake said he thought Natalie had gone with him out on the boat. He placed his face in his hands and said he couldn't remember.

Rosie said, hardly daring to hope, "Did something happen to Natalie?"

"Yes…no! Why do you ask?" His eyes darted around the diner like a wild man's.

"It's okay, Jake. Calm down and tell me what happened today."

After a few moments of urging, he finally said, "I remember a girl in a bright yellow bathing suit and cut-off jeans waving from her boat."

She reached for his arm, but Jake jerked when she touched him.

She drew back her hand. "That's good," she said. "You remember a girl waving from the boat, correct?"

Jake nodded.

"Now, where was Natalie when this happened?"

His face went slack. "Not sure, but her overnight bag is in the back of my truck."

Whatever had happened, Jake needed her now. Rosie told the cook to lock the front door and put out the closed sign. As soon as the last customer finished eating, they were to clean up and leave. In the meantime, Rosie pulled her phone from her apron pocket, called Officer Parker, and asked him to meet her outside the diner.

Rosie went into the kitchen for a minute, and when she returned, she had removed her apron and was carrying her pocketbook and a bottle of water. "Let's go, Jake. We're going to the emergency room in Brunswick."

She reached for his arm as Jake shuffled to the door and onto the steps. He appeared to be intoxicated, but Rosie knew he was just disoriented. Maybe even dehydrated, but the water should help with that.

Officer Parker pulled into the parking lot just as Rosie and Jake made it down the steps. He rolled down his window and looked at Jake. "Man, are you okay?"

Rosie said, "I need you to drive Jake and me to the emergency room in Brunswick."

"Sure."

She opened the passenger door and helped Jake inside. Then she jumped into the back seat.

Parker turned around and said to Rosie, "Has something happened?"

She explained that Jake acted like he'd suffered a concussion when he got to the diner.

"Why not take him to the clinic to see Natalie?"

"Jake doesn't know where Natalie is." Rosie lowered her voice, suppressing a smile. "She might be missing."

Chapter Forty-One

Parker

Parker swerved under the portico of the Thomas and Mildred Beach Emergency Care Center, killed the engine, and dashed inside the hospital to retrieve the nearest wheelchair. When he returned, Rosie was already standing at the passenger side door coaxing Jake to slide into the chair. Her urging seemed to have no effect, but finally, Jake stepped out of the car. He gave an audible groan as he tried to straighten.

Once they got Jake into the chair and inside the building, Parker rushed back outside to move his car to the visitors' parking lot.

While walking back to the emergency entrance, he tried to make sense of the information in his mind. The call from Rosie was about more than just needing someone to escort her and Jake to the hospital. He couldn't get his head around Rosie's theory that Natalie could be missing. The thought remained pure speculation because of Jake's lack of communication on the way to the hospital. Jake seemed so confused that he couldn't remember where he'd been, let alone Natalie's whereabouts.

As he climbed the steps to the entrance, it occurred to him that someone could have beaten Jake. He'd seemed oblivious to the cut on his head, but he'd winced when Rosie helped him into the patrol car and again when they helped him out.

He could have a cracked rib or two. He thought back to Jake's appearance as he and Rosie stood on the bottom step of the diner when he pulled in to get them. Wet hair, clean clothes, tennis shoes, and a fresh bandage covering a cut on his forehead.

Jake's decision to shower and change into clean clothes after a day on the water suggested he was filthy, but the nasty gash on his forehead implied he had either fallen or had been in a fight. But why?

Parker reviewed what he knew about Jake Ellis. Since he'd arrived on the island, Jake made it a routine to surf, sail, or snorkel every day after work. Most of those older cottages down on the beach had an outdoor shower attached to them, so it was reasonable to assume that Jake's place also had one.

Parker stood at the front desk and searched for a chair in the emergency room. The place was packed out—not a chair in sight. He suddenly recalled a conversation with Chris Rhodes, the investigator from the FBI. Earlier in the month, Rhodes had visited the island to investigate a break-in at Natalie's former residence. Although it was a long shot, Parker wondered if Natalie's alleged disappearance—if it was indeed a disappearance—and the break-in were connected.

While scrolling through his phone for Rhodes's cell number, Parker walked outside to get a better reception. Calling an officer outside his jurisdiction for help without permission from the police chief was against protocol, but he pressed the number, anyway. Rhodes answered on the first ring.

"Parker here, from St. Simons. We met at the diner earlier this month."

"Excuse me?" Rhodes said.

"I'm Officer Ben Parker from Glynn County Police Department. You asked me to call you if I heard anything unusual about Natalie Nieman."

"Yes," Rhodes said. "You were the officer who worked the double-suicide case, right?"

"Correct."

They talked for a few more moments. Then Rhodes asked, "Whatever happened to the man in the slicker running on the road behind the hotel? Did you ever find that guy?"

Parker explained the guy was in town training for a triathlon. It was a dead-end lead.

"Good work. That guy's been on my mind. Of all the scenarios I've encountered, I never considered he was preparing for a Triathlon. Hold on a minute." Parker heard the squeak of a man shifting in his chair. Then Rhodes said, "Glad you called, Parker. Do you have any information for me?"

There had been an accident, Parker clarified. Natalie and her friend, Jake, were supposed to have spent the night on the water, but when Jake returned home a few hours ago, Natalie wasn't with him. It was too soon to report her missing, but there was something in Rosie's voice that caused him to believe Natalie was in danger.

Rhodes hesitated. "Okay. Give me the chronological facts as you know them."

Parker complied. "Jake has a gash on his head and appears to have suffered a concussion. Rosie and I are getting him checked out at the hospital in Brunswick."

"I don't know, Parker. This isn't much to go on, but I'll trust your instincts. Did anyone actually see Jake and Natalie on the boat together?"

Parker couldn't answer, but he intended to find out. As soon as he could get clearance from the doctor, he planned to question Jake about Natalie's whereabouts.

Rhodes said, "Before you go into the hospital, why don't you call the clinic and find out when Natalie's assistant last talked to her? If you can find out the last time someone spoke with her, that will help narrow the search."

Parker could hear papers shuffling. Finally, Rhodes said, "Also, send someone to the docks. Find out if anyone saw Jake and Natalie together on the boat, and contact Jake's foreman. Jake could've fallen on a job site and hit his head. Let's explore every avenue until we locate Natalie."

Rhodes got another call and had to go. Before they hung up, he thanked Parker for calling and asked him to stay in touch. He hesitated, "Text me as soon as you find Natalie, but if you confirm she is indeed missing, I'll be on the next flight down there."

As the call ended, Parker was glad he'd contacted Rhodes. Although he had broken protocol, his gut told him Natalie was in trouble, and he respected Rhodes's opinion. If Rosie's hunch was accurate and Natalie was missing, then his expertise would be invaluable to the case.

Parker went back inside and stood close to the sliding glass door just outside the emergency waiting room. He had a clear shot to the wooden double doors going back to the treatment area, so if Rosie or a doctor came out, he could get inside fast. His first call was to dispatch. Parker needed to let the precinct know his whereabouts. He also needed to find out the name of Jake's construction company. A dispatcher in his precinct had dated Jake a time or two the previous summer. She gave him the name of the company, then told him that Jake rarely worked on the job sites anymore. He played more of a supervisory role, which included searching for properties to develop, preparing bids, purchasing building materials, and maintaining a close relationship with his clients. Despite living a simple, unassuming life, Jake had built a successful business since coming to the island.

He was a nice guy, she said, but their interests weren't compatible. She enjoyed shopping and eating at a different restaurant every night, and he wanted to be on the water every moment he could.

No red flags there.

After ending his conversation, Parker googled J Ellis Construction Company. A colorful picture of a vast ocean-side home appeared on the screen. He clicked the website and called the number.

He introduced himself and explained the nature of his call. At first, the receptionist refused to provide any information, but when Parker told her he was at the hospital in Brunswick with her boss, she started talking.

No, her boss had not been at work for two days. No, she had not spoken with him today. Yes, he had taken a few days off. Yes, he had planned to spend a few days on the boat with a friend.

Parker gave her his contact information and thanked her for her time. He looked through the glass doors, and there were several empty seats. It looked like the room had cleared out. While the corridor was quiet, it would be a good time to call the clinic.

"Hi Jennifer, it's Ben Parker. Is Natalie there?"

Parker looked up as Rosie exited the wooden double doors and walked in his direction.

He continued to make notes on his pad: Natalie had taken off… on the boat with Jake.

"She was terrified because of the note," Jennifer said. "They both thought it would be good for her to get away."

"What note?" Parker asked. "What are you talking about?"

Parker looked at his phone and shook his head. "Damn, she just put me on hold."

When she returned to the line, he reached for the pen in his uniform pocket. Quickly, he added her observation to his list— that there had been a second note, and the handwriting matched the one found during her house burglary.

Rosie flashed a questioning glance at Parker as she stood on her tiptoes, trying to read his writing.

Parker let out an ahem as he cleared his throat. "Are you sure Natalie went out on the boat with Jake? Is it possible she changed her mind and didn't go?"

While listening to Jennifer's response, he glanced at Rosie. There was something about her demeanor that made no sense. She seemed agitated at his last question. If Rosie seriously suspected her friend was missing, why wasn't she making calls? She knew everyone on the island. Surely someone had seen Natalie by now, especially if she'd returned with Jake.

His focus returned to Jennifer. "Okay, thanks, Jennifer. Call me the minute you hear from her."

He ended the call and asked Rosie, "How's Jake?"

"They're taking him to radiology for a CT scan." She looked around the waiting room and said, "How 'bout Jennifer? Has she seen Natalie?"

"No. Jennifer hasn't seen or heard from her."

Rosie flashed Parker a grin. "Ben, can I get you a cup of coffee?"

Rosemary had returned to Jake's hospital room when they brought him back from testing. He was groggy. She reached for a magazine and flipped through it while trying not to disturb Jake.

She had just finished an article about the advantages of planting perennials in southern states when Jake yelled, "Natalie, please!"

Rosemary looked over the top of the magazine. Jake appeared to be sleeping, but there was a smile on his face as he softly uttered Natalie's name. Natalie. Natalie. Natalie.

She threw the magazine on the floor and stormed out the door. Standing in the hallway outside Jake's hospital room, Rosemary leaned against the wall and held her face in her hands. Crying wasn't an option for Rosemary. Only weak people cried.

A nurse walked down the hall, stopped, and said, "Are you okay?"

"Yes," Rosemary said. "I'm fine."

The nurse gave her a measured look before going into Jake's room.

Rosemary watched the door close, and then she turned the other way. She thought about Jake. He was on the other side of the wall, dreaming about Natalie. She had taken him to the hospital, sat up with him, and seen to his every need.

Suddenly, she hit the wall. "This isn't acceptable. I was here first." As she turned to go back into Jake's room, she murmured, "I'm not losing him without a fight."

Chapter Forty-Two

Natalie

In her dream state, one moment Natalie was gazing into the crystal turquoise waters of the Caribbean Ocean while Paul lay face down on the white, sandy beach beside her lounge chair. The next moment, a sea of darkness surrounded her, and she'd developed a throbbing headache, the likes of which she'd never felt. Her eyes felt like sandpaper, and the movement of the room made her dizzy.

She couldn't figure out where she was. There was water close by. That was a given. But was she at her beachside cottage, or was she actually floating on a body of water? She couldn't be sure.

She felt something on the back of her arm. *Oh, please don't let it be a spider.* Natalie hated spiders. Lifting her hand to her arm, she felt a bandage. Well, that explained the weird feeling.

Someone had drugged her.

A pattern was establishing in her mind of drifting back and forth from the past scenario of Paul's last day in the NY hospital to her present dilemma of being held captive in the boat.

Natalie stood over her husband's gurney, trying to remember what she should do. She was a trauma specialist. She had been in this situation thousands of times, but now—for the first time in her life—paralyzed with fear, she looked at the pallid color of the man she adored.

Paul was breathing, but they were very shallow breaths. Tonight, Natalie was a wife, not a doctor. It didn't feel good being on the other side. She was too close to the patient to offer medical advice. Her skills as a highly trained specialist were no good to her now. At this moment, she knew all she could do was pray for her husband and hope that the divine hand of God was resting on his body.

The driver of the other car involved in the accident was in the unit next to Paul—separated only by a thick curtain. A police officer spoke with the driver's parents, who agreed to question their son. Natalie overheard the driver say that he'd been late to make "the drop." His class had run late, then he had to get gas. He'd run the red light near Paul's office. It was all his fault. He sounded young, late teens, maybe twenty.

Dr. Martin asked if there were drugs involved.

"But Doc, you don't understand," the kid said in an anxious voice. "I've got to get this bag of money to Mr. Nieman tonight. I was supposed to meet him at five."

Bag of money?

The comment shocked Natalie out of her dream.

***

She opened her eyes. It was dark. It took a minute to acclimate to the darkness, but a slight stream of light shone under what seemed to be a door on the other side of the room.

The cabin reeked of dead fish. A powerful thrust of water hit the outside. Fearing she might overturn, she clung to the side of the cot.

Suddenly, it hit her. She recognized the sounds of waves crashing against the boat's hull and the movement the waves created. She remembered the girl and the stalled boat she and Jake had stopped to rescue. And… there had been two other men, hadn't there? Judging from the size of her headache, they had given her a heavy dose of some strong narcotic before locking her in this tiny cabin, probably in the boat's bow.

She glanced around the room. What had they done with Jake?

When the waves subsided, she shivered from the cold. She explored the cot with her fingers until she felt a blanket near her feet. She spread it over her body and curled into a fetal position, pulling the blanket over her head. After a few minutes, her own body heat filled her little cocoon. The shivering stopped, and fight as she may, she couldn't keep her eyes open. Consumed by the drug-induced exhaustion, Natalie slowly lost consciousness as her mind drifted back to the night of Paul's accident.

***

The boy was getting more agitated with each word he spoke.

"Take it easy, son." The officer's voice was very calm.

"He specifically told me no later than five o'clock. He had to leave the office by 5:15." The boy choked back a sob and then gasped, "He depended on…"

The vital signs monitor beeped loudly. Then Natalie heard his mother scream, "What's wrong with him? Oh, my god! Do something, Dr. Martin!"

Dr. Martin yelled, "Get out. Everyone, get out."

The kid must have gone into cardiac arrest. Natalie had seen it in other trauma cases. One minute they were fine, and the next they were coding.

Muffled sobs and a shuffling of feet came from the other side of the curtain as the monitor continued to beep. It was such an annoying sound. She had worked twelve-hour shifts in the trauma unit and had never thought about the beeping of those machines.

Natalie strained to hear what was happening. Then she tiptoed to the end of Paul's bed just as Dr. Martin yelled, "One, two, three—CLEAR!"

Would someone please cut off that damn machine!

Again, Dr. Martin yelled, "One, two, three—CLEAR!"

Natalie's dream was interrupted by the sound of a man's voice from outside the cabin door. The faintness of the light and the increased temperature in the bow indicated it was late in the afternoon. She strained to listen to the conversation, but the boat's vibrations were deafening. After a while, they killed the motor. There was dead silence. The waves were smaller than before. Her body tensed. The silence felt like an ominous sign. A few minutes later, she smelled cigarette smoke. Someone coughed. It was a dry cough... a smoker's cough. It was the same type of cough her grandfather had, and he died from lung cancer when she was a young girl.

She forced her thoughts back to her present dilemma. Two men were on the boat when she and Jake stopped to rescue the girl, but she did not know how many more were down below.

When the coughing stopped, the man said something about the doctor and the massive amount of cash stashed away inside the car. It made little sense. What cash? What car? And what did that have to do with her?

The sound of his gruff voice startled her back into the moment. "If I could get my hands on that red Porsche, I'd rip through every inch until I found the money."

Natalie rubbed her sore head. Red Porsche. He'd actually said "red Porsche." That had to be Paul's car. The mechanic had said the repair would take a few days, which was the day she and Jake went out on the water. She couldn't be sure how long ago that had been.

At long last, another man spoke. His speech was softer and more polished than the first guy, perhaps because of his position on the boat. Natalie strained to hear him as he elaborated, "When we find the Porsche, we won't need to rip through it and ruin the car. If the money was hidden where he said, then we only need to find the secret compartment."

The men were suddenly quiet. Natalie thought it odd that they had stopped talking almost in mid-sentence. But then, sometimes, men were like that. Most women enjoyed sipping a glass of wine while chatting with a friend, but men appreciated sitting in silence while enjoying a drink.

Someone popped the top of a can. Soon, smoke from another cigarette filtered through the bow. Natalie shivered when darkness descended upon the interior, and the sounds of heavy footsteps moved across the upper deck.

"Where're you going?" the polished speaker asked.

The raspy-speaking man replied, "Going back down to check on the pretty lady."

"Leave her alone. Let her eat in peace."

Eat? Natalie looked around the hull and found a small cooler holding four water bottles. Next to the cooler, a loaf of Italian bread and a block of cheese lay wrapped in a paper bag. So they weren't going to let her starve. At least, not yet.

Natalie took a long swallow of water, pulled off a piece of the bread, and grabbed a chunk of the soft hoop cheese. She leaned back on the cot and arranged the food on her lap, grateful for the bread and water. Although she had never considered herself religious, Natalie offered a prayer of thanksgiving before peeling the red wax from the cheese and taking a bite of bread.

The humble meal made Natalie feel much better. Her thoughts were more precise, and she realized she had to find a way off the boat if she was going to survive. Then it would be her mission to go to Brunswick and search Paul's car.

Did I just call the Porsche Paul's car?

He'd never let her live that one down. Even so, she wished he were here now. She had questions, and it was time he answered them.

Laying awake for what seemed like an eternity, Natalie struggled to piece together what might have happened on the night of her fifth anniversary. She had difficulty comprehending the young man's involvement in delivering a bag of cash to Paul and how that connected him to the men sitting on the boat's deck.

The pulsating headache had finally subsided. Natalie willed herself to rest. At last, she slept:

The clock above the nurse's station showed ten o'clock. Natalie had been staring at it for what felt like hours, glued to her chair since her colleague and friend, Dr. Alex Martin, had declared the young man dead. She couldn't believe she hadn't even tried to help resuscitate the patient.

Yes, the renowned Dr. Natalie Howard-Nieman, one of the country's top trauma specialists, had stayed on her side of the curtain and not even tried to lend a hand to help save the panicked couple's son. Neither was she able to help her own husband. She was as useless as a zombie in a rom-com movie.

Natalie floated back to consciousness, then sank back into oblivion. She felt like she was adrift in time, wafting between the moment she first met Paul and her current predicament on the boat.

***

As soon as Paul finished his undergraduate degree in finance, he was determined to start his master's program in economics. After receiving his postgraduate degree, he landed the job of his dreams at JCMB…

Natalie could not possibly imagine her professional husband involved in what seemed to be a drug deal. How could that even be possible? He'd been assigned to a high-profile case. He worked long hours… she had considered the possibility that he was having an affair, but a drug deal? No way.

Was that kid hallucinating?

The young man clearly knew Paul's name. On two occasions, she'd heard him mention Mr. Nieman. But why would he be trying to deliver a package of money to Paul?

None of it made sense.

Natalie shook her head as if to clear her mind. Perhaps she was the one who had hallucinated. She looked at her watch and realized her husband had been gone for tests much longer than he should have been. What was taking so long?

Dr. Martin stepped from behind the curtain and sat in the chair next to her. "Listen, Natalie, they've just started running the MRI on Paul. It's going to be awhile before we know what's going on."

Natalie's eyes welled. "I was concerned. He's been gone awhile. Is he still unconscious?"

"Yes. Paul is still unconscious." He raked his fingers through his hair. "They're backed up in radiology tonight, and as you can see, we're covered up down here." He smiled at his friend. "It must be a full moon."

Natalie attempted a smile. "I read that a full moon is expected this weekend."

"Well, there you go." He slapped his hand on his knee. Then, sobering, he told her that the taxi driver had lost consciousness at the time of the impact. How could Dr. Martin possibly know that? Neither the police nor the emergency medical staff were at the scene at the time of the accident. But that was irrelevant. All that mattered was that her husband had blacked out sometime after the crash and had not regained consciousness.

"Is there anyone you need to call?" Dr. Martin asked. "A family member, close friend, a neighbor, perhaps... I'd love to sit with you, kiddo, but I've been here longer than my allotted time. I've got to get some sleep."

"You go." Natalie gave him another half-hearted smile. "I'm fine. Really."

It was getting close to shift change when they returned Paul to the emergency room. She hurried to his side and took his hand, waiting for the radiologist to review the results. "Hold on, honey," she told him over and over. "Okay, love. Stay with me."

She stepped aside as the attending nurse removed the sheet to insert the catheter, then drew in a sharp breath as her gaze fell on Paul's right leg, twisted beneath him, the foot lying backward on the gurney.

Her stomach rolled. "I need to see the EMT report. Dr. Martin didn't mention a broken leg earlier." She hugged herself to keep from shoving the woman away and setting the bone herself. "How could he have missed that?"

"Ma'am…" The woman's tone was curt. "We'll address the leg and other fractures once Mr. Nieman's condition is stabilized."

Quickly, the nurse removed her rubber gloves, reached for a squirt of hand sanitizer, and bustled out the door.

An hour later, the blood test results materialized. There were no traces of foreign substances in Paul's system. That didn't surprise her. Paul loved his body too much to take drugs or binge drink.

Feeling lightheaded, Natalie forced herself to concentrate on the report. A few nibbles of a peanut butter cracker were all she could manage before she pushed the rest of the package aside. It tasted like sawdust. She pulled the visitor's chair to Paul's side and laid her hand on his, too exhausted to talk, too worried to sleep.

It was after midnight when the attending physician stepped behind the curtain, followed by the attending nurse, to speak with Natalie about the results of the MRI.

When the doctor left, the nurse stayed behind and mentioned that Mr. Nieman's wife was being treated in Unit 3-B of the ER.

Natalie's head snapped up.

Wait. What? *Wife?*

She forced herself to focus on the nurse's words. Paul's "wife" was conscious at the accident scene but had lost consciousness when her lungs collapsed. Fortunately, the EMT acted quickly and inflated the lungs while they were en route to the hospital.

The woman prattled on. "The medics found them hunkered in the backseat of the taxi—it was adorable. They were holding hands. I've been working on her since she and Mr. Nieman arrived." She smoothed the blanket over Paul's chest. "The police will come back to finish their accident report now that she has regained consciousness."

Natalie tried to shake the fog from her mind. Perhaps her blood sugar level had dropped, and she was confused. Surely this person had not just told her that Paul had been with another woman.

The nurse held Paul's wrist while she checked the fluid port. "I'll be here for a few moments with Mr. Nieman if you want to walk over and check on his wife. I overheard the charge nurse tell her attendant that the police officer found her blue Michael Kors purse underneath the car seat. He's bringing it over when he comes to finish the report." The nurse looked at Natalie and smiled before she checked the monitor. "She might appreciate your support… since she's all alone."

Natalie looked up at her husband lying on the gurney. It was Paul, alright. There was no mistaking that gorgeous face. Talking to the nurse now felt like being in a *Twilight Zone* episode. She went and stood next to her husband. When the nurse turned back around, Natalie asked, "You're the new hire, aren't you?"

The attending nurse glanced at her and nodded. "Yes, this is my first day at New York Memorial. I've transferred here from Upstate."

Natalie paused, then reached for her husband's hand. "For the record—," her eyebrows went up, and a tight, nervous smile formed on her lips—, "*I* am Mr. Nieman's wife."

When the sun rose the following morning, Natalie's eyelids were heavy. The boat rocked beneath her, and slowly she remembered where she was. She knew someone had been there during the early morning hours. There was a stench in the air...a foul, cheesy odor like the smell from a male's armpits. She sat up and swung her legs over the side of the cot. A dirty undershirt and hypodermic needle lay on the ground next to her bed.

Her mouth was dry, and the pain in her head had returned. She noticed a fresh loaf of bread where the half-eaten bread had been the previous evening. Quietly, she tiptoed to the cooler, where she found two bottles of water and a bag of ice.

Following the same routine as before, she opened the water bottle, broke off a piece of bread, and sat back on the cot. Once again, Natalie prayed. This time, though, she recited The Lord's Prayer.

A sense of peace came over her as she bit into the bread. By the time she'd finished her food, Natalie had experienced a renewed strength. She surmised a story about Paul's involvement with his boss. Was it conceivable he had given Paul a stash of money to hide? It would explain why these men thought cash was hidden in his car. Although her rational mind found that hard to believe, given the right circumstances, it could have happened. If only she could get to the garage in Brunswick, she could check the door panels and secret compartment in the back and find out.

But first, she needed an escape route back to land.

Chapter Forty-Three

The second week of October

Lieutenant Parker stood on one side of the ER unit while Rosie sat in the only available chair. She seemed genuinely concerned about Jake's welfare, but there was more—like she was toying with an internal conflict. Rosie and Jake were friends, but as far as Parker knew, they weren't a couple.

Parker ran into Jake several times each week at the diner. They discussed politics and sports, but never women. If Jake had spent the night on his boat with Natalie, it seemed unlikely he had romantic feelings for Rosie, but that didn't necessarily mean Rosie didn't have feelings for Jake.

Parker scanned through his notes. "I've got a question. What was your relationship with Natalie? Were you ladies close friends?"

Rosie's smile came a beat too late. "We've spent a lot of time together. I'd say we were pretty close."

"My understanding is you and Jake used to be pretty close, too."

The tension in her jaw told him everything he needed to know.

THE EMPTY BEACH CHAIR

The nurse pulled back the curtain. "Mr. Ellis has finished his CT scan and is on his way back down."

When they rolled Jake back into the ER, he was dozing. The nurse dimmed the overhead light and then checked his vital signs. As soon as Jake opened his eyes, Parker leaned forward and said, "Man, do you feel like answering a few questions for me?"

The nurse looked over her glasses at Parker. "Officer, let's hold off on the questions. Mr. Ellis needs his rest."

"I understand that, ma'am, but we suspect someone might be missing, and I need to ask him a few questions to be sure."

"The doctor has given us orders to admit Mr. Ellis for the night. Why don't you come back after he gets settled into his room?"

"Jake," Parker said. "I'm going to run out to Natalie's cottage and see if any neighbors have seen her. Do you need anything from your house?"

The nurse cut her eyes at Parker again. Although he was an officer in uniform, the nurse was in charge of the patient. They both knew she trumped him.

Well, what could she do to him? Throw him out. He'd hoped the mention of Natalie's name would spark a thought in Jake's mind, and by the time he returned, Jake would have remembered what had happened.

Jake threw him the keys, "Grab a few things from my closet."

Parker checked his watch. It would be dark in a couple of hours. "No problem. I'll be back shortly. Get some rest while I'm gone." He winked at the nurse and whispered something to Rosie.

Rosie's eyebrows went up. Then she shrugged.

When Parker got outside the unit, he called the Brunswick Precinct. "Captain Wheeler, it's Lieutenant Parker, over on St. Simons. I've got a possible missing person." He gave Wheeler a quick recap. "Can you spare a team to begin a search of the island?"

"I'm on it. Do you need the search-and-rescue dogs?"

"Yes," Parker said. "I'll send over the details in an email."

Parker left the hospital, drove over the causeway, and headed straight to the diner. One of his buddies, Brent Sullivan, was turning around in the diner's parking lot. Parker pulled in and rolled down his window.

"What's up?" Sullivan asked.

"Not much," Parker said. "Have you got time to drive Jake's truck to his house? He was in an accident earlier in the day and is spending the night in the hospital over in Brunswick."

"Of course," Sullivan said.

The traffic was heavy for a Thursday night, and it took longer to get through town than Parker would have thought. They dropped off Jake's truck, and Parker went next door and walked around the house. Natalie's home appeared secure, and there were no lights on around the property.

Parker and Sullivan then walked to the neighbor's house across the street from Jake's. When he knocked on the door, his buddy stepped behind him. An older man came to the door. He had a toothpick in his mouth and was holding a mug of steaming coffee. The smell was comforting. Parker asked if he'd seen Natalie Nieman.

The neighbor said, "She left yesterday morning—not seen or heard from her since."

"Yesterday morning?" Parker suppressed a smile, hoping the neighbor's account meant she hadn't gone out on the boat with Jake. "What time?"

All the man could remember was that Natalie got into her car a little before nine o'clock and left; Jake had followed in his truck.

So she had probably gone with him after all.

After a couple of fruitless follow-up questions, Parker looked in the back of Jake's truck. Someone had tied a sweatshirt around the handles of an overnight bag. What was this? He unzipped the bag and found several items neatly rolled inside: a bathing suit, a pair of gym shorts, a long-sleeved T-shirt, and a black bra. Parker sniffed the shirt. A female scent of Chanel No. 5.

Parker grabbed the T-shirt and the sweatshirt, turned to Sullivan, and said, "Let's go."

They circled around to the marina on the way back to the diner. The deputies from Brunswick had just removed the dogs from the back of the van. He handed the officers the items of clothing and exchanged contact information.

"I need to take my friend to get his truck and then check on the patient at the hospital. I should be back within the hour."

Parker and Sullivan returned to the patrol car, but before they departed the marina, Parker pulled his car over to the van and said, "Hey guys, let's not let the media catch wind of this just yet."

As soon as Parker dropped Sullivan off at the diner, he headed back to the hospital. He glanced at his phone and pulled into the visitor's parking lot. He'd been gone almost two hours.

When the elevator doors opened, Rosie was standing in the hallway scrolling through her phone.

Parker held up the bag with Jake's clothing and said, "How's Jake?"

"The nurse said the amnesia caused by the concussion has almost cleared. They're going to wrap his torso and give him a mild sedative to help with the pain from his broken ribs."

"Do you think he's ready to answer some questions?"

She shrugged. "If he's awake, he shouldn't mind."

Jake was trying to sit up in the hospital bed when Parker and Rosie walked in. Parker perched on the edge of the windowsill while Rosie sat in the narrow recliner in the sparsely furnished hospital room.

Parker asked him if he and Natalie had gone out on the boat the previous day.

Jake gave Rosie a questioning look.

She chuckled. "Jake, he's asking you the question, not me."

When Jake didn't answer, Parker explained that he'd talked to his neighbor. "He told me he saw Natalie leave yesterday morning in her car. He said you followed her out in your truck."

Jake didn't respond.

Parker's eyebrows knitted in a frown.

Finally, Rosie went and sat on the bed and took Jake's hand. "Jake, you and Natalie were supposed to take the boat out and spend the night on the water." She smiled. "Jennifer from Natalie's office told Parker that Natalie found another note in her mailbox the night before, and the handwriting matched the note left on the table the night of the break-in."

Jake played with the remote, finally found a comfortable position in bed, looked at Parker, and then again at Rosie. "I remember the note."

"Okay. Good."

Parker released a breath and glanced at Rosemary. Jake was coming around.

"Where is Natalie now?" Jake asked.

Parker said, "We've got a team searching the island for her."

THE EMPTY BEACH CHAIR

The more Rosie and Parker talked, the more Jake fidgeted with his covers and moved the bed position so he could sit up.

"What are you doing?" Rosie asked, reaching for the remote control in his hand.

"Natalie's in trouble. I've got to find her." He struggled to rise.

Jake was strong, and once he understood Natalie could be missing or drowned, it took both Rosemary and Parker to keep him in bed.

Finally, Parker lay sideways across his legs while Rosie grabbed the buzzer from the side of the bed and said into it, "Would you get the doctor, please?"

***

When the doctor came in and saw Jake's angst, he glanced at Rosemary, reached into the pocket of his white coat, and said, "I'm giving him another sedative. With two fractured ribs, I'm afraid he'll puncture a lung if he continues moving around like this."

After administering the medication, he turned toward Rosemary and said, "Please try to keep him quiet and still."

"I'll try," Rosie said. *Don't know how I'm supposed to do that. He's stronger than me.*

Then, she added, "When can we take Jake home?"

"Perhaps tomorrow." The doctor told Rosie it would be the next day before he considered releasing Jake to go home. His amnesia was clearing up, but the broken ribs were still a significant concern. He'd need to take a few weeks off from work so his ribs could mend—he'd also need someone to stay with him for a few days.

"He can stay at my house until his ribs heal." Rosie wanted to take care of Jake while he recuperated. She'd show him the level of care only she could provide. And once she got him home, she'd convince him that Natalie was safe. That would be true—or mostly true—since by then, Parker would be forming a search party. But if Rosemary was lucky, Natalie would be gone long enough for Jake to realize who really deserved his heart.

Jake slung his sheet back and attempted to get up again. "We need to search for Natalie. She's missing, and we need to find her. I've got to get out of here, doc."

The doctor peered sternly over his glasses. "You're not going anywhere until I dismiss you. So lie back and let that sedative take effect. It'll be morning soon, and we'll reassess the situation then."

The doctor winked at Rosie when he left the room. "If he gets too agitated, have the nurse ring for me."

Rosemary swallowed a frustrated sigh and busied herself straightening the sheet on Jake's bed. She felt a little guilty for thinking ill of Natalie. As much jealousy as she'd felt toward her since she'd moved to the island, she didn't want anything to happen to her, either. Why did things always have to be so complicated?

If little 'Ms. Perfect' had just kept her mitts off Jake, then she and Rosemary could have been good friends.

She checked her phone. No messages. No texts. It had been almost twelve hours since Jake came off the water. If Natalie were anywhere on the island, she'd be trying to contact them.

At 2:30 a.m., when Officer Parker left the hospital, Rosemary followed him down the elevator and out into the night air. She liked Ben; he was a great guy, but she didn't like the way he'd questioned her earlier…as if he suspected her of something. She'd have to be careful around him.

She put on a worried expression. "Ben, do you think Natalie's okay?"

Parker turned to Rosie. "I know you're concerned, but the team from the Brunswick precinct are good at what they do." He touched her arm. "So far, no one has seen her car since Wednesday morning. She could've left the island and failed to tell anyone."

"That doesn't sound like Natalie," Rosie said. "She would have told Jennifer if she were leaving the island. Or me, for that matter."

When she was certain Ben had left the parking lot, she pulled out her phone and scrolled through her contacts. Chris Rhodes's name came up. The description under his name read FBI Task Force. She pressed the number and waited for him to answer.

He answered on the second ring. "Hello."

"Chris, it's me, Rosie. We've had a development here, and I thought you should be made aware."

"You've not found Natalie, have you?"

"How did you know?"

"Lieutenant Parker called me earlier. I've been waiting to hear back from him."

"So, you know the situation?"

"Yes," he said.

"It's been almost twelve hours. You need to get down here." She ended the call and smiled to herself. Her obvious concern should eliminate any suspicion. She put her phone in her pocket and went back upstairs.

Jake was sitting on the side of the bed, trying to put his pants on.

"What are you doing, Jake Ellis?"

"Natalie's in trouble." He continued nonstop chatter about his need to get up and find Natalie.

Rosemary went over to the bed and rubbed his neck. She spoke in a soft voice, trying to soothe his nerves. After a while, she helped him to lie back on the bed. He clung to her and finally stopped chattering. The physical contact was working.

Finally, she slid onto the bed and held Jake, continuing her soothing voice. "Everything is going to be fine. I've called for help. They'll find Natalie. You rest now."

Rosemary stayed by Jake's side throughout the night. The nurses' station wasn't far from his room. The medical staff shuffled in the hallway the entire shift. Phones pinged. The air conditioning system made a loud noise when it came on and then again when it went off. Patients called out for help. Orderlies dropped trays. Rosemary's heart pounded in her chest, and there was no way she could fall asleep. She had really botched it up! She should've gotten someone in the diner to drive her and Jake to the hospital and insisted Parker had formed a search party while it was still daylight. That would've proven beyond a doubt that she was truly worried—worried about the woman Jake was in love with.

She loved Jake. Jake loved Natalie, and Natalie was missing. What a cluster!

Chapter Forty-Four

Rhodes

Heading home to read the files and pack a bag, Chris Rhodes watched the traffic in front of him inch forward on the freeway. The report he'd just seen still niggled his mind, and he felt a surge of adrenaline, like a hound catching scent after losing a trail.

Mrs. Rockwell had always insisted that her husband was anything but suicidal. Rhodes knew you couldn't always tell from outward appearances, but the discovery of the photo and a reevaluation of the chemical substance found in the senator's body suggested he had not killed himself, but was murdered.

Strange how his current case, the break-in at Natalie Nieman's Brooklyn condo, had dovetailed with the death of two detectives investigating the Rockwell case. Like Rockwell, their deaths appeared to be suicide by carbon monoxide, and also like Rockwell, the autopsy reports showed a significant amount of fentanyl in their bloodstreams. One of the detectives had recently had knee replacement surgery and was dealing with the pain of scar tissue. The medical examiner compared the detective's prescription with the drug found in the two men's bodies. They didn't match.

It couldn't be just coincidental that the drug did match the one that had killed Senator Rockwell.

Rhodes had been home less than an hour when another urgent call came through. There'd been a second break-in at John Steelton's New York home. The perpetrators had caused significant damage, and the resemblance to the vandalism at Natalie's New York townhome was undeniable. The clues indicated the same group staged both crimes.

Interesting timing. Another coincidence?

Rhodes had spent the rest of the day at Steelton's home, inspecting every inch of furniture—dusting for clues and capturing fingerprints. When he completed his investigation of the premises, he made one final walk-through of the townhome. To his surprise, he'd found a secret door behind the wall in the master closet. The panel swung inward. A single light bulb hung from an exposed socket in the middle of the six-by-six darkly paneled room. An expensive Berber carpeting, similar to the floor covering in the master suite, covered the floor, and to the right, just inside the small storage area, a backpack hung on a metal peg.

Reaching for a fresh pair of rubber gloves, Rhodes unzipped the backpack. Someone had stuffed it full of unmarked bills. He felt around the inside edge. When he thought he had examined every inch and was about to remove his hand from the backpack, he discovered a small, thin piece of paper in the bottom corner. He carefully wiggled it loose. It was Mario Bernardi's business card—no cell phone. No address. No email. Only his name appeared in a heavy-block script: **Mario Bernardi**.

He stared at the card with disbelief. Benardi was the sole suspect in the 2014 murder case involving a prominent executive from the largest bank in New York's financial district.

THE EMPTY BEACH CHAIR

On the night of the murder, his car was seen parked around the corner from the home of the victim. The FBI intel suggested Bernadi had had secret dealings with the bank for years.

While affiliated with the NYPD, Rhodes was assigned to the murder case, working closely with the FBI to follow every lead in tracking down Bernardi. Rhodes' extensive knowledge of the case later led to his employment with the FBI.

Five years ago, an anonymous fax received by the FBI claimed Bernardi had fled to his homeland of Sicily, where he was possibly hiding in the mountains, with no sightings since the night of the murder. Bernardi's name appeared on the most prominent fugitive list of the FBI. Now suddenly, a card bearing his name had been recovered at a crime scene?

Bernardo was getting careless.

With flaring nostrils, he glared at the card. "You're back. Imagine. Your card, found in the home of another bank executive. We've got you now."

Later that night, while sitting at the office preparing a report for the case, he received a call from Lt. Parker. Natalie was missing. Parker's tone was composed and casual, like he thought Natalie might show up at any moment. He appeared to have the situation under control.

A few hours later, when the report was complete and he was adding a few finishing touches, Rhodes received a call from Rosemary. Nervous chatter, heavy breathing. "Natalie is missing." And an appeal for him to come to the island to head up a search.

"I'll be there as soon as I can," he said. How could he refuse? Especially when he'd already been assigned to go there.

As he ended the call, Rhodes closed his eyes, remembering back to his time at the NYPD, specifically the night he went to the theater to tell Natalie about her husband's accident. He vividly recalled the vision of her wearing a beautiful black dress and stiletto heels, her long brown hair seamlessly flowing onto her bare shoulders. He shook his head.

Natalie Neiman was in trouble. He couldn't ignore the parallels between the Steelton break-in and the vandalism at Natalie's former townhome. The similarities indirectly tied her to the Steelton case.

Did her presence on St. Simons Island tie her to the Rockwell case as well?

Rhodes texted Armstrong:

New development.

His cell phone rang. It was Armstrong. Rhodes had expected the call, but he thought it would come a few hours later.

Armstrong said in a raspy voice. "Did you send the report?"

"Yes, sir," Rhodes said. "It's in your inbox."

He heard the flick of the lighter. Then, a long draw from his cigarette. "What you got, Rhodes?"

Rhodes couldn't help but smile as his boss exhaled the smoke. He'd seldom seen the man without a cigarette in his hand.

Then Rhodes explained the details as he knew them.

"Damn," Armstrong said. "A new Rockwell development, another break-in at Steelton's, and now Natalie Nieman is missing. This is more than ironic. It has a bad smell to it. Get down to the coast ASAP, Rhodes. And keep me updated!"

Almost nine hundred miles between them, and he was drawn back to the island—back to Natalie.

Rhodes checked the airlines for a one-way ticket to the coast. No vacancies. All commercial flights to the coast were full. He called his friend, who owned a small plane and chartered trips.

"I need a favor. Can you fly me down to the Georgia coast this morning?"

The pilot chuckled. "If you don't mind flying with another client."

"I don't care. As long as you can get me there before daybreak."

Rhodes glanced at his watch. He had a little over an hour to catch the plane. He went to his apartment, changed clothes, and packed a few more items. When he got to the airstrip, a woman was boarding. The woman looked familiar, but Rhodes was so hurried that he didn't give her much thought. He reached inside his briefcase and retrieved a work file to review during the short flight.

Rhodes checked his bags with the pilot and then rushed up the steps. Much to his surprise, he recognized Tonya Rockwell sitting in the far seat. With a curious expression, he nodded and addressed her, "Mrs. Rockwell?"

"Good morning, Lieutenant Rhodes."

"Where are you going in the middle of the night?" Rhodes asked.

"St. Simons Island."

"Business or pleasure?"

"I'm on a mission to find this woman," Tonya reacted as she pulled a photo from her purse and gave it to Rhodes.

Rhodes looked at the picture. It was the one he had seen in the report. The photo showed a well-dressed woman entering the front door of the Alexandria townhome. It wasn't very clear, but the peripheral shot showed the woman's height and body type, along with a mane of curly, blonde hair and the wide headband that was the signature style of the woman who ran the senator's campaign.

Rhodes glanced at Tonya. "Do you know this woman?"

"Not personally, but she worked for Chad's senatorial campaign." Tonya pulled out a second picture of her husband and McKay on the night of his senatorial win...both broadly smiling and hands joined together in the air, and McKay's wide black headband holding back her blonde hair. They'd shown it on the news for days after Rockwell's death.

After he'd examined the second picture, Tonya continued, "According to our neighbor, she came to our townhome often and was there the day Chad was found dead in the garage."

"Which neighbor?"

"Gladys Kravitz, the widow next door. Poor thing has dementia. The only thing she really enjoys is taking pictures with her phone. Just random things, anything that catches her eye. And she loves to talk about her photos. Gives her something to talk about, I guess." She gave a little laugh. "Anyway, we were going through her pictures, and I was only half listening, when I saw this photo and the time/date stamp. For a minute, I couldn't breathe. Then I sent a copy to my cell, and... well, you know the rest."

He did. She'd hired two agents to find Alison McKay, and they'd ended up dead—in exactly the same way as her husband. He doubted she knew about that last part.

"But what are you doing here?" he asked.

"My private detective—"

"You hired a private detective?"

"Which I should have done in the first place. I should never have compromised those two agents. The guilt must have..." She looked away, "Anyway, my detective sent an update the day before yesterday. He found that Alison McKay was now going by Rosemary Delaney. He said she'd left the Chicago area after

Chad's death, and his firm had tracked her to St. Simons Island."

"That wasn't in the case file."

"I sent them the picture. That should have been enough to re-open the case. As for my private detective…" Mrs. Rockwell shrugged, "I'm the one paying him, which means that information is mine to deal with as I see fit. Of course, I plan to turn over the details once I'm sure it's accurate."

Rhodes let it go. "Has the investigator seen her on the island?"

She clicked on her phone and pulled up a picture. "Yes. Here she is working at Rosie's Diner. She's made a complete transformation in looks."

Alison McKay was the same Rosie he'd met at the diner. When he first met Rosie, he knew there was something familiar about her smile. Her hair was atrocious—grown-out gray roots and red ends. A wig. Makeup was so thick you could write your name on her face. Wow, he would have never put that one together.

Rhodes brought his attention back to Mrs. Rockwell. "So, you intend to approach her?"

Tonya nodded. "I want to ask her if Chad had been taking drugs while campaigning. She was with him on the campaign trail, and if anyone knew about his alleged drug use, it would be her."

Rhodes tapped the pictures on the back of his hand. Then he cocked his head to the left and asked, "Is that all?"

"I'd like to know what she was doing at our home on the day Chad died."

Tonya had left her little girl with her parents and taken a red eye on a chartered aircraft to pursue answers from McKay. She was one determined woman. Armstrong was right. She wanted to find out if her husband was having an affair with McKay, and she knew the only way to be sure was to go to St. Simons and look her in the eye. Woman's intuition: she'd know when she talked to her.

She hadn't shared her information because she didn't want the FBI to beat her to the punch.

He took a picture with his phone and then handed the photos back to Tonya. "Please text me that picture of Rosemary at the diner?"

"Sure."

Rhodes' thumbs moved across his keyboard. "Just forwarded those pictures to my boss, advised him of her name change, and told him you're on the same flight as me to St. Simons. Now, I must insist you let us take over from here."

"That's not gonna happen."

If this information was correct, Tonya Rockwell may have solved her husband's case. The recent development introduced a new twist, which he planned to investigate while on the island.

"Listen to me, Mrs. Rockwell, going after Rosemary Delaney without backup from the FBI could get you killed. You've got a daughter to raise."

"I know that..."

He gave her a severe look. "Well, this evidence adds a new twist to the case. I need your word that you won't contact Ms. Delaney without me."

Mrs. Rockwell looked away.

"Promise me, okay?"

She finally made eye contact with him and then nodded.

"Thank you," Rhodes said. He looked out the window of the plane. It spotlighted the white lighthouse that was in the distance. It was a comforting sight, like being welcomed back to the island. He had a lot of work to do once they landed.

There had been no phone service since he'd been on the plane. Rhodes had called his buddy at the Georgia Urban Search and Rescue Task Force on his way to the airport. The task force should be waiting for him at the docks.

Now that he had Mrs. Rockwell's promise, he could concentrate on finding Natalie.

When the Cessna 172 touched down at the McKinnon St. Simons Island Airport, Lieutenant Rhodes' cell phone showed 6:35 a.m. Normally, it would almost be daylight on the island, but the sky was gloomy with heavy cloud coverage—it was a perfect depiction of his mood. Despite having been awake for over twenty-four hours, his mind moved through various scenarios quickly.

He dressed in jeans, work shoes, and a black aeronautics jacket. Rhodes adjusted the aviator-style sunglasses perched on his nose and looked around the runway. He spotted the patrol car.

Parker flashed his headlights.

Rhodes reached back for his duffle bag and briefcase, closed the door, and saluted the pilot. He glanced over his shoulder when he heard the rackety sound of Tonya Rockwell's wheely suitcase as she pulled it behind her, going toward a long black limo. He had to admit, she traveled in style.

The plane's engine started, and the Cessna 172 taxied down the runway just as Rhodes opened the door to the patrol car.

"Good morning," Parker said. "That's a nice plane. Do you know the pilot?"

Rhodes threw the duffle in the back seat and climbed into the car. "Yep! He's a friend of mine."

After a few moments of exchanging information, Parker asked, "Where first?"

Rhodes explained he had already organized a search and rescue mission through Georgia's Urban Search and Rescue Task Force.

Parker absorbed the reality of organizing such an elaborate mission on such short notice. He drained the last of his coffee and said, "No questions for Jake Ellis right now?"

"Nope. I've got everything I need. We'll bring Ellis in once the hospital releases him."

"All right, then," Parker said.

Five minutes later, Parker steered onto a narrow sandy road adjacent to a lush green space covered in trees with long limbs draped in Spanish moss. A thick pole on which four colorful wooden signs faded from years of varying weather conditions pointed toward St. Simon's Marina.

Rhodes asked, "Is this the place Ellis stored his boat?"

"Yep. A guy by the name of Wilbanks called earlier to confirm." Cars were parked in every available space, leaving barely enough room for Parker to drive his patrol car down the tree-shaded, blacktop drive. Members of the task force were already organized and assembled. Outside the entrance to the office, next to the ice machine, was a picnic table with two flat boxes of donuts and a large container of coffee from Dulce Dough Donuts and Bakery. A fisherman was pouring a cup of steaming coffee into a Styrofoam cup.

Rhodes said, "Good deal. I gave him your number when I called to organize the search."

Parker pulled the car in front of a blue trash dumpster, above which hung an unassuming sign providing the hours of operation. The divers in their slick dark suits were assembled on one side near the three large boats while the other task force members huddled together on the nearby ramp.

The media had set up their cameras, and the reporters and their microphones were ready to record the day's events. Rhodes looked at Parker. "What are they doing here?"

Parker shrugged, "It's a small town—word spreads quicker than kudzu in a town of fifteen thousand."

As Rhodes walked closer, he spotted the mayor. Then a helicopter circled the tree-lined drive. When it landed, two members of the Georgia State Patrol jumped out, and then Bob Campbell, Georgia's governor, stepped onto the pavement. The press members made a mad dash for Governor Campbell, but to his credit, he waved them off, apparently not wanting to politicize the situation.

Rhodes grabbed a cup of coffee and stood ready to address the force when he received a text message. He glanced at his phone. It was the captain of the NYPD. The text message read:

I just received an anonymous tip about the abduction of John Steelton. We're awaiting the subsequent communication and DFM.

Demand for money?

Of course. When a corporate type was abducted, it was always about money.

Steelton was missing. Natalie was missing. Two intersecting cases, and now, Mario Bernardi's business card. It was an interesting triangle. The pieces of the puzzle were coming together—Rhodes pinched the bridge of his nose. Paul Neiman worked for John Steelton. *Well, I'll be damned!*

Rhodes looked around the marina at the dawn of a new day. No sleep and powered with soda and black coffee. *Barely seven hours into it, could this day get any worse?*

He immediately forwarded the text to his boss.

It had already been over eighteen hours since Jake returned home without Natalie. The overnight search, which he'd organized through the Brunswick precinct, had kept rescue personnel combing the island for four hours. They had found nothing. They were now loaded onto two patrol boats, with the search and rescue dogs, ready to search the island's periphery for anything that might have washed up on the shore overnight.

Rhodes stepped forward and raised his voice. "Good morning. Can everyone move in closer so you can hear the information we are about to discuss?"

The task force members were ready to get out onto the water, but they willingly moved closer. The press scooted behind Rhodes and Parker, extending their microphones high enough to pick up the sound of Rhodes's voice.

Rhodes turned to the press. "Do you people mind?" he said sharply. "Let's start this phase of the search, and then we'll give you guys a few moments for questions."

Members of the press group moved back a few feet, but there was rumbling among them.

Rhodes cleared his throat. "Good morning." He held up a blown-up picture of a woman. A member of the press flashed his light onto the image. Rhodes scowled at the journalist, then handed a stack of flyers to the man beside him, and said, "Pass these around."

While the picture circulated, he turned up his cup and finished the coffee. When he was certain each team member had at least looked at the picture, he said, "We have a forty-three-year-old female missing since yesterday. We now know that Dr. Natalie Nieman was last seen leaving her beachside cottage around 0900 on Wednesday morning. She was driving a red Porsche. Apparently, she and her friend Jake Ellis went out on Mr. Ellis' sailboat on Wednesday before noon, spent the night, and when he returned home yesterday afternoon, Dr. Nieman wasn't with him." Rhodes paused and looked at the faces of his team.

Someone from the back spoke up. "Is there any reason to suspect foul play?"

Rhodes lowered his Ray Bans and narrowed his eyes. "Who asked that question?"

The woman from the back raised her hand.

"There is no evidence at the moment to suggest Mr. Ellis was involved in any foul play."

There was mumbling amongst the gaggle of reporters, and someone else said, "It's a fair question, considering Mr. Ellis returned and Dr. Nieman did not."

Rhodes nodded. "It is a fair question. As you know, missing children are almost always assumed to be victims of foul play, but it's different with adults. In this case, because we know extenuating circumstances, we'll treat it as an abduction from the beginning."

There was more rumbling among the press.

Rhodes removed his reading glasses from his pocket. "Let me be clear: St. Simons is a relatively small island, and no one has seen or heard from Natalie… I mean Dr. Nieman… since Wednesday morning. While we have to prepare for any eventuality, we are praying that Dr. Nieman is found alive and unharmed. Now, I'll turn this over to Mr. Wilbanks with the Georgia Urban Search and Rescue Task Force for instructions on how to proceed."

Chapter Forty-Five

Natalie

The fire department at St. Simons was the main source of emergency services on the island. A fire station was located less than a mile from the clinic, which meant a safe haven was well within walking distance. After the uncertainty of being held captive in the hull of the boat, the familiar sound of the ambulance provided a source of comfort.

When Natalie woke, she immediately knew they had moved her. There was some sort of cloth around her head—a blindfold—and instead of the cot, she lay on a thin mattress. The smells of fresh wood and car grease replaced the stench of dead fish and stale cigarette smoke. Maybe an auto repair shop, or possibly, a home improvement warehouse? The continuous motion had ceased, exchanged for the distant honking of car horns, squeaking brakes, and the shrill wail of a siren.

Her feet and hands were bound, but her captors had left just enough leeway to negotiate the face covering.

Grateful for their carelessness, Natalie reached for the cloth around her head and pulled it below her eyes. The room was dark—pitch dark. But somehow, the darkness wasn't as frightening as being on the water. She had taken swimming lessons as a kid but wasn't a strong swimmer. At least now, she was on solid ground, and if she could get free of her bondage and escape the confines of the building, she'd run like hell.

And she *could* run. She was a distance runner in high school and continued her running routine to help reduce the stress of her job.

She fumbled with the knots and strained against the ropes until, trembling with exertion, she collapsed back onto the mattress. Whatever drug they'd given her, it was still wreaking havoc on her system. Her eyelids felt heavy. The familiar noises from traffic soothed her mind and tugged her toward sleep.

No. Paul's voice cut through the fog. *Natty, you've got to get out of here.*

The voice sounded urgent, but very far away. She'd try again soon, she promised it. She just needed to close her eyes for a few minutes. Another warning sounded in her mind—*The blindfold, Natty!*—and before she slipped back into unconsciousness, she summoned enough strength to push the cloth back into place.

A noise awakened her. The sun was up, and she was extremely thirsty. The effects of the drug had lessened, and she felt stronger than she had the last time she'd awakened. Natalie knew the lack of water was a danger. Food she could do without, but without adequate water, she would become dehydrated. After that would come the potential threat of organ failure, seizures, and possibly even death.

She lifted the rag just above her eyes. When her eyes adjusted, she saw a humble space. The air was damp and dusty, the gray cinder block walls unadorned. Perhaps it had once been a garage or a storage building, but not much more. There was a small cooler in the corner sitting on a small crate and several boxes stacked against the far side of the wall. A hook on the back of the door held a piece of clothing.

Natalie sensed someone else nearby. Her gaze swept the room, and then she saw a man, bound and blindfolded in the corner diagonally from where she lay. He looked to be in his early sixties, partially clad. His dark gray slacks looked like they belonged to an expensive suit. He wore black dress shoes and no shirt—only a stained undershirt, with circles of sweat under his armpits. Judging from his posture, he appeared to be drugged. Natalie shimmied up from the floor pallet and shuffled over to him.

"I'm...Natalie." She was breathless from the additional challenge of moving across the room with both her hands and feet constrained. Looking him over, she wondered if this stranger, who was also captive, posed any threat to her. The same person must have tied him, because they'd left the same leeway in his rope. She leaned forward and loosened the man's blindfold—just enough that he could lift it back into place when they heard the captors' approach.

When she finished adjusting the blindfold, he turned toward her. His eyes were wild and bloodshot. He looked vaguely familiar. Not a patient—she would have remembered that—but perhaps someone she'd seen in passing on the island.

"I'm... John." That was all she could get out of him. Finally, his eyes rolled back in his head, and he passed out again. She gently covered his eyes with the cloth.

As John slept, she removed the knot from the rope, wrapped tightly around her ankles. It was somewhat of a challenge, but finally, she created enough play to slip it off. Then, she removed the rope from her wrists.

A while later, John awoke and was still rather groggy. Curious and concerned, Natalie inquired about his physical condition, "Are you feeling any better?"

THE EMPTY BEACH CHAIR

At first, he was too disoriented to respond, and Natalie did not want to agitate him. She spotted a cooler in the corner of the room and reached in to grab a bottle of water. "Here," she said as she loosened the bottle cap. "You'd better drink this. I don't know how long you've been without food, but you can't live without water."

He took the bottle and turned it up. After drinking half of the liquid, he lay back on his pallet, turned toward the wall, and quickly drifted off to sleep. Natalie watched his chest move with each breath, and as soon as she was satisfied he was resting peacefully, she fell back into a slumber.

John's movement awakened Natalie. He seemed more alert as the drugs wore off, and he managed to sit up. Then he slid against the wall and sat with his head in his hands. Finally, he said, "I'm baffled." He paused and rubbed his head. Then he continued. "You look familiar. Who are you?"

"I'm Natalie Nieman."

John's expression changed when he heard Natalie's name.

"Any relation to Paul Nieman?"

The question startled Natalie. "How do you know Paul?"

"I'm John Steelton."

John Steelton! John Steelton was the vice president Paul had worked with the year before his accident. He'd been to their house on one occasion—before their New Year's Eve party. No wonder he looked familiar. But he looked different now, rumpled and wan, shrunken by fear and confusion.

Natalie knew she wasn't supposed to know anything about the account, but she asked anyway. "Why did you ask Paul to work with you on that account?"

Seeming to ignore her question, John rested his head against the wall and let a few minutes pass. Then he finished the bottle of water and cleared his throat. "Paul Nieman... he was a good guy." He paused again. "Whatever happened to his Porsche?"

As far as Natalie could remember, Paul had never socialized with Steelton outside the conference room that adjoined his office. That one New Year's Eve visit didn't count, not really. He had shown up an hour before the party started. Paul had taken him on a tour of their home, and then they had a drink in the library.

Otherwise, they had regular daily meetings, on the fourth floor. Paul even took a separate elevator up to the 'ivory tower.' An elevator only Steelton and the president of the bank used. Paul had described the process to her. Paul would take the steps down to the lobby and take the service elevator to the underground parking deck reserved for VIP members. From there, he walked inside a room disguised as a trash closet. It had a trash closet sign posted on the door, and the door required a specific code to enter. Paul's code, his driver's license number, was unique to him, so security knew when he was coming or going and if he used the access lift other than to meet with Steelton. It was very secretive and high-tech. Rich mahogany wood covered the disguised panels and brushed pewter covered the ceiling, the same as with the floor designator panel displayed on the wall next to the door. The panel had two buttons: one for up and another for down. It was simple.

Paul had even told her of a time he'd stopped by the management men's room on the fourth floor of the building before taking the elevator back to his office. While Paul was washing his hands, Steelton walked in, looked at him, and never said a word. They had just finished a two-hour meeting, and Steelton looked straight through Paul as if he'd never seen him before.

Natalie was confused about why or how Steelton would have any knowledge about Paul's car. As far as she knew, his and Paul's conversations were strictly limited to "the Boss."

Natalie didn't answer Steelton immediately. Then she remembered Paul telling her he'd let Steelton borrow his car to take "the Boss" to lunch one day. She had gotten furious because Paul had never let her drive his car. They had a massive argument about it.

Could Steelton be responsible for Paul's death?

The thought made her stomach clench, but she had no time to think about that now. Instead, she worked at loosening his knots and thought about the conversation between the men on the boat. She too had been drugged, but she was sure Steelton had not been on the boat at the same time as she. Pretty sure. If he was, they'd locked him in another area. His voice differed significantly from any of the men she'd overheard. One guy sounded more polished, but he had a mid-western dialect. The other one had spoken broken English in rapid fire, and she had to strain to understand what he was saying. In contrast, Steelton enunciated each word perfectly. His speech was soft and polished, with a refined southern accent.

Steelton got up and walked around the room, his movements stiff after his long confinement. The marks on his wrists were fresh and red. He walked closer and looked down at her like he was trying to memorize her face. Then he turned and walked back to his pallet.

"I'm not sure how much Paul told you about the account we worked on together," he said as he sat back down and leaned against the wall. "But you should understand it was a top-secret operation."

His voice increased an octave. "As the VP of global sales, I needed someone with Paul's intellect. The first thing I noticed about Paul when we interviewed him was his ability to adapt to different situations." Steelton paused, out of breath from talking so fast.

After a few moments, he continued, "Paul understood people, and he read body language well. He could also get on a personal level with individuals quickly. The account we worked on involved a client from a different culture than ours, and the first time Paul met the guy, they immediately connected."

He paused, dropped his head, and looked at the floor between his knees. "It was our largest account, and I needed someone with nerves of steel and a positive outlook. Someone who wouldn't back down from a situation."

Now, Natalie and Paul's conversations about "the Boss" were coming back to her. Her memories flooded back, leaving her torn about trusting the man who may—or may not—have killed her husband.

However, one thing was certain: her husband had been privy to far more information about the client than Natalie had been told.

She was uncomfortable but remained quiet. One thing Natalie had learned about being in stressful situations was that she needed to keep her mouth shut and her ears open.

Finally, Steelton said, "These people—our client—hid a large sum of money in Paul's Porsche." He looked at her and waited for a response. When she didn't give him one, he continued, "Maybe our client asked Paul to hide the money in his car. Or maybe he had someone hide it for him the day we drove the Porsche to lunch. I'm not sure... but they are looking for the car to retrieve the money." He paused again, short of breath. "Someone working for our client kidnapped me and brought me here." Steelton's hands were outstretched. "Wherever this is," he looked around the room, "he's hoping to find Paul's car."

Steelton removed his handkerchief and blew his nose, then stuffed it back in his pocket and added, "The only trouble is—I didn't know if you kept Paul's car after he passed."

Steelton coughed. Then he rubbed his chest. "I seem to recall it is red, but isn't it also a convertible?" His cough persisted.

"Sir, have you had that cough long?"

Sir? Why did I just call him sir?

"It only happens when I'm under a lot of stress. I've got high blood pressure and congestive heart failure. They diagnosed it not long after Paul... after Paul's accident. But I'm fine, really."

"Are you on medication to control your blood pressure?"

He nodded.

"How long have you been without your meds?"

With a grim smile, Steelton said, "Too long."

Just like that, John Steelton was no longer Paul's boss or a powerful businessman with a possibly shady past, or even a man who might know who was behind her husband's death. He was just a man with health issues. It had always been that way for Natalie. She was, first and foremost, a woman of medicine. Whatever else he was, she saw him as a patient now—a human being—in need of medical attention.

Natalie walked over to John and knelt. "Do you mind if I try something?"

He cut his eyes at her, obviously agitated and suspicious.

Natalie spoke in a soft voice, just above a whisper. "It won't hurt, I promise. This is a proven method to lower your pressure." She reached for his hand.

Reluctantly, he placed it on hers.

His hand was large, tanned, smooth, and well-defined. Finally, he relaxed, and Natalie placed her thumb on the webbing between his index finger and thumb. She pressed the area... stopped, then pressed again. She did three sessions, got up from her knees, and walked to her pallet.

By the time she sat down, Steelton said, "Wow! I feel better already. My headache is almost gone, and the heavy sensation in my chest is no longer there."

Natalie told him to tell her if the heaviness in his chest returned. Every nerve in her body told her to get out, get out *now*, but John still seemed weak. He would need some time to recover before they could make a move.

John walked over to the window. "Do you know where we are?"

"St. Simons Island." She hesitated, then said, "Did you and Paul know each other well?"

It took some time to draw him out, but eventually, perhaps because of their shared predicament, he opened up. She learned Paul had served as the intermediary to receive packages delivered by the Mob. The latest package was scheduled for delivery on the afternoon of her fifth anniversary. It was a large sum of money packed inside a backpack that had never been found. As John explained his need to find the backpack, Natalie realized Steelton had used Paul as his point man. Her husband was not directly working for the Mob, and neither was the delivery boy who had died in the emergency room the night of the accident. He, too, was an intermediary, or perhaps, he worked for a courier service. Courier services were popular in New York City.

The question was, how much had Paul known—or suspected—about the nature of his job?

As John looked out the window, he mumbled, "I should've known better than to risk the reputation of the firm on this deal, regardless of the exorbitant profits involved." After a while, Steelton looked around, found a steel crate, and slid it under the window. It was just the right height for him to peek outside. He turned around and said, "What do you say we break out of here and find a safe place to hide?"

Natalie walked over to the window. "What do you suggest?"

"Isn't there a deserted lighthouse here?" He stepped down from the crate. "I saw the top of it just beyond those trees. That would be a better hiding place until we figure out what to do."

"Yes. There is a lighthouse here."

Steelton looked around the garage. "We need to find you something to wear." He chuckled, "A woman running through the woods in a swim suit and sarong would attract too much attention."

Natalie started rummaging through boxes, looking for an old shirt or pair of pants. Then, she looked at the hook on the door and saw a mechanic's jumpsuit. Since it was short-sleeved, the heat wouldn't be too intense. She tried it on. The pants were too long. She searched through the mechanic's tools and found a pair of scissors. Natalie held the jumpsuit up to her body to determine where to cut off the remaining fabric of the hem.

Steelton was busy looking through boxes of tools. He tried several tools to remove the lock from the door before he finally found one that worked. The lock snapped, and Steelton carefully removed it. Then he cracked the door open and poked his head outside. When he came back in and saw Natalie, he shook his head. "That's perfect! If you can tie your hair up and put on one of those baseball caps, no one should recognize you."

Ignoring his stare, Natalie zipped the jumpsuit, reached for a rope, and tied it around her waist, hoping for a modern, industrial-chic look.

Steelton skimmed the outfit with an appreciative gaze. "All you need is a colorful scarf and a pair of shades, and you could pass as a tourist!"

With the lock removed, Natalie noticed Steelton had become more relaxed, but her anxiety only intensified as she contemplated escaping, resulting in nervous chatter. "I once hiked Cannon's Point Preserve." She said. "It has an elevation gain of 42 feet, the highest of all the trails on the island."

"I've had my share of hiking experiences, too." He turned to her and chuckled. The first real laugh she'd seen from Steelton. "At the time, I had a good pair of hiking shoes. Not like these." He said, pointing to his expensive Italian loafers.

Natalie liked the fact that Steelton was trying to diffuse the tension with humor. Paul would have done the same had he been in a similar situation. She turned and opened a tool drawer, found a large rubber band, and tied her long hair into a messy bun.

Steelton handed her the baseball cap. As she secured her hair inside the cap, Steelton reached and turned up the collar on her jumpsuit. "This way, you'll be further disguised." He stepped back and looked at her approvingly, "Perfect."

It was exactly like a father would do for a child, particularly for a daughter. There was something in his gesture that endeared him to her and gave her the confidence to trust him as they sought an escape from the dilapidated building. A few minutes had passed. It was hard to gauge without a watch, but it wasn't long. Finally, Steelton walked toward the window and peeped out.

"I don't see anyone. The area seems quiet." He stepped down from the metal crate and looked at Natalie. "Are those flip-flops all you've got to wear?"

She nodded.

"Okay. It'll slow us down a bit. Just let me know when you need to rest."

Steelton opened the door and stepped outside. He looked around the building. Nothing…no one. He motioned for Natalie.

When she got outside, they walked toward the lighthouse. Natalie followed his lead. Her mind raced in ten different directions. Then an idea struck her so hard it banished every other thought. The woman riding in the taxi with Paul on the way to the theater might know something about the cash. Paul never met a stranger. It would be like him to jump into the taxi and start rattling on about the reason he was late. Why had Natalie been afraid to talk to her that night at the hospital?

She didn't even know the woman's name.

Why didn't I walk across the emergency room and find out?

She remembered reading the headline of the local paper the following morning. Paul had been named in the article and so had the courier. Both had died at the hospital, but there was no mention of the lady in the car. Natalie had thought that odd at the time, but considering the woman didn't have proper identification when she was admitted to the hospital, Natalie had dismissed it. Now, however, in retrospect, it looked like the mystery woman may have been someone famous or well-known, and the authorities were trying to keep her name out of the limelight.

Prominent people and famous celebrities were like that— they'd pay large sums of money to keep their names out of the papers. Perhaps she was a politician's wife or someone's mistress.

Natalie knew she was just surmising now. How many times had they discussed similar scenarios in staff meetings? Each patient had an identity, and it was the responsibility of medical professionals to match the identity to the proper person. Any time a new staff member came on board, the new employee usually took a few days to acclimate. Almost always, these types of errors happened during frantic, short-staffed nights, and also when a patient came in by ambulance without a family member present.

This was what had happened the night of Paul's accident. An influx of patients, a short-staffed shift, a new hire, the head of the department off duty, and the assistant department head leaving the hospital because he'd surpassed the legal requirement of hours worked.

A perfect storm!

Chapter Forty-Six

The Chase

By now, traffic was moving along the primary thoroughfare. When Natalie and Steelton reached the business park on Mallery Street, several cars were already in the parking spaces, but the businesses were closed.

He looked down and noticed Natalie's bleeding foot. "Let's slow down," Steelton said as he caught his breath. "Your foot's bleeding."

Steelton took her arm and led her to a nearby concrete picnic table outside a burger joint. It was where the old Dairy Queen had been in years past. He remembered it from a trip he and his wife had taken decades ago.

No one was in the parking lot. The establishment was yet to open.

"Let's sit for a moment." The table was in the back of the building, surrounded by large trees, and farther behind was a wooded area.

As he sat, he felt something hard in his pocket. He reached inside and found his cell. Steelton remembered turning the phone off. "Holy crap, I would have thought my captors would have confiscated my phone."

He turned it on and looked at the face. Steelton had two text messages from unrecognizable numbers. He pressed the first text and read the cryptic message: **Call me when you get this!**

The second text mentioned the break-in at his New York home. He knew then it was some branch of law enforcement.

As if someone was watching his usage, a third text appeared from the same number. The message only contained his name and a single question mark.

Steelton's response was short: **Lighthouse SSI**.

He showed the text to Natalie.

She grinned. "Leave the phone on so they can track us."

Steelton nodded, despite his reservations. "Are you sure they can track us with this thing?"

"What version is it?"

Steelton shrugged.

"Here." Natalie reached for the phone. "I'll check for you." She pushed a few buttons and grinned again. "Yes, they can track us."

A helicopter came into view in the distance, but the closer it got, the lower it flew. A voice came over a loudspeaker. "Steelton, we've found you. Stop where you are. Put your arms over your head."

That voice, he would have recognized it anywhere. Mario Bernardi's voice sounded like no other in the world. He had a strong Sicilian accent and pronounced Steelton with one short 'e' rather than two.

But how had he found them so quickly?

Steelton closed his hand on Natalie's arm. "Can you run with those flip-flops on?"

"Yes, sir! I can run."

"Good, follow me."

They plunged deep into the woods. The helicopter hovered overhead. Finally, Steelton took a gamble and ran into The Village area, through the parking lot, and over to the front of the large brick structure at St. Simons Casino Building. He was certain someone would be there to help them, but as they ran through the courtyard of the library that connected the two buildings, there was no one to be seen. He went from door to door. No one...not even the cleaning crew was there yet. Breathless and with pains in his chest, he quickly went to the other side. There were brick steps, a green space, and then the vast body of water. Steelton stumbled to a stop, panicking at the sudden appearance of the Atlantic Ocean.

Natalie raced past him. "This way...," she said. She ran down the steps toward the playground at Neptune Park, ducking behind bushes and trees. There was no way he could keep up with her.

Maybe it was for the best. At least one of them might get away and find help.

Steelton hurried down the steps and started toward the park. He stumbled, lightheaded. A quick downward glance showed an untied shoelace. No time to stop. They were already encircling him. He caught a glimpse of Natalie in his peripheral vision; she had stepped behind a fallen tree and disappeared under twigs and brush.

Good girl!

Bernardi took a step forward. "Why did you tell the girl about us?" he demanded. "And don't you dare lie to me!"

Steelton knew then they had bugged him. He felt around his body and saw the tiny, purple, pin-like instrument on the sole of his shoe. Damn, he should have known.

Bernardi leveled a pistol at Steelton's chest. "No more funny business. Now, where did you hide the cash?"

He knew if he answered, he'd be of no further use. Before he could gather his thoughts, Bernardi backhanded him with the pistol. Steelton staggered backward, head reeling, and landed hard on the ground.

"I asked you a question, Steelton. Where did you hide the money?"

The second guy darted in, swinging a leather strap.

The sting of the strap on his bare skin took Steelton's breath away. With only an undershirt on, each blow felt like a hot branding iron. Steelton clamped his teeth together and tried not to cry out. He was almost unconscious.

Bernardi yanked Steelton's head up by the hair and leaned in close. "It would be a shame if we had to get our answers from the girl."

"In the Porsche," Steelton gasped. "Inside the door panels."

Bernardi asked one last question. "Where is the car?"

Steelton's eyes fluttered open and then closed. Where *was* the car? His mind aswirl with pain and panic, he flailed for an answer that floated just beyond his grasp.

It was the last opportunity he would get. The man raised his gun. Steelton heard a boom like thunder. Then, blackness engulfed him.

Natalie hid her eyes when she saw the leather strap. *Oh, John.*

When she heard the gunshot in the distance, she risked a peek through the twigs. Natalie watched as one of the kidnappers dragged Steelton to the water's edge, dropped him onto the large 'Johnson rocks', and began to weigh his body down.

She looked around as if seeing the landscape for the first time. She had to find cover before they did the same to her. As they dragged John deeper into the water, Natalie started digging a shallow trench to lie in. The ground was hard, and she'd barely made an indentation in the earth when the men turned back to shore. Natalie pulled the fallen limb across herself and tugged more twigs and brushes into the gaps between the branches.

As she shimmied into the shallow grave, she forced her breaths into a slow, gentle rhythm. She couldn't afford to let her breathing move the branches up and down.

With their task complete, the kidnappers returned and scanned the area looking for her.

Her pulse pounded so loudly in her ears, it seemed the kidnappers would hear it. She couldn't believe those men had shot John. He was trying to answer. Trying the very best he could…a terrified man with congestive heart failure and high blood pressure. Not that the kidnappers would have known all that, but even if they had, Natalie doubted it mattered to them.

They drew nearer, scanning the area. Natalie barely breathed as they stomped around her hiding place.

After what felt like hours, the Sicilian said, "She got away, but she couldn't have gone too far on foot."

"What do we do now? We still don't know where to find the car."

"Let's take the chopper up and scan the area."

The helicopter was facing the other direction, its rotors still.

Natalie watched the two men walk toward the chopper. When she guessed they were out of earshot, she crawled out of her trench and scooted on the ground until she reached the gazebo at the back of the lighthouse. A conversation she'd had with Jake popped into her mind. She remembered it verbatim—something she'd trained her mind to do in medical school—and she focused on it now, to keep at bay her fear of being caught.

"President Johnson came here in 1964," Jake had said, "after Hurricane Dora hit the island. He approved federal funding to protect the island's shoreline." The seawall, composed of massive granite rocks, stopped the erosion around the island and added a certain aesthetic beauty to the otherwise bland shoreline.

Jake's voice, even in her memory, calmed her and cleared her mind. Was there something he'd said about the lighthouse she could use to her advantage?

Waiting to hear the chopper start, she waited to catch her breath for a second. Then she ducked down, went around the side of the lighthouse, and checked one of the back doors. The knob turned, and she let out a relieved breath. It was a heavy metal door. She pulled hard and stuck her knee in front of the entrance to gain traction. The door finally opened, and she went inside and waited.

She heard the chopper fly away from her, circle back around, and then grow closer. The white paint made the cinder block walls look almost sterile. She thought of Jake, recalling the story he had told her the day they went out on the boat. It seemed like eons ago, but it was only two or maybe three days earlier.

She'd lost count.

Blood was oozing from the enormous blister on her right foot. The helicopter was directly above the lighthouse. She jumped when they said her name over the loudspeaker. It was loud, almost too loud to understand. She could hear the wind whirling overhead as the chopper hovered in the air. Natalie prayed Paul would whisper something in her ear. Tell her what to do and where to go.

There was only silence.

Natalie found the steps to the lighthouse and started to climb. She looked back and noticed she was leaving a trail of blood behind. Looking at the bottom of her pants, she tore a strip of fabric and wrapped it around her foot to stop the bleeding. The chopper moved away, just as she made the final tuck into the fabric. As she continued to climb the stairs, she could still hear the faraway sound of the rotors.

"Oh, Paul! Where are you, sweetheart? I need your help!"

Chapter Forty-Seven

Rhodes and Jake

The early morning search produced nothing. Boats and choppers were all over the water surrounding St. Simons Island, and there were no signs of Natalie. There were no signs of the boat Jake and Natalie had stopped to help, either.

Finally, after searching all day and night, Rhodes returned to the marina to get coffee and biscuits for the task force.

When they approached the first buoy, which slowed the speed to five miles per hour, Rhodes saw Jake standing on the ramp looking in a boat. It was white with a green stripe on the side.

Jake didn't hear Rhodes approach.

"Hi, Jake. Are you feeling better?"

"Yes, thanks." Jake extended his hand. The spot where they'd hit him on the head was still covered with a piece of gauze. He pointed to the boat. "This is the boat I was telling Parker about, the one where the woman flagged us down, and we went to offer help."

The boat's identifying number was also the same: GA1040. It was a simple number that anyone would remember.

There was a ping on Rhodes's phone. He read the text and looked up. "Grab yourself a cup of coffee and a biscuit from the table. You can ride with me."

"Where are we going?"

"A text just came back from Steelton." He showed his phone to Jake. ***Lighthouse. SSI.***

"Who the hell is Steelton?" Jake asked. Then, trailing behind Rhodes: "Should we let someone know where we're going?"

Agent Rhodes jumped into the patrol car. The keys were still in the ignition. "I'll text Parker. He can send backup when he frees up a team." He tapped a quick message and tucked his phone into his pocket. "This may change the trajectory of our search."

Jake jumped inside, balancing his coffee and biscuit while shutting the door. "What do you mean?"

Rhodes looked at Jake while cranking the patrol car. "First, it seems they brought the boat back to the marina overnight. Second, it appears Steelton is at the lighthouse. I need to check it out. Hang on to that coffee, Jake. I have a feeling that we're about to bust open this case."

"Who is Steelton?" Jake asked again. "Bring me up to speed."

"I've been texting John Steelton, the guy Natalie's husband worked for in New York. He finally got back to me. When I asked him where he was, he texted back, *Lighthouse SSI*."

Rhodes told Jake about the break-in at Steelton's New York home and how similar it was to the break-in at Natalie's condo. Then, he'd received word that someone had abducted Steelton.

Jake thought about it for a few minutes. Then he told Rhodes about finding the cash in the door panels of Natalie's car. "Could that have anything to do with their looking for Natalie and Steelton?"

"Very possibly."

After a moment, Jake said, "Natalie and I took her car to the shop in Brunswick the morning we went out on the water."

Rhodes pondered the information. "Okay," he said. "When we find Steelton, you will take off to Brunswick to get her car, or at least look for the cash. But we've got to find Steelton first. When we find him, we'll probably learn more about Natalie."

Rhodes pulled the patrol car into the empty parking lot. It was far enough away from the lighthouse to be noticed. They went up the steps in front of the library, through the courtyard between the two buildings, and down the steps on the ocean side. They immediately went to the left, toward the lighthouse. No one was around when Officer Rhodes and Jake came to the deserted lighthouse.

The door at the front was locked. Rhodes and Jake repeatedly beat on it, but no one answered. A sign by the door showed the hours of operation as 10-5 on weekdays and 12-5 on Sundays. One older couple was walking their dog in the distance toward the pier. Other than that, the area around the lighthouse was deserted…until they heard the helicopter in the distance.

It was closing in fast.

Jake said, "Let's go around to the side. I remember a door there. Maybe it was left unlocked. Otherwise, we'll have to wait until they open the building at ten o'clock."

Rhodes shook his head. Steelton must be around here somewhere. If not inside the lighthouse, then where?

The helicopter was getting closer. Someone was talking on the loudspeaker.

Jake said, "They're saying Natalie's name. Did you hear that?"

"Stay down," Rhodes said. "And walk close to the building."

Jake didn't wait to hear more. He edged around the side of the lighthouse and pulled on the door. It was heavy, but he jerked it open and walked inside.

He walked around inside, following the trail of blood. There was nowhere to go but up. Jake took two steps at a time until he'd almost reached the top of the lighthouse. When he took the final curve of the stairway, he saw Natalie sitting on the top step and slumped over. She was shivering, whether from cold or fear, he couldn't tell.

He wanted to rush up the stairs and put his arms around her, but if she'd been traumatized, that might only make matters worse.

Then Natalie turned, and their eyes met. At the profound look of relief on her face, Jake let out a breath. He had found her. After two full days of isolation in the hospital, and a twenty-four-hour manhunt, he'd finally found her.

She blinked, almost in disbelief that it really was Jake. Then she jumped up and rushed into his arms. "What happened to your head?" she mumbled into his chest. Then she pulled away and cupped his face with her hands. "Oh, my god! You found me! Jake, I was so worried about you!"

"Of course, I found you!" Jake laughed with relief. He held her close for a few minutes. Finally, he stepped back, searching her face for scrapes and bruises. "Are you okay?"

Natalie nodded.

Now that he had found her, he could have stayed in the lighthouse, protected by the concrete walls and the spiral cast-iron staircase, forever. Instead, Jake gave her one last hug and said, "Let's get you out of here."

When Jake opened the door, Rhodes was on the ground, lying on his back next to the building. Jake started toward him, but Rhodes motioned for them to stay inside. As soon as Jake closed the door, he heard gunfire. A bullet hit the pavement, going up to the side door of the lighthouse. Jake and Natalie both jumped and went back to the steps to get away from the only window in that part of the building.

As they huddled on the safest place on the steps, another round of gunfire struck the lighthouse walls, followed by a crash that could only be a helicopter plunging to the ground. One of Rhodes's bullets must have hit the pilot—or some vital part of the chopper.

Rhodes peeped around the building as Mario Bernardi exited the helicopter. The pilot was slumped over the instrument panel. He was pretty sure no one else was on board.

Bernardi looked much taller than the picture in the file showed. He'd aged in the decade since the photo was taken, but besides the facial lines and a few silver streaks in his hair, he looked the same.

A few minutes later, a door slammed shut, and Rhodes yelled, "FBI. Stop! You're under arrest!"

Bernardi fired his pistol, and a sharp pain shot through Rhodes's left shoulder. It felt like the bullet had shredded his rotator cuff. He couldn't lift his arm beyond his chest. Blood trickled down his shirt, but not too much. He could tend to it later. For now, he had a job to finish.

Rhodes crept around the back of the lighthouse while gripping his injured shoulder and staying close to the ground. He removed the belt from around his waist, made a makeshift sling, and settled in to wait. His pulse evened and slowed, and finally, Bernardi came around the lighthouse.

Rhodes shot him center mass. Bernardi fell, and his pistol skittered across the concrete walkway. Rhodes stepped on the gun and rolled Bernardi onto his stomach, wincing as another wave of pain pulsed through his shoulder. Then he yanked Bernardi's hands behind his back and slapped on the cuffs.

"You're trapped, Bernardi! After ten long years of running, how does it feel now?" Rhodes rolled him back over and checked the bullet entry. A through-and-through. Not much blood. Bernardi would live to stand trial. Smiling, Rhodes tugged his spare cuffs off his belt and struggled to secure a glowering Bernardi to the handicapped rails.

It had taken a decade to get it done, thought Rhodes. But we finally got him.

He stepped away from Bernardi and took a few minutes to catch his breath and let the pain in his shoulder subside. When it had eased to a dull throb, he went inside the lighthouse. He was standing at the bottom of the steps, holding his shoulder, when Natalie and Jake came down the stairs. He felt a twinge of jealousy as he watched Jake holding on to Natalie; it was like they were one body.

Finally, Rhodes said to Natalie, "I can't believe Steelton's text brought us to you! What are the odds of that happening?"

"Were you hit in the shoulder?" Natalie asked.

"Yes," Rhodes said. "Did you know Steelton? Had you ever met him?"

Natalie teared up and said, "Yes. Once. He came to our townhome." She wiped her eyes. "Steelton didn't make it. They shot him and dragged his body over those rocks." She pointed toward the pier. "Then they dropped him into the ocean."

"That's the price he paid for getting in bed with the Mob," Rhodes said. At her gasp, he softened his tone. "I've dispatched a couple of ambulances. They'll be here in a moment. I've got

Mario Bernardi handcuffed to the handrails outside. The bureau has been trying to get him for years." He looked down and pointed at Natalie's bleeding foot. "What happened there?"

"It's a long story," Natalie said, gripping Jake's arm even tighter.

Chapter Forty-Eight

Tonya Rockwell

Tonya was on the island for over twenty-four hours before leaving her suite at the resort. She had honored Agent Rhodes's request to let the FBI handle the case. Now that she had been there for a full day and hadn't heard from him, she decided it was time to get to work. She missed her daughter. The sooner she uncovered the truth, the quicker she could return to everyday life…if there was such normalcy for a thirty-two-year-old widow with a toddler.

Room service had just delivered another meal and a carafe of steaming coffee. Tonya poured a cup and went out onto the porch. The sky was a beautiful shade of blue, and a few clouds wisped across the horizon. It should have been a relaxing scene, but its placid beauty only made her feel more restless. Her body thrummed like an overcharged battery. Tapping her fingers on the railing, she waited for the fresh brew to cool. The first sip scalded her tongue anyway, and she set the mug down with a frustrated sigh. She couldn't stand the thought of staying inside the hotel room for one more day.

Boredom was driving her crazy, similar to the anxiety she experienced when learning about Alison's frequent visits to their condo. She revisited in her mind the earlier conversation with Agent Rhodes. She'd been chatting with her elderly neighbor, Mrs. Kravitz, who delighted in sharing the pictures she'd taken on her phone. They'd scrolled through several hundred photos when they came across the one of Alison in front of the townhouse owned by her husband.

The lady might be eccentric, but the photograph was the very proof for which Tonya had been searching. The time/date stamp put Alison there on the day Chad died.

Game over.

At that moment, Tonya's suspicions were validated. When she returned to her condo, she called the medical examiner's office and asked if he had time to meet with her. She had a few questions about her husband's death certificate and asked him to retrieve a copy of the autopsy report before her arrival.

Tonya's father-in-law had refused to accept that his son had committed suicide. As soon as he learned of his son's death, Mr. Rockwell called an old friend from the D.C. Circuit, and when the official announcement was released, it stated that Senator Chadwick Rockwell had died of cardiac arrest. When the death certificate arrived, it listed cardiac arrest due to natural causes.

At first, Tonya had reluctantly accepted the FBI's explanation of her husband's suicide. The medical examiner's cover story spared both her and Chad's family weeks of unrelenting media attention—and it had also saved Chad's sterling reputation.

But as time went on, she began to have more and more misgivings. What reasons could Chad have for killing himself? He had been elected Illinois junior senator; he was a bright political prospect and dedicated family man. His political career was in its infancy.

The medical examiner worked out of a cramped office in the basement of the northern regional area. A dozen half-filled coffee cups sat on his desk surrounded by piles of manila folders. He stood when Tonya walked in and held out a folder with her husband's name typed neatly on the label.

"Are you sure you want to see all this?" he asked, a pitying look in his eye. "I'm afraid you might find it painful."

"I'm sure," she said. She took the seat across from him and opened the folder.

When she'd turned the last page, she looked up at him. "What does it mean that the amount of fentanyl found in Chad's bloodstream registered over three milligrams? Is that what killed him?"

His shoulders lifted almost imperceptibly. "Two milligrams would be considered fatal for a man of his size. But it's unclear whether the carbon monoxide played a role."

Chad was opposed to recreational drugs. He'd never had any injury or surgery requiring an opioid drug prescription. So, where did the drugs come from?

She'd never found out.

Now, as she sat on the balcony of her suite, reviewing the autopsy report, she stopped reading and looked out over the ocean. She thought about her reasons for coming to the island: to deliver the anniversary gift Paul Nieman had purchased for his wife and to find Alison McKay. Ironic, that both women were on the same island.

Chapter Forty-Nine

Tonya

Tonya was dressed in a pair of black leggings, a lightweight sweatshirt, and an Atlanta Braves baseball cap. She had considered wearing one of Chad's long-sleeved T-shirts, but a shirt with Harvard Law imprinted on the front might stand out too much in this southern town. She'd bought a Braves cap at the store when she arrived on the island, which ended up being the perfect accessory.

She pulled into the driveway at Rosie's Diner and sat in her rental for a few minutes as she considered how far Alison McKay's career path had changed. She'd been a rising star in her husband's senatorial campaign—but of course, Tonya and Chad weren't married at the time.

Tonya knew Alison was the mover and shaker—the journalist who could open any door and write a compelling speech on the back of a napkin if necessary. She'd heard Alison had written a novel, although she'd never gotten a copy. What was the use? She had no interest in reading anything that woman had written.

Alison and Chad had spent a tremendous amount of time traveling through the state together during the campaign. Alison and Chad. Tonya hated to link their names together like that, but she couldn't deny that Alison was his right-hand person during the campaign. Chad owed his election to her. It usually took one brilliant person, or sometimes several brilliant people, to get a young politician elected to the Senate. Well, it also took some deep pockets, but Chad's family had that covered from the start.

Tonya drew in a long steadying breath, then got out of the rental and walked toward the diner's entrance. When she opened the door, a flash of cold air hit her in the face. Her eyes immediately teared. She sat at the first available booth and grabbed a napkin from the silver canister. When her eyes dried and her vision cleared, she looked around the diner and marveled at the place. At nine o'clock in the morning, the packed restaurant was buzzing with activity.

Rosie's Diner must be the place to eat.

The diner smelled of strong coffee and bacon. Tonya's mouth watered as she looked at the plate of pancakes on the counter. They were thick and fluffy with a large dab of butter dripping across the top. There must be a thousand calories on that one plate alone.

A woman in a short, white uniform moved through the crowd with practiced ease, pouring coffee with one hand while balancing multiple plates along the other forearm.

"Hey Rosie," someone called. "Got any of those famous muffins?"

Rosie.

Rosemary Delaney.

Tonya blinked. She would never have recognized this woman as Alison McKay. Her hair differed from the pictures in the paper—no black headband. Gone was the blonde hair, only gray roots with reddish-brown ends, and her hair was long…not the short sleek style she had worn during the campaign. Something didn't add up, but Tonya filed that away for the time being.

It took a few moments for Rosie to notice her. Then she grabbed a fresh cup and a pot of coffee and headed in her direction. Rosie was almost at her booth when Tonya used her left hand to reach for the bill of her cap, releasing her long red hair to cascade onto her shoulders. Her big diamond ring flashed in the morning sun as she combed her fingers through her hair.

Rosemary stopped in the middle of the diner—eyes dumbfounded and mouth wide open. The look on her face was priceless. If only Tonya had snapped a picture!

When Rosie finally approached the table, Tonya said, "Hi! You're going by the name of Rosemary Delaney now, right?"

Rosemary nodded, looking around to see if anyone was listening.

Tonya extended her hand. "I'm Tonya Rockwell…Chad's wife. You worked for Chad's senatorial campaign."

"Yes," Rosemary said. Her face was pasty, as if she had just witnessed evil spirits in the diner. Or maybe her coloring looked off because of that hideous hairstyle. It had to be a wig. Either way, her coloring was off.

"What are you doing down here, girl?" Tonya asked. Rosemary poured coffee into the cup but never answered the question. Then Tonya said, "I wanted to ask you about Chad's drug use."

Rosemary paused. "I don't remember any drugs used by anyone on the campaign trail. Chad would never have allowed it, anyway."

No, she said, as Tonya peppered her with questions. He didn't suffer any pain: no leg or back pains, allergies, or indigestion. Tonya was surprised by how easily the conversation flowed. Rosemary was straightforward and kind. She acted like a woman who'd had a professional relationship with Chad. Nothing more.

The knot in Tonya's shoulders eased.

Only once did Rosie say something that she probably would like to retract. "I only saw him take something for sinus pain on one occasion. He'd had a hard day on the trail, and the barometric pressure had caused him to develop a severe headache. He couldn't sleep. I encouraged him to grab a Tylenol from the medicine cabinet, and he did. He'd often wake up in the middle of the night, but I never saw him take pain pills."

Tonya sat up straighter. Rosie had just admitted that she and Chad had slept together. Tonya wondered if that had been intentional. Maybe she was proud of it.

Tonya let the implication slide. "Never? Chad's autopsy report showed a large amount of foreign substance in his bloodstream." She hesitated as if searching for the correct word. "Fentanyl. Yes, that's the name of the drug, Fentanyl."

Rosemary's eyebrows lifted an instant too late. Before she could speak, Tonya reached for her spoon and asked if she could get her some cream.

"Of course." Rosemary looked toward the kitchen and said, "Excuse me, I'll be right back."

Tonya sipped her coffee. She wanted to ask Rosemary if she considered Chad an excellent lover. Was he patient with her? He could be very sensuous during their lovemaking, nuzzling her neck or nibbling her earlobe, just the way she liked. Or was their time together all about him? He could also be narcissistic at times, especially when he came home from the campaign trail. He just wanted her to stop at a moment's notice and give him what he wanted, without regard for her schedule or feelings.

Tonya shoved her coffee away with such force that the hot liquid sloshed over the edge of the cup. Had Chad ever really loved her? Or was their entire marriage a lie?

By the time Rosemary returned with the cream, Tonya had soaked up the spill and folded her napkin to cover the stain. She noticed Rosemary's hands shaking as she placed the small silver pitcher of cream on the table. . .a few tiny crystals floated on the top. It looked like sugar, maybe salt. Or maybe a drug component. She would not take the chance.

Rosemary gave a nervous laugh. "I thought you had died. I haven't heard or read anything about you since in... in a while."

There was something in the way Rosemary said it that made Tonya's skin prickle. The falter in the voice, the nervous laugh, the averted gaze. Together, they painted a picture of guilt. And then, there was the wig. The only way any sane woman would wear a repulsive-colored wig like that was if she were trying to hide her identity.

Was it possible that the car accident wasn't random? That Rosemary had orchestrated the entire thing? Surely not. And yet …

Tonya forced a smile. "Oh, no. I'm very much alive. However, Paul Nieman died later that night from the crash. You may know his wife, Natalie Nieman. She lives on the island."

The vein in Rosemary's forehead bulged.

She looked like a deer in headlights.

BINGO!

But what possible reason could this woman have to arrange the car wreck that had injured Tonya and killed Paul?

Fortunately, Tonya's cell pinged before she was forced to decide on a course of action. She glanced at her phone and read the message. Then she reached for her pocketbook, retrieved a five-dollar bill, and placed it on the table. "Thank you for the coffee," she said. "But I have to get across town and pick up a friend. Hopefully, we can talk again later."

She would have to remain on her guard. That conversation had flowed altogether too smoothly, almost as though she and Rosie were old friends.

Friends. That was an unusual description, but then, they had a lot in common. They'd both loved the same man.

Had Rosemary's love driven her to kill him?

Chapter Fifty

Natalie and Tonya

Natalie shifted in the hospital bed, gripping the edge of her sheet so hard her fingers were cramping. She'd spent the last twenty-four hours in the observation unit, and she still couldn't shake seeing John Steelton killed and dumped into the ocean. Each time she closed her eyes, she saw the soles of his Italian leather shoes as Bernardi's goon dragged him to the ocean's edge.

She could still hear the shame in his voice as he confessed to accepting a client he should have avoided, seduced by the extremely high fees the account would bring to the firm.

He'd paid a high price for his actions, but as much as she had gotten to know and like John, Natalie couldn't find it in her heart to forgive the man whose choice to use her husband as a pawn had led to Paul's death and very nearly caused her own. She hoped that, in time, she'd be able to summon that grace. For now, though, her mind was caught in a traumatic loop—John's murder interspersed with a flood of memories from the night Paul had died.

She glanced at the nurses' call button, tempted to ask for a mild sedative. But no. She was stronger than that.

Her door opened, and Officer Rhodes stuck his head inside, breaking her brain's infernal loop. He cleared his throat as he looked behind him and said, "Hi, Natalie. Do you feel like a visitor?"

"Sure," she said, grateful for the interruption.

An attractive woman with long red hair followed Rhodes into the room. Together, they approached the foot of her bed. Rhodes said, "This is Tonya Rockwell, the woman who shared a cab with Paul in New York on the night of the accident."

Tonya extended her hand.

Natalie shook it, stilling her face into a blank mask. So, this was the woman Paul was with that night. She didn't look like Paul's type, but then, "other women" never were. After all that had happened in these past few days, why was she here now? Coolly, she said, "Are you from New York City?"

"No," Tonya said. "I'm from Chicago. I was in the city that day to meet with my husband's attorney."

Natalie leaned back on the bed and put her arm over her eyes. Finally, she found the words to ask, "How did you know my husband?"

"We shared a taxi. I didn't know your husband for long," Tonya said, "ten minutes tops. He was late leaving work to meet you at the theater. Tina Turner, right?"

Ten minutes tops. A wash of relief swept through Natalie. She lowered her arm. "Yeah, Tina Turner."

"Your husband was so excited. He said he'd tried several times to get tickets, but you guys had such crazy schedules, it had never worked out." Tonya chuckled. "He said you had planned your anniversary because he was so busy at work. You kept it a secret about where you were going for several weeks, and the suspense was killing him. He said you told him that afternoon that you had gotten tickets to the show and then he experienced a delay while waiting for a courier delivery."

She wasn't Paul's lover. The tension Natalie hadn't realized she had been holding since that night loosened and tears welled in her eyes. Regret at the grudge she'd held against Paul warred with relief that the pretty lady wasn't his mistress. Finding her voice, Natalie said, "I wanted it to be a surprise, but when I realized he'd have to meet me at the theater, I told him so he would leave the office in time to make the opening." Fresh tears rolled down Natalie's cheek. "I'm so glad I did. You should have heard his voice when I told him we had tickets to Tina Turner. He sounded like a kid on the phone."

Tonya handed the box of tissues from the bedside table to Natalie. "Well, he loved the surprise. Unfortunately, the timing was all wrong. He got into the wrong cab... it was the wrong place, wrong time, sort of thing."

While Natalie blew her nose, Tonya reached into her purse and handed her a small turquoise box with a white satin ribbon.

Natalie could barely breathe when she saw the small box. Without explanation, she knew it was Paul's anniversary gift. It was such a Paul thing. Every significant gift he'd ever given her came from Tiffany's.

"The last words he spoke were about you," she said. "After he told me about the surprise you planned for your anniversary, Paul said you were the best thing that ever happened to him. He raised his hands in the air like he was making a grand gesture!" She laughed at the memory.

A wistful expression crossed her face. "Imagine meeting a man in a cab, and fewer than ten minutes later, he declared his love for his wife, without reservation and unashamed. It was such a sweet moment... I remember thinking that you were one lucky lady."

I was, Natalie thought. *I really was.*

Growing more somber, Tonya glanced at the window and said, "And that was it—a split second later, I saw a car approaching us from the corner of my eye. There was a loud crash...the cab started spinning, and everything turned black."

Natalie closed her eyes, imagining it.

Tonya said she had felt so alone in the dark—when a streetlight came on and shone into the car before the authorities arrived on the scene. "The light," I believe, "was Paul's spirit."

For a moment, Natalie saw it, too. A blazing white light with Paul standing at the center of it. Then it faded, and she opened her eyes. "Thank you for taking the time to find me. I've often wondered if Paul's last conscious moments were peaceful."

"Yes, they were peaceful moments." Tonya smiled. "You know, Natalie, the two of us share a common thread..."

Natalie glanced at her, frowning. "What thread?"

"I'm also a widow, and I was in New York settling my deceased husband's estate on the day of the accident. I told you earlier that I'm from Chicago...At least, I was. My husband was Illinois Senator Chadwick Rockwell. You may have heard about him. Someone murdered him one afternoon at our townhome in Alexandria." Her voice broke. "He died from fentanyl poisoning." Her hand found its way to her chest, as though she had difficulty breathing. "It was cleverly disguised as a suicide."

Tonya paused, as if allowing the gravity of the situation to set in.

Natalie's hand covered her mouth. "I'm so sorry. I remember seeing that story on the news. He was so young... He was polished and well-spoken and had a bright political future."

Wait. This sounded familiar. Something Rosemary said...

Natalie grasped Tonya's hand. "Thank you for coming down here." She lifted the box. "And for giving me this gift of closure." Natalie placed a fist under her nose as she pushed back a sob. "But more importantly, for showing my husband compassion on the night of the accident."

Tonya laid a hand on Natalie's. "He gave me something, too." Tears glistened in her eyes. "He showed me that real love is out there."

When Natalie regained her composure, she wiped her eyes. Even in the darkest hours, it was that gentle human touch, or in this case, a simple ray of light, that confirmed no one was ever completely alone.

Tonya glanced toward Rhodes and then back at Natalie. "While I'm here, there's something else I need to discuss with you."

Natalie looked at Rhodes, and he nodded for her to listen.

She sat up straighter and said, "Go on."

"Your neighbor, Rosemary Delaney, worked for my husband's senatorial campaign. They became very close while working together."

Natalie leaned back against her pillow, emotionally spent and trying to follow the story. She'd heard it before, hadn't she? Rosemary and a senator? Slowly, the memory came back to her. Chatting on the beach in lawn chairs behind Rosemary's house. She could still remember the crisp, clean taste of the ice-cold beer. But Rosemary's senator had died from a heart attack the night he and Rosemary broke up, and Tonya's had been poisoned.

Still, the stories were so similar, it had to be the same event. Natalie kept looking at Rhodes for reinforcement, and he kept nodding for her to listen.

"Chad and I married and soon welcomed our little girl. We were a happy family of three, and then a wife's worst nightmare happened." Tonya reached for the tissues and dabbed at her eyes. "I should have known it wasn't suicide."

She gave Natalie a watery smile and went on. "I went by the diner to talk to Rosemary earlier today. I'm sure she orchestrated the car accident."

"Are you kidding me?" Natalie asked. "What makes you think that?"

"I just know." Tonya's tone made it clear that was all she intended to say about the accident. "But if you'll come with me to ask Rosemary about it, I think you'll have the answer to your question."

"Rosemary is my neighbor," Natalie said, "and a friend of mine. She was one of the first people I met when I came to the island."

Tonya shrugged. "It's your choice, of course. I just thought you would want to know the person responsible for your husband's death."

"But I didn't even know Rosemary then. That was before I came to the island. How can you be certain Paul was the target?"

"I'm not saying he was." Tonya crossed her arms and continued, "It was a coincidence that Paul was even in the cab. He wasn't the target. I was. As I said earlier, Paul was in the wrong place at the wrong time. But, listen to me, Natalie, your friend Rosemary's true identity is Alison McCay. She was my husband's speech writer. I suspected they were having an affair, and I'm convinced that she was. I also think that she killed Chad, because she found out he was married to me. She made it look like an accidental fentanyl poisoning. Then she tried to kill me while I was in New York. Guess she still had a grudge."

Tonya looked down at the Tiffany's box in her lap. Wrong place, wrong time. If Paul hadn't been running late, if he hadn't shared the cab with Tonya, if, if, if...Paul's death was reduced to a cosmic roll of the dice.

Tonya looked at the package. "Aren't you going to open your gift?"

Natalie held it to her chest. "Not now. I'm going to wait until I get home."

Tonya nodded. "And when will that be?"

"Hopefully, in the morning." Natalie forced a smile. "Fingers crossed."

Tonya and Officer Rhodes thanked Natalie for her time and turned to leave. They were walking out the door when Natalie remembered the look on Rosemary's face the day at the beach when she told her the story about Chad's heart attack. Finally, she said, "Tonya, it's making sense now."

Tonya walked back to the bed and said, "Will you go with me to confront her? We're stronger together than we are apart."

"Will Rhodes go with us?"

Tonya nodded.

Rhodes said, "Of course, I will."

He obviously took Tonya's suspicions seriously. Which meant Natalie needed to take them seriously, too. Slowly, she nodded.

When Tonya and Rhodes left the hospital room, Natalie closed her eyes and clung to the turquoise box that held her anniversary present from Paul. One of the last items his hand had touched before he lost consciousness…it would be the last gift she would receive from him in her lifetime. She tried ever so hard to smell his scent, but the sandalwood aroma had been replaced by sweet memories. She hoped she'd have a chance to tell him what those memories meant to her.

Natalie was awake before the sun came up the following morning. The hospital walls were as thin as tissue paper…every conversation, tray accident, and footstep echoed through the hallway. She heard them all.

Clop. Clop. Clop. It went on all night. She'd slept very little. Natalie closed her eyes, willing the noise to subside, but sleep wouldn't come.

She replayed the visit from Tonya and Rhodes. It had never occurred to her that Rosemary could have battled with a personality disorder. Rosemary was quirky, but that only added to her charm. Lying in the bed and gazing at the ceiling tiles, Natalie remembered the times when Rosemary, Jake, and she were together. Rosemary was transparent. She wore her jealousy like a band of armor. Natalie had almost felt sorry for her.

Natalie placed her arm over her eyes. The woman Tonya had described was a ruthless individual. Was Rosemary really capable of murder? It seemed impossible. But the FBI was now involved, which meant Tonya's story was plausible. Still, Natalie struggled to believe it.

The problem was, she was too close to the situation. She needed to think like an neutral observer—like the professional she was. Shifting her mindset to a medical perspective, she removed their 'friendship' from the equation.

Who am I kidding? Rosemary was never my friend.

Natalie gave her pillow a strong punch and assumed her previous position...even if Rosemary had experienced trauma in the past, perhaps even abuse, it couldn't be severe enough to justify this kind of bizarre behavior. Maybe an act of self-destruction...but not murder. Yet, that was what the facts suggested.

Natalie closed her eyes, questioning her conclusion.

"Killing," she whispered.

Natalie looked at the clock. It was time for breakfast. She caught a whiff of cooked bacon and fresh coffee, the comforting fragrances lingered in her room. She had been in deep thought for two hours. Natalie turned onto her side and watched the sun burst through the clouds. She realized if she didn't go with Tonya to confront Rosemary, the killings would continue, and Rosemary would keep destroying innocent families. She'd already killed Paul, and Tonya's husband, Chad—leaving behind two widows and one little girl. That was enough!

Natalie sat up in bed. How many more people had Rosemary killed?

Rosemary may be ruthless and hardhearted, but Natalie knew she loved Jake. She saw it in Rosemary's eyes and had heard it in her voice many times. What was it worth for her to keep Jake close?

A chill spread over the room. Natalie shivered as she laid her head back on the pillow and snuggled under the covers.

Could she be Rosemary's next target?

Chapter Fifty-One

Tonya

Later that night, Tonya lay in bed thinking about the look on Natalie's face when she saw Paul's gift. The fifth-anniversary gift.

Tonya had laughed when she'd impulsively asked Paul what was in the box. Being so nosey with a stranger was totally out of character for her. Although she had just met Paul, he didn't seem like a stranger—more like an old friend. He had a charming, childlike quality about him. He was so proud of himself for buying his wife the very best gift he could imagine. Paul had told her about the ring Natalie had fallen in love with when they last went into Tiffany's.

Tonya pulled out her phone and googled anniversary gifts by year. The only official wedding anniversary list on the internet showed a traditional fifth-year gift of wood. Had Chad lived, next year would be their fifth anniversary. Tonya scrolled down the list and found that a diamond was featured at the bottom, next to the sixtieth anniversary. Paul had covered the entire span of their marriage… to the sixtieth year, with a diamond eternity ring.

Tonya reached to cut off the lamp, knowing she had done the right thing by returning the gift to Natalie.

As she drifted into sleep, her final thoughts were of Alison McKay, aka Rosemary Delaney, and their impending confrontation. One way or another, there was going to be a reckoning.

Chapter Fifty-Two

Tonya and Alison aka Rosemary

The following morning, Tonya slept late and spent the rest of the day lounging around the pool at the resort. Although it was early October, the temperatures were in the lower eighties—perfect weather to enjoy a day in the sun. As Tonya sipped her iced tea, she looked over the beautiful horizon. It seemed vaster and more open. With no haze to veil the sky, its blue hue appeared purer—something Tonya had grown to appreciate while on the island.

By late afternoon, bored with people-watching, flipping through magazines, and checking her phone for messages from Rhodes, she realized that contacting Alison was not a priority for him. He had no concrete evidence that Alison was responsible for Chad's murder.

A strong gut feeling, along with her neighbor's picture and Alison's vague admission at the diner, was all Tonya had to go on…none of which were hard facts. The only one that might hold up in a court of law was the latter.

As she packed her towel and book into her beach bag, she would give Rhodes until after dinner. If he hadn't called by then, she would go without him.

While walking through the lobby, her bag slung over her shoulder, she glanced toward the restaurant. All day, Tonya had looked forward to a delicious meal there. The website displayed the dishes with an exquisite flair—the thick, juicy filet mignon topped with deep grill marks featured on a fresh vegetable medley. A platter of jumbo shrimp dusted in seasoned breadcrumbs with creamy tartar sauce. The photos alone made her mouth water, and each time she walked past the restaurant, she thought it would be a place she and Chad would have loved when he was alive.

After showering, instead of styling her hair as usual, she walked into the bedroom, toweled it dry, and stared at the dress she'd draped across the bed. She lifted the hem of the delicate fabric and frowned. The elegant outfit seemed too posh for her mood, and she found no appeal in the idea of eating alone.

She had more important things to do.

She placed the dress on the padded satin hanger, hung it back in the closet, and dressed in a pair of shorts and a sweatshirt. She grabbed her keycard, phone, bottled water, ball cap, and a protein bar, went to the pool area and headed toward the steps to the beach.

The quiet solitude took the edge off her frustration. She strolled along the water's edge, her feet marred with clumps of sand, leaving her imprints trailing along the beach. The sparkling moonlight danced off the water, painting a spectacular scene as if the entire cosmos of stars had assembled just for her. She simply wasn't in a state of mind to appreciate it.

After walking a half mile down the beach, Tonya came to three small cottages. The same three she had seen the previous morning as she ran on the beach. From the outside, it looked as if the builder had used an identical floor plan, with screened porches added to the back overlooking the ocean.

Was this where Alison lived?

According to Natalie, Alison lived in a small beachside cottage to her left, and Jake lived on the other side.

A woman stood at the window of the first cottage and then moved out of sight. Tonya stopped far enough away not to be noticed. Then the woman moved back into view. Tonya knew it was Alison. It was only because of the bright fluorescent light above the kitchen sink that she had seen her. The lighting showed the beautiful blonde hair that she remembered from the campaign, minus the black headband.

Tonya stood on the beach and nibbled her protein bar, watching Alison through the window. She appeared to be making dinner. The hideous wig was gone, her blonde hair cut in a stylish, messy bob. It was much shorter than when she had worked on the campaign. How strange that she had changed her identity and ended up in a beach town so far from home, only to publish popular novels with her picture on the book jacket.

Alison reached for a bottle of wine.

Was she deliberately hiding from the truth?

The folks at the diner loved her, and her business seemed to flourish. However, did her customers realize she lived a double life: a loud, red-neck waitress at work and a refined journalist and published author at home? Of course, it was really a triple life, wasn't it? Waitress, author, murderer?

After standing in the backyard, staring at the kitchen window a moment longer, Tonya decided she was right to leave Rhodes out of it. She took the last bite of the protein bar, wadded the paper, and stuck it in the pocket of her shorts before moving further down the beach.

As she got closer to Natalie's cottage, she thought how tragic it was for Natalie to find out her friend was responsible for her husband's death.

Tonya approached Natalie's well-lit cottage and knocked on the screened porch door.

A tall, tanned man with his arm in a sling answered the door. *This must be Jake.*

Tonya introduced herself.

***

When Natalie heard Tonya's voice, she yelled from the other room, "Be there in a moment...just need to get my shoes."

Natalie had not mentioned to Jake that Tonya had come to the hospital. When Natalie returned with her shoes in hand, Tonya stood on the porch, her feet covered with clumps of wet sand. Natalie told Jake her detailed story, complete with Tonya's theory that Rosemary had coordinated the accident that caused Paul's death.

"What?" Jake looked from Natalie to Tonya. "You're saying that Rosemary killed your husband?"

"Yes."

"And mine," Tonya said.

Natalie touched his arm and said, "Tonya has some very compelling evidence to suggest that Rosemary orchestrated the accident that killed Paul. Rhodes is on board, too."

"Then let Rhodes handle it," Jake said.

Natalie and Tonya spent a few minutes deciding how to approach Rosemary.

Jake leaned against the door with his arm folded, listening to their discussion. He finally said, "Natalie, think about this. You've just gone through a traumatic experience. You've been in the hospital."

"I've got to get to the bottom of this, Jake." She looked at him with pleading eyes. "Otherwise, I'll never be able to put this behind me...and move on with my life."

Jake let out a long breath. He looked from Tonya to Natalie and back at Tonya. "If Rhodes told you he would handle the case, then let him do his job." He paused. "It's hard to believe that Rosemary is a murderer...although I've always thought she had a dark side...anyway, this could go south in a hurry."

Tonya fidgeted. "I haven't heard from Rhodes since we landed on the island. He hasn't called or texted."

Jake combed his fingers through his hair. "The man's been kind of busy. He suffered a pretty nasty gunshot wound to his shoulder, but if I know Rhodes, he's got it under control. He's got the support of the FBI to back him up, and it's not like Rosemary is going anywhere."

Tonya looked at Natalie and said, "I'm going next door. You can come along if you like. Your choice."

Natalie gently touched Jake's arm and gave him an apologetic smile. Then she followed Tonya outside and walked toward Rosemary's cottage. At one point, she glanced back toward her cottage and saw Jake standing at the door, his arm propped up against the door frame. She'd learned to read his body language pretty well. His posture suggested he didn't know whether to follow them or stand there waiting for their return. She hoped he'd wait.

The previous day, when they released her from the hospital, Jake insisted on staying with her until she regained her strength. He'd slept in the club chair at the end of the sofa. When she woke during the night, Jake was watching a football game on the television with the volume muted. He was very protective of her, even more so than Paul had been.

Natalie looked back at Jake again while waiting for Tonya to put on her shoes before entering Rosemary's house. He had walked out to the fire pit, but his gaze kept shifting to follow her.

It was a typical October evening. The direction of the wind had changed, as sand whipped across the beach. Natalie knew Jake didn't want her to go. She could see it in his eyes, but she had to find out if Tonya's story was true.

They approached the door, and Natalie knocked.

Natalie put her ear to the screened door. "No one seems to be moving around."

She knocked again, louder.

Finally, a door slammed, and they heard the sound of footsteps moving across the floor.

"Rosemary," Natalie yelled. "Are you home?"

In a few moments, Rosemary appeared at the kitchen door.

Tonya stepped forward. "Hi Rosie, it's me, Tonya. I thought I'd drop by since we didn't have time to finish our visit at the diner." She nodded toward Natalie and said, "Natalie came with me, too."

Rosemary's hand shook as she reached to unlock the screened door and let them in. She looked from one to the other. Finally, she hugged Natalie. "How are you feeling?"

"Better, now that I'm home."

Tonya explained she had gone for a walk on the beach.

Rosemary gave them a stiff smile. "Would you like a cup of tea?"

"Thank you," Natalie said, "but please don't go to any trouble."

Rosemary offered them a seat at the small round table on the screened porch. "No trouble. I'll be just a minute."

As they waited for Rosemary to return to the porch, Natalie wondered what was going through her mind. She wondered if Rosemary remembered telling her about Chad that day on the beach. Of course, she did. It was clear from the way Rosemary had looked at her when she came to the door.

The bigger question was why Rosemary would admit to sleeping with Chad. What was she thinking?

Natalie could see Jake's silhouette through the screened porch. He was sitting in her chair at the firepit, facing Rosemary's cottage. Her only intention was to stay long enough for Rosemary to confess to orchestrating the car crash that took Paul's life. While it wouldn't bring Paul back, finding out who was responsible for his death would provide some peace of mind.

Although Natalie and Tonya were sitting on Rosemary's screened porch facing the beach, a round mirror suspended from the ceiling allowed Natalie to see Rosemary in the kitchen behind her.

As she watched Rosemary in the mirror, Natalie thought about the evenings she had spent on this very porch with her and Jake. Good times. Fun times. A few times were not so fun when Rosemary was spiteful or drank too much, but even then, because of Jake, there was a bit of humor in the situation.

Then again, when a person moved to a new area, it was nice to find a few individuals who would become friends, and Rosemary and Jake were those people—her people.

While looking around the screened porch, Natalie wondered if their friendship would have survived under different circumstances.

Natalie glanced at Tonya. They made small talk while Rosemary made the tea in the next room. She, too, seemed nervous. It was a bizarre situation. Although Natalie and Tonya had different reasons for being there, it ultimately came down to one psychopath, two dead husbands, and two grieving wives.

Chapter Fifty-Three

Rosemary

The minute Rosemary saw Natalie and Tonya together by the door, she sensed trouble. Not yet, maybe, but sooner or later, it was inevitable. Tonya had seemed to accept her as nothing more than a romantic rival. By the end of the visit at the diner, Tonya had all but welcomed Rosemary into the sisterhood. No, Rosemary was sure Tonya didn't suspect her role in Chad's demise. But Natalie's presence was problematic. How had she and Tonya even met?

Well, it was a small island. The real question was, did Natalie know their friendship was a fraud? Rosemary didn't have many friends. Ironically, she thought Natalie was different, they could've been best friends.

Replaying the greeting at the door, Rosemary decided the answer was no. There was no way a gullible, goody-two-shoes like Natalie would suspect that her "best friend" had ordered the hit that ended up killing her husband. If she did, it would be written all over her face.

As she filled the tea kettle with water, anxious thoughts flooded Rosemary's mind. How had Tonya found her? Rosemary had been careful to cover her tracks, even using a photoshopped picture of her on the book jacket. She had changed her name when she left Chicago. The hitman she'd hired didn't even know her real name. The very presence of the woman on her doorstep was a threat to her new life.

Waiting for the water to boil, Rosemary fought back the panic she'd been battling since Chad's wife had shown up at the diner. Tonya had survived the accident, after all.

It only took one mistake to bring a world crashing down. Rosemary's mistake was not verifying that night's fatalities.

Waiting for the tea to steep, she remembered the events of that stressful day.

Chapter Fifty-Four

Alison aka Rosemary

Two and a half years ago...

Alison McKay slid a picture of a woman and a young child across the table and said, "Tonya Rockwell flew into LaGuardia earlier today to wrap up the last of her late husband's estate."

The gentleman had been careful to sit facing the door of the coffee shop with his back to the large 72-inch screen that hung on the wall at the end of the restaurant.

He cut his eyes at Alison as he pushed the picture away with a nicotine-stained hand. "You're paying me to crash into the car. That woman riding in the car may be the ultimate target, but don't personalize it." A cigarette dangled from his lips, which he only removed to sip his scalding black coffee or chew on the yellow pencil he held when it wasn't resting behind his ear. There was a significant round discoloration on the side of his cheek—perhaps a birthmark of some sort.

Alison looked out the window of the coffee shop, wondering if this was the best guy for the job. They could quickly identify him with that birthmark; otherwise, he was as plain as the next thug on the street. But in a city of almost two million people, who would even notice?

She'd always heard that most criminals were brilliant. Well, almost brilliant. If they'd used their intelligence for anything other than crimes, they'd be very successful.

Alison was surprised when he told her he had not seen the ten-second clip on the noon news. He probably didn't watch the news. His type seldom did. Either they didn't care what happened in the world, or they were too busy making a living to keep up with current events. Of course, the events that would concern a person like him took place in the back streets and alleys of the Bronx.

Alison released a long breath. The technology of the twenty-first century allowed for news feeds to arrive in his inbox almost instantaneously, but he probably wouldn't subscribe to those either.

Alison sat in her parked rental car and watched her former fiancé's wife walk out of the One Park Avenue building near Billionaires' Row in New York City. It was the stretch of high-end property on Manhattan's 57th Street, between Park Avenue and the iconic Hudson River.

From the looks of it, the meeting with the senator's attorney had gone well. Chad's widow, Tonya Rockwell, wore a black Chanel suit, black stilettos, a blue Michael Kors bag, and an Armani multi-colored scarf with blue accents artfully tied around her neck. A prestigious Fifth Avenue boutique had the same scarf featured in its display window.

Mrs. Rockwell walked with her head held high, shoulders squared, and her back as straight as a metal rod. A tiny waist and minimal body fat—perhaps she had a personal trainer to keep her body toned. Impeccable complexion and gorgeous hair. Her skin glowed. Thanks to her deceased husband's money, she could afford to buy all that and more. His life insurance money alone could pay the health care costs for a small country, but money was just a commodity, right? Well, that's what Chad had always said. Easy enough to say when you come from 'old money.' Alison had grown up in a tumbledown trailer and scrabbled for everything she'd ever gotten.

Tonya Rockwell smiled and exuded confidence while clutching the manila envelope in her left hand. A three-carat diamond engagement ring sparkled from the movement of her hand. Her long, manicured fingernails only accentuated the size of the rare diamond. Alison had noticed the ring in the picture on the bedside table at the Alexandria townhome the day the senator's body was found dead in the garage. Later, a former staff member confirmed the size of the stone. Alison had been desperate for an engagement ring from Chad. Then this gold-digger had swept in and gotten one. With a heavy sigh, Alison glanced at her chapped hands, noticing her nails bitten down to the quick, a recent habit she had developed.

The doorman walked to the curb and waited for the next cab. When the taxi arrived, he opened the back door for Mrs. Rockwell. Suddenly, a sharply dressed man carrying a briefcase and a small turquoise bag from a prominent Fifth Avenue store ran from across the street and yelled for the doorman to hold the cab.

Alison was disgusted with herself for not considering something like this might happen. She closed her eyes, willing him to wait for the next taxi.

The doorman tapped on the window and slipped the driver a bill. Then the man with the briefcase jumped into the backseat.

Damn.

The doorman said something to Tonya. She flashed a broad smile and touched his arm. The taxi driver fiddled with the screen on the dash for several minutes. Finally, the taxi took off toward the intersection.

Alison murmured to herself, "This is going to complicate matters." But she refused to stop now. Things were already in motion. She texted Joe the number of the taxicab, hoping he remembered her instructions. Immediately, her phone rang.

She saw his number and accepted the call. "Joe, did you get my text?"

"Yep! Right here. How close?"

"They're within seconds of the intersection."

Alison heard the sound of the revved engine as he applied the gas. "Consider it done."

A moment later, a dirty white van came charging through the intersection.

There was a loud sound of squealing tires as glass shattered from the windows. The taxi spun several times, skidded for ten feet, and crashed into the base of the light pole.

Alison watched the mission unfold in real time. It was like watching a slow-motion picture. The dirty van continued through the light without even tapping its brakes.

Slowly, Alison pulled the rental car out of the parallel parking space and onto the street. Traffic had already begun to stop. People gawked at the disfigured taxi, while trying to avoid the broken glass on the street. The dirty van was long gone from the scene.

Alison looked in the rearview mirror. The doorman retrieved his cell phone from his pocket, his arms waving toward the accident.

Time to get out of here before the authorities arrived.

She paused too, as she passed the wreckage. A streetlight came on and shone in the window. The senator's wife lay in the floorboard behind the front seat. Her body facing backward, head slumped. The driver's head lay back on the headrest, eyes closed, mouth ajar, and blood streaming from his nose. The stranger was not visible from the street. Neither passenger could have survived that crash—with or without restraints.

The hitman had delivered. She could not have asked for a more perfect accident. Quickly, she dialed his number. Voicemail. He had already disposed of the phone. He proved to be not just a skilled driver, but also more intelligent than she had first assumed.

She wiped her sweaty hands on her pants and glanced at the clock on her dashboard. Alison smiled. She had just enough time to stop by the post office and get to the airport in time to catch her flight back to the coast.

Chapter Fifty-Five

The Confrontation

The element of surprise. Rosemary had studied it in her creative writing class. Her editor had even presented a Zoom webinar on the subject, which she had watched one rainy afternoon. Now, Rosemary stood in her kitchen, frustrated with herself. The perfect example of surprise sitting on her porch. She had been outwitted by the person she had presumed dead. If Tonya had come this far, it was only a matter of time before she uncovered the truth.

Rosemary drained the last of her wineglass and glanced at the near-empty bottle. *That wasn't a good idea.*

Why hadn't Tonya called first? Or, at least, Natalie. She'd always called before.

Rosemary's hands were almost steady as she poured the tea, lifted the tray, and then quickly spun back toward the counter. She reached into the cabinet and removed the pill container from the shelf. The position of her body would prevent her visitors from identifying the item in her hand.

Rosemary grabbed a clean spoon from the drawer and stirred the tea.

Beads of sweat popped out on her forehead. It could be because she'd already drunk over half of the bottle of wine. It could also just be nerves.

Rosemary listened as Natalie and Tonya continued their small talk in the next room. They talked of nothing serious. The beautiful sky over the ocean. The tourist season, stuff like that. Nonetheless, it grated on her nerves. She wondered what Natalie would think if she knew she was responsible for her beloved Paul's death.

Karma has its price, she thought as she poured the tea. She stole Jake from me. I killed her husband. Even.

A few minutes later, Rosemary swept onto the porch with a tray carrying three cups of tea. She placed the tray on the table and was careful to remove her cup first. There were three cocktail napkins on the tray along with three teaspoons, a cream pitcher, and a bowl of sugar.

Tonya glanced at Natalie and then said to Rosemary as she placed the cups before them, "I prefer lemon juice. Do you have any?"

Rosemary looked from Natalie back to Tonya. If she said no, they might suspect she'd done something to the tea. She looked into Natalie's guileless face and saw nothing to alarm her.

"Sure." She hurried into the kitchen.

Natalie could hear Rosemary scurrying around in the cabinet. Leaning back in her chair, she had a view of Rosemary opening the fridge. Then she snapped her gaze forward as Tonya quickly switched Rosemary's cup of tea with Natalie's, making sure the handle of Rosemary's teacup remained at the exact angle as before.

Natalie cast a quizzical look at the cup Tonya had placed before her. Tonya put a finger up to her lips and nodded toward the mirror.

Rosemary returned to the porch, placed the lemon juice on the table next to Natalie, and sat down. With a trembling hand, she lifted her cup to her lips.

"Thank you." Natalie moved the lemon juice across the table. Tonya gave her a stern look as she poured a dash of juice into her tea and then pushed her cup farther away.

She finally understood what Tonya was doing.

Rosemary asked about Natalie's boating accident and apologized for not stopping by the hospital, as Tonya continued to stir the hot liquid.

As the conversation continued and Rosemary sipped her tea, her hand steadied, and her posture relaxed. Gradually, her shoulders slumped, her reflexes weakened. She gave a nervous laugh. "I thought you had died in that accident. I haven't heard or read anything about you since that night."

Tonya said, "Are you still talking about Natalie's accident here, or the one in New York?"

The drug was affecting Rosemary. It was difficult for her to lift the cup to her lips, and when she did, she missed her mouth. The liquid ran down her chin as she said, "What?"

Tonya glanced at Natalie and said, "Paul was on his way to the theater to meet Natalie that night. They had tickets to see the Tina Turner musical."

She looked across the table and watched the pathetic woman wiping her mouth with the sleeve of her shirt.

Natalie had made excuses for the way Rosemary had treated her regarding Jake. Jealousy, that's what she'd told Jake one time. Rosemary was just jealous of their friendship. But her relationship with Jake was more than friendship. It had been obvious to everyone from the start.

Tonya couldn't stop talking about Paul. Perhaps she was enjoying watching Rosemary's discomfort.

Rosemary's eyes were already dilated as she looked at Natalie and said, "I didn't know until yesterday… that was your husband."

Natalie's heart was beating so loudly that she could hear it. She had wanted to know the truth, but now that she knew, she was doubly hurt. Rosemary had pretended to be her friend.

As Natalie continued to stir her tea, she realized they were in over their heads. Jake was right. Rhodes should be there. She looked at Rosemary and forced herself to say, "It was very unfortunate. Paul was in the wrong place at the wrong time." She stopped to clear the lump in her throat. "Rosemary, you're a smart woman, but you'll never know how it feels to be loved by a man, because your heart doesn't have the capacity for love."

She got up and took her cup and saucer to the kitchen sink, then calmly walked out of the house.

Tonya watched Natalie leave. She knew there was nothing more to say, and Tonya was glad Natalie had come with her to see Rosemary.

When Tonya looked back at Rosemary, Tonya wanted to ask her if she ever wondered what Chad was feeling during the moments before *his* death.

Chad…then Paul. Natalie had been right. Was this woman even capable of feeling?

It was plausible that Rosemary would never remember the question anyway. Sure enough, when Rosemary spoke, her speech was even more slurred. After the screen door slammed, Rosemary was several beats off when she said, "Bye, Natalie, see you tomorrow."

She pushed to her feet, then blinked unsteadily at Tonya. "I'm... not... feeling... well," she said. "I need to lie down."

Tonya insisted, "You go on to bed. I'll let myself out."

Rosemary staggered toward her bedroom while Tonya watched from the porch. Once Rosemary was out of sight, Tonya peeped over at her cup. There was a small amount of tea remaining, along with the sediments of the drug at the bottom.

Suicide by carbon monoxide—that was Rosemary's trademark move. But there was no need for anything so elaborate now.

Tonya carried her spoon, cup, and saucer to the kitchen sink. She had been careful to only touch the spoon, and neither she nor Natalie had drunk their tea. When she'd washed the spoon and both cups with hot soapy water, she opened a drawer next to the sink, grabbed a clean dishcloth, dried the dishes, and positioned them in the cupboard.

She went back to the porch and placed hers and Natalie's cocktail napkin in the sleeve of her sweatshirt, but left Rosemary's napkin next to her cup. Then she used her elbow to open the screen door. Tonya looked back at the teacup that Rosemary had left behind on the table.

Fentanyl cocktail.

As she closed the door and turned toward the resort, she murmured, "But this time Alison McKay aka Rosemary 'Rosie' Delaney has killed herself."

Chapter Fifty-Six

Natalie and Jake

Natalie couldn't wait to get out of Rosemary's house. She felt dirty, betrayed, and used.

The full moon was bright. She walked as fast as her legs would carry her toward her cottage, but when she saw Jake sitting in her beach chair, she let out a deep, cleansing breath and smiled.

She stopped at the firepit and looked down at him. "Were you afraid something would happen?"

Jake reached for her hand. "How did it go?"

"Rosemary admitted she didn't know the man in the car was Paul. Tonya was correct in assuming she was the target."

"I find it hard to believe that Rosemary orchestrated that wreck," Jake said. "All that time, she acted like we were all friends…"

"Well, Rosemary wasn't a nice person, Jake…but thanks for letting me go alone. I had to find closure."

Jake kissed her hand and looked up at her. "Did you find closure, Natalie?"

"Yes." Her last glimpse of Rosemary's slack features flitted across her mind. Whatever was happening to her now, Natalie was complicit. Well, she could live with that. Rosemary may not have known it was Paul in that cab, but she'd known it was someone.

Was it cowardly not to stay and see it through?

Perhaps. But Natalie could live with that, too.

She pulled Jake out of the beach chair and encircled his waist with her arms. "Enough about that. It's cold out here."

Jake looked down and kissed her nose. "Let's go inside. It's been a long day, and you need your rest."

Chapter Fifty-Seven

Natalie

The following morning, Natalie took a cup of coffee and the turquoise gift bag to the beach and sat in her Adirondack chair. She leaned her head back and enjoyed the beauty of the cloudless sky. A gentle wind caressed her face, while the soothing waves lapped onto the beach, as if the ocean welcomed her back home.

She leaned forward in her chair as a car rounded the curve and pulled into her driveway. She had expected the detectives to stop by, but maybe not so early in the morning. She looked up as Officer Rhodes came around the side of the cottage. He stopped and yelled at Jake through the screened door. Jake handed the backpack to him and explained that he'd gone over and gotten the money out of the side panels of the Porsche's doors.

"Where's the car now?" Rhodes asked.

"It's still in the shop," Jake said. "They're waiting for a part to come from California."

Natalie held her breath when Jake asked Rhodes about Rosemary. "Is it true that she's dead?"

Rhodes put the backpack on the porch step. "Yep, an apparent suicide. But, of course, there will be an autopsy to confirm."

Jake said, "What a shame. Rosemary was a tormented soul."

"She was, indeed." Rhodes sat on the porch step, unzipped the backpack, and removed a stack of what appeared to be bills. He stuck his hand down to the bottom and retrieved another one. Uniformly wrapped in cellophane, each brick had a one-hundred-dollar bill on either side.

Rhodes sniffed both packs of bills. Then he removed his pocket knife, opened it, and gently stuck it in one of the packs. When he removed the blade, it was covered in a white, powdery substance.

He looked up at Jake, who was standing on the porch watching his every move, and said, "Looks like we've just recovered the drugs from that operation. Those guys didn't care about Natalie or Steelton, it was the cocaine they were after."

Jake looked horrified. "I wonder when they made the swap. Four months ago, I discovered cash in the door panels. And, not too long ago, a drone kept shining over Natalie's house. I bet they made the switch that night."

Rhodes shrugged. "There's no telling how long the cash had been in her car. It proved to be a safe hiding place." He recited the scenario as he surmised it had happened. "Then they needed a place to stash the drugs for a short while, and when they came back for them, the car was gone. They panicked."

Shaking his head, Rhodes placed the bricks of cocaine back into the backpack, then turned and walked toward the beach chairs.

"Are you okay, Natalie?"

"Yes. Better."

"I'm sorry about your friend."

Her friend. Of course, he would say that, and it was almost true. At first glance, they seemed like friends. Natalie had tried her best to be a friend to Rosemary.

"Thank you."

"I'll be questioning Rosemary's neighbors and close friends as part of the investigation. First, I've got to get these drugs secured—I'll be back later."

Natalie leaned back in her chair. Later, she thought. Yes, I'll deal with that later.

She hoped she could keep a good poker face.

When Rhodes was ready to leave, he stopped by the porch to pick up the drug-filled backpack. Jake stood with his arm resting on the door frame. Rhodes nodded toward Natalie and said, "Take care of her, Jake."

"I plan on it."

"You're a lucky man, my friend. A very lucky man."

Jake grinned and said, "Don't I know it!"

As Rhodes drove off, Natalie thought about her decision to move to Georgia. She had come to the southern coast unsure of what she would find, but soon realized beach life suited her. Even the disturbing events of the past few weeks had served a purpose. She had finally learned the truth about Paul's death and the strength of his love for her.

She hadn't counted on Rosemary being a criminal. She had a strange personality, yes, but she would have never taken Rosemary for a criminal. That one had surprised her, even though throughout her life, she'd learned that people's secret selves were often different from their public personas.

Chapter Fifty-Eight

Natalie and Paul

Natalie glanced at the porch step where the backpack had remained until Rhodes left. Jake had taken an enormous risk sneaking in the window of the repair shop to remove the bricks from the car panels, only to find out it wasn't money, but cocaine. She sure could use a portion of that drug money to build a modern clinic for the island.

Her eyes welled up with tears as she reflected on Tonya, contemplating the many occasions she had wondered about the woman who had been with her husband during his last conscious moments. It was as simple as walking across the emergency room and initiating a conversation, but she'd made a choice. A decision that morphed into a whirlwind of ifs and maybes. A decision that had caused her much pain.

She closed her eyes and drifted back in time for a few moments. It was the afternoon of their fifth anniversary. Natalie had just hung up talking with Paul about meeting her at the theater. It was a bittersweet moment. Excited for the night ahead with her husband, but disappointed he hadn't come home in time to ride together.

Looking into the mirror on the dining room wall in their Brooklyn townhome, she spotted the champagne chiller. She popped a chocolate-covered strawberry into her mouth and pulled the bottle from its cradle. As tempting as it was to open the two hundred-and-ninety-dollar bottle of champagne, she gazed at the label instead, licking the excess sugar from her lips.

The rich ornate foil of the Krug Grande Cuvee Brut champagne label looked like liquid gold. The bottle was ice cold. Made in Reims, the center of the Champagne region in France and, of course, her husband's favorite. Only the best for Paul… Touching a bead of cold sweat dripping from the bottle, she placed it back inside the wine chiller and recalled a memory from their previous anniversary. She could still see Paul's cocky grin as he had expertly removed the cage from the bottle.

He had performed the task so many times throughout their marriage: birthdays, Christmas Eve, New Year's Eve, each anniversary, and with such flair, he had made it look like an art form. She smiled at the memory. The way his hands moved with the deftness of a magician. The way he'd held up the bottle with a flourish. The flash of his eyes as he glanced at her over the bottle and said she was the absolute best thing to happen to him.

He had made that same remark many times during their marriage, and each year, he'd said it on their anniversary.

Slowly, the delicious dream faded. Natalie had relived that day a thousand times since Paul's death. She opened her eyes and raised a hand to shield them from the glaring sun. There was a man silhouetted on the beach in front of her house, surrounded by a bright light. The easy stride and muscular physique were Paul's, but she couldn't see his face. She felt a moment of panic as she tried to remember the exact angle of his jaw, the perfect brown of his eyes. The picture was there, but the edges seemed faded, like a photo left too long in the sun. "Talk to me, Paul," she called. "I've missed our talks."

Paul ran up from the beach and sat in the empty beach chair. "I'm here, Nattygirl."

Natalie had delayed opening the gift until she was home. The place where she felt closest to Paul. She glanced at him as she hugged the gift. It was so good to be home—good to be in her safe place, where she felt the safety of his presence.

Paul looked at her with that devilish grin, enjoying every second of her suspense. "Aren't you going to open it?"

She stared at him, grateful she could see his handsome face. Then she meticulously removed the beautiful satin ribbon. When she opened the box, she found a diamond-studded band. Simple. Elegant. Exactly what Natalie would have chosen for herself. Natalie slipped it on her finger.

She reached for his hand and said, "It's lovely, Paul." Holding her hand out in front of her for him to admire. "No, it's perfect!"

Paul leaned close to her and said, "Are you still mad at me?"

Surprised, Natalie replied, "What do you mean, am I still mad at you?"

Paul looked at the sand beneath his feet and said, "You know you've been angry with me since the crash."

"Well, I wasn't exactly angry, but I was upset with you for not coming home in time for us to go to the theater together." She sniffed. "It seems silly now, now that I know you were just caught in the middle of a violent act."

"Are you sure that's all it was?" He laid his hand on hers. It felt like a breath of warm air. "It felt like there was something off between us, even before the accident."

"We were both so busy, it seemed like we were growing apart. Then at the hospital, when the nurse said there was a woman with you in the cab…" Her eyes brimmed. "I can't believe I ever doubted you."

Paul smiled. "Do you feel better now that you've gotten that off of your chest?"

Natalie nodded and wiped her eyes with the beach towel.

"I need to ask one more question, Paul."

"What is it?" he said.

"Did you know Steelton was working for the mob?" Natalie's chin quivered. "You're such a smart man…a man of integrity. I just have to know…."

Paul looked away. When he turned back to her, there were tears in his eyes. "I told myself I didn't. But, yes, on some level, I knew. You know how ambitious I was…I got caught up in the moment, trying to make my mark within the firm. I wanted that promotion."

Paul leaned forward in his chair and at last said, "I wanted to give you the world. There were so many plans I had for us, Natty…making VP would have made it all possible." His gaze drifted toward the ocean. "I thought we had thirty-forty more years together. We were so young, with plenty of time ahead of us."

Natalie reached over and rubbed his back. "But there's never enough time, is there? I'm not sure even a hundred years together would have been enough."

"True, and now that I'm on this side, I realize life is fleeting. I'm willing to bet that if you asked a thousand men whether they'd spent enough time with their wives at the end of their lives, every one of them would say no."

"Not just men," Natalie paused. "Paul, I had dreams, too."

"I know you did." Paul looked around at the beach and said, "We should've come here for a vacation."

They sat in silence for a few more minutes. Then Paul turned and looked back at her cottage. "Natty, it feels right here. Relaxed and peaceful, not like the crazy pace of our previous life."

Natalie thought about the late-night dinners she had kept warm for Paul. The mornings they had passed each other on the front steps, her coming home from a twelve-hour shift, and Paul going to work. It was their life, and at the time they thought that was all there was. Success had its price, and they had certainly paid a huge one for theirs.

Paul's description of her beachside cottage pleased her, and she knew it would be her forever home. "You're right, this is a peaceful place. It's like a different world down here."

He looked over at her and pulled on his ear, something he always did when he was nervous. In all of these months, she hadn't seen him do it. "Do you remember the night we met at Rue 57," he said. "You never told me who you were meeting that night."

Natalie grinned and inhaled a deep breath. Paul had asked her that same question many times, and she had never told him the truth. It was a game they used to play, and it had seemed trivial. Today, she felt compelled to explain it to him. "It's the only secret I've ever kept from you. I guess it's time I clear the air."

"Oh, so you weren't so perfect, were you?" he teased.

Natalie rolled her eyes. "Well, almost...the truth is, I'd met someone at a party in the city. Tall. Gorgeous. He'd asked me to meet him for a drink the next night, and he didn't show up. Later, I learned he was engaged. I felt foolish for falling for that line." She paused. "If I hadn't agreed to meet him that night, I would have never met you. So I guess his standing me up was all part of the divine plan."

Paul pointed his crooked finger at her and said, "I knew I had you when you stole the last chocolate-covered strawberry from my plate. And when you bit into the fruit, there was a speck of white chocolate on your chin. I debated about whether to remove the speck or leave it for you to find later, but I didn't want it to get on that pretty winter white sweater."

Natalie pulled the beach towel up under her chin and turned her head toward his chair. "You reached over and wiped my chin, and then you put your finger in your mouth. You made the cutest face. I fell in love with you at that moment."

Now, after two and a half years, she had received answers to all of her questions. It was nice to feel Paul's presence in the Adirondack chair beside her. Natalie turned her head and peeped through partially closed eyelids. He smiled that beautiful smile that she loved so much.

"So, you liked the gift?" he asked.

"Like it? It's the most gorgeous thing I've ever seen." Natalie clung to the box and held it near her chest. "It's the ring I saw at Tiffany's. I didn't think you noticed how much I liked it."

"I noticed." Paul hesitated. "I couldn't wait to see your face when I surprised you with it."

She gave him a watery smile. "Was it worth the wait?"

"It was." Paul crossed his legs and shifted his body closer to Natalie. In a soft voice, he said, "Natty, I'm sorry I let you down. I should have focused more on the time we had together, instead of on my job. I let a lot of time slip away that we could have spent together. You know if I had a choice, I would have never left you."

"I know." She did know, but for the past two and a half years, she'd let her mind convince her otherwise.

He fidgeted in his chair. "I wish I could stay, make that life with you we never got to have. But I have to let you go, so you can move on, Nattygirl."

Paul's time was almost up. She heard it in his voice and saw it in the way he pushed his feet across the sand.

She closed her eyes. Now that she knew what had happened, she wanted just a little more time with her husband. "Do you know you are the only person, other than my daddy, to call me Nattygirl?"

He reached for her arm and gently rubbed the tiny hairs. "Eternity is a long time, sweetheart." He stumbled over his words. "Promise me that you'll live an adventurous life— and that you'll find someone to live it with. Do all of the things we could only talk about. Do them for us..." He paused. "Do them for me."

Natalie turned toward Paul and opened her sleepy eyelids. "How will I know it's right? With you, I knew from the very first night that you were the one. Next time, I might not be so lucky."

Paul placed her hand in his, "You'll know..."

Natalie could feel him drifting away. She just wanted one more minute with him. "How will I know, Paul? Tell me, how will I know for sure?"

He touched the new ring, lifting her finger to get a better look. "It'll be something he says...the way he looks at you, perhaps the lyrics in a song, or a quote in a book." He chuckled. "Or maybe he'll have a piece of white chocolate on his chin or stuck between his teeth!" He became more somber as he looked into the distance. Paul was drifting from her again.

The screened door slammed, and Natalie turned as Jake walked toward her. Jake had effortlessly assumed the domestic role since she came home from the hospital. His blond hair was damp from his morning shower, and his sun-kissed muscular body glistened from working long hours in the sun. There was a dish towel hanging out of the waist of his khaki shorts, only enhancing his charm.

Paul nodded. "You're a smart lady, Natalie. Trust me, you'll figure it out."

As she watched Jake stroll through the backyard holding two coffee mugs, she looked at him differently. Natalie tried to think of a correct description. He was comfortable. That was the word she was searching for. Jake, like Paul, was a confident man, and comfortable with himself. Whereas Paul was always in a rush, looking forward to tomorrow, attracting the next client, the next vacation. Jake moved slower through life. He lived in the moment, enjoying every second of every day. Living at the beach had something to do with it.

In many ways, Jake had taken over Paul's role since she'd moved to the coast. She now realized Jake had been waiting all along—for her heart to heal.

When Jake reached her side, Paul rose from the beach chair and stepped away. Natalie felt the distance between them.

"Who have you been talking to?" Jake asked as he looked around, "Is Paul here?"

"He was here earlier."

"I made a fresh pot of coffee for you, Nattygirl."

Paul turned and winked at Natalie. He raised his eyebrows and pointed his finger toward Jake. Natalie felt her face turn red.

Natalie hesitated as she glanced back at Jake. *Maybe Paul was right.* Perhaps it *was* time... for a new beginning.

"Thank you, Jake. The coffee smells wonderful."

"Your favorite—white chocolate mocha. I found it in your fridge."

"Mmm," she said.

Placing her cup on the arm of the chair, he gently touched the side of her face. He nodded toward the empty beach chair and asked, "Is this chair taken?"

Was it taken?

Natalie looked up. Paul was walking down the beach. Suddenly, he pivoted, lifted two fingers to his lips, and playfully blew a kiss. She felt the familiar touch of his lips on her forehead and smelled the scent of his cologne in the air. The sandalwood scent faded away as Paul vanished into the clouds.

Natalie watched until he was completely out of sight. Then she smiled up at Jake and said, "Not anymore."

The End.

ACKNOWLEDGEMENTS

The Empty Beach Chair is a women's fictional suspense novel that includes two of my favorite places, New York City and St. Simons Island.

A special thanks to my friend, Susan Daniel, for her research regarding the St. Simons Lighthouse and other bits of historical information.

This book would not have been possible without the beta readers who combed through the pages of this manuscript at different intervals, looking for inconsistencies within the story. Thanks to Charlene DeWitt, Marie Franklin, Beth Grindle, Sydonna Hardin, and Martha Megahee. You ladies are simply the best! Thanks for the time and energy you gave to this project. I cannot thank you enough.

Many thanks to Kay Paschal and Kim Conrey; both are exceptional writers and very busy women who took time away from their careers to provide the blurbs for the back cover. Thank you, ladies!

Thanks to my grammar guru and friend, Elizabeth Waidelich. Liz has been involved in all four manuscripts and provided constant encouragement throughout this process. Thanks for your friendship, Liz.

A huge thank you to my publishers at The Kimmer Group—you guys are the best!

To my editor, Beth Terrell, thanks for sharing your invaluable editorial insights and encouragement throughout this lengthy process. I'm grateful you fell in love with this story from the very beginning. As editors do, you have nudged and pushed to make my story the very best it could be. Thank you for demanding the very best from me!

Many thanks to my treasured friend, Jean Ellis, who provided edits and honest commentary throughout the writing of *The Empty Beach Chair*. Every writer needs at least one friend who is well-read, vastly knowledgeable, and understands the rules of creative writing. Jean is my person. Nothing overshadowed her unwavering support and encouragement for this venture. Your friendship knows no bounds. Thank you, sweet friend!

A special thanks to all the small-town boutiques across America and the world who support local authors. Several local businesswomen have graciously supported me by showcasing and selling my books or sponsoring book signings. Mary Beth Wood at The Crystal Plate, Elizabeth Waters at Elizabeth's Clothing Store, Jane Green Truelove at J. Green Salon, Carole Hudgins at The Little Ladybug, and Teryl Worster at The Spa on Green Street have all been generous in supporting my writing career. I am blessed to be surrounded by a group of women who truly understand the impact of encouraging each other.

I would be remiss if I did not thank my family for their love and support throughout this two-year process. A special thanks to my husband, Hardy, for those special nuggets of wisdom he tossed my way at the most opportune moments, and for believing in my ability as a writer. To my son, Zach, and daughter-in-law, Katie—thanks for always giving me an honest answer. Lastly, I'm grateful for my granddaughter, Emmy, whose presence fills a void in my life that I didn't realize existed, and to whom this book is dedicated. You guys fill my heart!

Above all, thanks to my sweet friend, Jesus, for His mercy and grace.

ABOUT THE AUTHOR

Renee Propes writes women's fiction and southern suspense. She lives in Gainesville, Georgia, with her husband, Hardy, and their Yorkshire terrier, Lucy.

Also by Renee Propes
Duplicity-A Story of Deadly Intent
Fractured-A Story of Broken Ties
Redemption-A Story of Grace

If you enjoyed *The Empty Beach Chair* and are so inclined, please leave a review on Amazon.
You may visit Renee's website at: authorreneepropes.com

Made in United States
Cleveland, OH
09 April 2025